Praise for the Hope Harbor Novels

"Award-winning Hannon steps away from romantic suspense in this inspiring tale. As her characters come closer together despite their fears, they find that their lives are growing rich again in ways they thought were lost forever."

—***Booklist*** on *Hope Harbor*

"Gorgeously rendered romance."

—***RT Book Reviews*** on *Hope Harbor*

"Fan favorite Irene Hannon brings a whole new cast of characters to life in a charming Oregon seaside village. Emotional and heart-warming, this story invites readers to come home to Hope Harbor."

—***Christian Retailing*** on *Hope Harbor*

"What a beautiful romance! Hannon has a true gift for creating real-life characters readers can connect with."

—***RT Book Reviews*** on *Sea Rose Lane*

"Summer romance doesn't get much better than this."

—**Examiner.com** on *Sea Rose Lane*

"Will surely be a favorite for Hannon's faithful fans."

—***Publishers Weekly*** on *Sandpiper Cove*

"A beautiful love story, yet it is also such a gorgeous picture of acceptance, learning to trust, and becoming a new creation."

—***RT Book Reviews*** on *Sandpiper Cove*

"Reminds readers of the power of faith and love to transform lives and lead to a future beyond what most people could imagine for themselves."

—***Booklist*** on *Sandpiper Cove*

Pelican Point

Books by Irene Hannon

HEROES OF QUANTICO

Against All Odds
An Eye for an Eye
In Harm's Way

GUARDIANS OF JUSTICE

Fatal Judgment
Deadly Pursuit
Lethal Legacy

PRIVATE JUSTICE

Vanished
Trapped
Deceived

MEN OF VALOR

Buried Secrets
Thin Ice
Tangled Webs

CODE OF HONOR

Dangerous Illusions

That Certain Summer
One Perfect Spring

Hope Harbor
Sea Rose Lane
Sandpiper Cove
Pelican Point

Pelican Point

A Hope Harbor Novel

IRENE HANNON

Revell
a division of Baker Publishing Group
Grand Rapids, Michigan

Published by Revell
a division of Baker Publishing Group
PO Box 6287, Grand Rapids, MI 49516-6287
www.revellbooks.com

Printed in the United States of America

ISBN: 978-0-8007-2880-9

Library of Congress Cataloging in Publication Control Number: 2017052816

This book is a work of fiction. Names, characters, places, and incidents are the product of the author's imagination or are used fictitiously.

18 19 20 21 22 23 24 7 6 5 4 3

In loving memory of my wonderful mother,
Dorothy Hannon,
who had a deep affection for lighthouses.

Although you've been gone more than a year,
the light of your love continues
to shine in my heart,
guiding and blessing my days.

As it always will . . .
until we meet again.

1

He'd inherited a *lighthouse*?

Ben Garrison stared at the dark-haired attorney, inhaled a lungful of the tangy, salt-laced air drifting in through the open window, and wiped a hand down his face.

No way.

Skip wouldn't do that to him.

It must be jet lag playing tricks on him. After all the flights he'd taken through multiple time zones to reach the Oregon coast, he was definitely in zombie land. And frequent changes in air pressure could mess with a person's ears, distort words.

At least he hoped that was the explanation.

Otherwise, this say-goodbye-and-take-a-few-weeks-to-decompress trip was going to turn into one gigantic headache.

Gripping his mug of coffee, he gave the view from the window a sweep. Usually the peaceful scene of bobbing boats in Hope Harbor's protected marina had a calming effect.

Not today.

Bracing, he refocused on the man across from him. "Tell me you didn't say lighthouse."

"Sorry." Eric Nash folded his hands on the round conference table and gave him a commiserating grimace. "I wish I could."

Ben closed his eyes and stifled a groan.

"I take it you weren't aware of this . . . unique . . . asset in your grandfather's estate."

"No." Ben took a long slug of his coffee, willing the caffeine to kick in.

Nada.

Too bad this brew wasn't as potent as the stuff they chugged in the forward operating base hospitals where he'd spent his days for the past seven years. He could have used a high-octane boost about now.

"It's the one on Pelican Point." The man motioned toward the north. "You might remember it from your visits. Your grandfather said the two of you used to walk up there in the evening."

An image of the fifty-foot-high weather-beaten lighthouse dating back to 1872 flashed through his mind—and despite the ache beginning to pulse in his temples, the corners of his lips rose.

Yeah, he remembered those walks. They'd been a nightly ritual during the summer visits of his youth. Fair skies or foul, they'd trekked from Skip's small house in town up the winding, rocky path to the lighthouse after dinner. The view was amazing, and the stories Skip had told about shipwrecks and danger and the steady beacon of light that guided frightened sailors home on stormy nights had stirred his youthful imagination.

But his grandfather hadn't owned the place.

And in the almost two decades since his last summer-break stay at age sixteen, Ben couldn't recall Skip ever mentioning it. Nor had the subject come up during any of his whirlwind visits through the years.

So what was going on?

"I have clear memories of the lighthouse—but how did he

end up owning it?" Ben held tight to the ceramic mug, letting the warmth seep into his fingers.

"After it was deactivated and decommissioned by the Coast Guard three years ago, the government offered it to Hope Harbor. But the cost of restoring and maintaining the property was too high and the town declined. In the end, it was put up for auction."

Ben knew where this was heading. Skip had loved that lighthouse—and all it symbolized. Light in the darkness. Guidance through turbulent waters. Salvation for the floundering. Hope for lost souls.

"I'm assuming my grandfather offered the highest bid."

"He offered the *only* bid. It's been his baby for the past two years. The price was reasonable—as lighthouses go—and from what I gathered, restoring it was a labor of love. However, it was also a money suck. I'm afraid there isn't much of an estate left, other than his house and personal possessions."

"I didn't expect a lot, even without the lighthouse expenses." No one who spent his life mining the sea for Dungeness crabs got rich—except the big operators. And if the cost of restoring and maintaining the structure was too high for a *town*, it was surprising Skip had anything left at all.

Other than the lighthouse.

An albatross that now belonged to him.

The throbbing in his temples intensified, giving the pounding bass beat of a rock band serious competition.

What in tarnation was he supposed to do with the thing?

"I'm afraid the lighthouse isn't in the best shape, either—despite your grandfather's efforts to restore it. After his knee issues began, he wasn't able to do much physical labor, and contractors charge a lot for that kind of work. Some people in town lent a hand on occasion, but progress was slow."

Tucking away the bad news that the lighthouse might be

crumbling, Ben homed in on the other piece of information the man had shared. "What knee issues?"

The attorney cocked his head. "You didn't know?"

"No. In his emails, he always said everything was fine. We didn't often talk by phone, but whenever we did, he was upbeat."

"Maybe he didn't want you to worry, given the demands of your job."

Yeah. That sounded like Skip. His grandfather knew army surgeons working near the front lines had a high-stress, high-adrenaline, fast-paced lifestyle. They'd discussed it often. And Ned Garrison had never been the type to burden other people with his problems.

But Ben wasn't other people.

He was family.

And he owed Skip. Big-time. Without those summer visits to look forward to after the acrimonious divorce that had rocked his childhood, who knew how he'd have ended up?

There was nothing he wouldn't have done for the man who'd been his lifeline.

Ben took another sip of the cooling coffee, buying himself a few moments to rein in his wobbling emotions. "Tell me about the knee issues."

"Your grandfather wasn't one to dwell on unpleasant subjects, but I understand he had bad arthritis and opted for a knee replacement not long after he acquired the lighthouse. An infection set in, requiring revision surgery. When that didn't work, a third surgery was done to insert a metal rod—which left him with a permanent limp and hampered his physical activities. He couldn't do much on the lighthouse anymore, so four months ago he decided to sell."

"Who was his surgeon?" Ben's jaw tightened. If someone had botched this job, they were going to be held accountable.

And why hadn't Skip taken advantage of his expertise? No, he hadn't done many battlefield knee replacements—but he was an orthopedic surgeon, for crying out loud. He could have consulted on the case, vetted the specialist his grandfather had chosen.

Eric riffled through the papers in front of him and extracted a sheet. "Jonathan Allen in Coos Bay. I don't see a primary care doctor listed for your grandfather. He must have done what most of the locals do and simply visited the urgent care clinic in town for everyday medical needs. They may have recommended Dr. Allen."

"Thanks." Ben jotted down the man's name. Before he left Oregon, he intended to pay the doctor a visit and review his grandfather's medical records.

But it wasn't likely the knee procedure had anything to do with the massive heart attack that had felled him.

Swallowing past the lump in his throat, he shifted gears. "If my grandfather put the lighthouse on the open market, I'm assuming the town still doesn't want to buy it."

"Correct. A few residents tried to stir up some interest, but the effort petered out. Even if the structure was in pristine condition, Oregon has an abundance of lighthouses already—many much more impressive than ours—so it's not as if it would draw tourists who might contribute to the local economy."

Hard to argue with that logic—or fault the town for passing on the purchase.

"So a private buyer is the answer."

"If you can find one." The attorney didn't sound any more confident than Ben felt. "Your grandfather listed it with an agent, but I don't believe there have been any inquiries."

Of course not.

That would be too easy.

"I'll go up and look it over after I arrange the memorial

service for my grandfather. Is there anyone in town who might be able to do a structural assessment?"

"My wife's an architect and runs a local construction firm." Eric rose, crossed to his desk, and extracted a business card from a drawer. "She went out before your grandfather bought it to give him her thoughts. She won't mind running up there again to reevaluate it." He returned to his seat at the table and handed over the card.

"Thanks." Ben pocketed it. "Is there anything else we need to discuss?"

"No. Your grandfather's estate was in order. Transitioning the assets will be simple. You have the keys to his house and car, and the paperwork's been signed. You're set." Eric pushed an envelope across the table. "This is the key to the lighthouse."

For a fraction of a second, Ben hesitated.

But there was no avoiding the truth.

He owned a lighthouse.

One that apparently no one wanted.

Including him.

Heaving a resigned sigh, he picked up the envelope and rose.

Eric stood, too, and extended his hand. "My condolences again on your loss. Your grandfather was a wonderful man—and an asset to this town."

"Thanks." He returned the attorney's firm clasp.

"If I can be of any other assistance while you're here, don't hesitate to let me know."

"I appreciate that. But I don't plan to stay long." Or he hadn't, until he'd inherited a lighthouse. "Thank you for delaying our meeting a few hours."

"No problem. I know how hard it can be to maintain a schedule on travel days. With all the ground you've covered, you must be operating on fumes."

"I am." Hard to believe he'd been in the Middle East thirty-six sleepless hours ago. "I'm going to crash at my grandfather's house for a while until I feel more human."

"Sounds like a plan. The Myrtle Café is open if you want to grab an early dinner first. Or you could swing by Charley's on the wharf. You might have gone there with your grandfather as a kid."

"I did. Often." His mouth watered just thinking about the savory fish tacos the man concocted. A visit to Charley's was on his Hope Harbor must-do list—but not until he got some z's. He needed sleep more than food.

The attorney walked him to the door, and Ben exited into a steady drizzle typical of the Oregon coast in mid-April—or any month.

Tucking the paperwork the man had given him under his jacket, he hit the remote and jogged toward his rental car.

Fifteen seconds later, he put the key in the ignition. Tapped the wheel.

Should he drive up to Pelican Point and pay Skip's folly a quick visit, or save that disagreeable task for later?

No contest.

Later.

He was fading fast—and the lighthouse wasn't going anywhere.

Unfortunately.

After checking for traffic, he pulled onto Dockside Drive. Maybe, as with the prophets of old, a solution to his dilemma would come to him in a dream.

And if it didn't?

He was going to be beating the bushes to find a buyer for his unexpected—and unwanted—legacy.

At the sudden peal of her doorbell, Marci Weber's fingers tightened on the tube of toothpaste, sending a minty-striped squirt arcing toward the mirror over her bathroom sink.

Who could be on her front porch at this hour of the night? No one in Hope Harbor came calling after eight o'clock, let alone ten-fifteen.

Pulse accelerating, she dropped the tube onto the vanity, ignoring the sinuous line of goo draped over her faucet and coiled in her sink.

Rubbing her palms down her sleep shirt, she crept into the hall, sidled up to the window in her dark bedroom, and peered down into the night.

Drat.

The tiny arched roof over her small front porch hid the caller from her sight, despite the dusk-to-dawn lights flanking the front door.

And the notion of going downstairs to get a better view from one of the front windows goosed the speed of the blender in her stomach from stir to puree.

No surprise there, given her history.

The bell pealed again, jolting her into action. She scurried over to the nightstand, snatched her pepper gel out of the drawer, and yanked her cell from the charger. Finger poised to tap in 911, she tiptoed back to the window, heart banging against her ribs.

Breathe, Marci. This is Hope Harbor. Bad stuff rarely happens here. They caught that teenage vandal who was getting his jollies destroying other people's property, and there haven't been any serious incidents since. You're overreacting.

True.

Nevertheless, she kept a tight grip on the phone while she waited for her visitor to vacate the porch and walk away.

But if he or she didn't leave . . . if her uninvited caller *did* have malice in mind . . . she had a first-rate alarm system that was already armed for the night, the Hope Harbor police would be here in minutes, and a faceful of pepper gel would stop anyone in their tracks.

She'd be fine.

Still . . . why couldn't Great-Aunt Edith have chosen to live in the middle of town rather than on the fringes? The Pelican Point cottage might be charming, but the old saying was true.

There was safety in numbers.

If no one answered the door, what was he supposed to do about the stuck cat?

Ben planted his fists on his hips and frowned. There were lights on upstairs. Someone must be home.

On the other hand, it *was* kind of late. Not by his standards, perhaps, but Hope Harbor tended to shut down by ten o'clock on weeknights, as far as he could recall. He might have caught the owner preparing for bed.

The very thing he should be doing instead of prowling around in the dark.

Except he was too wired and wide awake for sleep, thanks to the four hours he'd spent comatose in Skip's guest room after meeting with the attorney. Much as he'd needed to rack out, he should have forced himself to wait until a normal bedtime. Now his body clock was more out of whack than ever.

The hike up the rocky path to the lighthouse, with only a peekaboo moon and flashlight to guide him, had dispelled some of his restless energy, but if he'd known a stuck cat was waiting for him on the winding Pelican Point road, he'd have returned to town on the more dangerous cliff path.

Giving up on the occupants of the Cape Cod–style cottage, Ben expelled an annoyed breath and stepped off the porch.

A plaintive meow greeted him as he circled around the house to the adjacent tree, and he aimed his flashlight at the amber-eyed feline.

If the cat didn't have a bleeding paw, he'd walk away. It might be easier for kitties to climb up trees than descend, but hunger motivated most of them to return to solid ground on their own.

Unless they were hurt or scared.

And the cowering cat above him was both.

Ben eyed the limb-free lower trunk of the hardwood tree. No way could he climb that. Besides, an encroaching human might further freak out the cat.

He could rouse the volunteer fire department—but asking them to rescue a kitty at this hour wouldn't endear him to the locals.

Stymied, Ben surveyed the yard. A weathered garden shed off to the side might hold some useful implement.

He strode over to the structure and tested the door. Open.

Aiming the flashlight inside, he poked his head in and swept the beam over the contents, taking a fast inventory. Six-foot ladder. Broom. Twine.

Those would work.

And if the occupants of the house didn't like him borrowing their stuff? Tough. They'd surely heard the cat's pitiful meows of distress. If they didn't want to deal with the little critter, they should have called someone for assistance instead of letting a helpless creature suffer.

Mouth tightening, he stripped off his knit hoodie, wrapped it around the bristles of the broom, and secured it with the twine. Ladder hooked over his shoulder, he returned to the tree.

"Hang in, kitty. We'll get you down and fix that hurt paw." He used his most soothing tone as he set the ladder against the tree. The one he reserved for the hurting, frightened civilian children he'd treated, casualties of a vicious war that spared no one, who'd understood only his inflection, not his language.

After testing the ladder, he ascended to the second-highest rung, lifted the broom above his head, and nudged the cat with the fleece-covered bristles. The mouser wobbled, clutching the hoodie to stabilize itself.

Mirroring the rescue technique he'd seen a friend use, Ben eased the broom away from the tree. With its front claws locked into the fleece, the cat's back claws lost their grip on the tree. As the distance between tree and broom widened, it scrabbled to snag the hoodie with all four claws.

The instant the writhing cat latched onto the broom, Ben slid the handle down through his fingers and gripped the kitty gently by the scruff of its neck. Dropping the broom, he supported the cat in the crook of his arm while descending the ladder one careful rung at a time.

Back on firm ground, he turned—only to be blinded by a piercing beam of light.

"What the . . ." He released the cat's scruff and lifted his hand to shade his eyes.

Apparently the cat didn't like the intense light any better than he did. With a banshee-like screech, it swiped a claw down his forearm, twisted free, leapt to the ground, and vanished into the darkness.

"Keep your hands where I can see them while we have a little talk. I'm Officer Jim Gleason with the Hope Harbor Police Department."

The disembodied voice came from the blackness behind the light.

Squinting against the glare, Ben watched a rivulet of blood run down his arm from the claw gouge as the theme song from *The Twilight Zone* began to play in the recesses of his mind.

How could so much go so wrong so fast?

From the moment the call had come in with the bad news about Skip, he'd known this trip would be difficult—but that word didn't begin to describe his first eight hours in Hope Harbor.

And if inheriting a lighthouse and being mauled by a cat weren't bad enough, now he'd attracted the attention of the police.

This visit was beginning to border on surreal.

Even worse, it was going downhill fast.

"His story checks out, Marci. We can cite him for trespassing if you want, but . . ." Officer Gleason lifted one shoulder.

He didn't have to finish the sentence for her to know what he was thinking.

But it would be pretty low to punish a man who's come to town to bury his grandfather and who just got mauled trying to do a kind deed.

From the shadows inside the front door where she'd tucked herself, Marci peeked out at the tall, lean intruder.

He was standing ramrod straight at the edges of the light cast by the lanterns on either side of her front door, a shredded hoodie clutched in his hands. His dark hair was beginning to glisten from the heavy mist descending on Pelican Point, and while his features were dim, his pallor was impossible to miss.

The man's face was as white—and tense—as her own had been when she'd glanced in the mirror after throwing on jeans and a sweatshirt while waiting for the police to arrive.

He did *not* look like a troublemaker.

He looked like someone who'd found himself caught in a nightmare.

"So what'll it be, Marci?" The law officer flipped up the collar of his jacket as the mist intensified.

She hesitated. If the story the man had told Jim Gleason was true, he was more a cat rescuer than a cat burglar.

"You're certain he's legit?"

"I ran his ID, and Eric verified that the two of them met this afternoon. He also has a fresh scratch. I only caught a quick glimpse of the cat before it zipped into the darkness, but I heard it screech. The evidence supports his story."

Yes, it did. Annabelle got stuck in the same tree every few days. She'd rescued the feline herself after several similar incidents until she'd realized Mrs. Schroeder's pet was perfectly capable of getting down herself, despite her yowls for assistance.

But the stranger in her yard didn't know that—and how could she punish a good Samaritan?

"Okay. Let it go. Sorry to have bothered you."

"No bother at all. That's what we're here for." He tipped his hat. "I'll let him know he's off the hook."

The officer started to turn away, but Marci stopped him with a touch on his arm. "Did he say why he was up here at this hour?"

"Yep. He's fighting a serious case of jet lag and couldn't sleep, so he went for a walk. He flew in today from the Middle East. Can you imagine how many time zones he must have crossed?"

She did the math.

Middle East.

Grandfather's funeral.

Compassion for an injured animal.

Gaze fixed on the man, who was keeping his distance, Marci leaned closer to Jim and lowered her voice. "Is that Ned Garrison's grandson?"

"None other."

Her stomach bottomed out.

She'd called the cops on the army surgeon Ned had loved to brag about. The one who'd won medals for heroism and spent years near the front lines patching America's fighting men and women back together.

Major Ben Garrison deserved far better than the homecoming she'd given him.

"I, uh, think I owe him an apology."

Jim gave the man a dubious once-over. "You might want to wait on that. I think he's had about all he can take today—and he'll be soaked if he stands out here much longer. I'm going to run him back to Ned's house."

Marci bit her lower lip. Jim was probably right about the timing—but if she didn't try to make some initial amends she wouldn't sleep a wink tonight.

"I won't delay him long." She edged past the police officer. "Give me one minute."

The shadowy figure at the edge of the light stiffened as she approached, and her step faltered.

Just do it, Marci. Say you're sorry and get it off your conscience.

Right.

She straightened her shoulders and picked up her pace, stopping a few feet from the man. "I want to apologize for the hassle I caused you. I live alone, and I'm not used to callers at this hour. Officer Gleason explained what happened."

"You're not going to file a complaint?"

"No."

"That's one bright spot in this day, anyway."

Weariness—and a hint of sarcasm—scored his words.

Jim's assessment had been correct. The man wasn't in the mood for conversation.

Time to retreat.

"Well . . . I'll let you go before this mist becomes a full-fledged rain." She swiveled away.

"In case you're interested, the cat was hurt."

Stomach flip-flopping, Marci swung back.

Ben Garrison's arms were crossed tight against his broad chest, and though the murky light made it difficult to read his expression, disapproval oozed from his pores.

"What happened to her?"

"I have no idea. All I know is her paw was bleeding. Didn't you hear her crying?"

"I heard her *meowing*—but Annabelle gets stuck in that tree on a regular basis. She always manages to get herself down. How was I supposed to know she was injured?"

"Would it have hurt to check?"

"I don't wander around outside at night."

"Or answer the door."

"Not for strangers."

"You could have called through a window, acknowledged I was there. I would have explained what I was doing and saved us both all this aggravation."

That was true.

In hindsight, her lapse in judgment was obvious.

But why did he have to be snippy about it? She'd apologized, hadn't she? What more did he want? She couldn't go back and restage the whole scene, for pity's sake.

"Look . . . I said I was sorry. That's all I can do at this point."

"Does the cat belong to you?"

"No. My neighbor. And I expect by now she's receiving plenty of TLC for that hurt paw."

"Do you plan to verify that?"

What did he think she was, some callous animal hater?

Bristling, she glared at him. "I intend to call her as soon as you leave."

"Fine."

Sheesh.

This guy had attitude with a capital *A*.

Turning on her heel, she stomped back to the house, passing the police officer halfway.

He gave her an I-warned-you shrug and continued toward the cruiser parked at the end of her drive.

Fine.

Maybe it would have been wiser to hold her apology for a day or two.

But if she'd learned one thing over the past few years, it was to speak up and do what needed to be done instead of pussy-footing around until it was too late.

Putting off the hard stuff was a recipe for trouble.

However . . . not every situation required an immediate fix. Jumping into the fray too fast could cause problems too.

Tonight was proof of that.

Huffing out a breath, she climbed the two steps to her porch. Had she waited until Ned's grandson logged some sleep and recovered from jet lag, he might have been more receptive to her apology—and less judgmental.

Too late to fix that now, though.

Behind her, car doors slammed and an engine rumbled to life. By the time she let herself into the house and peeked through the window, red taillights were disappearing down the road.

Thank goodness the unpleasant episode was over—or it would be, as soon as she talked to Mrs. Schroeder and confirmed Annabelle was safe.

Marci reset the dead bolt and secured the sliding lock on the front door, armed the security system again, and retreated upstairs.

What a night.

As for that story about Ned she'd planned to write for the *Hope Harbor Herald*, filled with quotes from his beloved grandson?

She had a feeling it was toast.

2

The church was packed.

From his front-row seat, Ben gave the standing-room-only crowd at Skip's memorial service a quick sweep over his shoulder.

What a fabulous tribute to the man who'd been part of Hope Harbor for seventy-eight years. As the minister had said in his sermon, Ned Garrison had embodied the spirit of this town, with his upbeat attitude, giving heart, passion for life, and abiding hope.

Saying goodbye over the past three days as he'd wandered around his grandfather's tidy bungalow, paging through photo albums and examining the well-worn books in the modest library, had been gut-wrenching.

Yet the hardest task lay ahead.

And it had nothing to do with the eulogy he was about to deliver, even though public speaking wasn't high on his list of favorite activities.

As if on cue, Reverend Baker called him to the pulpit.

Taking a deep breath, Ben moved forward and stepped behind the microphone.

From up front, he had a much more expansive view of the congregation. Pressure built behind his eyes as he scanned the people who'd given up their Saturday morning to honor the man he'd loved. Most of them were strangers, but he did recognize a few faces.

White-haired Eleanor Cooper, who'd always plied him with her famous fudge cake when he and Skip had dropped in to say hello during his summer visits.

Charley Lopez, resident taco maker and renowned artist, who dished up philosophy along with his mouth-watering tacos.

Eric Nash and his wife, BJ, who'd visited the lighthouse and confirmed Skip had put no more than a small dent in the work that needed to be done.

And in a pew near the back, sitting beside the older man from the cranberry farm he'd loved to visit as a kid, was the red-haired woman who'd sicced the police on him Wednesday night.

A woman whose generous lips and heart-shaped face had been popping up far too often in his mind since their inauspicious meeting.

Marci Weber.

Not that she'd introduced herself that evening. She'd been too busy morphing from penitent to piqued once he'd lit into her about leaving the cat in the lurch.

But on the drive home, Officer Gleason had offered a few details about her, including her name and profession.

So was she here to pay her respects to Skip—or to cover the memorial service of a lifelong resident for the *Herald*?

Not that it mattered. Their paths weren't likely to cross much during his brief stay. And that was fine by him. He didn't need any more grief, and she appeared to be capable of dishing out plenty.

Redirecting his attention to the sheet of paper he'd placed on the podium, Ben launched into his eulogy, keeping it brief—as Skip had requested in the directions he'd left behind.

How like his grandfather to plan the whole service and tie up all the loose ends with his estate so his sole heir wouldn't have to deal with an overwhelming amount of hard stuff.

Other than a lighthouse.

But Skip *had* been trying to sell the thing. No one—least of all the man himself—could have envisioned his shockingly sudden end.

Ben's voice wavered, and he paused. Dipped his head. Cleared his throat.

Hold it together, Garrison. You can get through this if you stay the course and keep your eye on the horizon, like Skip always counseled.

He lifted his chin . . . and his gaze landed on Marci.

Compassion had softened her features, and the sheen on her cheeks gave him the answer to his earlier question.

She was here to pay her respects as a friend of Skip's, not as a reporter.

For some reason, that comforted him.

Grasping the edges of the podium, Ben held on tight as he wound down.

"I know my grandfather would have been touched—and taken aback—by the large turnout here today—but it doesn't surprise me. He was a very special man." He glanced toward the photo of Skip on the deck of the *Suzy Q*, which rested on an easel next to the urn holding the ashes of the man who'd loved the sea almost as much as he'd loved the woman he'd exchanged vows with more than fifty-five years ago.

"I'll close by sharing a piece of wisdom he offered me during one of my visits here two decades ago. Not much sticks in a teenage boy's mind, but as most of you know, Skip knew how to turn a phrase. He said, 'Always remember that life moves as fast as a mole crab—and it can disappear just as fast. Live every day. Plans are fine and dandy, but if all we do is think about the future, we throw away the gift of today for a tomorrow that might never be.'"

Ben folded his notes with hands that weren't quite steady. "Thank you all for coming this morning. I know each of us will miss my grandfather in our own way, but we can take comfort in the assurance that he's home—and happy. While he always called Hope Harbor a little piece of heaven, he knew this special town was only a tiny preview of what God has in store for those who love him. So I'll repeat to him now what he always said to me when my visit ended each summer." He angled toward the urn. Swallowed. "Godspeed, Skip—and God bless."

The last word scraped past his throat, and the room blurred.

Before he lost it completely, Ben tucked the notes in his jacket pocket and escaped back to his seat.

Reverend Baker took his place at the podium. "Thank you, Ben, for that beautiful send-off for your grandfather. He was a man of firm beliefs who lived his faith every single day. And he has, indeed, gone home." The minister then addressed the whole assembly. "Following the service, please join Ben in the fellowship hall for refreshments. Now let us join together in song as we conclude with Ned's favorite hymn."

The organ launched into the introduction for "Amazing Grace," but Ben didn't attempt to sing. Instead, he closed his eyes and let the comforting lyrics wash over him, soaking up the much-needed interlude of contemplation and peace.

Unfortunately, his serenity was short-lived—because for the next ninety minutes, it seemed everyone in town wanted to talk to him and share their memories of Skip.

If he wasn't still jet-lagged, Ben would have enjoyed their humorous and heartwarming stories. But even the full plate of food someone pressed into his hands and the piece of Eleanor's sugar-packed fudge cake he wolfed down weren't sufficient to restore his flagging energy.

When he was at last left alone for a moment, he skimmed the hall. If he could sit for five minutes, he might be able to . . .

"You look like you're ready to fold."

The mellow baritone voice transported him back twenty-plus years, to a sunny day on the Hope Harbor wharf.

Summoning up a weary smile, he swiveled around. "Hello, Charley. Thank you for coming."

"No thanks necessary. Ned was a remarkable man—and a blessing in many lives. It was a privilege to know him."

"I agree. Having him as a grandfather was a gift."

"Indeed it was. You two had a special bond."

"That's because he saved my life—metaphorically speaking."

"I know."

Doubtful. Skip wasn't the type to air dirty family laundry to friends and acquaintances.

Then again, Charley had always inspired confidences—and he had uncanny intuitive abilities. How else could he have picked up the turmoil in a young boy's heart within minutes of their meeting all those years ago?

Apparently, his acuity hadn't declined with age.

Nor had his appearance changed, come to think of it.

Ben sipped his lemonade and took a quick inventory.

Same weathered, latte-colored skin. Same long gray hair pulled back into a ponytail. Same keen, insightful eyes—now tinged with amusement.

"I feel like a bug under a microscope."

Warmth crept up Ben's neck. "I was thinking how nice it is to see some familiar faces in town." Close enough. "But I have to admit that outfit threw me." He swept a hand over the man's dark suit, crisp white shirt, and string tie. "I've never seen you wear anything but jeans."

"I do dress up on occasion if the event or the person warrants the effort. Ned did."

"He'd be honored."

"A tribute well deserved." Charley nodded toward some empty chairs tucked into a corner against the far wall, away from the clusters of people chatting and eating. "I think one of those seats has your name on it. No one will mind if you take a break for a few minutes."

"I don't know . . ." Ben assessed the crowd. "There's been a steady parade of people passing by, and I don't want to be rude if someone wants to talk to me."

"Everyone seems to be otherwise occupied for now."

Ben took another survey of the hall. No one appeared to be in the least interested in approaching him.

Perfect.

"You're right. Would you like to join me?"

"Thank you, but I need to get back to the stand. Weekends are busy, and I hate to disappoint customers. You're planning to pay me a visit soon, aren't you? I have a complimentary order of tacos with your name on it."

"Trust me, you're on my list. A trip to Hope Harbor wouldn't be complete without a visit to Charley's."

The man smiled, displaying two rows of gleaming white teeth. "I'll look forward to seeing you again soon. And now, I'll leave you to chill for a few minutes." He gestured to the chairs.

Except they were no longer empty.

Marci Weber had claimed one of them.

Ben sighed.

So much for his quick break.

"I think I'll hang out here after all and hope people give me a little space."

"Marci won't bother you—and she doesn't bite, despite that red hair."

Right.

"That hasn't been my experience."

"You two have met?" Interest sparked in the man's dark brown irises.

"The day I arrived. It wasn't a pleasant encounter."

"No?" Charley studied him. "That's odd. Marci's a very agreeable person. She's only been here two years, but everyone likes her."

He squinted at the man.

Was Charley suggesting *he* was at fault for their rough start?

No.

That would be ridiculous.

The man had no idea what had taken place on Pelican Point three days ago.

Yet truth be told, he hadn't been as kind to her that night as he could have been.

Should have been.

Calling the police might have been overkill, but her reasons for ignoring the cat's yowls were plausible—as was her caution about answering the door at that hour, especially with the nearest neighbor around a bend a couple of hundred yards away.

As Officer Gleason had pointed out in her defense during the drive back to town, a woman living alone needed to be careful, even in a town like Hope Harbor.

And she *had* apologized—or tried to.

Until he got snippy.

Ben kneaded his forehead.

Maybe he owed *her* an apology.

"Don't overthink it, Ben." Charley gave his shoulder a gentle squeeze. "Claim a chair and put the rest in God's hands."

"She might not be happy if I invade her space, given our rocky beginning."

"Rocky beginnings have a way of smoothing out. Ask Eric and BJ about that sometime—and come visit my stand soon."

Before Ben could respond, Charley ambled away to join the small group clustered around Eleanor and a fortyish Latino man.

The buzz in the hall had subsided somewhat as the crowd began to thin, and Ben tossed his empty plastic cup in a nearby trash can.

Should he follow Charley's advice—or walk a wide circle around the redhead and leave his apology for another day?

As if sensing his perusal, Marci looked up from her phone. Her eyes widened, and she dipped her chin, picked up her oversized purse, and stood.

Perfect.

If she left, he'd have the corner to himself.

But instead of waiting for her to vacate the spot, he found himself walking toward her.

What on earth . . . ?

He jolted to a stop.

What had prompted *that* impulsive move?

Could he blame it on Charley's encouragement?

Or perhaps Marci's flashing green eyes, which had sucked him in the other night despite his annoyance, were the culprit.

The sheen he'd seen on her cheeks during the service—and the compassion he'd felt emanating from her despite the distance separating them—could also have spurred his impulsive behavior.

Whatever the reason his feet had carried him toward her, he was going to have to follow Charley's advice and put this in God's hands.

Because she was standing frozen in place, cell clutched to her chest, waiting for him to approach.

It was too late to turn back.

He could only hope their second meeting was a whole lot more civil than the first.

He was coming over.

Marci's heart skipped a beat as Ben started toward her again, looking very *GQ* in his dark suit, crisp white shirt, and a subtly patterned tie that matched the cobalt blue of his eyes.

Whew.

She'd known he was handsome the night of the cat incident. Despite his mist-dampened hair, casual attire, and dour demeanor, he'd radiated a potent masculinity no woman would fail to notice.

But today?

It was everything she could do not to fan herself while he approached.

He stopped a few feet away from her, a heady hint of sandalwood tickling her nose as he offered a tentative smile. "I don't mean to intrude if you're busy"—he motioned to her phone—"but I wanted to thank you for coming today, introduce myself more formally, and ask if we could start over."

"I'm not busy." She attempted to shove the phone into a pocket on her purse. Fumbled it. Tried again while heat crept across her cheeks.

Good grief.

She was acting like a besotted schoolgirl!

"I, uh, liked Ned a lot. Coming to the service was a no-brainer." She finally managed to jam the phone into its slot. "He wrote a history column for the paper . . . the *Herald* . . . and he liked to stop in at the office and chat. We had some fascinating conversations, and along the way we got to be friends. Sometimes we even met at Charley's for lunch and ate on a bench by the wharf. I'm the editor of the paper, by the way. Well, editor, owner, publisher, reporter—in other words, jack-of-all-trades. It's a very small operation."

Enough already, Marci! You're running off at the mouth like a politician who likes to hear herself talk whether or not she has anything worthwhile to say.

She clamped her jaw shut.

If the man across from her thought her rambling discourse odd, however, he gave no indication of it.

"I didn't know about the column for the paper—but I did know Skip was a history buff. I'd enjoy reading some of his write-ups. I'll have to look around the house. He must have them stashed somewhere."

"I'll be happy to give you copies."

"I don't want to create work for you."

"It won't take but a few minutes—and I'd like to make amends for the cat incident."

"Actually, I think I'm the one who needs to say I'm sorry."

She blinked at him. "But . . . *I* called the police."

"And I'm the one who wasn't very receptive when you tried to apologize."

"Forget it." She waved a hand in dismissal. "Jim Gleason told me you'd been in the air all day. You had to be seriously jet-lagged. Not to mention the fact you were grappling with the bad news about Ned."

"That doesn't excuse bad manners."

"It does in my book."

"Does that mean you're willing to start over?"

"Yes."

"In that case . . ." He extended his hand. "Ben Garrison."

Not Dr. Ben Garrison. Not Major Ben Garrison. Just Ben Garrison.

Nice.

She took his hand and found her fingers enfolded in a firm, steady grip. "Marci Weber."

"It's a pleasure to meet you."

"Likewise. The cat's fine, by the way. I called her owner, who lives down the road. It wasn't a bad cut. Not close to being worthy of a trip to the vet."

"I'm glad to hear that."

"It was kind of you to try and help her, though—and it fits with how Ned described you. He told me you were born with the healing gene."

"Sometimes that can be more of a curse than a blessing." A flicker of pain darted across his features, gone so fast Marci wondered if she'd imagined it. "Wednesday was one of those times—and I have the scar to prove it." He tapped his forearm.

She winced. "Annabelle can be prickly if she gets spooked or annoyed."

"She's not the only one."

Marci squinted and tipped her head. "Is that a dig?"

"I was referring to myself, but if the shoe fits . . ." His eyes began to twinkle.

Whoa.

The man had breathtaking baby blues.

"Sad to say, it does." She did her best to maintain a conversational tone, but her response came out a bit breathy. "I do have a few stereotypical characteristics of redheads. On the positive side, my temper dies as fast as it flares."

"Good to know. Being friends with Skip is also a check in your plus column. He was an exceptional judge of character."

"He had many fine qualities—as you communicated so well in your comments at the end of the service. There wasn't a spare tissue in the house."

"Thanks. I wanted to give him a memorable send-off, and I had a lot of hours in the air to work on the eulogy."

"Jim Gleason said you came straight from the Middle East. That's a long haul for a short trip. How much leave did they give you?"

"Unlimited. I was a week away from mustering out, and they expedited the paperwork."

So he was *ex*-army now.

For some reason that pleased her.

"At least you don't have to rush back. How long do you plan to stay?"

"Until I wrap up Skip's affairs."

"I assume that includes dealing with the lighthouse."

"Unfortunately, yes—and that glitch could slow things down. I understand there isn't much of a market for lighthouses. Even Hope Harbor doesn't want it."

"I know, and it's a shame. The light is such a town landmark. But maintenance costs are high, and that's a hard sell in this tough economy."

"So I've been told."

"It would be terrific if you could find a buyer who would finish the restoration job Ned started." As far as she could see, that was the best possible outcome at this stage.

"I can try. Well . . ." He glanced around at the dwindling crowd, then at his watch. "I need to move on to the final good-bye."

Marci frowned. "I thought we did that in church."

"That was the public farewell. This is the private one. Skip wanted his ashes buried at sea. He made arrangements with the man who bought the *Suzy Q*—his crab boat—to provide the transportation. It was a condition of the sale. In fifteen minutes the captain will be waiting for me at the wharf, and I want to walk rather than drive."

The sentimental streak that had earned her the Weepy Weber nickname in grade school reared its head, and Marci mashed her lips together. She was *not* going to get emotional again. She'd already spent half the service blubbering, and her tissues were gone. "A perfect resting place for a man who loved the sea as much as Ned did." Somehow she managed to get the comment out without a quiver.

"I agree. Some of my happiest hours were spent with him on the deck of the *Q*, and his love of the ocean was infectious." Ben swallowed, the corners of his mouth flexing up a hair. "I better get going. I don't want to keep the captain waiting. I'm glad we had a chance to mend our fences today."

"Me too. Is, uh, anyone going with you on the boat?" Ned had always said Ben was his only family, but surely the man standing in front of her had a relative or two on his mother's side. Someone . . . anyone . . . who could have met him here and offered some moral support.

Yet he'd been the solitary occupant of the front pew at the service.

Meaning if he did have any other family, they hadn't bothered to come.

How sad was that?

"No. Just me and the captain."

"You know . . . I was getting ready to leave myself. Would you like some company on your walk?" The question spilled out before she could corral it.

He narrowed his eyes . . . and her stomach clenched.

Would she never learn to curb her impetuous streak?

"Sorry." She flashed him a grin. "I tend to rush in where angels fear to tread. It's a bad habit of mine. I walked over from my office on Dockside Drive, and I'm going that direction anyway, but I totally understand why you'd want to be alone."

As Eric and his wife stopped to say goodbye, she dug a card out of her purse. As soon as he refocused on her, she held it out. "If you have a few spare minutes later today or tomorrow,

I'd love to talk with you more about Ned. I'm working on a feature about him for the next issue, and having a few quotes from you would give it a more personal touch."

He took the card and slipped it in his pocket. "I'll be happy to call you." A few seconds of silence ticked by, his expression unreadable. "Listen . . . if you'd like to walk with me to the wharf, that's fine."

She bit her lip.

Was he trying to alleviate her embarrassment for putting him on the spot, or did he *want* her company?

He spoke as if he'd read her mind. "I've been by myself most of the past couple of days. Much more than I'm used to. I could answer a few of your questions for the article between here and the wharf."

Unless her people-reading skills were failing her, he was sincere.

"If you're certain . . ."

"I am."

"Okay. Let me get my coat from the rack."

"No hurry. I need to say a few goodbyes and go collect Skip. Why don't I meet you at the exit in five or ten minutes?"

"That works."

While he walked back toward the small group hovering around the food table, Marci went to claim her jacket—and tried to ignore the tiny buzz vibrating in her nerve endings.

The kind she felt whenever an attractive man caught her attention.

The kind that intensified when said man noticed her in return.

The kind that had gotten her into big trouble back in Atlanta.

But this wasn't Georgia.

And Ben wasn't . . . *him*.

The ex-army officer was a skilled and courageous doctor. The grandson of a man she'd admired and respected. A good Samaritan who rescued cats and wrote touching tributes.

He was the real deal.

Or he seemed to be.

And there was the rub.

Three years ago, she would have taken him at face value—and the buzz of attraction would have been exciting rather than unsettling.

But despite Ben's stellar credentials and Ned's glowing comments about his grandson, guys who came with first-class recommendations and looked superlative on paper weren't always what they seemed.

3

Skip's urn cradled in the crook of his arm, Ben paused in the back of the church and leaned against the wall.

Letting Marci accompany him to the wharf was a mistake.

A big one.

He hadn't planned to have any company on his walk.

Hadn't *wanted* any company.

Yet he'd hesitated no more than a few heartbeats before accepting her offer, despite the out she'd given him.

It didn't make sense.

Hadn't he decided nine months ago to walk a wide circle around women for a year or two? To focus on settling into his buddy's practice in Ohio and getting reestablished in civilian life without taking on any other complications or obligations?

Yes and yes.

However . . . a two-block walk to the wharf didn't break any of those rules. So what was the big deal?

You know what it is, Garrison. Stop playing dumb.

He huffed out a breath.

Fine.

The big deal was that he liked Marci Weber.

Too much.

Too fast.

Despite their rough start, something had clicked between them—and unless he was reading her all wrong, she'd felt the electricity too.

Then again, in light of recent experience, his instincts could be dangerously off.

He shifted toward the deserted sanctuary and examined the photo on the easel.

If Skip were here now, he'd no doubt have some witty advice to offer, all wrapped up in a sea analogy. Like, *Go with the flow—because you can't fight a tide God sets in motion.*

Yet as his grandfather had also once warned, setting sail toward stormy waters was foolish.

So which was this—a God tide or a storm?

Hard to say.

But what did it matter? Marci Weber lived in Hope Harbor. He was heading east as soon as Skip's estate was settled and his medical licensing paperwork went through in Ohio. There was no chance anything serious could develop between them during his short stay.

As long as he was careful, spending a few minutes in her company on occasion wouldn't be dangerous.

And truth be told, having her along on this sad, final walk might help mitigate the surge of grief threatening to swamp him now that his jet-lag-induced fog was lifting and the harsh reality of his loss was setting in. It would be harder to succumb to melancholy in her animated, vivacious presence.

Maybe her offer had been a blessing that would lessen the trauma of this last, most difficult chore.

So for today, he'd go with the flow rather than fight the tide.

Two minutes later, he found her waiting for him at the exit, her belted emerald green raincoat an exact match for her eyes. It was cinched at the waist with a sparkly belt that emphasized her trim figure—a touch of bling that would add shimmer and shine even to gray, rainy days.

Kind of like the lady herself.

Squelching that line of thought, he lengthened his stride.

"Sorry." He stopped beside her. "I got tied up with my good-byes."

"No worries. My office schedule today is lighter than the rest of the week."

"You work on weekends?"

"Half a day every other Saturday. A necessity with a paper that comes out on alternate Tuesdays. But I try to take some comp time on Wednesdays."

He pushed the door open and let her precede him, inhaling the whisper of jasmine that wafted toward him as she passed—the same sweet scent released by the flowers on the vine covering the arbor Skip had built for Gram at the house.

How odd that her perfume—or perhaps shampoo—would remind him of the happy hours he'd spent here, and the TLC his grandparents had . . .

"Ben?" Marci angled back toward him, eyebrows peaking.

"Coming." He put his feet in gear and followed her out, motioning toward the blue sky to divert her attention from the delay. "I got lucky on the weather. After all the mist this morning, I was afraid I might be doing this in the rain."

"It wouldn't dare rain on Ned's parade." She fell in beside him as they left the church behind and started toward the curving path that rimmed the harbor.

They walked in companionable silence for a few minutes in the salty breeze, until Marci spoke again.

"Ned liked to stroll here. He never missed his daily walk along the wharf unless his knee was bothering him. I could see him from my office." She waved across the wide street, where storefronts adorned with bright awnings and flower boxes faced the sea. "Sometimes he'd sit for a while and enjoy the view. It's hard to beat, isn't it?"

Ben gave the scene a slow sweep.

Above the sloping bank of boulders that led to the water, benches were spaced along the sidewalk between overflowing planters, offering a vista of boats anchored in the marina or tethered to a dock. The deep blue water, protected by the long jetty on the left and the pair of rocky islands on the right that tamed the turbulent waves, was placid. At the far end of the harbor, Charley's taco truck was parked near the white gazebo in the tiny park.

It was as picturesque as he remembered it.

"Yes. I liked hanging around down here as a kid. In fact, I loved everything about Hope Harbor. My visits were the highlight of my year."

"Would you mind sharing some of those memories while we walk? I have my digital recorder with me." She dug it out of her bag.

"You came prepared."

"As any first-class reporter would."

He could buy that.

But why would a first-class reporter spend her life running a podunk paper like the *Herald*?

Major disconnect.

Frowning, he took her arm and guided her around a pair of seagulls who'd planted themselves in the middle of the sidewalk.

Marci appeared to be bright, smart, and personable. The kind of woman who would rise quickly in any field.

So what had brought her here two years ago? Where had she lived before? What had she done in her previous life? Who had she left behind—or come to Oregon to be close to? Why wasn't she working for a big-name publication? How could she make a living publishing the eight-page, every-other-week *Herald*?

Why wasn't she married?

Most important, could he ask a few of those questions without getting her hackles up?

"Being prepared is smart in any job." He chose his words with care as the gulls fluttered along behind them—likely hoping for a handout. "But tell me about the *Herald*. I thought it went out of business six, eight years ago."

"It did. I revived it."

"So it's been back in business for about two years."

Her step faltered, and she stiffened. "Yes. How did you know that?"

"Officer Gleason mentioned your tenure here. Charley did, too, after the service. They're staunch fans, by the way."

Her posture relaxed a hair. "Both are super guys. They've been very supportive of my attempt to get the paper going again. The whole town has been."

"It's a risky venture, though. Papers are struggling everywhere these days."

"That's why I do PR work on the side. Those clients provide my main income—but journalism is my first love. And every town deserves a newspaper. The *Herald* is small, but I like that I can be hands-on with every aspect."

"Do you do everything?"

"Not quite. I have a part-time assistant at the office and a freelance designer who takes care of the layout."

"Still sounds busy."

"It is."

"Have you worked on larger publications?"

"No. Newspaper slots are hard to come by for newly minted journalism majors. After college I took a job with a PR firm in Atlanta."

"That's a long way from Hope Harbor. What brought you here—aside from the beautiful setting?"

She watched a black oystercatcher dip low over the harbor, its distinctive yellow-tipped, orange-red bill a blaze of color against the blue sky. "My sister and I inherited our great-aunt's cottage on Pelican Point. I came to clean it out and put it on the market, but I fell in love with the town. Since I was ready for a change of job and lifestyle, I bought my sister's share of the cottage and stayed."

Her straightforward explanation covered all the basics, and she'd delivered it in a casual, relaxed tone.

Except she wasn't relaxed.

A thrum of tension radiated off her, and her response came across as too glib and practiced—as if she'd expected to be queried on this subject and had written out and memorized her answer.

Suggesting this wasn't a topic she liked to discuss.

Why?

Before he could figure out how to finagle an answer to that question, she held up the recorder. "Let's talk about Ned. We're going to be at the boat soon, and you haven't told me a thing yet. Why don't you share a story or two about your visits here, and what you most remember about him?"

Her request was reasonable. She'd joined him on this walk to hear about Skip. But they'd be at the boat in less than three minutes, and that wasn't long enough to do justice to *any* story about his grandfather.

"I have a better idea."

Marci slanted him a cautious look. "What?"

He hesitated, already besieged by second thoughts about the suggestion that had popped into his mind. After all, he'd planned to use his time on the boat to reminisce about the happy days he'd spent with Skip, not entertain a passenger.

But he wasn't yet ready to let Marci go—leaving him just one option.

Dismissing his qualms, he plunged in. "Why don't you come out on the boat with me? That's where Skip spent his happiest hours . . . and I have a lot of memories of the *Q* too. I could share a few of them while we're on the way to the spot he chose as his resting place."

She jolted to a stop. "I'm, uh, not exactly dressed to go out on a crab boat."

"You're wearing flat shoes, the weather's fine, and we can stay inside the cabin if you prefer that to the open deck. It's a beautiful day to be on the water . . . and I have a feeling Skip wouldn't mind if I brought one of his friends along. Besides, don't first-class reporters go where the stories are?" He gave her his most persuasive grin and tapped the recorder clutched in her fingers.

"Yes, but . . . but we could also meet after you get back. I'll be in my office for a while."

That was true.

Yet the idea of concluding the funeral ritual accompanied only by a complete stranger—accommodating though the captain might be—was quickly losing its appeal.

"Are you certain you want to pass up a ride on the *Suzy Q*?" He conjured up another charming smile. "She's a great boat . . . and that's where my grandfather spent a significant portion of his life. It would give you some—is color the right word?—for your story."

The wry tug at the corners of her lips told him he'd convinced her to come even before she responded.

"You win. I'm in."

"You won't be sorry."

But as they continued down the wharf and the captain welcomed them on board, Ben wasn't as certain about his own feelings.

It was very possible he might live to regret this.

Because the more he talked to Marci, the more intrigued he became . . . and he'd had enough intrigue to last a lifetime.

Hope Harbor was as beautiful from the sea as it was from the land.

As the *Suzy Q* left the protected harbor and picked up speed toward open water, Marci held on to the corner of the wheelhouse and surveyed the town nestled at the base of low hills.

Strange that in all these months here, she'd never ventured out to sea. Any number of her friends and acquaintances had connections to boats and would have been happy to arrange for her to take a spin.

But perhaps it was fitting that her first trip on the water was in honor of Ned.

"Beautiful view." Ben spoke close to her ear, raising his volume to be heard above the rumble of the engine.

"Very."

"The only thing that made Skip happier than standing behind the wheel of this boat and setting off in search of crabs was coming back with a huge catch on a beautiful day like this. But more often than not, the weather during peak crabbing season was dismal."

"He told me once that crabbing was a family tradition."

"It was—until my dad became an engineer and took a job in San Francisco."

"That's what he said. He must have been disappointed."

"I'm sure he was. Dad was an only child, so that was the end of a three-generation crabbing business. But Skip understood that people need to follow their own dreams."

"Are your parents still in California?"

"No. Dad died twelve years ago of a stroke."

It was difficult to read Ben's expression under the dark sunglasses he'd put on, but she had no difficulty picking up a trace of melancholy.

"I'm sorry."

His forehead knotted. "Thanks. The two of us had drifted apart, but losing him was still a shock."

He didn't offer more—and for once she reined in her unruly tongue and moved on to a safer subject.

"Since you were alone at the service, I assume there are no brothers or sisters?"

"No."

"Did your mother stay in California?"

The bunching muscle in his jaw told her she'd miscalculated.

Apparently family in general wasn't a safe subject—other than Skip.

"No. She and Dad divorced when I was ten. A few years later, she remarried and moved to the East Coast."

If his tone was any indication, he didn't much care where she was.

Not the best family situation.

He offered nothing else, and save for the powerful throb of the engine and the caw of a gull following in their wake, silence fell between them.

Time to change the subject.

"Why don't you share one of those stories you promised?" She dug out her recorder again. "Readers would enjoy hearing about an adventure the two of you had that can still brighten your day when you think about it."

His mouth curved up, erasing some of the tension in his features. "There are dozens of those."

"I'm ready whenever you are." She held up the recorder.

He launched into a story about his first crabbing excursion

with Ned, who'd taught him to distinguish between keepers and throwbacks, adding touches of humor as well as details that illustrated his grandfather's patience and deep love for the sea.

From there, he went on to reminisce about their evening treks to the lighthouse and the tales Ned had told about the seafaring life, their walks on the beach that were filled with folksy wisdom, and the summer the two of them had surprised his grandmother by baking her a lopsided birthday cake and preparing her favorite meal while she was at a garden club meeting.

By the time the boat slowed, Marci had plenty of memorable quotes and stories to flesh out the article she'd already drafted.

The captain cut the engine and opened the door to the wheelhouse. "This about the spot you had in mind?"

Ben scanned the scene, and Marci followed his lead. To the right, part of the Hope Harbor wharf was visible in the gap between Gull Island and the jetty. On the left, the lighthouse on Pelican Point soared above the sea.

"Yes. This is perfect." Ben retrieved a small New Testament from the inside pocket of his jacket and picked up the simple, sand-colored urn that held Ned's ashes.

The captain removed his hat. "I rigged up a net so you can lower that over the side, if you like. It seemed more respectful than dropping it into the water."

"Thanks. I appreciate that."

The captain dipped his head, ducked back into the wheelhouse, and returned with a small net attached to two ropes.

"Would you hold this?" Ben extended the Bible to her with a hand that wasn't quite steady.

Marci took it in silence.

With the help of the captain, he nestled the container in the net. "For the record, Skip was an environmentalist to the end." His voice rasped as he rested a hand on the urn. "Just like crab pots have biodegradable panels to let crabs escape from lost traps, this is ecofriendly. It will float for several minutes, then sink to the bottom and dissolve within twenty-four hours—and Skip will become part of the sea he loved."

Marci's lower lip began to quiver, and her vision misted.

Shoot.

Weepy Weber was back.

Struggling to stem her tears, she surreptitiously felt around in the pockets of her coat for a tissue.

Zilch.

So much for her claim to Ben that she was always prepared.

Stifling her sniffles as best she could, she watched as the captain eased back and Ben lowered the urn to the sea.

Less than a minute later, he retracted the ropes and the empty net, set the makeshift contraption on the deck, and turned to her, his gaze on the New Testament clutched against her chest.

Her cue.

She walked toward him, doing her best to maintain her balance on the undulating deck. Falling flat on her face at his feet in the midst of this solemn moment would rank right up there with calling the police on him.

He met her halfway . . . gave her a fast scrutiny . . . then fished out a neatly folded pristine handkerchief and traded her the white square for the compact volume.

Despite his sorrow, he'd noticed her tattered emotions.

Which only made her more weepy.

Back at the railing, he read the twenty-third psalm in a quiet, choked voice as the urn floated away from the boat, rocking gently in the waves.

After he finished, he slid the book back inside his jacket but remained at the railing, back ramrod straight, watching the urn.

When it at last sank beneath the waves, he gripped the railing and bowed his head. A few moments later, his shoulders began to shake.

Sweet mercy.

He was weeping.

As her own eyes filled again, Marci pressed the handkerchief against her lips to smother the sob threatening to erupt.

Of course she'd feel compassion for anyone mourning a loss—but somehow it went deeper than that with Ben, despite their short acquaintance.

Maybe because she'd known Ned and grieved his death too.

Maybe because Ben had touched her heart by inviting her to share in this final, personal farewell.

Maybe because it had been a long while since she'd felt such an instant connection to another person.

Maybe because she couldn't imagine how difficult it must be to say goodbye to the last person in the world who mattered to you.

Whatever the reason, his almost palpable sorrow infiltrated her soul—and she didn't want him to feel alone.

Following her instincts, she crossed the deck, stood behind him, and rested her hand against his back.

He froze—and she held her breath. Then, ever so slightly, he leaned back into her touch.

The air whooshed out of her lungs.

He hadn't rejected her overture.

Two long, emotion-laden minutes later, after swiping the arm of his suitcoat across his eyes, he turned.

The pain of loss was carved into his features, grooves bracketing his mouth, lashes spiky with moisture.

Once again, the waterworks erupted, and she dabbed at her tears with his handkerchief.

"Hey." He took her hand, his voice husky as he wove his fingers through hers. "As Skip used to say when I was down, dry your tears, lift your face to the sun, and trust that God will give you a better tomorrow."

"That's a b-beautiful thought." The last word came out in a hiccup. "But I should be the one c-comforting you."

"You've already done that. It's amazing how one caring touch can make a person feel less alone. Thank you for that—and for being Skip's friend."

"He was an easy man to like."

"Yes, he was." Giving her fingers a squeeze, he spoke to the captain. "We're ready to go back."

The man disappeared inside, and a few seconds later the engine revved up.

As the deck began to vibrate and the boat swung around in a slow arc, Marci lost her footing and groped for the railing.

Ben's grip on her fingers tightened, and he motioned to a small bench tucked beside the wheelhouse. "Why don't we sit?"

"I vote for that—although you don't appear to be in the least bothered by the motion."

"I spent hours on this deck in all kinds of weather. I got my sea legs long ago. But there is a bit of a chop now. I think a storm may be brewing." As he spoke, the sun disappeared behind a dark cloud and the wind picked up.

He held tight to her hand as she lurched across the deck, then sat beside her on the bench.

It was a tight fit—but cozy.

Very cozy.

Best of all, he didn't let go of her fingers during the entire ride back to the wharf.

Only after the boat nudged into the dock and the captain emerged did Ben relinquish his grip and stand to thank the man again.

"I was glad to do it, Doctor. I could tell your grandfather loved crabbing as much as I did and hated to give it up. He sold me a gem of a boat, and being part of his final trip to sea would have been my privilege even if that hadn't been part of our agreement."

Once they were on the dock, the captain lifted his hand in farewell, disappeared into the wheelhouse, and aimed the *Suzy Q* back toward the sea.

With one last look at the boat, Ben focused on her. "I guess that wraps up today. Thank you for coming along. It helped."

"Thank you for inviting me. It was an honor to be there."

"Are you going to your office now?"

"Yes." Unless he made a better offer.

Not happening, Marci. The man just buried his grandfather. He doesn't have socializing on his mind—and you're not interested anyway. Remember—caution is your operative word around men.

"Do you need anything more from me for your article?"

For a split second, she hesitated. If she said yes, she might be able to prolong this interlude.

But that would be a lie—and given the persistent buzz in her nerve endings, it was far safer to say goodbye and be on her way.

"I don't think so. You gave me plenty. But if you don't mind sharing your cell number, I'd appreciate having it on hand in case any follow-up questions arise."

"Sure."

She retrieved a pen and a small notebook, jotting down the numbers as he dictated them. "Thanks. Watch for the story on Tuesday."

"I will."

She extracted his soggy handkerchief from the pocket of her coat. "I'll return this after I restore it to its original condition."

"Don't bother. I have plenty." A raindrop hit the tip of his nose, and he inspected the sky. "We better go our separate ways or Mother Nature will be laundering that handkerchief—and us too."

A raindrop bounced off her cheek, confirming his assessment.

She forced herself to back off a few steps. "Well . . . maybe I'll see you around."

"I wouldn't rule out that possibility. Hope Harbor isn't very big."

In other words, he wasn't planning to seek her out. If they met again, it would be by chance.

Her spirits nosedived—a reaction that was just plain dumb.

She didn't *want* him to have any interest in her. Romance would only complicate her life.

Lifting her chin, she pasted on a smile. "Take care, Ben."

"You too." With a lift of his hand, he strode away.

She watched him surreptitiously as she crossed Dockside Drive and trudged toward her office.

He didn't look back once.

Which was for the best. Even without her other issues, getting involved with a Hope Harbor short-termer would be a mistake.

And if she ever did meet a charming, eligible man who was going to stick around town for more than a week or two, she still wasn't going to let herself get carried away.

She'd think the relationship through and do some due diligence instead of letting electricity short-circuit her brain.

Because she was done making mistakes that led to trouble.

4

Skip's neighbor needed help.

Juggling a box of his grandmother's quilting fabric, Ben paused at the kitchen window. As far as he could tell, the twenty-something guy next door hadn't made much progress on the hole he'd been trying to dig for the past fifteen minutes.

A swirling cloud of dust motes rose from the box, and Ben waved them away as the younger man placed the shovel in the ground, steadied himself on what appeared to be a bum leg, and pressed down on the blade with the other.

As had happened with his previous attempts, he lost his balance. Teetered. Attempted to right himself.

But this time he failed.

And he fell.

Hard.

Ben dropped the box on the kitchen table.

Enough.

If Skip were here, he'd have offered to help four-trips-from-the-basement ago.

Pushing through the back door, he searched his memory for a fact or two about the next-door neighbor. Came up blank. Skip might have shared some tidbits—but with all the stuff going on overseas, Ben hadn't always absorbed the details about his grandfather's everyday life or the minutiae of the various Hope Harbor residents who peopled his world.

For now, though, this was *his* world—and while in Rome, it was important to do as the Romans did.

In a small town, that meant stepping up to the plate if someone needed help.

The guy was still struggling to get back on his feet as Ben approached the weathered picket fence separating the yards, and he held back until the man was upright. No reason to embarrass him.

Sixty seconds later, Ben strolled over to the fence. "Good morning."

The guy swung around . . . tottered again . . . but used the shovel to steady himself.

"Morning."

Based on his clipped delivery and fierce scowl, there was nothing good about *his* morning—and the man didn't seem receptive to chitchat . . . or an offer of help.

Better proceed with caution.

"I noticed you from the kitchen window. I'm Ben Garrison, Ned's grandson." He extended his hand over the pickets.

Using the shovel almost as a crutch, the younger man closed the space between them with a not-quite-normal gait and returned his clasp.

"Greg Clark. Sorry for your loss." His voice was gruff, but a flicker of sympathy softened his angular features. "Your grandfather was a good man."

"Yeah, he was. Thanks." Ben surveyed the potted rosebush and half-dug hole in the center of a small, well-tended plot that appeared to be under development. "You chose a perfect spot for your garden. You'll be able to see it from the kitchen window."

Greg gave the bed a fast, annoyed sweep. "It's not mine. This is my wife's project."

"Looks like she recruited you to help, though." He motioned to the rosebush.

The corners of Greg's lips dipped south. "She's always finding some chore or other for me to do." Bitterness soured his inflection.

"I've heard about those never-ending honey-do lists." Ben kept his tone light.

"Yeah. She's a master at that. But I'm not into gardening."

"In that case—could you use a little help? Two sets of hands might speed up a disagreeable chore."

A flush mottled Greg's face. "I don't need help."

At the defensive jut of the man's jaw, Ben hooked his thumbs in the front pockets of his jeans and hitched up one corner of his mouth. "To tell you the truth, I wouldn't mind taking a break from cleaning out the basement. I can't believe how many boxes of quilting fabric my grandmother squirreled away. I'd be glad to have an excuse to get some fresh air for a few minutes and let the dust settle before I dive back in."

Greg hesitated . . . eyed the half-dug hole . . . shrugged. "If you want to help, fine. The sooner I can get this done, the sooner I can have the beer that's waiting for me inside."

Beer at ten in the morning?

Maybe there was more to the man's surliness than anger at being recruited to do a distasteful job in the garden.

Ben sighed.

And maybe he should have stayed in the kitchen.

Getting embroiled in someone else's problems wasn't part of his agenda for this visit.

Too late now, though. He'd already stuck his nose in. His only option was to finish the task on the double and retreat to Skip's house.

"I'll circle around the front and join you."

"Whatever."

Less than a minute later, as he approached the garden from the other side of the fence, the guy was once again trying to dig the hole for the rosebush.

He didn't appear to be any more stable now than he'd been before.

Since Greg hadn't mentioned his leg issue, however, it must be an off-limits subject—and it was hard to help a guy who didn't want to admit he needed assistance.

Ben wiped a hand down his face.

His second attempt to do a good deed in Hope Harbor seemed fated to fail as dismally as his first.

At least this guy didn't have any visible claws.

Psyching himself up for an awkward exchange, he crossed to the garden. "Why don't I get this out of the pot while you finish the hole—or I could dig if you'd rather tackle the rosebush."

"I'll dig." The man ground out his reply as he jabbed at the soil.

"Works for me."

Ben knelt on one knee while Greg continued to use the shovel for balance as he stepped on the edge of the blade.

The technique wasn't working. Every time the blade sank into the soil, he wobbled.

Tension oozed off the man as Ben loosened the dirt in the pot around the root ball.

This guy was seriously stressed.

And Ben had a feeling his mood had little to do with the rosebush his wife had asked him to plant.

All at once, after a particularly aggressive application of foot to shovel, he lost his balance and pitched sideways.

Ben sprang to his feet and managed to grab him before he hit the dirt again.

As he sagged and flailed for support, he let loose with a string of curses while Ben absorbed his weight.

"I've got you, buddy. Give yourself a few seconds to get your legs under you." Ben maintained his conversational, no-sweat tone.

But the instant Greg regained his footing, he pushed away, bright splotches of color once again staining cheeks that were too pale even for a resident of the cloudy Oregon coast.

"I'm done with this stupid project." He spat out the words, hands fisted at his sides. "If Rachel wants a rosebush, she can plant it herself. Fiddling with flowers isn't fit work for a real man."

Greg clumped back to the house, slamming the door behind him.

In the silence that descended, Ben took a long, slow breath. Let it out.

Wow.

That was one angry dude.

Shoving his fingers through his hair, he eyed the half-dug hole.

He could walk away and leave the garden in disarray—or he could spare Greg's wife the dirty work and complete the chore.

Given that neither choice was likely to endear him to her husband, there was no reason to saddle her with the messy job. She had plenty to deal with already, if his brief encounter with Greg was any indication of the man's temperament.

Without further deliberation, Ben picked up the shovel, finished the hole, planted the rosebush, and went in search of a hose.

Once he'd watered the plant in, he cleaned the shovel, placed it and the empty rose container beside the rear door, and hightailed it back to Skip's.

Playing good Samaritan was definitely not working for him on this trip.

So from now on, he'd keep to himself, do what needed to be

done to settle Skip's affairs, and get out of town as fast as he could without creating any more trouble for anyone—including himself.

"Here are all the columns Ned wrote, Marci. If you don't need anything else for a few minutes, I'm going to take my lunch break."

Marci swiveled around in her chair as Rachel placed the newspaper clippings on her desk. "No problem. Is Greg joining you?"

Her part-time assistant dipped her head and smoothed down the edge of her sweater. "No. He's, uh, got other plans for today."

Based on the few insights about the man Marci had gleaned, that meant Rachel's husband was either sulking in the shadowy house with all the shades drawn or sitting up at Pelican Point by the decrepit lighthouse, staring out to sea.

Not much of a life for a bride of eighteen months.

"How's he doing?" She tapped the columns Rachel had given her into a neat stack. *Careful, Marci. Don't push too hard.*

"Okay."

"I haven't seen him around town."

"He doesn't socialize much."

Like not at all, as far as she could tell.

"How are *you* doing? I know how hard it can be to move to a new town filled with strangers."

Not exactly true. Unlike Rachel, by her four-month anniversary in Hope Harbor, she'd already dived into town life and sent down deep roots.

Of course, her time and energy hadn't been sapped by a taciturn husband battling physical and emotional challenges.

"I'm fine." Rachel pulled her sweater tighter around her and averted her gaze—as if she was afraid her boss would see through her lie.

Marci reined in a surge of frustration.

Every overture she'd made in the eight weeks they'd worked together had been rebuffed.

But Rachel needed a friend. Someone she could vent to, who would listen without judging.

Too bad her assistant wasn't on better terms with her parents. Texas wasn't easy commuting distance, but surely they'd offer moral support if she worked up the gumption to let them know what was going on here.

Or perhaps not, if they'd been less than thrilled about their daughter's elopement—as Rachel had hinted.

Meaning she had to keep offering a hand of friendship.

"You know . . . I've been thinking about running down to the new native-plant nursery near Sixes. Would you like to come along?"

A spark of interest brightened the other woman's face—just as Marci had hoped. The one subject Rachel talked about freely was gardening.

But the tiny glimmer of animation flickered . . . and died.

"Thank you for asking, but I need to be available for Greg when I'm not working."

"You also need some time for yourself—and your own interests. There's nothing wrong with setting aside a few hours here and there for fun." She tried to infuse her comment with caring rather than criticism.

Rachel's throat worked. "Fun hasn't been part of my life for a while."

That was the closest the woman had come to a direct confidence—although the admission was no big revelation. Based on the sheen in her eyes after most of the hushed phone conversations she held with her husband in this office, laughter and joy weren't part of her standard fare.

Thank goodness she'd applied for the job here. At least it got her out of that depressing atmosphere for fifteen hours a week.

"Why don't you think about that trip south? We could stop for tea at the lavender farm too. It's charming."

Rachel hesitated—but in the end she shook her head. "I appreciate the offer, but this isn't the best time. Maybe down the road?"

So much for her powers of persuasion.

"Sure. And don't worry about hurrying back. I'm going to review the ads for the next issue of the *Herald*. I can't believe you convinced Lou Jackson to commit to a regular slot for the bait and tackle shop—but I'm thrilled. We can always use another steady revenue stream."

"It wasn't a hard sell after I suggested he use the ad space to not only promote his shop but indulge his penchant for trivia. To be honest, it was Greg's idea."

"Really?"

"Yes. I mentioned at dinner one night that you'd asked me to contact a few businesses about buying an ad. Greg knows Lou from way back and remembered how he likes to entertain customers with obscure facts. He said including a trivia tidbit in ads would attract readers—and potential customers—especially if Lou ran a special on one of his more eclectic items."

"Well, it's a very creative idea. I love the copper hummingbird feeder he's featuring in the first ad. Who'd expect to find such an item in a bait and tackle shop? Tell Greg I said thanks for the suggestion."

"I will." She retreated to her desk and picked up her purse. "Be back soon."

As Rachel pushed through the door, Marci exhaled and sank back in her chair.

Such a sad situation.

At twenty-two and twenty-three, Rachel and Greg had their whole life ahead of them.

Yes, they'd had a serious setback.

Yes, they'd need to alter the plans they'd made.

Yes, they'd been given a tough row to hoe.

But if they stuck together—and accepted the help that was available—they could weather this storm.

Unfortunately, as far as she could tell, neither of them was ready to admit they needed outside assistance. Pride, embarrassment, insecurity—whatever their reasons, they were hunkering down and trying to get through this alone.

Or Rachel was.

Greg appeared to be on the verge of giving up.

What a mess.

And despite the save-the-world gene her mother always claimed was embedded in her DNA, there was nothing she could do about it except pray—and watch for any opportunity that came along to offer a helping hand.

With a quick glance at her watch, Rachel pulled into the driveway of the tiny bungalow she now called home.

She had twenty-two minutes left on her lunch break—even if lunch wasn't on her noon agenda. Checking on Greg was more important than food.

Not that she'd tell him that. He'd probably go ballistic if she did.

And she wasn't up for one of his angry tirades today.

She surveyed the sweet, furnished rental cottage, with its rose arbor on the side and hanging fern on the front porch. It was just the kind of home she'd envisioned for them when she'd been a smitten college student in Austin and he'd been a strapping army cavalry corporal.

How could she not have fallen in love with the charming military man who'd painted such a rosy picture of their life together in this idyllic town—especially after he'd made the hour-and-fifteen-minute commute from Fort Hood to spend time with her every chance he got?

It had felt like a match made in heaven.

Until the vows they'd taken on that sunny October day a year and a half ago had been put to a harsh test.

She choked back a sob.

In hindsight, her parents' advice to wait awhile before getting married seemed spot-on.

As they'd pointed out, if it was meant to last, what was the rush? Why not plan a wedding a bit further down the road, after she finished school and her love-at-first-sight romance with Greg had sustained a few challenges?

But no. From the day they'd met at a party given by a mutual friend, she'd been convinced Greg was her soulmate.

Rachel pulled the key from the ignition and clenched her fingers around it.

Maybe the man she'd fallen in love with was still inside his body somewhere.

Maybe.

But if he was, he'd retreated behind a barricade she hadn't been able to breach.

And after four depressing months in a town that wasn't living up to its name, she was running out of ideas.

Yet short of going home and admitting she'd made a mistake, all she could do was hang in and pray their situation would improve.

With a weary sigh, she pushed the door open and circled

around to the back of the house. Jolted to a stop at the shovel and empty rose container.

Had Greg read her note and actually planted the bush instead of wadding up the slip of paper and tossing it in the trash?

She hurried to the back of the yard and the in-progress garden where she spent her happiest hours.

The bush was there, in the spot she'd marked.

Her spirits took an uptick.

Was it possible they'd turned a corner?

Trying not to get her hopes up, she continued to the back door, unlocked it, and walked in.

"Greg?"

Silence.

A niggle of unease raced up her spine.

"Greg, are you here?"

More silence.

It was a foolish question, anyway. She had the car, and he wasn't inclined to do much walking, despite the urging of the physical therapist.

Dread pooling in her stomach, she walked down the short hall, stopping on the threshold of the master bedroom.

He was lying on his back in the dim room, fingers linked over his stomach, eyes closed.

His body was so motionless, her lungs locked.

Had her fears finally come to pass? Had he crossed the line and decided to escape from his problems once and for all?

No.

His chest was rising and falling.

He was still with her—in body, if not spirit . . . or heart.

Fingers curled into tight balls at her sides, she refilled her lungs. "Thank you for planting the rosebush. It will be much happier in the garden than in that pot."

Several endless, silent seconds ticked by.

"What are you doing here?"

"I live here." Her attempt at humor had zero impact on the rigid set of his mouth.

"I'm not in the mood for jokes, Rachel."

He never was—unlike the old days, when his ready laugh had brightened her world.

"I had an errand to run on my break and decided to swing by and have some yogurt." Not far from the truth. She did need to eat some lunch. "I noticed the rosebush as I walked around the back. I appreciate your . . ."

"I didn't plant it."

At his harsh cutoff, she blinked. "What do you mean? It's in the ground, exactly where I asked you to put it."

"Our neighbor did it."

"What neighbor?"

"Ned's grandson. I think he said his name was Ben."

She tried to make sense of that. "Why would he plant my rosebush?"

"Because your husband couldn't!" He pushed himself upright and swung his right leg to the floor, the stump below his left knee protruding over the edge of the bed.

Rachel gave the room a quick scan.

The utilitarian tube that functioned as his new leg, along with the hard, flesh-colored shell that fit over his stump, were jumbled on the floor in the corner—as if he'd hurled them from the bed.

Above them, the mar on the paint confirmed her suspicion.

The rosebush story was less simple to sort out.

"How did Ned's grandson get involved in this?"

He glared at her. "He must have seen me struggling. When he offered to help, I figured the sooner I got done, the sooner I could move on to a few beers." He swept a hand over the three cans lined up on the nightstand that she hadn't noticed until now. "So I said fine. Then I fell while he was here. Or I would have if he hadn't caught me." Bright spots of color reddened his cheeks. "Do you have any idea how humiliating that was?"

"I'm sorry, honey. I know it—"

"No!" His bellow reverberated off the walls, and she flinched. "You don't know anything! Not what it's like to lay here at night needing to pee and hoping you can get onto your crutches before you wet the bed. Or to live with the reality that you'll never lead a group of soldiers into battle again, or win a marathon, or be a firefighter." He rubbed his forehead. "You don't know squat, Rachel."

"I know you." She tried to keep her voice steady. "Or I thought I did. The man I married wasn't a quitter."

"Yeah, well, he's long gone."

"I don't believe that."

"Believe it."

"No!"

At her uncharacteristic vehemence, his eyebrows rose . . . and her heart stumbled.

What on earth had prompted her heated—almost belligerent—rebuttal?

Until now, she'd absorbed all the verbal abuse he'd dished out, pussyfooting around the hard issues, giving him space to deal with anger and grief over his loss, afraid that if she took a hard stand, she'd further damage his delicate psyche.

Yet the kid-gloves treatment hadn't worked—and she was sick to death of being patient.

Apparently some of the advice she'd picked up while scouring the internet for guidance had sunk in.

And with their relationship deteriorating anyway, what did she have to lose by taking a harder-line approach?

Steeling herself, she marched over to the bed. "I have a few things to say."

"Then sit down so we're on the same level."

"No. You stand up."

A muscle spasmed in his jaw. "I need my stuff." He gestured to the corner.

"How did it get over there?"

He glowered at her in stony silence.

But no response was necessary.

They both knew the answer to that question.

Instead of retrieving his prosthesis as she would have in the past, she strode to the small side chair in the corner, picked it up, and placed it in front of him. Once seated, she twisted her fingers together, hoping she wasn't about to make a big mistake.

"For the past eight months, I've watched you struggle to accept the new reality—and I'm not seeing any progress. I've listened to you complain, endured your bad moods, let you vent your anger and hostility and resentment on me. Well, I'm done. Things need to change around here. We're supposed to be partners in this marriage, for better or worse, in sickness and in health. I'm trying to keep my end of that bargain. You need to keep yours."

His features hardened. "I'm doing the best I can."

"No, you're not."

A spark of anger ignited in his eyes. "What gives you the right to make that judgment?"

"I know you. I've seen how hard you can work and how goal-driven you can be. If you applied the same single-minded focus to rebuilding your life that you used to woo me, we wouldn't be having this conversation. Our life might be different than we planned, but it would be good . . . and happy."

"That's easy for you to say. You have both legs. There's nothing holding you back from doing anything you want to do."

"There's nothing holding you back, either—except anger. You need to get over it and move on."

"To what? All I ever wanted to be was a firefighter like my dad and brother. No chief is going to hire a man with a fake leg." He threw the prosthesis a venomous look.

She wasn't going to dispute reality. Facts were facts.

"There are hundreds of other jobs that don't require two perfect legs."

"Firefighting is in my blood. It's been my goal since I was a kid."

"Goals can change. I have a variety of interests. You must too. Pick a new field and pursue it. You have two years of junior college—go back to school and get a bachelor's degree."

"I'm not college material. And who's going to support us? You?"

"The VA is covering most of our expenses. My job is nothing more than a supplement."

"I didn't sign up to be a parasite."

"Then what's the plan? Are you going to mope around for the rest of your life?"

"I might."

She let a few beats pass while she gathered up her courage.

"Then you're going to do it alone."

At her firm, quiet statement, Greg froze. "You're leaving?"

"That's up to you." She stood, returned the chair to its place, and walked to the door, her legs quivering as she angled back to him. "I still love you, Greg. You—not your leg. And I'll help you in any productive way I can. But the next move has to come from you."

For one tiny second, she hesitated. His prosthesis was across the room, in the corner. Retrieving it would be a struggle for him while maneuvering on crutches.

But he'd caused that problem himself . . . and cleaning up avoidable messes for him wasn't productive.

It was enabling.

Shoring up her resolve, she turned, left the room—and kept walking until she reached her car.

After she slid into the driver's seat, her trembling fingers fumbled three attempts to insert the key.

Once she succeeded, she expelled an unsteady breath and rested her forehead against the wheel, doubt gnawing at her already shaky composure.

Had she been too hard on him?

Was she wrong to set some ground rules?

What would she do next if this didn't work?

The answers eluded her.

All she knew was that countless articles she'd read on the net over the past few months had emphasized the need for tough love in certain cases.

Like this one.

Greg hadn't been happy about it—but as long as there was a chance it might work, she had to stick with the program.

Even if it broke her heart.

5

She needed a taco.

Bad.

Marci scrolled through her email, stopping to read yet again the note Ben had sent her after the article about Ned appeared in last week's paper.

It was cordial, complimentary, appreciative—and totally impersonal.

If she'd had any doubts about the finality of their parting at the wharf, his polite communiqué dispelled them. It was clear he had no intention of seeking her out.

Which was excellent news, given her aversion to dating at the moment—wasn't it?

Yes.

Of course it was.

The best strategy would be to forget about him—and she would, as soon as she convinced the right side of her brain to get with the program.

In the meantime, a stroll to the wharf and some spicy fish tacos should distract her from imprudent fancies on this first day of May.

She rose and moved over to the window, wedging herself against the frame as she peered toward the far end of the wharf.

Rachel eyed her. "What's up?"

"I'm trying to see if Charley is cooking before I trek down there. Mondays are iffy." She squinted. The serving window on the truck appeared to be open. "I think tacos have trumped painting today."

"Lucky you." Rachel refocused on the half-finished article displayed on the screen in front of her. "I was in the mood for one of his creations myself an hour ago, but the truck was shut up tight."

"Want me to bring you back an order?"

"No, thanks. I got a bowl of soup at The Myrtle instead. That will hold me until dinner."

Marci returned to her desk to retrieve her purse, giving her assistant a discreet scan.

Rachel needed more than a bowl of soup to fill out the hollows in her cheeks.

But an infusion of hearty food wouldn't erase the smudgy half-moons under her lower lashes that grew darker with every passing day.

Apparently the situation at home wasn't improving.

She slid the strap of her purse over her shoulder. "I'll be back in ten minutes."

"No worries. I've got it covered here."

Marci left her office behind, inhaled the tantalizing scent of cinnamon rolls as she passed Sweet Dreams Bakery, and crossed Dockside Drive toward Charley's.

Her favorite taco chef raised a hand in greeting as she approached, treating her to one of his trademark all's-right-with-the-world smiles. "Good morning . . . or should I say afternoon?" He perused the sky. "Afternoon it is. The sun's on a downward slide."

She twisted her wrist. "For the record, it's one-thirty. How do you manage without a watch?"

"Why would I need one?"

True. Charley marched to the beat of his own drummer and set his own schedule—which accounted for the erratic hours at the taco stand.

"I see your point. Unfortunately, most of us can't live without our watches."

"More's the pity. Life's too short to spend it yoked to a clock. So what are you having today—a late lunch or a very early dinner?"

"Knowing how filling your food is, probably both. What's the fish of the day?" Not that it mattered. She'd never met a Charley's taco she didn't like.

"Mahi-mahi, with a chipotle lime sauce."

"Yum."

He pulled some fillets out of a cooler, set them on the grill, and began chopping a tomato. "I enjoyed your article about Ned in the paper last week."

"Thanks."

"I bet Ben was pleased with the tribute."

"He seemed to be, based on the note he sent."

"Considerate of him to invite you out on the *Suzy Q* for the final farewell."

Marci furrowed her brow. "How did you know about that?"

Grinning, he pulled out three corn tortillas and laid them on the grill. "It's a small town. People talk. I listen. Right, Floyd?" He tossed the remark toward a seagull pecking around on the nearby pavement.

The bird nudged his feathered companion, and the other gull cackled in what almost sounded like a laugh.

"I agree, Gladys." Charley opened a bottle of his homemade sauce.

"You talk to seagulls?" Marci's lips twitched.

"As long as they talk back." He winked at her. "One-sided conversations aren't much fun." He removed the tortillas from the heat and flipped the fish, his manner growing more serious. "I expect Rachel knows all about that."

She scrutinized him.

Had her clerk confided in the taco-making artist?

"Has she talked to you about her . . . situation?"

"We've chatted now and then. But Greg's only been by once since they arrived."

"I think he keeps to himself."

"Not the best idea when you're feeling blue."

Marci assessed the man as he began assembling her tacos. Did he know more than she did about Greg's mental state—or did that comment just reflect Charley's keen intuition?

Best to proceed with caution.

"I feel bad for both of them. I can't imagine being hit with such an immense challenge that early in a marriage."

"I hear you. Storms can throw us off course whatever our stage in life, but they're harder to weather if you're inexperienced or unprepared. As Ned would have said, in a rough sea, it takes a lot of hands working together to get a boat back to safe harbor."

"My hands are available—but Rachel isn't receptive."

"That could always change. You might still get your chance." He lifted his arm and waved at the city manager, who was crossing the street toward them. "It seems you aren't the only one having a late lunch today."

Brent Davis strode up to the truck and sniffed. "I could smell your tacos all the way to city hall."

Charley chuckled. "You must have a world-class nose."

"My mother claims I do. Wherever I was in the neighborhood as a kid, I could smell her chocolate chip cookies baking and always managed to arrive at the back door as she was pulling them out of the oven. Put my order in the queue, okay?"

"You got it."

Brent turned to her as Charley wrapped her tacos in white paper. "Hey, Marci. How's the world treating you?"

"No complaints. Anything new at city hall?"

"As a matter of fact, yes." His smile faded.

"Care to share?"

"As long as it's off the record."

"Sure. The *Herald* isn't the *New York Times*. I'm not trying to scoop anybody."

"New York wouldn't have any interest in this story—but Hope Harbor will. We had an inquiry from a law firm in Eugene on behalf of a client who prefers to remain anonymous. This client has an interest in buying the Pelican Point lighthouse, and they were asking a bunch of questions about zoning regulations."

"What kind of questions?" Charley set her bag on the counter, faint vertical creases scoring his forehead.

"It seems this client wants to purchase the adjacent parcels of property as well as the lighthouse and build a luxury weekend home that could also be used for corporate retreats and meetings with his senior management."

"Why does he want a lighthouse?" Marci dug some bills out of her shoulder bag and passed them to Charley.

"He doesn't. He wants the view. That's the problem. He's already checked state and federal laws, but he wanted to verify there were no issues from our end if he tears it down."

"What?" Marci's heart flip-flopped. "He plans to level a town landmark?"

"Apparently."

"We can't let him do that!"

"How are we supposed to stop him? There's no zoning

ordinance that would prevent him from combining parcels of land up there, and the lighthouse is privately owned."

"But . . . but it's been part of this town for more than 125 years!"

Charley set her change on the counter. "I agree."

"Hey." Brent held up his palms. "Don't shoot the messenger. I'm just giving you a heads-up. I wish the town had the means to buy it, but we've already been down that road, and it's a dead end."

"Ned would be sick about this." Marci swiped up the coins and dumped them in her bag. "Does Ben know what's going on?"

"The attorney said the firm had been in touch with him."

"And he's going to sell to someone who plans to tear the light down, knowing how much it meant to his grandfather?"

"That I can't answer. But I have to believe he's receptive to their offer if the firm is conducting due diligence with city hall."

"I suppose it's hard to fault a man for entertaining a reasonable offer." Charley pulled some more fish out of the cooler. "I'm sure Ben wants to settle the estate and move on with his life. He has no reason to linger in Hope Harbor."

"It seems to me he could have tried a little harder to find someone who respected the heritage and history the lighthouse represents. I mean, selling it is bad enough, but tearing it down . . ." Marci snagged her bag of tacos, trying without much success to rein in her temper. "Someone ought to talk to him."

"Are you volunteering?" Charley threw the question over his shoulder as he laid Brent's fish on the grill.

"I did promise to give him copies of Ned's columns, so I have an excuse to drop by."

"I say go for it." Brent pulled a few napkins from the dispenser on the counter. "What can it hurt to have a calm, rational discussion about what the lighthouse means to the town and politely ask him to see if he can find a buyer who's willing to preserve it?"

Calm.

Rational.

Polite.

Marci wasn't feeling any of those things at the moment.

But maybe that was okay.

Maybe this situation called for passion and fervor and zeal.

Those she had in spades.

"I'll do it—as soon as I eat my tacos and pick up Ned's columns from the office."

"Good luck. We're behind you 100 percent." Charley gave her a thumbs-up.

"Thanks."

But as she crimped the top of the brown bag between her fingers and hurried back to the office, she had a feeling she was going to need a lot more than luck to convince Ben to walk away from someone who was ready to take an unwanted lighthouse off his hands for a sum no one else might be willing to top.

"Greg! I know you're in there! Answer the door!"

As the banging on the front door intensified, Greg muttered a few choice words.

He was *not* in the mood for a visit from his big brother.

But if Dan had made the long drive down from Florence over eighty-plus miles of winding coast road, he wasn't going to leave without doing whatever he'd come to do.

"Keep your shirt on! I'm coming."

The banging ceased as he struggled up from the recliner where he spent most of his days—but knowing Dan, it would resume within sixty seconds if he didn't unlatch the door.

And he wouldn't put it past his overbearing brother to call the police and claim it was an emergency if his noisy summons went ignored.

Once he was steady, Greg clumped to the door and flipped the lock. "I thought you were going to knock the door down."

"My next step if you continued to ignore me."

"I wasn't ignoring you. I just don't move as fast as I used to. What are you doing here, anyway?" He narrowed his eyes. "Did Rachel call you?"

"No. I'm here because you don't answer my texts or return my calls." Dan gave him a slow, disapproving survey. "You're a mess."

"It's great to see you too."

"I didn't come down here to exchange niceties. And I don't intend to tiptoe around your delicate sensibilities, like Rachel does." He shouldered past him into the house.

"I can see that."

Dan stopped in the middle of the room and did a slow 360. "At least you haven't trashed the place. I was half expecting to see piles of pizza boxes and junk food containers in addition to these." With his toe, he toppled a small pyramid of empty beer cans beside the recliner.

"Rachel is a neat freak."

"So the pristine condition of the house is her doing."

"Yeah."

"And how do you contribute to this household?"

Heat flooded his cheeks. "That's none of your business."

"You're my brother. Rachel is my sister-in-law. If there's trouble in your lives, it's my business."

"Who said there was any trouble?"

Dan snorted. "Look at you. When did you last shave? Or comb

your hair? Or do your PT? Your mobility isn't going to improve if you don't put some effort into it. And what's with all the booze?"

"I'm not answering any of those questions."

"Then you're going to be enjoying my handsome face for the next two days." He dropped onto the couch and folded his arms. "My duffel bag is in the car."

Based on the set of his jaw, his brother was serious.

Blast.

"Why aren't you at the firehouse?" He didn't try to hide his annoyance.

"I finished my rotation. I have two days off. Start talking."

"I don't have anything to say."

"Fine. I'll talk to Rachel. Where is she?"

"Work—and I don't want you talking to my wife."

"Why not?"

Three reasons: she was fed up with him, she liked Dan, and his brother could get anyone to spill their guts if he turned on the charm.

"This is between you and me."

"Nope. In marriage, two become one—remember?"

Greg hesitated. Rachel would be home from work in less than two hours. If he didn't talk, Dan would follow through on his threat and pick her brain.

"Fine." He walked back to his chair in as normal a gait as he could manage and sat. "I'll answer your questions. Three days ago, yesterday, this morning, and I acquired a taste for beer in the army."

"That's a start, anyway." His brother unfolded his arms. "So what's with the radio silence from your end? You don't return my calls, and I could count on two hands the words in the few texts you've deigned to answer."

"I don't have anything to say. My life isn't exactly brimming with news or excitement."

"There could be . . . if you got out of this house once in a while."

"I do."

"When's the last time you ate at a restaurant with your wife or poked around at Lou's shop or had a taco at Charley's?"

"I've done all that since I've been back."

"How often?"

He clamped his teeth together and glared at his brother.

"That's what I thought. You know, hiding in a dark house with all the shades drawn isn't healthy."

"I'm not hiding."

"You could have fooled me. Some fresh air and physical activity wouldn't hurt you."

"I get out."

"Where? To the lighthouse?"

"How do you know about that?"

"I called one day, and Rachel said you'd gone up there alone. Again. She sounded worried."

No surprise there. Rachel had been worried since the day the IED had shattered his leg—and ruined their life—eight months ago.

But it wasn't going to ruin her life much longer, if he continued to ignore the ultimatum she'd issued.

And that might be the best outcome—for her.

"Rachel worries too much." He gave a dismissive wave, all the while fighting back a rush of panic at the very real possibility that she might disappear from his life.

"No, she doesn't. The woman you married has a sunny disposition and a glass-half-full outlook—or she used to. If she's worrying, there's a reason." His brother leaned forward and clasped his hands together. "You need to get your act together, Greg. Dad and Mom would tell you the same thing if they were still here."

"Well, they're not. And I'm sick of being lectured. I don't need you giving me grief too."

"Too?" Dan's eyebrows rose. "Who else is rattling your cage?"

Whoops.

Bad slip.

"No one."

Dan inspected him with that X-ray vision unique to big brothers. "Given how you've been Mr. Antisocial since you came back to Hope Harbor, I'm guessing Rachel finally decided to play hardball."

He could deny it—but if Dan hung around until Rachel got home, he'd pick up on the tension between them and know he'd nailed the situation.

"You sound like you're happy about that."

"I'm not sad, if that's what it takes to bring you to your senses."

"I don't respond well to intimidation."

"It's not intimidation if someone has your best interests at heart. That's called love." He leaned closer. "And Rachel loves you every bit as much as you love her."

As his brother's quiet comment hung in the air between them, Greg dipped his chin, clasped his hands together, and watched his knuckles turn white. "I'm not certain that's true anymore."

"She wouldn't be here if it wasn't."

"She might not be for long."

"Sounds to me like that's up to you."

Exactly what Rachel had said.

"I'm not the same man she married."

"True—but you could be even better. Positive change can come out of bad experiences. It's a choice."

"It's tough finding anything positive in losing a leg."

"Could be you're not trying hard enough—and are too fixated on anger and bitterness to appreciate the blessing of a woman whose world has also been rocked but who's stuck around and tried to shake some sense into you." He stood.

"Where are you going?"

"Home. Now that I know Rachel is putting on the pressure, my work here is done. But a piece of advice. Don't let her do all the heavy lifting. Make an effort. I bet that's all it would take to smooth off some of the rough edges in your relationship. You could start by shaving."

"I like this look."

"Trust me—it doesn't suit you. Clean-cut all-American is more your style."

"Thanks for the fashion advice."

Dan gave him a crooked grin, crossed the room, and squeezed his shoulder. "That's what big brothers are for. Call if you need anything."

"Yeah. Listen . . . you want to hang around for dinner?" After his brother's long drive, he ought to at least offer to feed him.

"No. I don't want to intrude on your evening together."

"Rachel wouldn't mind."

"She might—if you gave her a reason to be glad I decided not to stay." Dan arched an eyebrow.

A surge of heat swept up Greg's neck.

Dan winked and sauntered to the door. "Hold that thought."

"Listen . . ." Greg tried to will away the flush. "Thanks for coming down."

"No sweat." Dan paused, hand on the knob. "But it's not a relaxing road trip. So answer my calls—and try responding to my texts with more than three words."

"I'll keep that in mind."

"Tell Rachel I said hi—and hang on to her. She's a keeper."

Dan exited, closing the door behind him.

For a long while after his brother left, Greg remained in his chair, head tipped back, gaze locked onto the blank ceiling.

He couldn't argue with a thing Dan had said—especially his last comment.

Rachel *was* a keeper.

He'd known that the day they met.

But *should* he keep her? Was it fair to saddle such a young woman with a disabled husband? Didn't she deserve more than he could offer?

I still love you, Greg. You—*not your leg.*

As her declaration from last week echoed in his mind, he closed his eyes. Swallowed.

Hard as it was to believe after all the garbage he'd heaped on her for eight long, painful months, that must be true. Otherwise, she'd have left long ago.

Dan was right.

He needed to start appreciating the blessing Rachel had been in his life and cull back some of the orneriness.

If he didn't, she might follow through on her threat.

And he wasn't strong enough to let her go yet . . . if ever.

Meaning he needed to get his act together and begin rebuilding his life—and behaving like the husband he'd promised to be on their wedding day.

But how was he supposed to do that? The career he'd expected to have was toast, and he had no clue how to provide for his wife's material—or emotional—needs.

He *could* make a few changes in his behavior to ease her worry, though . . . and hope inspiration struck about how to tackle the rest of his issues before she got totally fed up and walked out the door without a backward glance.

6

Seated on the soaring headland, his back against the weather-beaten wall of Pelican Point light, Ben tried to ignore the vibrating cell against his hip.

Why ruin the ambiance of this peaceful scene with conversation? Far better to enjoy the view of the distant horizon, where indigo sea met cornflower blue sky, and watch gulls float lazily on a capricious wind current above the jagged sea stacks offshore.

But after all his army and medical training, he wasn't wired to blow off a summons.

Heaving a sigh, he pulled the cell out of his pocket and skimmed the screen.

Marci.

Why would she be calling him?

As his pulse picked up, he frowned.

Not good.

In light of all the sparks that had pinged between them nine days ago on the *Suzy Q*, further contact with the *Herald* editor wouldn't be wise. Even if he was in the market for romance, getting too friendly with a woman in Hope Harbor would be foolish. As soon as he settled Skip's estate, he was out of here.

Yet before the phone completed its fourth buzz and rolled to voicemail, his finger pressed the talk button.

He scowled at the errant digit. Did it have a mind of its own, or what?

"Hello?" Marci's voice was whisper soft on the other end of the line as he held the cell at arm's length.

What in blazes had compelled him to answer?

"Is anyone there?" Her tone was less certain now.

Talk to the woman, Garrison. Don't compound your first mistake by being rude.

Resigned, he put the phone to his ear. "Hi, Marci. Sorry for the delay. I was, uh, distracted for a minute." Definitely not a lie.

"No problem. I'm just glad I caught you. I stopped by Ned's house to drop off copies of his columns, but you weren't there. I was afraid to leave them on the porch in case the fog rolled in. They could get soggy." She sounded a tad breathless.

Strange.

"I appreciate you following up. Despite all the cleaning-out I've been doing at Skip's, I haven't come across his articles. If you're going to be at your office in an hour or so, I'd be happy to swing by and pick them up." A gull swooped low with a loud caw and landed a few feet away from him.

"I hear seagulls. Are you at the wharf?"

"No. Up at the lighthouse. I had some errands to do and stopped by to enjoy the view."

"That's a coincidence. I ran home after I went to your place, and I'm still here. If you don't mind sharing the view for a few minutes, I could stop by and give you the articles."

Alone with Marci at a rugged lighthouse in a spectacular—and romantic—setting?

That could be dangerous.

But hard as he tried, he couldn't come up with one valid reason for refusing.

"That works." He hoisted himself to his feet. Better to face this standing up. "I'll be here for another ten minutes or so." Setting a time limit might help keep their exchange focused and businesslike.

He hoped.

"Look for me in three."

The line went dead.

While Ben slid his phone back into its holster, another gull fluttered down to join the one sitting on a rock a few feet away. They nestled close together, watching him.

"Sorry, guys. No handouts today."

The lack of food didn't appear to bother the duo. They seemed content to sit and wait, like theatergoers anticipating the next act of a show.

As long as they didn't act like typical seagulls and make a nuisance of themselves, he didn't care how long they hung around.

The faint sound of an approaching car registered, and he turned his back on the cozy couple.

Fifteen seconds later, as a royal-blue Civic came into sight around the final curve in the road, his lips tipped up. Emerald green raincoat, blue-blue car.

The lady did like her color.

She parked next to Skip's pickup on the gravel turnaround at the end of the road, hopped out of her car, and strode toward him, a manila envelope in hand.

Unlike her dress-up attire at the memorial service, today she wore jeans and a gauzy top crisscrossed with green ribbons.

It was kind of retro—but it suited her.

It suited him too.

Can it, Garrison. Keep your mind on business.

Check.

Still . . . he could appreciate Marci Weber's charms without succumbing to them.

At least he was pretty certain he could.

She stopped a few feet away from him. "I'm glad I caught you up here while I was close by. It will save me another trip to Ned's . . . although I would have called before my next attempt."

"It's a fluke I wasn't at the house. I'm almost always there. Thanks for persisting." He held out his hand.

She gave him a blank look—as if she'd forgotten why she'd tracked him down.

He leaned toward her and tapped the envelope.

"Oh. Sorry." Her cheeks pinkened, and she passed it over. "I, uh, think you'll be impressed. He was quite a writer. A number of the stories relate to this lighthouse."

"That doesn't surprise me."

The two seagulls hopped off their rock and waddled closer.

"Friends of yours?" She nodded toward them.

"Hardly. They showed up a few minutes ago. I think they're hoping for a handout."

The first bird nudged his feathered companion, and the other gull gave a laugh-like cackle.

Marci's brow puckered. "Those two remind me of the gulls I saw earlier at the wharf."

"Yeah?" He gave them a dubious once-over. "They all look alike to me."

"That sound was kind of unique, though." After giving the birds one last wary perusal, she dug around in her shoulder bag and pulled out a folded white square of fabric, ziplocked into a plastic sandwich bag. "I owe you this too."

"You didn't have to bother. I have plenty of handkerchiefs." He took the tidy packet she extended.

"I always return borrowed goods. So . . ." She shifted her weight. Like she was nervous. "I ran into Brent Davis, the city manager, an hour ago at Charley's. He mentioned you've had an offer on the lighthouse."

Wow.

News must travel super-fast in small towns.

Faster even than gossip at a forward operating base hospital.

His stomach clenched, and he took a steadying breath.

Don't go there, Garrison. The lighthouse situation has nothing to do with your army career—and that incident is history.

"Yes." Remarkable how calm and controlled he sounded despite the sudden surge of gut-churning memories. "The Hope Harbor grapevine must be major league. I only got the call yesterday afternoon."

"I understand the buyer plans to tear down the lighthouse."

Her tone was conversational, but the sudden tautness in her posture put him on alert.

"My contact didn't say that, but based on how the buyer intends to use the site, I assume he does."

"Ned would be devastated."

He already knew that—but what choice did he have? No one else had come forward with an offer.

"I know Skip loved the light—and I'm sorry there isn't a better option. But look at it." He waved a hand toward the battered tower. "If someone doesn't invest a sizable amount of time and money in it soon, the walls are going to crumble. And no one else wants it."

"They might."

"It's been on the market for more than four months and there hasn't been a single nibble, according to the real estate agent."

"It wasn't an emergency until now."

He squinted at her. "What's that supposed to mean?"

"I doubt anyone in Hope Harbor expected the light to be torn down. Now that we're faced with that reality, the town might rally behind the cause and come up with a way to buy it."

"From what I understand, they didn't want it for *free* when the government offered it to them three years ago."

She narrowed her eyes. "How much is this person paying you for it, if you don't mind me asking?"

"More than Skip paid." As he gave her the number, she winced. "And that doesn't take into account the cost of restoration and upkeep."

"But . . . but what about Ned's legacy? Don't you care about preserving that?"

"It's hardly a legacy. He only owned the light for two years."

From somewhere on the rocks below the point, a seal belched.

"My sentiments exactly." Marci dipped her chin in agreement as her mouth flattened into a taut line. "Ned cared about the light long before he bought it."

She was right. The title might have been in Skip's possession for a mere twenty-four months, but he'd loved that lighthouse his whole life.

Ben tried to ignore the latest prick on his conscience—one of dozens since he'd agreed to mull over the offer.

"And it *is* a legacy." Fire ignited in Marci's green irises as she continued without giving him a chance to respond. "He wanted to preserve this little piece of Hope Harbor history. That's why he bought it rather than let it fall into the hands of an outsider. Maybe he wouldn't have been able to accomplish his dream, but I know this. He would never, ever have sold it to anyone who planned to tear it down."

Man, this woman knew how to lay on the guilt.

He planted his fists on his hips and locked gazes with her. "Why do you care so much, anyway? You're a newcomer. You have no history here." Certainly no evening hikes to this spot with a beloved grandfather.

She bristled, sparks pinging off her as she straightened to her full five-foot-fourish height. "I might be new, but I love this town—from Charley's taco stand to Sweet Dreams's cinnamon rolls to the one-for-all mentality of the people who live here. We may not have the kind of funds your buyer has, but what this town lacks in money it more than makes up for in spirit and hope and a can-do attitude. And we stand together when the chips are down."

"You don't have to defend Hope Harbor to me. I have fond memories of this place."

"Not fond enough to find a way to save the lighthouse."

"That's not fair. Skip would have—"

"Wanted you to at least *try* to save it."

Good grief.

This woman had a runaway mouth.

"You don't know that."

"Yes, I do! I often come up here in the evening, like Ned used to, and we spent many a night sitting on that rock watching the sun go down." She waved a hand toward the perch the two seagulls had abandoned. "I got to know him well. In fact, he lit such a fire in me for lighthouses in general and this lighthouse in particular that I logged quite a few hours inside, working alongside him on the restoration."

Marci had invested sweat equity in Skip's project?

No wonder she was riled about the sale.

"Listen . . . I'm not going to dispute anything you've said. But Skip's gone—and without a person who shared his passion spearheading a project like this, the light wouldn't survive anyway. The practical choice is to sell it and move on."

Eyes thinning, she mimicked his confrontational pose. "Not every decision in life has to be based on practicalities."

"What do you expect me to do? I'm leaving as soon as I wrap up Skip's estate. Four or five weeks, max. If I turn down this sale, the light will just sit here and continue to deteriorate."

"A lot can happen in a handful of weeks."

"Like what?"

"I don't know." She gave a vague flip of her hand. "Something that would help preserve the light."

"That would take a miracle."

"They do happen."

"Oh, come on. Be realistic. That's as crazy as"—he homed in on the two sets of unblinking avian eyes watching the exchange—"as thinking our seagull friends here might peck some gold pirate coins out of the sand that would cover all the lighthouse expenses."

As if on cue, the two gulls rose in a flutter of wings and raucous squawks, circled close to his head until he was forced to duck, then landed on the ground next to Marci, one on each side—like sentries.

Weird.

"I don't understand how you can be so callous about this. Ned was your grandfather!"

If the weather were colder, Ben wouldn't have been surprised to see steam coming out of Marci's ears.

His own temper was heating up too. What right did this woman he barely knew have to throw a guilt trip on him?

"Don't you think you're being too emotional?"

"No!" The slight frizz in her red hair fairly quivered with indignation. "There's nothing wrong with honest emotion. Sometimes a healthy dose of passion is what it takes to make a person see the light. I'm not going to apologize for how I feel. You need to do the right thing."

Ben froze as another woman's similar words echoed in his mind.

"I'm not sorry for how I feel, Ben. Just do the right thing. It can all be so simple."

But it hadn't been.

Nor was it now.

Selling a lighthouse might not have the same fallout as his previous dilemma, but it, too, was ripping a hole in his heart.

And he didn't need another emotional woman compounding the problem.

He backed off a few steps and fished out his keys. "I'm doing what I have to do to wrap up all the loose ends before I leave for Ohio."

"The lighthouse isn't a loose end. It's a legacy. A landmark."

"Depends on your perspective. Thanks again for the clippings."

Without waiting for a response, he circled toward his car, giving her and the birds a wide berth.

"Hey!"

He paused. Hesitated. Angled back.

She glared at him. "Walking away in the middle of a discussion is rude."

So he'd been told.

But sticking around could be worse.

Even dangerous.

"The discussion is over."

With that, he turned his back on her and strode toward his truck.

Only after he was speeding down Pelican Point Road, the lighthouse receding in his rearview mirror, did he venture a glance back.

Marci was standing where he'd left her, hands on hips, the gusty wind whipping her glorious hair.

He pressed harder on the gas.

No doubt her intentions were honorable. It was clear she cared about Hope Harbor and wanted what was best for the town.

But excitable women were also unpredictable. If he gave her an inch, she might take a mile.

So barring a better offer for the light, he'd stick with his plan—get Skip's house ready to put on the market, sort through the rest of his grandparents' personal belongings, and go as many rounds as necessary with his conscience to vanquish his doubts before he signed on the dotted line and ditched the lighthouse that had become one more unwanted complication in his life.

Gee.

That had gone well.

As Ben's truck disappeared around the curve in the road, Marci exhaled and dropped onto the large rock that offered the best seat in the house for the daily sunset show.

The two gulls waddled over and settled at her heels.

"I guess I might have come on a little too strong, huh?"

They observed her in silence.

Too bad she didn't have Charley's skill at communicating with birds—and people.

Would she never learn to curb her tongue?

She tucked her windblown hair behind her ears, massaged her forehead, and admitted the truth.

Diplomacy was *not* her forte.

Yes, some positive passion would have been fine. Persuasive, even.

But angry, accusatory passion?

Different story.

It was hard to blame Ben for shutting down. Had the situation been reversed, she would have been livid if someone tried to ladle on guilt and dictate what she should do with a piece of property she owned.

Perhaps if she'd come to him with a constructive idea or two and funneled her passion into productive enthusiasm instead of antagonism, he might have been more receptive to exploring other options.

Considering the cold mask that had slipped over his face near the end of their heated exchange, however—and the speed with which he'd vacated the premises—there wasn't much likelihood he'd be open to a second go-round, even if she extended an olive branch.

Why, oh why, had she been cursed with fiery hair—and a disposition to match?

The upbeat strains of "Zip-a-Dee-Doo-Dah" drifted from her purse, and Marci dug out her cell. Smiled at the screen.

Perfect timing.

A quick chat with her mother always gave her spirits a boost.

"Hi, Mom." She leaned back on one hand and filled her lungs with the fresh, salty air. "I've missed talking with you. How was the fortieth anniversary cruise?"

"Fantastic. Your dad and I felt like honeymooners."

Marci grinned. Her mom *sounded* like a honeymooner. Sort of giddy and girly.

Hard—and kind of disconcerting—to picture a parent in that role, though.

"I'm glad you had fun. Did you and Dad boogie the nights away?"

"I don't know if I'd call it boogying, but those ballroom dancing lessons we've taken for years came in handy. I wish we could have convinced you to sign up for a few."

"Dad taught me enough to get by—not that I need those skills very often. Most guys in my generation wouldn't know a foxtrot from a tango."

"More's the pity. They have no idea what they're missing. There's nothing more romantic than dancing to a classic tune.

Maybe if you beat the bushes, you'll find a few men who know a step or two."

An image of Ben flashed through her mind.

Did he know how to dance? And if he did, what would it be like to sway in his arms to a slow, romantic melody?

A soft sigh escaped her.

"Marci? Are you there?"

"Uh, yeah." She shot to her feet, and the gulls scuttled back with an accusatory glower. *Focus, Marci.* "I haven't run into any Fred Astaires out here."

"Have you been looking?"

She stifled a groan.

Of course her mother would bring up her love life—or lack thereof.

"I'm occupied with the *Herald* and getting my business established. That doesn't leave me much free time."

"You've been there two years, honey. I know you're busy, but don't you think it might be healthy to carve out a few hours for a social life? We all need balance to thrive." Unlike her daughter, Laura Weber knew how to tactfully discuss a sensitive subject.

Why couldn't she have inherited her mom's ash-blonde hair and calm temperament instead of her grandmother's ginger mane and unruly tongue?

"I'll get there at some point, Mom."

"Are there many eligible men in that small town?"

Again, Ben's image strobed across her mind.

How ridiculous was that?

The man didn't like her, she wasn't altogether sure about him, and he was leaving in a handful of weeks.

That was *not* the definition of eligible.

She erased his face from her mind.

"A few."

"Not as many as in Atlanta, though. You had an active social life there. I bet you miss that."

Her stomach kinked.

No, she didn't.

Not one bit.

Thanks to Jack.

The moratorium she'd declared on dating suited her fine.

But she'd never shared that bit of her history with her parents—and she had no intention of starting now.

"Believe it or not, my life has been too full to think much about dating. Hope Harbor may be small, but there's always interesting stuff happening here. Wait till you hear the news about the lighthouse."

She proceeded to fill her mother in on the impending sale, downplaying her involvement with the cat-rescuing army surgeon who now owned the property.

"I can see why the town would be upset about that." Her mother's comforting empathy filtered over the line—another trait Marci wished she'd inherited. "Since you run the newspaper, is there anything you could do to rally support for a save-the-lighthouse campaign?"

"That might be a possibility if we had more time—but the owner has an offer on the table, and he wants to close the deal before he leaves town in four or five weeks."

"Ouch. That's a tiny window. Still . . . it couldn't hurt to talk to a few people, generate some ideas, could it? When you're all fired up, you're a force to be reckoned with. Your zeal could create a lot of enthusiasm."

Not with Ben—but in all fairness, she hadn't applied it very well, either.

"It's worth thinking about."

"Seems like the only reasonable option, short of finding a wealthy benefactor."

"Not likely in this area. Hope Harbor is rich in many ways, but money isn't one of them."

"Why don't you sleep on it? Give the situation some thought—and prayer. God's help desk is always open."

The corners of Marci's mouth twitched. "Cute analogy."

"Also true. Will you keep me informed?"

"Sure."

"I'll say a few prayers myself. I remember the light from our visit last summer. It would be a shame if it disappeared."

"I agree—and I appreciate the prayers. Tell Dad I said hi."

"Will do. Take care, sweetie. We love you."

The line went dead, and Marci tucked the phone back into her purse.

"It's always comforting to talk to your mom, you know?" She addressed her comment to the two seagulls.

One of them made a purring noise that sounded like an affirmation.

Or had that come from Annabelle? Maybe the feline was prowling around nearby, in search of another tree to climb.

She scanned the windswept terrain.

Nope. Her neighbor's cat was nowhere in sight.

Marci checked out the seagulls again. They appeared to be grinning at her.

Rolling her eyes, she strode toward her car. She was as bad as Charley, talking to seagulls.

Yet somehow she felt better.

Go figure.

In any case, her mother was right about the light. She did have tons of enthusiasm, and she'd always believed that old saying about obstacles being nothing more than stepping-stones.

So what if she'd ticked off Ben? That didn't mean the cause was lost.

If she could recruit some volunteers to form a think tank, they might be able to come up with a plan he could accept and the town would find financially palatable.

It was possible.

And if, in the end, they failed to stop the sale, at least she'd be able to sleep at night knowing she'd tried her best to preserve a treasured piece of Hope Harbor history.

7

What was that appetizing aroma?

Pulling a bag of groceries from the back of her car, Rachel sniffed again.

It smelled like Italian spices.

Not pizza, though. *That* scent was all too familiar after the countless takeout they'd ordered over the past two months.

Or rather, the ones Greg had ordered while she was at work, so he didn't have to sit with her during a meal.

He might never have admitted that was the reason for his sudden pizza craving, but why else would he eat while she was away unless it was to avoid her at the dinner table?

And maybe this was no more than a continuation of that pattern. He could have found some other place with more than pizza on its takeout menu.

Spirits sinking, she hefted the second bag out of the car and shut the door with a hip-check. If he'd ordered out again, she'd be eating another solitary dinner while he watched TV or played video games.

At least she wouldn't have to cook tonight—assuming he'd left a portion for her in the fridge, as usual.

After setting one of the bags down at the door that led into the house, she inserted her key in the lock and shouldered into the kitchen.

Stopped.

Gaped.

The small café table was set for two—sort of. A knife and fork rested on a paper napkin at each place, and a container of parmesan cheese was in the middle. Not fancy . . . but an effort.

She glanced at the stove.

Two pots were steaming—boiling water in one, and what appeared to be spaghetti sauce in the other. The kind Greg had made for her from his mother's recipe on a few occasions during their courtship and in the early days of their marriage.

There was also a bag of salad on the counter beside a large bowl.

He'd been busy while she'd run up to Coos Bay to do some errands.

But what in the world was going on?

As if he'd heard her unspoken question, Greg appeared in the doorway from the living room. "Are you hungry?" He continued toward the stove without meeting her gaze.

"Um . . . yeah. I am."

He stirred the sauce, then crossed to her and took one of the bags. After setting it on the counter, he opened one of the utensil drawers and poked around.

Feet rooted to the spot, she studied his taut posture. "Greg?"

"Yeah?" He pulled out a pair of scissors and cut open the bag of salad, his voice gruff.

"Why are you cooking?"

"I got hungry for Mom's spaghetti sauce. You don't have to eat it if you don't want to."

"No. That's fine. I like your mom's sauce."

She moved to the counter and deposited the other bag, keeping a surreptitious eye on her husband while she put away the groceries.

He wasn't just fixing dinner. He'd also combed his hair and shaved.

Something was up.

But what?

If she got him talking, she might be able to find out—though that was a difficult-to-impossible chore most days.

"I've been meaning to tell you . . . my boss asked me last week to pass along her thanks for your idea about the ad for Lou's Bait and Tackle shop. He went for it hook, line, and sinker—pardon the pun."

She braced for a smart-aleck comeback.

It never came.

"Good." He bent down to get the colander, keeping his face averted.

It was a start—but one-word answers weren't going to tell her why he was cooking dinner.

She needed to ask more open-ended questions.

"Do you remember any of the weird trivia Lou shared with you when you visited his shop as a kid?" Lame, but the best she could come up with on the fly.

Several silent seconds ticked by, and her spirits dipped.

He wasn't going to respond.

Whatever the reason he'd decided to clean up and prepare dinner, he wasn't going to . . .

"That the Mayflower landed at Plymouth Rock because they ran out of beer. As a teen beginning to sneak a few sips of alcohol here and there, that stuck with me."

She froze.

He'd not only answered but offered a tiny personal insight.

Stay cool, Rachel. Keep the conversation going.

"Are you certain he wasn't pulling your leg?"

He stiffened—and she sucked in a sharp breath.

How stupid could she be?

Any reference to legs was bound to shut him up as tight as one of Oregon's butter clams.

So much for . . .

"Yeah." He resumed stirring. "I checked it out later. He had his facts straight. A few people tried to call him on trivia over the years, but he could always back up his claims."

Rachel slowly exhaled.

He hadn't closed down.

Thank you, God!

"I don't know what fun nugget he's going to share in the first ad, but the featured item is a copper hummingbird feeder."

"That should sell well. I saw quite a few of the birds darting among the flowers up by the lighthouse on Sunday."

She masked her dismay.

He must have taken the car up there—again—while she walked to church.

Lovely as the spot was, thinking about her brooding husband sitting on the edge of a cliff did not leave her feeling warm and fuzzy.

But she wasn't going to try and dissuade him from his solitary trips again tonight. That would only raise his ire and shut him down.

"The lighthouse has an incredible view." She tried for a pleasant tone as she crossed to the counter and began to toss the salad. "Sad to say, though, it may be off-limits soon."

He finished dumping the limp noodles from the pot into the colander and swiveled toward her, brow furrowed. "What do you mean?"

She told him what Marci had passed on yesterday after her

encounter with the city manager at Charley's—and with Ben later at the lighthouse.

Frown deepening, Greg ladled sauce over the noodles while she put the salad on the table. "That stinks. Everyone in town loves Pelican Point light."

"That's what Marci said. She's planning to get some people together to brainstorm ideas about how to save it."

"When?"

"She made some calls yesterday afternoon while I was at the office." Rachel filled two glasses with water and set them on the table, homing in on the spark of interest in Greg's eyes. "Would you like to get involved?"

He carried their plates of spaghetti to the table. "I don't know what I could offer."

"You're very creative. You were the brains behind that successful charity fund-raising drive your unit had in Fort Hood, and you had a very creative idea for Lou's ad."

"Your boss is a pro at this stuff."

"No, her background is journalism and PR, not marketing. She's looking for help."

"I don't have any training." He opened the lid on the can of parmesan but weighed the container in his hand instead of sprinkling any cheese on his pasta.

"You have excellent instincts—and you know this town. Better than Marci."

He refocused on the task at hand, dousing his spaghetti with the parmesan before handing her the can. "I'll have to think about it. We better eat or this will get cold."

Rachel bowed her head, said a short blessing, and dug into the spaghetti.

"I got some chocolate chip cookie dough at the grocery store." An impulse purchase that for once might pay off. "I could bake a few after dinner—if you'd like some dessert."

"Yeah. That'd be okay." A moment of silence passed . . . and when he spoke again, his inflection was a tad too casual. "Dan would have enjoyed those if he'd stuck around for a couple of days, like he said he might. They're his weakness."

She stopped eating. "Your brother was here?"

A faint flush spread over Greg's cheeks as he continued to chow down. "For a little while yesterday. He drove down to say hi."

All the way from Florence?

Not likely.

Dan was one of the most single-minded men she'd ever met—next to her husband. If he'd made the long, winding drive, he'd had an agenda.

One that involved his younger sibling.

And whatever he'd said must have hit its mark.

Yet curious as she was about what they'd discussed, a different question was front and center in her mind as they chatted more than they had in months during the remainder of the meal.

Was tonight the beginning of a permanent course correction—or no more than a blip on the radar that would disappear by morning?

As the chime of the doorbell echoed through the house, Ben yawned, took a slug of coffee, and padded barefoot toward the front door.

He'd need a gallon of caffeine to perk him up after the hours he'd spent tossing and turning for the past two nights, thanks to his less-than-pleasant encounter with Marci at the lighthouse on Monday.

It was downright irritating to be that discombobulated by a woman.

Even more annoying?

He still found the *Herald* editor appealing despite her over-the-top emotions and penchant for poking her nose in other people's business.

His business, anyway.

And it didn't help that she'd been dead right about most of what she'd said.

Trouble was, no matter how much he racked his brain, he couldn't come up with a solution that would preserve Pelican Point light.

Smoothing a hand down the hair he hadn't yet bothered to comb, he pulled open the front door.

His neighbor stood on the other side. The one he hadn't seen since *their* less-than-pleasant encounter a week ago.

Wonderful.

If the man was as ill-tempered on this Wednesday morning as he'd been in his backyard, Ben might as well write this day off as a total loss.

And it wasn't even nine o'clock yet.

"Good morning." He managed a stiff smile, fingers tightening on his mug.

"Morning." The guy cleared his throat. "I, uh, wanted to stop by and thank you for planting the rosebush for my wife—and apologize for my bad manners."

A few beats ticked by while Ben absorbed the man's words.

Maybe the guy wasn't a total jerk after all.

Some of the tension in his shoulders evaporated.

"No worries. We all have bad days."

"Or months. Eight of them, in my case." His Adam's apple bobbed. "I lost my leg in the Middle East, and the adjustment has been hard."

Ah.

Stiff gait explained.

Along with the man's testy attitude.

Given all the mangled limbs he'd seen, all the desperate please-save-my-leg/arm/foot/hand pleas he'd heard from soldiers, Ben knew as well as anyone could who still had both legs how devastating a loss like that was to a young person in their prime.

"I'm sorry to hear that. I just got back from my last tour over there myself, at a forward operating base hospital."

"You're a doctor?"

"Yes. Orthopedic surgeon."

A muscle ticced in Greg's jaw. "You cut off a lot of limbs while you were there?"

"Some—but I saved every one I could. We all did."

"So I was told. But in Landstuhl they said mine was too far gone. You ever work there?"

"For about a year." He'd seen more trauma cases at the military hospital in Germany than most doctors saw in a lifetime. "Did you run into an IED?"

"Yeah. After only six weeks." Disgust flattened his features. "All that training for nothing. I didn't have a chance to do anything worthwhile while I was over there." He eyed the mug. "Except learn to like super-strong coffee."

At the sudden turn in the conversation, Ben regarded his visitor.

Was the guy angling for an invitation?

Could be.

He might want to talk about his experiences with someone who'd seen battlefield trauma up close and personal.

"Same here. That's the kind I brew now. Would you like a cup?" He lifted his mug and motioned toward the back of the house.

"I wouldn't mind. Thanks."

Ben eased aside to let him pass. "Straight back to the kitchen."

He followed as his neighbor walked with a not-quite-normal gait toward the rear of the house. At eight months out, it was possible he was still using a temporary prosthesis. Depending on the extent of any other IED-related injuries, his progress might have been delayed. Hopefully he was following whatever PT regimen had been recommended.

Based on their previous encounter, however, the man had anger—and depression—issues.

Marital ones, too, given his comments about his wife.

Could he build some rapport with the guy, who seemed in need of a sympathetic ear?

Might be worth a try.

After all, if he couldn't save the lighthouse for the town, he might be able to at least lend a hand to one of the town's residents.

"Have a seat." Ben motioned toward the table and removed yet another box of fabric he'd dragged up from the basement. Thank goodness the quilting club at Grace Christian was willing to take them off his hands. "Cleaning out the house is taking longer than I expected. I had no idea my grandparents were such packrats. Cream or sugar?"

"Black is fine."

He filled a mug for the man and joined him at the table. "I'd offer you a donut or Danish if I had either, but Cheerios are my breakfast staple."

"They were mine too, in my bachelor days." One side of Greg's mouth hitched up. "For lunch and dinner too."

"I hear you. Been there, done that."

"I eat better now, though. My wife made some kind of baked omelet before she left for work. Her cooking beats Cheerios and army grub any day."

"Lucky you."

"Yeah." His smile faltered. "I'm definitely the lucky one in our relationship. She had no idea what she was in for when we got married a year and a half ago."

They were almost newlyweds?

Ouch.

"Tough break to be hit with a big challenge so early in a marriage."

"It wasn't what we planned, that's for sure." He stared into the black depths of his coffee.

"Are you both from Hope Harbor?" It would be helpful if they had a support system . . . but the lack of visitors to the house suggested otherwise.

"I am. Rachel's from Texas."

"So you have family in town?"

"Not anymore. My mom and dad are gone, and my brother lives in Florence. I have some friends here . . . but I haven't been in the mood to socialize."

Meaning the two of them were trying to muscle through on their own.

Not the best idea.

"How's your wife settling in?"

"Okay, I guess." He took a slow sip of his brew. "But it isn't the life we expected. After I got out of the service, she was going to finish her degree and I was going to be a firefighter. You know what they say, though. If you want to make God laugh, tell him your plans." A thread of bitterness curdled his words.

His neighbor may have corralled his anger to some degree since the day in the garden, but it continued to lurk, as insidious as a staph infection.

And potentially as lethal.

Ben debated his next move.

He could tell the man it was better to lose his leg than his life, that he was fortunate to have a supportive wife, that there might be opportunities out there he'd have missed if he'd stuck with his original plan.

But platitudes or pep talks weren't going to pull him out of his funk.

Ben swigged his coffee.

Too bad he hadn't opted for a bit of psychiatric training in med school.

As it was, he'd be safer to sympathize with the man's plight and offer a few open-ended comments to get the guy talking rather than attempt any armchair counseling.

"Life can definitely throw curves."

"Yeah." Greg set his mug on the table and gave him an intent look. "I heard you got hit with one yourself when you arrived in town. Inheriting a lighthouse had to be a shock."

He tried to mask his surprise.

That had come out of the blue.

Given the active local grapevine, he wasn't surprised his neighbor had heard about the lighthouse—but why bring it up?

"That's putting it mildly." He took a slow sip of his joe, trying to figure out how to play this. "I can't believe my grandfather never told me he bought it, given how close we were."

"Maybe he was afraid you'd think it was an impractical purchase."

"It was."

"Yeah—but it meant the world to him. I didn't know him well, but after Rachel and I moved in next door, he'd stop in on occasion with a bag of donuts or some cinnamon rolls from Sweet Dreams to shoot the breeze."

That sounded like Skip. Always tuned in to the needs of others, always willing to lend a hand to help a lonely person.

Or an abandoned lighthouse.

"My grandfather did have a touch of Don Quixote in him."

"There are worse things, I suppose. My wife told me last

night that you're planning to sell the property to someone who intends to knock down the light."

Uh-oh.

Unless his listening skills were failing him, there was a very slight undercurrent of censure in that comment.

Was this guy going to reward him for his hospitality by jumping all over him too?

And how did he and his wife know about that brand-new development? Hope Harbor might have a warp-speed grapevine, but you had to mingle to tap into it, and they didn't seem to socialize.

"Where did you hear that?"

"Rachel's boss told her yesterday afternoon."

That made sense. His wife did come and go on a regular basis, suggesting she had some kind of job.

"It's not easy to keep anything private in this town, is it?"

Greg's lips quirked again. "Welcome to small-town America. Rachel's not nosy, but when you work for a newspaper editor, you hear stuff."

Newspaper editor?

Greg's wife worked for Marci?

No wonder this guy and his wife were both in the loop about town happenings.

"I assume you're talking about the *Herald*?"

"That's the only paper we have. I heard you met Marci Weber."

"Uh-huh."

"She's a firecracker."

No kidding.

"Do you know her well?" *Keep it conversational, Garrison.*

"No, but Rachel told me how passionate she can be about causes she believes in. Like the lighthouse."

Had Marci told Greg's wife details about their volatile encounter on Monday—or was the man's comment more generic?

A proceed-with-caution warning began to beep in his mind.

It might be best to tiptoe around this and approach from the side rather than head-on.

"What does your wife do at the *Herald*?"

"Whatever needs to be done. She's only been there eight weeks."

"She like it?"

"Yeah. She's just a year short of her journalism degree, so the work is right up her alley. Having a great boss helps too."

Marci the firecracker was a great boss?

"I take it the editor hasn't blown up at your wife."

"No. Rachel's pretty easy to get along with. She has to be, to put up with me." He gave a self-deprecating shrug. "So is it true about the buyer tearing down the light?"

"I think that's his plan."

"Bummer."

"I agree. But no one else has come forward, and I can't afford to turn down the offer. I want all the loose ends tied up before I leave in four or five weeks."

The man traced a finger around the rim of his mug. "Would you consider putting off your buyer until then if there was a chance the town could come up with a way to buy the lighthouse?"

This guy was as pie-in-the-sky as Marci.

"Yes—but as I told your wife's boss, I don't see that happening."

"I agree the odds are long, but Marci is putting together some sort of think tank to tackle the issue. They might come up with a plan that could be feasible."

A think tank spearheaded by Marci.

Why was he not surprised?

"I don't know how agreeable the buyer would be to me deferring my decision."

"Would you be willing to ask? All he could do is say no."

That was true.

And if there was even a remote possibility of saving the light Skip had loved, why not put the question on the table?

"Sure. I can do that. I'll have my realtor contact him. But I'm curious. Why are *you* so interested in the light?"

"I used to hang around up there with my friends when I was a kid." His features softened, and the corners of his lips rose a fraction. "Some of my happiest memories are the hours I spent there in the imaginary worlds we created, defending the place from pirates and rescuing ships in distress, or pretending it was a castle under siege. Going up there gives me a lift."

It appeared everyone in town had a soft spot for Skip's folly.

"I'll call my agent this morning and let you know what the buyer has to say."

"That'd be super." He finished his coffee and pushed himself to his feet. "I've taken up enough of your time. I wouldn't want to keep you from that." He waved at the dusty boxes from the basement lining one wall in the kitchen.

"Trust me, I'm in no rush to plunge back below deck."

He followed his neighbor to the door, where the man shook his hand, apologized again for his prior rudeness, and thanked him for the coffee.

Yet as Greg walked down the path toward the street and Ben closed the door, he had a feeling the man's visit had been prompted as much by his concern over the fate of Pelican Point light as by his apology.

And truth be told, he'd like to see a different outcome too.

In fact, if Marci had been willing to discuss the situation rationally on Monday, they might have been able to find some common ground.

But no.

She'd waved her hands in the air and spouted nonsense about miracles and accused him of betraying Skip's legacy.

His mouth tightened as he strode back to the kitchen.

He hadn't exactly been Mr. Congeniality himself—but anyone would have gotten defensive in the face of such an onslaught. Short of yelling back at her, walking away had been his only option.

However . . . he wasn't an unreasonable man. While Greg's idea might not lead anywhere, he was willing to ask the buyer to wait four weeks for an answer. If the nameless man with deep pockets said yes, Marci and her think tank would get their opportunity to come up with a viable alternative.

It was the least he could do for Skip.

And it will make Marci happy too.

He blew out a breath and set his mug down on the counter with more force than necessary.

So what?

He didn't give a lick whether she was happy or not.

Liar, liar.

Ignoring the taunt from his conscience, he plunged back into Skip's black hole of a basement that seemed to produce two new boxes for every one he hauled up the steps.

At this rate, it would take a full three weeks to empty the place.

In the meantime, he'd stay far away from the fiery redhead. Now that he and Greg were communicating, he could funnel any news about the light through him to his wife, who could in turn inform her boss.

It was a perfect plan.

Because while life might be more boring without Marci's jade eyes flashing his direction and her sizzling energy setting off sparks to rival Fourth of July fireworks, his heart would be much, much safer.

8

Rachel checked her watch.

Ten minutes until her workday ended . . . and another thirty before she got home after a quick detour to the local grocery store for the OJ she'd forgotten on her trip to Coos Bay yesterday.

Her nerves began to ping.

What would be waiting for her at the house tonight?

Would Greg be like he'd been last night, genial and communicative . . . or would he default to his previous ornery, taciturn behavior?

And if he did regress, what was she going to do about it?

Her stomach knotted.

Maybe she shouldn't have issued the ultimatum that could hold dire consequences for both of them.

But if she hadn't, would whatever Dan had said to his brother have had as much impact?

Closing the document on the screen in front of her, she massaged her temple.

It was so hard to know what to do.

Counseling might help them sort through the mess, but Greg had been clear that he'd had his fill of what he called psychobabble before he mustered out of the service.

And she doubted whether a solo trip on her part would resolve their issues.

Her phone began to vibrate, and she pulled it out, keeping an eye on Marci, who was frowning at her laptop screen and typing at a furious pace. She must be working on next week's editorial about the proposed commercial building code revision that would clean up the disreputable Sea Haven Apartment complex on the outskirts of town.

A short, quiet conversation shouldn't distract Marci while she was in passionate prose mode.

Rachel scanned her cell—and her breath hitched.

Uh-oh.

Greg never called her at work. All phone communication originated with her.

Pulse accelerating, she put the phone to her ear and angled away from Marci. "Hi. What's up?"

"Sorry to bother you at the office, but I have some information you might want to share with your boss."

As she listened to him recount his visit with their neighbor this morning, her eyebrows rose.

She definitely owed Dan a thank-you call.

Whatever he'd said during his visit on Monday appeared to be having a domino effect. A shared spaghetti dinner last night, evidence in the spare bedroom that Greg was buckling down on his PT, and now an impromptu social visit with a neighbor.

Her spirits began to lift, like one of Hope Harbor's whimsical mists.

". . . defer for four weeks."

Drat.

She'd lost the thread of the conversation.

"I'm sorry . . . I missed the last couple of sentences."

"I said, Ben checked, and the lighthouse buyer agreed to give him four weeks to consider the offer. That should buy your boss and her think tank some breathing room."

Rachel stared at the poster on the wall across from her.

"Shoot for the moon. Even if you miss, you'll land among the stars."

The words were pretty . . . and they summed up how Marci approached life . . . but the sentiment had never resonated with her.

Until now.

Maybe *she* needed to shoot for the moon . . . with Greg. Push him to build on whatever Dan had started during his visit and the ultimatum she'd issued. She might not manage to fully restore the relationship they'd enjoyed during their courtship and early days of marriage—but they'd have to end up in a better place than they were now.

It was worth a try, anyway.

"I'll let her know. Thanks for asking him to do that." She curled her fingers tighter around the phone and dropped her volume yet again. "By the way, Marci's having an open meeting about the lighthouse tomorrow night. She sent an email to the *Herald* mailing list and I put up a few flyers around town for her. After that, she'll form her think tank committee. Why don't you attend?"

Please, Lord, let this project pique his interest so he has something to do all day besides sit in the dark house or up on the cliff lamenting over everything he's lost.

A few silent seconds passed, and her heart sank.

He was going to refuse.

Without giving him a chance to reject her suggestion, she

jumped back in. "It's going to be in the fellowship hall at Grace Christian. I think she's expecting a large group. You could sit in the back and listen in if you want to. You don't have to participate."

"I haven't been inside a church in months, Rachel."

"This is the hall, not the sanctuary. And Reverend Baker is very laid-back. I don't know if he'll attend, but you don't have to worry if he does. He welcomes everyone. He won't make you feel uncomfortable for not coming to services with me."

"I know him. He came to Grace Christian when I was thirteen." A beat ticked by. "Have you talked to him about our . . . situation?"

As his voice took on a harder edge, she lifted her chin. "No. That's between us—and God."

"You wanted us to go to a counselor."

"I still think that might be helpful—but I wouldn't share our history with anyone without talking to you first."

"Okay." He exhaled. "I'll think about the meeting. Are you coming home soon?"

"After I pass on the news about the reprieve to Marci and swing by the grocery store."

"I put a chicken in the oven. It'll be ready at five-thirty."

He was fixing dinner *again*? The man whose entire culinary repertoire included his mom's spaghetti sauce and throwing some meat on the grill?

"I . . . uh . . . didn't know you knew how to cook chicken."

"I didn't—until about three hours ago. I found a recipe for beer-can chicken online that sounded . . . unique. But I've got the pizza place's number on hand if this is a bust."

Beer-can chicken.

Yeah, they could end up eating pizza.

But hey, he was making an effort.

"We might be surprised." She tried for an optimistic tone.

"That's what I'm afraid of. See you soon."

The line went dead . . . but a surge of new life infused Rachel's heart.

For the past two days, a glimmer of the old Greg was back. And now, a touch of humor.

Meaning that maybe . . . just maybe . . . her newly adopted town might live up to its name after all.

Was it possible life at home was improving for her assistant?

As she continued to type, Marci peeked at the woman.

Rachel was still sitting at her desk, phone in hand. But in the past, a conversation with her husband often left a glimmer of tears in her eyes.

Today, however, she looked happy—and a distinctly positive emotion was wafting across the room.

It felt a lot like hope.

Rachel swiveled in her chair and faced her, too quick for Marci to avert her gaze.

Whoops.

No way to hide the fact she'd been watching her.

Marci stopped typing. "Everything all right?"

"Yes. Fine. And I have some news I think you'll be happy to hear."

As her assistant told her about the lighthouse sale reprieve Greg had negotiated with his next-door neighbor—none other than Ben Garrison—Marci's mouth dropped open.

The man who'd cut her off cold on Monday and walked away after she'd asked him to do the right thing . . . well, okay, *demanded* might be a more accurate word . . . was having second thoughts?

"Your husband must have powerful persuasion skills."

"He does. Greg can be calm, rational, and diplomatic if he chooses to be."

Yeah, those would be handy skills to have instead of getting all worked up and flying off the handle. It was always better to cool off before flinging yourself headfirst into a potentially volatile discussion.

She'd have to work on that one of these days.

But for now . . . she had a four-week grace period to come up with a solution for the lighthouse.

Hallelujah!

"This is huge, Rachel. When I tell the group tomorrow night that Ben's receptive to ideas to save the light and won't finalize the sale for a month, everyone will be pumped. Is Greg coming to the meeting?"

"I'm going to try to persuade him, but he doesn't think he'd have much to offer."

"That's crazy! He has a history in this town, he loves the lighthouse, and I know he's creative. He came up with the idea that sold Lou on a regular ad, didn't he? I got nowhere with the man for two years. Please tell him I'd appreciate it if he'd attend."

"I will—but I can't make any promises." She stood. "Do you need me to do anything else today?"

"No. Go on home and enjoy your evening."

"You know . . . I think I will." She grinned, slung her purse over her shoulder, and walked out with a new bounce in her step.

As Rachel exited, Marci sank back in her chair, swiveled toward the window, and watched her assistant pass by.

Life sure could take some curious twists.

She might not be happy with how she'd handled her last encounter with Ben, but if they'd parted on more pleasant terms—perhaps even arrived at a compromise—Greg might not have come out of his cave and gotten involved.

Whatever the reason for this hopeful development, if he showed up for the meeting tomorrow night, she wasn't going to let him get away until she had a commitment from him to serve on the think tank. Working on a project like this could offer him a new perspective . . . which in turn might help bolster his marriage.

She tapped her fingers on her desk and watched two seagulls circle over Rachel as she crossed the street toward her car.

All these weeks, her efforts to offer her assistant a sympathetic ear had met with zero success. But now—thanks to an endangered lighthouse—the tide might be turning for both her and her husband.

Could this be the opportunity to help that Charley had suggested might come her way—albeit in a form she'd never expected?

It was possible.

All she knew was that she was going to run with it—for the sake of Pelican Point light, for Ned's dream, and for a young couple who were in desperate need of a fresh start.

"Dr. Garrison? I'll show you back to Dr. Allen's office now."

Ben closed his email, stowed his cell, and rose from his chair in the Coos Bay orthopedic surgeon's tastefully decorated waiting room that was as warm and inviting as a space like this could be.

At least the man hadn't left him to cool his heels for an hour.

One mark in his plus column.

But he was more interested in the physician's skill than his punctuality.

Ben followed the scrubs-clad woman down the corridor in the office Allen shared with another orthopedic surgeon. The place appeared to be white-glove clean, and the equipment he glimpsed through a couple of doors was state of the art. The office staff also came across as professional and buttoned up.

All of which fit with the research he'd done online—as well as the brief chats he'd had with two patients in the waiting room.

Unless everything he'd discovered was off base, Jonathan Allen hadn't made any missteps with Skip's treatment.

But he needed to be certain about that.

"He'll join you as soon as he finishes with his current patient, Doctor." The woman stopped at an office doorway. "Make yourself comfortable. Would you like some coffee?"

"No, thanks." He crossed the room, claimed a cushioned chair in front of the desk, and gave the room a methodical survey.

The diplomas on the walls matched his research, including one from Johns Hopkins School of Medicine, which boasted a top-ranked orthopedic program. There were also a number of Best Doc certificates from national magazines and organizations. And the framed letters thanking Allen for his service on the board of the American Academy of Orthopedic Surgeons and the editorial board of the *American Journal of Orthopedics* were impressive.

Allen had some prestigious professional credentials.

The personal items in the office were also instructive.

A photo featuring a couple in their forties surrounded by three smiling children ranging in age from about eight to mid-teens hinted at a happy family life.

Two bookshelves displaying numerous medical titles along with volumes on sailing suggested he had a serious hobby.

And front and center on his desk, a small, lopsided box made of popsicle sticks—perhaps crafted by his youngest daughter?—and filled with Tootsie Rolls indicated the man had a sweet tooth.

That sweet tooth, however, wasn't apparent when the doctor entered the office a few moments later and extended his hand.

He was fit and trim, the brush of silver at his temples and the fine lines at the corners of his eyes the only indications he was on the cusp of middle age.

"Please." He waved Ben back into his chair as he started to rise. After snagging a file off his desk, the man took the seat beside him rather than across the expanse of mahogany—a gesture that leveled the playing field by positioning them as colleagues.

Courteous touch.

"Thanks for meeting with me." Ben settled back into his chair. "As I explained to your office manager on the phone, I'm an orthopedic surgeon too. Fresh out of the army. Since my grandfather didn't tell me about his knee problems, I'd like to get a sense of what was going on."

Empathy filled the man's eyes. "Of course. I'd want to do the same in your place. And please accept my condolences on your loss. Ned was an exceptional person."

"Thank you. He'll be missed." Ben indicated the folder in the man's hands. "I'm sure you're busy, and I don't want to encroach too much on your day. If you could give me a quick briefing on his treatment and the issues that came up, I'd appreciate it."

"I'll be happy to." Allen flipped open the folder and essentially repeated the story Eric Nash had relayed in his law office, embellished with more detail—including MRI scans and various other test results.

By the time he finished explaining the case and answering questions, Ben was satisfied. The protocols the man had followed, his thoroughness, and the reasons for his treatment decisions were beyond reproach. Infections did happen with knee replacements, and Allen had addressed the complications exactly as he would have done.

"I tried to avoid the intramedullary arthrodesis, because your grandfather was a vigorous man and I knew fusing the femur and tibia would restrict his activities." The doctor's brow furrowed, and he shook his head. "But we couldn't get the infection under control—and that choice was better than the alternative."

Yes, it had been. Skip would have hated the notion of amputation.

Kind of like his neighbor did.

"I agree with every treatment choice you made. I just wanted to review the case for my own peace of mind."

"Understood." Allen closed the file folder and laid it back on his desk. "If you'd like a copy of any of the records, we'll be happy to provide them."

"Not necessary."

The man leaned back, as if he was in no hurry to end their conversation. "Are you in town to wrap up your grandfather's affairs, or are you settling here?"

"The former. I'll be joining a friend's practice in Columbus, Ohio."

"Given your credentials, I can understand the appeal of a big-city practice. I imagine you've amassed more experience than most doctors acquire in a lifetime."

"A degree from Johns Hopkins would also provide entrée to an established, big-city practice." Ben indicated the diploma on the wall. After everything he'd read and observed about this man, Allen could have aimed higher than a small practice in a town the size of Coos Bay.

"True—and that's where I thought I'd end up while I was in medical school and during my residency. As a matter of fact, I had my eye on a practice in Chicago."

"What happened—if you don't mind me asking?"

"Not at all. After I met my wife, who's from Coos Bay and has strong family ties here, my priorities shifted."

"Ah." Ben smiled. "The power of love can be mighty."

"Yes, it can. Besides, patients are patients wherever you treat them, and the needs here are as pressing as those in Chicago or Seattle or San Francisco. Plus, to quote that old movie, *Field of Dreams*, I've learned that if you build it, they will come—assuming you offer first-class care, which we do. The truth is, we can't keep up with the demand."

"So you never had any regrets about passing up the Chicago opportunity?"

"Not a one. I'm as busy as I want to be—too busy at the moment, as is my partner—a situation we need to address soon. I also live in one of the most beautiful spots on the planet surrounded by a wonderful family. What more could I ask?"

"That sounds like something my grandfather would have said."

"Come to think of it, I may have stolen a few of those lines from him." One side of Allen's mouth hitched up. "He was a smart man—and quite the armchair philosopher."

"Yes, he was." Ben stood. He'd used up too much of this doctor's busy day. "Thank you for all you did for him."

Allen rose too and extended his hand. "It was a privilege to have him as a patient. Let me show you out the back way."

As they walked down the hall toward a door that bypassed the waiting room, Ben asked a few polite questions about the other physician in the practice and the hospital facilities in the area.

Yet as he said goodbye and left the Coos Bay orthopedic surgeon's office behind, one of Allen's comments kept replaying in his mind.

"Patients are patients wherever you treat them, and the needs here are as pressing as those in Chicago or Seattle or San Francisco."

That was true.

However . . . big-city practices had more resources available. More hospital options. Potentially a bigger variety of cases.

And that had been Allen's first choice too—absent a strong personal incentive to make Coos Bay his base.

Ben stepped outside the medical building, into bright sunshine, and struck off for his truck.

But his mind remained on the conversation with Allen rather than the buzz of activity around him on the busy street.

If his circumstances were similar to the other man's, he might choose a different route too. Other than his med school buddy in Columbus, he didn't know a soul in the city. And while the professional challenges might keep him busy during the workday, his after-hours life was liable to be lonely for the foreseeable future.

And Columbus would be nothing like Hope Harbor, where everyone knew everybody else's business—and almost the entire population showed up to bid farewell to a beloved, longtime resident. Where people cared about their neighbors, and the pace of life felt slower . . . and more reasonable.

Small towns had much to recommend them.

Maybe someday, once he was ready to think about romance again, he might relocate to a place like Hope Harbor. With his credentials, he should be able to find a slot in a practice like Allen's without any difficulty—and a small town would be an ideal place to raise a family.

Truth be told . . . with the right incentive, he might consider staying *now*.

An image of Marci's face flashed through his mind, and he scowled as he thumbed the automatic door opener and strode across the parking lot toward Skip's truck.

She was *not* an incentive.

Just the opposite.

The *Hope Harbor Herald*'s editor was the last woman on earth who should be on his radar screen.

If or when he fell in love, he intended to pick someone with a placid, even-keeled temperament who thought before she spoke and who knew how to present a calm, reasoned argument instead of going ballistic and hurling insults and accusations.

In other words, the polar opposite of Marci Weber.

He slid behind the wheel, started the engine, and pointed the truck toward Hope Harbor.

Too bad about those flyaway emotions, though—because she did have some fine qualities. She cared deeply and wasn't afraid to put herself on the line for people—and things—she loved. Her tears on the *Suzy Q*, her attempt to apologize the night she'd called the police on him, her efforts to save a town landmark were all admirable.

Not to mention that she was one gorgeous woman. Long after he left Hope Harbor, he had a feeling her sparkling green eyes, slender curves, and vibrant hair would continue to strobe through his mind.

But he'd had enough of volatile women to last a lifetime. Unruly emotions were a deal breaker, plain and simple.

He paused at a stoplight and leaned forward to switch stations on the radio. Halted mid-reach to squint across the street.

Was that Marci now? Coming out of what appeared to be a vintage clothing store?

She stopped and pivoted, as if someone had hailed her, and he followed her line of sight.

Charley was strolling toward her.

Suspicion confirmed.

It was Marci.

Odd that she'd show up while he was thinking about her.

He watched the two Hope Harbor residents chat until an impatient beep from behind forced him to accelerate through the now-green light.

With Marci's hair glinting in the sun, it wasn't difficult to keep tabs on the duo in his rearview mirror for a full block.

But at last they disappeared from view.

And that was just as well, based on the sudden jump in his pulse when she'd walked out the door of the shop.

At another time . . . with another woman . . . he might have let himself fall for a local resident and altered his career plans, as Jonathan Allen had done for the woman he loved.

Yet even if the perfect match came along, the timing in his case was just plain bad. He needed some distance from the last woman who'd complicated his life before he trusted himself to dip his toes into romance.

So he'd keep his eyes fixed on Columbus . . . and pray that when the day came for him to leave Hope Harbor, he could walk away and forget all about lighthouses, legacies—and the lovely Marci Weber.

9

Almost all hundred seats in the fellowship hall had been claimed, and the meeting wasn't scheduled to start for fifteen minutes.

They needed more chairs.

Marci scanned the room, homing in on Reverend Baker, who was having what appeared to be a lively conversation with Father Murphy from St. Francis church.

Weaving through the clusters of people grouped around the edges of the rows, she approached the two clergymen.

". . . and alternate the sessions between our churches." Reverend Baker consulted his cell phone. "Would Wednesday night be a possibility?"

"No. Our men's club meets then. What about Tuesday?"

"That should work." Reverend Baker caught sight of her and lifted a hand in greeting. "Hello, Marci. You've got quite a turnout."

"Of course she does. Saving the lighthouse is a worthy cause. We all love our landmark." Father Murphy beamed at her. "I can't recall the number of times I've used that icon in a homily."

"Better you should use a biblical analogy." The minister sniffed.

The priest narrowed his eyes. "I use plenty of those too. And speaking of the Bible . . ." He redirected his attention to her. "We have some news for the *Herald*."

"No, we don't." Reverend Baker sent the padre an exasperated look. "Not yet, anyway. We only came up with the idea today. There are a host of details to work out."

Father Murphy dismissed his objection with a wave. "We'll get to those. But we're in agreement on the concept, and since it's never been done here, I think the idea is worthy of a small mention in the next issue of the *Herald*."

"Why don't we let Marci decide?"

Both clergymen turned to her—but before they could launch into their spiel, she held up a hand.

"I'm always interested in news, but I have a more immediate concern." She swept a hand over the room as the last few seats were claimed. "We're running out of chairs."

The two clerics surveyed the hall.

"Indeed we are." Reverend Baker slid his cell back into his pocket. "I'm afraid we got carried away with our discussion and lost track of what was going on around us."

"Evening, everyone." Charley materialized at her elbow, dressed in his usual jeans, T-shirt, and a Ducks cap. "I think we need more seats. Why don't I round up a few men to set up some more chairs?"

"Would you, Charley? That would be a huge help!" She smiled her thanks.

"No problem. I'm glad to see such a big turnout for the meeting." He touched the brim of his cap and moseyed back toward the crowd.

"Now that we've solved the seating issue, we'll tell you about the brainstorm we had today—on the golf course, no less. And they claim nothing productive happens on the links." Father Murphy grinned and nudged her arm with his elbow. "Now for the big news—St. Francis and Grace Christian are going to sponsor a joint adult Bible study class this summer. Isn't that an inspired idea?"

"Yes. Inspired." She peeked at her watch. "I'll tell you what. Why don't I get with you both tomorrow to talk about it some more?"

"That would be wonderful."

"Of course, your parishioners will have to do some remedial work before the first session." Reverend Baker's tone was serious, but the twinkle in his eye tipped Marci off that she was about to witness some of the clergymen's good-natured jibing.

"Hmph." Father Murphy adjusted his clerical collar. "Despite your misguided notions, Catholics are not Bible illiterates."

"I guess we'll find out."

"This is supposed to be a learning session for everyone, not a contest."

"True. I don't plan to keep score—do you?"

"Certainly not. I only keep score between the two of us."

Reverend Baker tut-tutted. "That must be a very depressing exercise. Remind me how far you are in the hole."

"Hey!" Father Murphy bristled with mock indignation. "I've bested you the last two out of three."

"I do have to admit your game is improving." The minister's lips twitched.

"More than your golf score is." Father Murphy winked at Marci as he delivered his zinger.

She covered her chuckle with a cough. "I'll let you two finish this discussion in private. I have a meeting to start."

Leaving them to their friendly sparring, she moved to the front of the room, collected her notes, and took her place behind the microphone.

As the crowd settled down, she gave the attendees a quick once-over. After two years here, she recognized many of the faces.

Michael and Tracy from the cranberry farm. Eric Nash and his wife, BJ. Sheriff Lexie Graham Stone and her new husband, Adam. Eleanor Cooper, seated beside Luis Dominguez, the Cuban immigrant who'd lost so much in his flight to freedom. Anna Williams, who had apparently once been a recluse but was now front and center at every civic event. Charley. Brent Davis.

Even Jeannette Mason from Bayview Lavender Farm had come. She might not be an official Hope Harbor resident, but she was a regular at the weekly farmers' market in the summer and a familiar face around town.

But the one person she'd most hoped would attend was nowhere to be seen.

Greg Clark.

Stifling her disappointment, she forced herself to focus on the agenda in front of her. She could always make a personal pitch later for his involvement.

After welcoming everyone, sharing the news that they had close to four weeks to come up with a solution, and explaining the think tank she'd be forming after the meeting, she opened the floor to discussion.

As the first person walked toward the microphone in the center aisle, the rear door opened. Greg Clark slipped inside and claimed a seat near the back.

Yes!

Even if he didn't contribute, he was here.

That was huge.

For the next twenty minutes, a number of people claimed the mic to reminisce about Pelican Point light or offer suggestions to save it while Marci took copious notes.

Only after the comments waned did Greg rise and approach the microphone.

He introduced himself, and Marci smiled her encouragement.

"I arrived a little late, but I did hear all the input. I'm not an expert on this sort of thing, but I do have a few thoughts that might be worth considering."

"All ideas are welcome." Marci held up her pad of paper. "I'm recording every one, and the think tank committee will review each of them over the next few days."

"Well . . ." He rubbed his palms down his jeans. "It seems to me we need a rallying cry. A slogan people can latch on to. Something like 'See the Light.'"

A smattering of applause and "hear, hears" echoed throughout the room.

"I like that." Marci wrote it in the notebook. "Much catchier than 'Save the Lighthouse.' Please, go on."

"Even with serious effort over the next four weeks, I don't know if it's possible for us to match in one fell swoop the price offered by the anonymous person who wants to buy the property."

When he relayed the amount, a collective groan rippled through the group.

"But . . ."—he held up his hand—"if we can generate sufficient interest in the project and lock in some longer-term commitments to assure funds will continue to come in, we might be able to work out a payment plan with Ben Garrison."

Ha.

Maybe Greg could do that—but she doubted the army doctor would be amenable to anything *she* proposed.

"It's still a pile of money." The callout came from someone sitting near the back.

Greg angled that direction. "We could also ask him if he might be willing to take part of the value as a tax write-off, which would reduce the price."

"I like it. That could have possibilities." Marci continued to scribble. "Any thoughts on how to deal with the costs of restoration and ongoing maintenance?"

"There are resources in town we could tap for some of that. For example, the Hope Harbor garden club might be willing to take care of the grounds, at least initially."

Rose Marshall, the club president, jumped up. "I'd be more than happy to broach that with the group. Given the desperate situation, I'm confident we could find enough volunteers to handle the site for a few months—at the very least."

"That's wonderful, Rose. Thank you." Marci grinned at her, then looked back at Greg. "What about restoration?"

"That could also be done by volunteers, as long as the work was supervised by a professional."

Eric's wife stood. "I'd be happy to volunteer my services in an oversight capacity. I've done a couple of assessments of the light, and the good news is that it has no lead paint and only moderate water damage. There's a lot of work to be done, but volunteers could handle the bulk of it. And some contractors might be willing to tackle the more dangerous exterior work pro bono if we can generate some positive PR for them."

"Thank you, BJ." Marci continued jotting on her pad. "I can help on the PR front."

"Once the light is restored and the grounds are maintained, the biggest expense will be ongoing upkeep." Greg shoved his fingers into the back pockets of his jeans. "If we could make the lighthouse a paying proposition—perhaps create a venue for special events, like weddings—and market the property that way, the lighthouse upkeep might pay for itself in the end. It could even be profitable."

"Are you thinking the town would own the lighthouse?" Marci paused, pencil poised above her tablet.

"That's one option. Or we could form a nonprofit lighthouse foundation that would oversee the property, supported by various organizations in town—like the garden club."

"I'm liking this." She scrawled a few more notes . . . weighed the odds of taking a risky plunge . . . decided to go for it. "I'm going to be assembling a committee later tonight that will pursue all these ideas, but I think you need to be a member." She gave the assembled group a sweep. "How does everyone else feel about that?"

Resounding applause echoed through the room.

She smiled at him as his complexion reddened. "That sounds like a mandate to me. May I sign you up, Greg?"

Putting the man on the spot might backfire—but if he agreed to assist in front of all these people, she was certain he'd honor the commitment.

A few beats passed . . . a few more . . . and finally he gave a slow nod. "Sure."

In short order, Marci closed the meeting and flipped off the mic, mentally ticking off all the positive outcomes from this evening.

The large turnout suggested the town was behind the campaign.

Lots of innovative ideas had been put forward.

Several people had volunteered their own services or the services of their organizations.

And the icing on the cake?

Greg Clark had not only come to the meeting but agreed to be part of her committee—surely a boon for both the lighthouse and his marriage.

As she left the podium, Marci's gaze landed on Charley, seated in the middle of the crowd.

The corners of his mouth lifted . . . and he gave her a thumbs-up that felt like a stamp of approval.

Did he, too, recognize that both Pelican Point light and a young man's life—and marriage—might have been given a second chance this evening?

Or was she reading too much into their quick, silent exchange?

Hard to say.

Yet both were true.

And Marci wasn't about to let either backslide in the days ahead.

With one final scan of the stunning view from Pelican Point, Ben pulled out his keys and headed back to Skip's truck.

Taking a Saturday lunch break at the light while feasting on Charley's tacos had been an inspired idea. Best seat in the house, no question about it—even if the place was wild and overgrown.

Back behind the wheel, he wadded up his empty brown bag, downed the last swig of his soda, and stuck the key in the ignition.

Some yard work, a trip to Grace Christian with all the boxes of quilting fabric he'd stacked in the kitchen, and a meeting with the realtor to discuss putting Skip's house on the market would round out his afternoon.

And tonight, maybe he'd treat himself to a movie in Bandon or Coos Bay. After more than two weeks without a break, he was ready for some R & R.

As he approached Marci's bungalow, which was tucked into a curve on the winding road that led to the headland, he frowned.

Her bright blue Civic hadn't been parked in the gravel drive when he'd passed by forty-five minutes ago. Nor had he expected it to be. Hadn't she told him the day of Skip's service that she often spent part of Saturday at the *Herald*?

It was past noon now, though. She might have clocked out for the weekend.

Just because she was home didn't mean they had to cross paths, however. She was probably inside, doing laundry or cleaning the house or dealing with some other typical Saturday chore.

He'd be willing to bet she wasn't the outdoorsy type who might be puttering around in the . . .

Whoops.

She came around the side of the house, a ladder hooked over her shoulder—and he pressed on the brake.

A futile attempt to avoid detection if ever there was one.

There was only one driving route down from Pelican Point—and it went right past her house.

Ben sighed.

Too bad he hadn't followed his first instinct an hour ago and hiked up.

As it was, he'd have to tool on by. If she noticed him, he could offer a casual wave and keep going.

Armed with that plan, he picked up speed again while she propped the ladder against the side of the house, pulled on a pair of gloves, and climbed up.

All the way to the top.

The very top.

His foot shifted back to the brake.

Was the woman crazy?

Climbing that high up a ladder was dangerous.

With one hand, she gripped the edge of the gutter, reached up into it with the other, and removed a handful of . . . stuff.

She let the glob of nature's castoffs fall to the ground and repeated the process.

He slowed the truck to a crawl.

After lobbing two more handfuls of gunk onto the grass, she descended the ladder, repositioned it, and climbed back up.

It teetered, and his heart lurched as she grabbed the edge of the gutter to steady herself.

Good grief.

The woman needed someone to save her from herself.

Since the closest neighbor was out of sight around the next

bend in the road, and there was minimal car traffic on this winding, dead-end route, it appeared he was elected.

Expelling a resigned breath, he parked on the shoulder and slid out from behind the wheel.

Skip's truck wasn't the quietest-running vehicle he'd ever driven, and he was only a couple hundred feet from Marci, but she didn't acknowledge his presence in any way.

Odd.

Unless she was concentrating so hard on her task she was oblivious to her surroundings.

The best strategy might be to move close enough to assist if necessary and wait until she descended before announcing his presence. Startling her would only exacerbate an already dangerous situation.

As he approached the ladder, however, a scampering squirrel suddenly appeared around the corner of the house—with Annabelle in hot pursuit. Both of the critters barreled straight toward him.

Ben jolted to a stop.

A second later, Marci noticed the racing duo. She jerked . . . tottered . . . clutched the edge of the guttering . . . and stabilized.

Until she spotted him.

Eyes widening, she jerked again . . . and the guttering wobbled.

As Ben vaulted into a full-out sprint, the metal channel separated from the roof and Marci pitched sideways.

He dove for her.

Absorbed her weight.

Fell to the grass in a tangle of arms, legs—and guttering.

Once his lungs kicked back in, he turned his head . . . and found a pair of wide green eyes less than twelve inches from his own.

And for just a moment, he got lost in them.

Totally.

How had he never noticed the flecks of gold in those jade irises? Or the long sweep of her thick lashes? Or the fine sprinkling of freckles across her nose? Or the . . .

"Oomph." With a sudden shove, Marci extricated herself and scooted back on the grass, one earbud dangling. "What were you trying to do, make me fall and break my neck?"

The scorching glare she lasered at him would ignite a fire better than a stack of dry kindling . . . but had there also been an infinitesimal flare of panic? Like she was afraid—of *him*?

No.

He must be mistaken.

They might not be best buds, but she ought to know there was nothing to fear from him except a temporary hike in blood pressure thanks to their relentless sparring.

He sat up. "You were standing on the top rung of a ladder!" Hiding behind righteous indignation would buy him a few seconds to get a grip on the unsettling emotions their close encounter had stirred up. "Nobody with any sense does that!"

"They do when they have clogged gutters. Why did you sneak up on me, anyway?"

"I didn't sneak. How was I supposed to know you'd tuned out the world?" He waved at the hanging earbud. "And I had nothing to do with the cat-and-squirrel chase."

With one more withering look, she scrambled to her feet.

But she left some blood behind.

Ben stared at the bright red splashes staining the grass a few inches away and sprang up, doing a head-to-toe inspection as he spoke. "You're bleeding."

"What?" She gave a slow blink.

"You're bleeding." He motioned to the grass and closed the distance between them, homing in on a dark-edged tear in the arm of her purple sweatshirt. "There." He took her cold hand. "Let me see."

Before she could protest, he gently peeled back the sleeve to reveal a three-inch-long gash on her left forearm.

She gave a small gasp. “Yikes.”

“It’s not long, but it could be deep. I need to wash it off and see. Let’s go in the house.”

“Um . . .” She swayed.

He grasped her shoulders, a surge of panic wicking away some of his professional composure. “What’s wrong? Did you hit your head?”

“N-no. I just . . . I don’t do b-blood well.”

The firecracker was squeamish?

Not what he’d expected.

“Don’t look at it. Lean on me and we’ll walk to the house together.”

Without waiting for her to respond, he tucked her close to his side and urged her toward the Cape Cod structure—prepared to scoop her up into his arms if she showed any signs of doing a face-plant.

At the back door, he tried the knob.

It didn’t budge.

Strange.

“Did you lock this when you came out?”

“Y-yeah.” She fished around in the pocket of her jeans and pulled out a key ring. Fumbled through until she found the right one. Missed as she attempted to slide it into the slot, thanks to a bad case of the shakes.

She hadn’t been kidding about being squeamish.

“Let me.”

He took the key from her icy fingers, inserted it, and pushed the door open.

Once inside the kitchen, he guided her to the sink and twisted the faucet.

“I think . . . I think I’m going to . . .” Her words faded out.

Clapping a hand over her mouth, she leaned down and yanked open the cabinet door.

She barely got the small trash can out before she lost her lunch. Breakfast too.

He supported her while she retched, then snagged a dish towel that was draped over the adjacent oven handle, wet it, and did a fast cleanup job.

If misery could be personified, Marci was it. Distress pooled in her irises, and the corners of her mouth sagged.

"S-sorry."

"Don't be." He tucked her hair behind her ear and gentled his voice. "I've seen worse. Now let's get that arm cleaned up. I need to evaluate the cut. You might want to close your eyes."

He didn't have to repeat the suggestion. She instantly squeezed them shut.

Keeping one arm around her, he adjusted the water temperature and guided her arm under the flow.

"H-how bad is it?" Her eyes were still clamped shut as she propped herself against him. Like she was afraid her legs might give out.

"Not terrible. But it will need a few stitches."

She emitted a small groan. "This was so not on my agenda for today."

His either.

But he couldn't leave her in the lurch. Any other woman, he might be able to bandage up and send off to the nearest medical facility.

That wasn't an option with a fainter.

"It shouldn't take long to get this fixed up." He shut off the water, pulled a bunch of paper towels off the roll, and guided her toward a chair. After padding the kitchen table with most of the towels, he set her arm down and draped a few loosely over the gash. "Do you have any first-aid supplies?"

"In the linen closet. End of the hall on the left."

"Got it. I'll be right back."

He passed through the kitchen, giving the adjoining open eating area and living room a fast survey.

Smiled.

The place felt like Marci.

She may have inherited a furnished house, but unless she and her great-aunt had the exact same taste, she'd infused it with her personality.

Bright cushions and wall hangings steeped the rooms with energy, while the open-hearth fireplace added a touch of warmth. None of the furnishings matched, yet somehow the overstuffed sofa draped with a quilt, a crammed bookcase, a crab pot topped with a piece of glass that served as a coffee table, and a collection of beach flotsam on a side table that had begun life as a large wooden industrial spool, all worked together to create a comfortable, inviting vibe.

The house was also neat as the proverbial pin.

Her emotions might be messy, but Marci's living space was well-ordered.

A charming dichotomy.

He continued to the end of the hall, passing a guest bath that was also pristine, and quickly located the supplies in a box labeled First Aid beside neat stacks of towels, sheets, and extra blankets.

The lady was more organized than he'd expected.

By the time he returned to the kitchen, blood was seeping through the draped paper towel—and Marci's complexion was pasty.

She shouldn't have opened her eyes.

"Do you have a pair of scissors?" He picked up his pace.

No response.

"Marci." He firmed his tone.

She lifted her chin, her eyes slightly glazed, and he repeated the question.

"Y-yes. First drawer. There." She waved toward a kitchen cabinet.

He found them and rejoined her. "You might want to close your eyes again."

She didn't argue.

As he put some antiseptic ointment on the wound, applied a sterile pad, and secured it with gauze, he assessed her.

She was as white as a sun-bleached bone—and he doubted her color would improve until the laceration was sewn up and the bleeding stopped.

His next order of business.

"Where's the closest medical facility that can handle stitches?"

"The urgent care clinic in t-town. I think they're open on Saturday. If not, I'll google Bandon or Coos Bay."

"Let me check the local place first." He pulled out his cell and found the clinic website in less than a minute. "They're open until two. Let's go."

Twin furrows creased her brow as he stood. "You don't need to take me. I can drive myself."

He hesitated.

If he dug in his heels, she'd probably blow her top—as usual.

Better to set this up so she was forced to admit she needed help.

If that didn't work—he'd dig in his heels.

"Fine. I'll walk you to your car."

"Um . . . I think I'll sit here for a few minutes first."

Ah.

First step accomplished.

She knew she was too shaky to get to her car.

"I'll wait until you're ready to go." He sat again.

A tiny bit of color stole onto her cheeks. "That's not necessary."

"Yes, it is. I take the Hippocratic Oath seriously. Walking away from a patient who needs treatment isn't in my playbook."

"I don't want to hold you up." She fiddled with the edge of the temporary bandage. "I guess I'll go now."

"Okay." He stood again. "Is that your purse?" He indicated a shoulder bag on the counter.

"Yes."

He snagged it as she sucked in some air. Stood. Held on to the back of her chair until her knuckles whitened.

"Ready?" He indicated the back door.

"Uh-huh." She peeled her fingers off the chair and managed to cross the kitchen without swaying.

At the door, she stopped at a security system keypad.

He frowned.

That was a first in Hope Harbor—as was all the defensive hardware on the back door.

Sliding lock.

Dead bolt.

Knob lock.

There was more security in this place than a government office building. Far more than the average citizen of this town would need.

What was the story behind it?

"We have thirty seconds to get out." Key in hand, she opened the door, twisted the lock in the knob, and exited onto the small landing.

He followed her out and took the key. "I've got this."

Alarm system still beeping, he secured the door and turned to her. If she were any other woman, he'd take her arm and help her down the one step to the path that led to the gravel driveway.

With Marci, though, he needed to stick with his plan. Let her realize on her own that she wasn't in any shape to get behind the wheel of a car.

But Lord, she was stubborn as she plodded toward her car, one careful step after another, obviously determined to do this on her own.

And he was running out of time.

He'd wait until the last possible moment to intervene—but no way was he letting her drive to the clinic, even if that meant he was in for another argument.

Not until she reached the car and opened the door did she falter.

"You know . . . I'm a little shaky." She exhaled as she clung to the door. "I'm sorry to impose, but would you mind very much driving me to the clinic? I can find a ride home later. You can just drop me off and be on your way."

Finally.

"I don't mind in the least. I'm going that direction anyway." Now he took her arm.

Again, she leaned into him as they walked to the truck—the gesture telling him more eloquently than words how unsteady she was.

Nor did she talk much as they set off on the short drive to town . . . another indication she was feeling rocky.

And although she'd probably rouse enough to argue with him about waiting around while she was treated, that topic wasn't up for discussion.

Because he was sticking close for as long as she needed someone to lean on.

10

Why, oh why, did she have to be such a baby about blood?

Grimacing, Marci clutched her stomach as Ben negotiated a curve on the winding road that led down to Hope Harbor.

Heights, small spaces, spiders, snakes, thunder, lightning, roller coasters—bring 'em on. Not one of those common phobias scared her.

Just blood.

Especially her own.

She tucked herself into the corner of the seat, closed her eyes, and leaned her head back.

Lord, please let me get to the urgent care center before I further embarrass myself by hurling in Ben's truck.

"The road will straighten out in a minute. That should help with the nausea."

Ben's voice was soothing—but his ability to read her mind? Not so much.

Of course, his assumption that her stomach was preparing to revolt again might not have anything to do with telepathy.

Could be he'd had sufficient experience with blood-shy patients to know the drill.

For now, she'd go with the latter, less unsettling, explanation.

"I'll be fine."

She hoped.

"Don't worry about it if you're not. There's an empty plastic bag in the glove compartment if you need it. Now tell me about this urgent care place. Have you ever been there?"

"Not as a patient, but I did a story about it after I relaunched the *Herald*. It's well equipped." She opened the glove compartment.

Yep. Bag was there.

No need for it—yet—but why not leave the door open just in case?

He asked more questions about the center as she leaned back into the corner, keeping her focused on conversation rather than her roiling stomach.

Smart tactic . . . honed through much practice, no doubt . . . and it diverted her attention for the entire drive.

Marci straightened up as he swung into the parking lot adjacent to the facility at the far end of Main Street.

"It's small." He gave the storefront location a dubious perusal.

"It's bigger than it looks from the outside. They even have an X-ray machine." She fumbled with the handle of her door.

He touched her arm. "Sit tight. I'll get that."

After a brief hesitation, she dropped her hand.

If he wanted to walk her in, why not let him? Her legs hadn't quite regained their starch, and what would another three- or four-minute delay matter? He could drop her in the reception area and be on his way while she was checking in.

Her door swung open. He leaned in to close the glove compartment and extended his hand. "Take it slow and easy."

"That was my plan."

Tucking her injured arm against her body, she slid out of the truck. His grip tightened as her feet hit the pavement, but thank goodness her knees didn't buckle.

"It doesn't appear we'll have a long wait." He surveyed the empty parking spaces in the lot as he shut the door and walked her toward the entrance.

We?

"You don't need to stick around. Once we get inside, I'll be in capable hands."

"I want to look the place over."

"Why?"

"Call it professional curiosity."

Sounded more like an excuse to her.

But why argue over a short additional delay?

"Fine. Once you do that, you can be on your way."

One side of his mouth quirked up. "Trying to get rid of me?"

Yes—but not for the reasons he might suspect.

In fact . . . the temptation to hold on tight to his muscled arm and lean into his solid strength until this was all over was strong.

Too strong.

But he couldn't be thrilled about spending his Saturday afternoon babysitting a wimpy woman.

"I don't want to intrude on any more of your day."

"No worries. You've saved me from my to-do list, which is full of items I'm happy to defer. A couple of phone calls, and I'm free for the afternoon." He pushed through the front door and guided her inside, to an empty waiting room. "It's not very busy here. Are you certain . . ."

The door to the back opened, and she called up a smile for Ellen Bennett.

"Marci! Another visit from the *Herald*. What a surprise."

"For me too. And I'm here today as a patient, not a reporter."

"I assumed as much." Ellen eyed the bandage. "What happened?"

Marci opened her mouth to respond, but Ben beat her to it.

"She's got a one-by-seven-centimeter linear incised wound, mid-right forearm, smooth edges, down to—but not through—deep fascia. A close encounter with some guttering. It needs to be stitched."

Marci stared at him. His authoritative tone and concise evaluation were all doctor—and offered a glimpse of the commanding presence he must have displayed during his years as an army surgeon.

Ellen scrutinized him. "You're Ben Garrison, right? Ned's grandson."

"Yes."

"I thought I recognized you from the service for your grandfather. Would you like to come back while I examine the wound?"

"Yes."

"No."

At their simultaneous response, Ellen looked from one to the other.

"You don't need to stay, Ben." Marci tried to pull her arm free.

He held tight.

"Yes, I do." He shifted his attention to Ellen. "FYI, she's a little squeamish around blood."

"Thanks for the heads-up. Why don't you both come back, at least for the initial evaluation?"

Without giving her a chance to protest, Ben guided her through the door.

Fine.

He could stay for a few minutes—until she got to one of the examining rooms and no longer needed his arm for support.

"Where's Chuck today?" She tried to sound nonchalant as

she followed the woman down the hall . . . but Ben wasn't likely to miss the tiny quaver in her voice.

"He had a family wedding in Portland this weekend, so we told him we'd cover the front desk yesterday and today. Have a seat there." Ellen motioned toward an examining table in the first room off the hall.

"Chuck's the office manager for the center." Marci scooted onto the table, directing her comment to Ben. "I know him from Grace Christian."

"He's been a tremendous asset to our operation. Very responsible and buttoned up." Ellen began to unwrap Ben's makeshift bandage.

"I could tell that from . . . ouch!" Marci looked at the wound.

Big mistake.

The room began to ripple, and another wave of nausea swept over her.

A plastic kidney-shaped dish was thrust under her chin—just in time to catch the remaining contents of her stomach.

As soon as she stopped retching, strong arms guided her back and down, until she was lying flat.

Good grief, could this get any more humiliating?

"I see what you mean about being squeamish." Ellen patted her arm.

"Close your eyes and take some deep breaths." Ben touched her shoulder.

Sound advice.

As she sucked air in and blew it out, a cool, damp cloth was draped over her eyes and forehead.

Heaven.

"Is there a doctor on staff?" Ben was back in professional mode.

"Yes, but he's not here today. I'm a one-woman show at the

moment." Ellen removed the rest of the bandage. "You're right about the stitches."

"Should we go to Bandon or Coos Bay?" A note of concern threaded through Ben's words.

Remarkable how you could pick up tiny nuances in inflection when you focused on sound rather than visible cues.

"Not necessary. I'm a physician's assistant. Believe me, I've done more than my share of stitching, a lot of it much worse than this."

Silence.

"Okay."

I guess.

Marci heard Ben's unspoken caveat even if Ellen didn't—and a wave of warmth percolated through her.

He was concerned about her and wanted to be certain she got first-class care.

Sweet.

"It might help if you stick close to her while we get this done." Ellen was all business now, brisk and professional.

A few seconds later, her hand was enfolded in a comforting clasp. "I'm here, Marci. This won't take long."

She ought to tell him to go.

Ellen had this under control.

But the words stuck in her throat.

"I'm going to numb your arm and clean up the wound before I stitch it, Marci. Hang on. I'll be back in a minute." Ellen's voice faded, as if she'd walked out the door.

"The worst part will be a few pricks of the needle." Ben squeezed her hand.

Nope.

The worst part was puking twice and almost fainting—and that was over.

It was a downhill coast from here.

"I'm fine. Needles don't bother me."

"Lucky you. I've seen hardened soldiers carrying assault rifles keel over at the sight of a syringe."

Really?

Or was he trying to make her feel better by downplaying the spectacle she'd made of herself?

Whatever his motivation for sharing that tidbit, she *did* feel better.

"In case no one's ever told you, you have a terrific bedside manner."

Rather than offering a verbal response, he squeezed her fingers.

"We're all set, Marci." Ellen spoke again. "You'll feel a few pinches while I numb the area. Ready?"

"Yes." She held on tight to Ben's hand.

The shots weren't fun—but at least they didn't make her nauseous or dizzy.

"The lidocaine will take effect very fast. I'm going to get set up to clean the wound, and I'll have this stitched in less than ten minutes. How are you doing?"

"Fine."

Ellen and Ben chatted while the woman worked, and Marci was content to zone out, her hand in his—until the gist of the woman's comments began to register.

". . . finding someone to take Dr. Logan's place."

"What? Is Dr. Logan leaving?" Marci almost tugged her hand free from Ben's to remove the cool cloth. Caught herself in the nick of time.

Her hand could stay right where it was while she talked. No need to see the players.

"Yes. He accepted an ER position with a hospital in Portland."

"But what will happen to the urgent care center?"

"We're not sure. I can't blame Dr. Logan for moving on to a bigger opportunity now that he's got some experience under his belt, but it will be difficult to find a replacement. Getting a highly qualified resident fresh out of training to take Doc Walters's place after he retired was an incredible blessing—but we may not be that fortunate again."

"What happens if you *don't* find someone? Can't you and Barb run this place alone, maybe hire a nurse?"

"No. We need an MD as a director. A physician's assistant and nurse practitioner can do a lot—but a doctor has to be in charge." The woman sighed. "I'd hate to see it happen, but we might have to shut our doors."

"That would be terrible! All of us would have to go to Bandon or Coos Bay for minor medical emergencies—like my arm. And a lot of Hope Harbor residents have come to rely on this place as their primary medical resource."

"I know. Dr. Logan is putting out feelers, and we're going to run ads in medical media, but I'm not holding my breath. We do have three months to search, though. He was able to negotiate a delayed start with his new boss. I know he doesn't want to leave us in the lurch."

"When did you find out about this?" Marci felt a tug on her arm and tried not to think about what the woman was doing to her skin—or the blood that might be oozing from the wound.

"Last week. I probably shouldn't have said anything. It's not public knowledge yet."

"I won't tell anybody."

"Neither will I." Ben rejoined the conversation. "I hope you find someone, though."

"You wouldn't happen to know a qualified physician who might be interested in the job, would you?" Ellen didn't sound too hopeful.

"No. Sorry. My contacts are either in the service or in private practice."

"I figured that—but it was worth asking." A final tug on her arm. "All done, Marci. You're good to go."

Someone removed the damp cloth from her face. She blinked at the bright light and focused on Ben, seated beside her.

He smiled. "You did great."

"I'm fine as long as I don't see any blood."

And as long as you're holding my hand.

A thought she throttled before it could spill past her lips.

"Do you know when you last had a tetanus shot?" Ellen disposed of some wrappings in a trash receptacle.

"About nine years ago. I cut myself at work, and one of my colleagues took me to the ER—after I fainted. From the blood, not the cut."

Another embarrassing faux pas that would live in infamy.

"We should do a booster while you're here. Do you feel steady enough to sit up?"

She risked a peek at her arm. The cut was covered by a sterile pad Ellen had taped in place. No blood visible.

"Yes." She pushed herself up and swung her legs over the edge of the table.

Ben rose, keeping a firm grip on her—as if he wasn't certain he believed her.

No problem.

He could hold on to her for as long as he liked.

"What's under the sweatshirt?" Ellen moved beside her.

"A tank top."

"Perfect. I'll help you get the sweatshirt off."

Less than five minutes later, after taking care of the injection with quick efficiency and copying Marci's insurance card, Ellen handed over a printed page of instructions and made an appointment for her to return in a week to have the stitches removed.

"You shouldn't have any trouble, but if you do, don't hesitate to call." She frowned at Marci's tank top as she walked them to the door. "Whoops. We forgot your sweatshirt. Let me get it for you."

As Ellen turned away, Marci clasped her arm. "Don't bother. It's not repairable." And seeing that blood-soaked tear again was the last thing her stomach needed. "Could you pitch it?"

"Sure. You take it easy for the rest of the day."

"I will. Thanks again for everything."

"That's why we're here—for the next three months, anyway." She glanced out the window, where a swirling mist obscured the street view. "Drive safe going home."

Ben said goodbye too, complimented the woman on the job she'd done with the stitches, and guided Marci outside.

At the distinct chill in the early-May air, she shivered.

"Here . . . take this."

Without giving her a chance to protest, Ben pulled off his sweatshirt, revealing a snug black tee that outlined impressive pecs and biceps.

Another shiver rippled through her—one that had nothing to do with the cool air.

"Let me help you put this on. Watch your arm."

Somehow he managed to get the much-too-big shirt over her head and guide her arms through the sleeves with very little help from her.

It was kind of hard to think . . . or coordinate her limbs . . . with the warm, fleecy shirt gliding over her exposed skin and surrounding her with the subtle but potent scent that was all him—and all man.

Whew.

Despite the chilly mist, she could use another cool rag on her forehead.

"Better?" He studied her.

"Much warmer."

"Good."

Not really.

Getting all hot and bothered about a man who would be leaving in a month would be foolish—even if she happened to be in the market for romance.

Which she wasn't.

Not yet, anyway.

Or she hadn't been until a certain army doctor walked into her . . .

". . . home soon."

As the tail end of Ben's comment registered, she tuned back in to her surroundings.

They were halfway to his truck.

"Wait." She jolted to a stop. "I can get a ride home. You don't need to take me all the way back to the Point."

"All the way?" The skin at the corners of his eyes crinkled. "Nothing in Hope Harbor is more than ten minutes away."

"Still. You must have better things to do with your Saturday than chauffeur me around."

A parade of intriguing emotions passed across his face before he exhaled and locked gazes with her. "No. As a matter of fact, I don't."

What did that mean?

Was it possible he *wanted* to spend time with her?

"Why not?" The question was out before she could stop it—as usual.

The corners of his mouth twitched, as if he'd expected no less from her. "You're an . . . interesting . . . woman. And as a physician, I'd feel better seeing you safely home after watching you almost hit the mat twice in the past hour."

"There's no blood now." She tugged on the hem of his sweatshirt. "And I know lots of people in town who'd be happy to run me home."

"Including me."

For personal—or professional—reasons?

Hard to tell without a bit more probing.

"I, uh, don't know why you want to bother—aside from some sense of professional obligation. We didn't exactly part on the best terms after our last conversation."

He shoved his free hand in his pocket. "I might have overreacted at the lighthouse that day."

He'd overreacted?

Not even close.

"The blame is all mine. I can get kind of emotional about causes I believe in."

"I figured that out." A trace of amusement glinted in his blue irises as he urged her forward. "If we stand here talking any longer, we're going to be soaked. We could have been halfway to your house already if we'd left five minutes ago."

Give it up, Marci. Whatever his reasons, let him take you home. It's what you want him to do, anyway.

"I bow to your logic. Let's go." She started walking again.

He held her arm until they reached the truck, then gave her a boost up.

Another whiff of the subtle masculine scent she'd first noticed on the *Suzy Q*, after the service for Ned, wafted her way.

The one that had fixed itself in her memory like a barnacle to a boat hull.

And it was very, very potent.

She cracked her window and sucked in some cool air as her pulse stumbled.

This was not good.

Ben Garrison might have much to recommend him—but he wasn't for her.

Maybe, at another time, if their paths had been destined to intersect for more than a handful of weeks and her memories from Atlanta no longer had the ability to spook her, exploring the electricity zipping between them might have been an option.

But this wasn't that time.

And letting herself get carried away would be a bad mistake.

It was a shame, though. If their timing had been better, who knew where this might have led?

She sighed as Ben circled around the front to the driver's seat.

Wishing the circumstances were different was foolish. She needed to accept reality and be strong.

So when they got back to the house, she'd thank him for all his help today—and for his willingness to work with them on the lighthouse project—then send him on his way with a polite handshake and a goodbye at her front door.

No matter how much she wanted to invite him in.

11

He didn't want to say goodbye at her front door.

As Ben rounded the last curve on Pelican Point Road, he slid a glance toward Marci.

She'd been quiet on the short ride back from the urgent care center. Now, her lower lip was caught between her teeth, and parallel grooves scored her forehead.

Not a promising sign that she was going to invite him in.

In fact, she probably wanted to ditch him as fast as possible once they got back.

And that would be a prudent move—for both their sakes—even if a different outcome held more appeal.

But while his reasons for walking a wide circle around emotional women were sound, why was *she* reluctant to spend time with *him*?

Could be she just didn't want to form an attachment to a guy who was only passing through . . . yet that didn't explain the flicker of fear in her eyes when they'd tumbled together onto the ground after the guttering gave way. Or all the security at her house.

Was there a more disturbing reason she wanted to keep her distance? A bad experience somewhere in her history?

If so, could he convince her to tell him about it?

He risked another peek at her furrowed brow.

Nope. Not based on that off-putting expression.

And why should she?

People didn't share personal secrets with new acquaintances.

"Annabelle's back in the tree."

At Marci's comment, he shifted mental gears and squinted through the mist. "She's on her own this go-round."

"Unless she's hurt."

"What are the odds that would happen twice in the space of two weeks?" He swung into the driveway.

"Very low." She gave him a slow smile. "But I bet you're going to check anyway."

Maybe she knew him better than he thought, despite their short history.

"I might take a quick look."

"I'd be disappointed if you didn't."

Was that a compliment?

"You approve of my compulsiveness?" He set the brake.

"No. Your compassion."

His hand stilled.

Okay.

It was a compliment.

And while mist might be obscuring the sun, his day inexplicably brightened.

"Wait here while I scope out the situation. Then I'll walk you to your door."

Without waiting for a response, he slid out of the truck and strode over to the base of the tree.

As he approached, the amber-eyed feline gave a loud meow.

She was in the exact same spot she'd occupied two weeks ago—but this afternoon she didn't appear to be injured.

"Sorry, Annabelle. You'll have to find your own way down today."

She gave another plaintive yowl and extended a paw toward him.

"I'm on to you, kitty. Marci clued me in. Enjoy the view up there—until you get hungry and decide to come back to earth for a meal."

With that, he pivoted, retraced his steps to the truck, and opened Marci's door.

"No rescue today?"

"Nope. Fool me once and all that. Except the night I arrived in town she wasn't fooling, so I'll cut her some slack."

"You wised up faster than I did. She got me quite a few times with that trick until I figured out her scam. What some creatures won't do for a little attention."

He stiffened as Marci scooted out of the truck, but he managed to mask his reaction before she looked up at him. No reason to let her know she'd touched a nerve with a remark meant in jest.

Forcing up the corners of his lips, he waved a hand toward her door. "Better get inside. The mist is heavier up here."

"And it's chillier." She fished her keys out of her purse. "You must be cold."

While he was standing within touching distance of her, inhaling that distinctive whisper of jasmine?

Not one bit.

"I'm fine."

"I'll give you your sweatshirt back once we get to the porch."

Suspicion confirmed.

She wasn't going to ask him in.

Stifling a foolish surge of disappointment, he took her arm

and guided her toward the door. "No hurry. You can give it to me tomorrow when I stop by to change the dressing on your arm."

As the words spilled out of his mouth, he frowned.

What on earth had prompted *that*?

She came to an abrupt halt at the steps to her front porch, looking as surprised as he felt. "You don't have to do that."

"I know, but . . ." He scrambled to come up with a logical reason for his impromptu offer. "There, uh, will be some blood."

Some of the color leached from her face. "How much?"

"Not a lot. How much does it take to make you queasy?"

"Not a lot."

That's what he'd assumed.

"It's up to you . . . but in light of what happened today, you might want to let me handle wound care tomorrow. After that, there should be minimal, if any, blood on the dressing."

Grimacing, she fingered her key ring. "At this rate, you're going to be sorry you ever crossed paths with me. I'm becoming a pest."

"I wouldn't use that term."

"Thanks for being diplomatic."

More like honest—but better to leave that unsaid.

"What time would work best for you?"

"Are you going to services in the morning?"

Good question.

He hadn't attended any yet, other than the one for Skip—but he ought to get back into the habit. Now that he was stateside again, with a more reasonable schedule, there was no excuse to skip a weekly visit with God.

"Yes."

"Which one?"

"I haven't decided."

"I'll be at the eight-thirty. We have donuts afterward, and I always help serve. I should be home by ten-thirty."

"Why don't I meet you here about noon?"

"Would you rather I come to Ned's house?"

"No." He flashed her a grin. "And you wouldn't offer if you could see the place. All the rooms are piled with boxes, and the dust bunnies have taken up permanent residence. I was planning to swing by the lighthouse tomorrow anyway. Skip and I used to do that every Sunday after church."

Another wave of mist swept in, and she moved up under the porch roof. "I'll let you go before you get soaked . . . but I do want to thank you for asking your buyer to wait four weeks for an answer to his offer. I've formed a committee to work on ideas. Our first meeting is tomorrow afternoon."

"I heard about that from Greg. And for the record, I hope you succeed. You may not believe this after our last discussion at the lighthouse, but I'd like to save it too, if possible."

"I'm glad to hear that." More damp air coiled around them. "You'd better get going or you'll be socked in. I'll thank you properly tomorrow for the lighthouse reprieve." She stuck a key in the knob and turned it. Fitted a second one into the dead bolt that was inches from a security system sticker.

As she pushed open her door, the alarm began to beep.

His cue to exit. "I'll see you tomorrow."

"Thanks again."

She closed the door, and as he stepped off the porch, a slider lock was pushed into place with a muffled *snick*.

Marci had a serious hang-up about security.

Perhaps tomorrow he could find out what was up with all her defensive measures.

Curious as he was about her private Fort Knox, however, it was her parting comment that kept replaying in his mind while he jogged toward the truck.

"I'll thank you properly tomorrow for the lighthouse reprieve."

Of course she hadn't meant anything personal with that remark.

But the image running through his mind of what a proper thank-you from her *could* entail was very personal.

And inappropriate.

Ben slid behind the wheel and clamped his jaw together as the irony of his situation registered.

Since the day they'd met, he'd been skittish about Marci's volatile temperament. Out-of-control emotions were very, very scary.

Yet he'd begun succumbing to the same affliction in her presence.

Fingers gripping the wheel, he ticked off the evidence as he backed out of her driveway and accelerated toward town.

The night she'd called the police on him, he'd been rude and terse. At the headland on Monday, he'd lost his usual cool. Earlier today, after she'd fallen off the ladder and tumbled into his arms, his emotions had been as tangled as their arms and legs.

While he might hide his roiling feelings better than she did, they were there, no more than a microscopic layer below the surface.

As for the electricity sparking between them—that, too, appeared to be short-circuiting the left side of his brain . . . and his common sense.

It was almost as if Marci had infected his emotions with jumble-itis.

Ben slowed to negotiate one of the trickier curves in the road, and the small, rustic wooden cross that had hung from Skip's rearview mirror for as long as he could remember began to swing.

Too bad his grandfather wasn't around to offer some of the folksy, sage counsel he'd spouted each summer, some of it on this very road . . . and one particular piece on a misty day like this, not long after his parents separated during his tenth year.

From the depths of his consciousness, the memory of that exchange surfaced.

He and Skip had been driving through the fog, and during a lull in their conversation, he'd begun to think about the pending divorce. Tears had welled in his eyes—and much to his chagrin, one had spilled out.

Naturally, Skip had noticed—and he'd reacted in his usual address-the-problem-rather-than-let-it-fester style.

"It's okay to have feelings, son. Good and bad. Never be ashamed to let them out."

"Grown-ups don't c-cry."

"Who says?"

"D-dad never cries."

Skip gave a dismissive wave. "He cried plenty growing up—and I expect he's crying this summer too. It's rough when two people who stand before God and vow to love each other forever decide they can't keep that promise anymore."

Funny how Skip always seemed to know what was on his mind.

"Maybe they didn't try hard enough."

"Maybe. Or it could be they should never have made the promise in the first place."

"I wish they hadn't." He kicked at a piece of gravel on the floorboard. "I wish they'd never gotten married!"

"No, you don't." Skip's voice was calm and measured. "You wouldn't be here if they hadn't—and I wouldn't have the finest grandson in the whole country."

"But . . . but how can people just stop loving each other?" Hard as he'd wrestled with that thorny question since Mom and Dad had told him the news, the answer had eluded him.

"They don't—if the love is real. The trick is to do everything you can to be sure it is before you say 'I do.'"

"How do you do that?"

Skip smiled as he negotiated a curve. "If I had a magic formula to guarantee happy endings, I could make a million bucks—or two. Best I can offer is take your time, ask the good Lord for guidance . . . and cross your fingers. But you have a while yet until you need to worry about that."

"I don't ever have to worry about that. I'm never getting married." He clamped his arms across his chest. "It's too scary."

"Yes, it is—but it's also a beautiful adventure if you find the right mate to share it with."

He sidled a look at Skip. "Do you think Gram was the right one for you?"

"No doubt about it."

"But I heard you arguing the other day, when she got mad because you wouldn't go to that town council meeting with her."

"Well, I never said love was always smooth sailing. Your grandmother can be a spitfire if she gets riled. She has more spirit than any woman I've ever met. But as long as you agree on the fundamentals, some feistiness can add tang to a marriage, like a brisk sea breeze can spice up a trip on the Suzy Q. *It's all a matter of balance. Too much breeze, the ride is rough. Too little, the journey is boring."*

Frowning, Ben stopped at the intersection of Pelican Point Road and Highway 101. Waited until he had a clear view of the pavement through the fog to confirm it was safe to turn. Hung a right, back toward town.

He didn't want a rough ride once he got married—but a boring one didn't hold any appeal either.

And boring might be what he'd get with the placid, even-keeled type of woman he'd decided would make the perfect mate.

Marci, on the other hand, would add a heaping measure of spice to a marriage. Whoever exchanged vows with her would never be bored. She was, as Greg had declared, a firecracker.

Trouble was, while firecrackers were fun, they could also burn.

So would Marci lead her husband into rough seas . . . or simply add tang to a marriage with her vivaciousness and spirit?

Hard to say, thanks to the skewed perspective that had been Nicole's legacy to him.

Ben shuddered as an image strobed through his mind of the blonde woman who'd come within an inch of ruining his life.

Talk about a close call.

And until the sting of that experience faded, he needed to be vigilant—and wary—around every female he encountered . . . especially ones who wore their emotions on their sleeves.

Like Marci.

Even if every encounter with her made it more difficult to think about the not-too-distant day he would leave her—and Hope Harbor—behind.

12

"It's about time you came back for another taco. How's it going?"

As Charley greeted him, Greg circled around two seagulls camped on the sidewalk near the taco stand and continued toward the counter. "Hanging in."

"More than that, I'd say. You were a force to be reckoned with at the lighthouse meeting. I'm not surprised Marci signed you up on the spot for her committee. The first gathering tomorrow should be lively."

"Did she rope you in too?"

Charley chuckled. "Yep. It's not easy to say no to our *Herald* editor. She's a dynamo."

"I'm finding that out. But given our short timeframe, it might take a miracle to save the light."

"They do happen."

Greg let out a slow breath. "Not in my life."

"You don't think so?" Charley rested his forearms on the counter and leaned down, his manner conversational.

"Saving my leg would have been a miracle. Losing it wasn't."

Hard as he tried to rein it in, a thread of bitterness wove through his words.

"I guess it's one of those glass half full/glass half empty situations." Charley's tone remained mild. Nonjudgmental.

But Greg wasn't touching that comment. Plenty of people had already told him to be grateful his life had been spared. He didn't need another pep talk.

"Yeah. Listen . . . can I get two orders of tacos?"

"Sure. Saturday dinner for you and Rachel?" Charley moved over to the cooler and pulled out some fish fillets.

"Uh-huh. She's been working in the garden most of the afternoon. I told her I'd pay you a visit so she didn't have to cook."

"Very considerate." He laid the fish on the grill. "How's that new rosebush doing?"

Charley knew about the bush he'd refused to plant?

"Fine . . . I think." He narrowed his eyes as he watched the man. "Did Rachel talk to you about her garden?"

"Yes. We've had several conversations about it. I can tell she loves working with flowers—but she's in new territory here in Oregon. She'll have to adapt what she knows to suit a very different climate."

That was true about more than gardening, given the unexpected twist their lives had taken.

"I'm sure she'd welcome any advice you can offer."

"That's what she said." Charley pulled a bottle of one of his homemade sauces out of the cooler, along with bags of shredded lettuce, red onion, and an avocado. "But that David Austen Munstead Wood rose I recommended should do well for her. It has a spicy old-rose fragrance, and it's disease resistant."

Was there no end to the taco-making artist's knowledge?

"I didn't know you were a rose expert."

"I'm not—but I do love all of God's flora and fauna." He flipped the sizzling fish and pulled out some corn tortillas. "Right, Floyd?"

As he directed his comment to the pair of seagulls who seemed to have claimed squatter's rights at the taco stand, the one on the left cooed and ruffled his feathers.

"You have a pet seagull?" Greg arched an eyebrow and scanned the bird.

"No. Floyd and his wife, Gladys, are friends of mine."

Greg grinned. "They're married, huh?"

"Sure. Seagulls mate for life—like humans are supposed to do."

Greg's lips flattened, and despite the savory aroma of the grilling fish, his appetite tanked. "That's not always easy to do."

"Never said it was. And not all marriages survive. But sometimes people give up too fast when a hard challenge comes along instead of making a course correction and continuing the journey. You should ask Floyd about that."

Greg inspected the bird again, and the seagull stared back at him. "He's not much of a talker."

"He is if you learn how to listen. Most creatures are once you discover how to communicate with them. Floyd, for example, went through a rough spell a while back. He lost his first wife a few years ago and was down in the dumps until Gladys came along. Now he has a whole new outlook."

"Cute story." But a seagull's woes had nothing to do with him—even if Charley appeared to be implying otherwise.

"Also inspiring—as many stories are." Charley began assembling the tacos. "The Bible, for example, is packed with some beauties."

The Bible?

Greg gaped at him.

In all the years he'd known Charley, the man had rarely made more than a passing reference to God or religion or faith.

"You read the Bible?"

Charley smiled over his shoulder. "That surprise you?"

"Yeah. I mean . . ." He shrugged. "I've never seen you at church. Unless . . . do you go to St. Francis?"

"I've been to both of the churches in this town on many occasions."

"But not every week, right?"

"If you're asking me whether I worship regularly, the answer is yes—and not just on Sunday."

Charley could be as slippery as a slime eel if he didn't want to be pinned down.

"You don't have to go to church every week to be a person of faith, though." Hard as he tried to contain it, a trace of defensiveness crept into his voice.

"True." Charley wrapped the two taco orders in white butcher paper. "But Rachel's a regular, isn't she?"

"Yes." She must have mentioned it to Charley on one of the occasions she'd stopped at the stand for tacos.

How else would the man know his wife's worship habits?

"Well, that old saying we've all heard may be trite, but it's also true. 'The family that prays together stays together.'" He slipped the tacos in a brown bag and slid the sack across the counter. "Two orders to go."

Greg pulled out his wallet. "Are you ever going to take credit cards?"

"Nope." He tapped the small cash-only sign taped to the serving window. "I like to keep life simple. You two enjoy those tacos."

"That goes without saying." He handed over the cash and picked up the bag.

"By the way—they're having donuts at Grace Christian tomorrow after the services. I can recommend the chocolate custard." Charley winked.

Greg froze.

Strange that the taco chef would happen to dangle his favorite variety as bait—although it was possible he'd mentioned his preference to the man years ago.

"How do you know what they're serving tomorrow?"

"I have inside information." He gestured toward Sweet Dreams Bakery on the other side of Dockside Drive.

"I'll have to think about that."

"You do that—and give Rachel my best. Tell her to drop by if she wants to talk gardens again. I don't imagine she has many friends here yet."

No, she didn't—and that was his fault. Thanks to his hermit-like ways and gloomy mood, she'd felt compelled to stay close unless she was at work.

Not much of a life for a young bride.

Greg lifted his hand in farewell, skirted the seagulls again, and trudged toward the car.

If he wanted her to stick around, he needed to resolve his issues before she got fed up and followed through on her ultimatum.

No, scratch that *if*.

He definitely wanted her to stay.

The real questions were what did *she* want to do—and what was fair to her?

If she was only staying with him out of a sense of duty, he ought to cut her free . . . despite Charley's commentary on marriage, and despite the knot that formed in his stomach whenever he thought about her leaving.

Transferring the bag of tacos to his other hand, he dug out his keys and pushed the auto-lock button.

Maybe it was time to unlock the truth at home too. Have

the hard discussion he'd been dodging for months and find out where Rachel stood.

And hope that whatever the outcome, he could find the courage and strength to move past the trauma of these past few months and create a new future.

"Hi, honey. It's been months since we talked, and your dad and I, we were . . . well, we wondered if it might be better to schedule a call instead of playing phone tag. Let us know what might work for you. We're flexible. Take care, and we . . . we hope to hear from you soon."

As her mother's message finished playing, Rachel set her cell back on the patio table, wiped her grimy palms on her jeans, and sank into one of the molded plastic chairs.

Three calls from her mom in the past six weeks—and in every succeeding one, she'd sounded more distressed.

Rachel filled her lungs with the fresh salt air and rotated the kinks out of her neck.

She ought to respond with more than a one-sentence email.

But how did you put aside hurt that ran bone deep—especially when not once in their limited communication since the wedding had her mother apologized for the grief she and Dad had given her about rushing into marriage?

And they must still be miffed that she hadn't followed their advice to defer the wedding for a few months. Otherwise her mom would have uttered the two magic words during one of her messages.

An *I'm sorry* would go a long way toward bridging the rift between them.

Rachel rubbed at a streak of dirt on the back of her hand and sighed.

The stubborn gene was strong on both sides of her lineage.

In fact, without the Hope Harbor address change she'd emailed—and her oblique reference to an injury that had resulted in an early discharge for Greg—her mother probably wouldn't have started calling.

At some point, if her mom persisted, she'd have to share the news about Greg's leg.

But she'd do that by email. A phone call would be too revealing. Her mom would pick up the undercurrent of strain and realize the marriage she and Dad had advised against was in serious trouble.

They might be right—but Rachel wasn't ready to admit that.

Yet.

Not after the positive developments of the past few days.

"Tacos are here."

At Greg's announcement from the back door, she swiveled around. "I'll be there in a minute."

"You want to eat outside? The mist is clearing. We should have sun soon."

"That's fine. I'll get us some sodas."

"I already put them on the counter. I can go back for them."

"I need to wash up anyway. Why don't you divvy up the tacos?" The savory aroma wafted toward her as they passed on the patio, and her stomach rumbled.

She should have eaten some lunch—but until their recent dinners of spaghetti and surprisingly tasty beer-can chicken, food had held little interest.

At least her appetite was improving, if not her relationship with her parents.

After scrubbing her hands, she scooped up the sodas and joined Greg on the patio.

He'd pushed her phone aside but tapped it as she sat. "Anyone call?"

"Yes." She opened the first taco, peeling back the white paper. "My mom left a message."

"I didn't know you and your parents were communicating again, except for an occasional email."

"We aren't. The phone calls have all come from their end."

"How many is 'all'?"

"Three in the past six weeks."

"Have you returned them?"

"By email." She took a bite of her taco. Since talking about her relationship with her parents would only ruin her appetite, a change of topic was in order. "Are you still planning to go to the lighthouse committee meeting tomorrow?"

"Yes. I said I would . . . and it's important to keep promises."

A subtle nuance in his inflection put her on alert, and she stopped chewing as their gazes met—and locked.

Was he talking about the lighthouse commitment . . . or an even bigger promise?

"I agree." She wadded the taco paper in her fingers, studying him.

His Adam's apple bobbed. "I, uh, haven't done the best job of that with the promises we made to each other."

"No. You haven't." She was done coddling him. They either had to fix their problems or . . .

No.

She wasn't going to think yet about following through on her ultimatum.

A muscle flexed in Greg's cheek, and he played with a piece of red onion that had fallen out of his taco. Took a swig of soda.

She waited him out, forcing her lungs to keep inflating and deflating.

"We need to talk." The hoarse statement scratched past his throat. "Decide how to go forward . . . or if we should."

Her stomach bottomed out—but she forced herself to ask the hard question. "Do you want to call it quits?"

He looked past her, toward the rosebush their neighbor had planted in his stead. "What I want and what's best for you might be two different things. I need to make the right choice."

What?!

He was trying to call the shots in her life, just as her parents had?

Anger goosed her pulse.

She slammed her taco on the table. "You know what? I am sick to death of people deciding what's best for me. First Mom and Dad, now you. When is everyone going to realize I'm an adult who is perfectly capable of making my own decisions?"

"Whoa!" He held up a hand, furrows creasing his forehead. "I didn't mean it that way."

"No? Then how *did* you mean it?"

"Look, I'm trying to take the honorable course, okay?" He raked his fingers through his hair. "You deserve more than this." He swept a hand over his leg.

"I didn't marry you for your legs. I told you that days ago."

"I know—but I also know you married a man who was capable of contributing to this partnership on an equal level. Instead, you've got a husband who can't even plant a rosebush." Disgust laced his words.

"You could if you worked harder at the physical therapy."

"Even if I work my butt off, I won't ever be a firefighter."

It always came back to that.

"So because one career avenue is closed, your life is over?"

"The life I planned is."

"I thought *I* was a big part of the life you planned?"

"You were. You are."

"Well, I'm still here. That hasn't changed. Why can't we accept what's happened and move on?"

"To what?"

"I don't know—but we could figure it out together if you'd communicate more."

He focused on the rosebush again, a flush creeping over his cheeks. "I don't know why you'd want to talk to me—let alone hang around—after these past few months."

"For very simple reasons. I took the same vows you did—and I meant it when I said through better or worse, in sickness and health." She gentled her tone. "And I fell in love with a handsome soldier who swept me off my feet with charm and wit and intelligence and strength and compassion and joie de vivre."

"Most of those have been in short supply since the IED."

"Yes, they have. I can't remember the last time you laughed or joked or . . ." Her voice rasped . . . but the rest of the sentence echoed in her mind.

Or touched me.

A wave of yearning swept through her, so strong it stole the breath from her lungs.

What she wouldn't give for a loving caress or gentle kiss or warm hug. Any of those simple gestures would chase away the soul-sapping loneliness that had plagued her these past months.

Especially at night.

Except they slept in different rooms, with far more than a few inches of wall separating them.

Her vision misted, and she gripped the arms of her chair.

Don't you dare cry, Rachel. Tears haven't helped in the past—and they're not going to solve the problem now. Stay strong.

"I'm not sure the man you married exists anymore, Rachel."

"I don't believe that." Somehow she managed to choke out the denial.

"I wish I had your confidence." He slumped back in his chair, shoulders hunched. "My life's been one giant train wreck for the past eight months. I don't think anyone who's been through what I've been through emerges unscathed."

"Neither do the witnesses." She spoke quietly, but every muscle in her body was taut. "Do you know how hard it is to see someone you love sink deeper and deeper into darkness? To sit here day after day while you shut me out, watching your pain and feeling helpless and useless and lonely? To wonder if life will ever be happy and normal again?" Her voice broke, and she gritted her teeth.

Don't cry!

His features twisted, and pain shimmered in his eyes. "I'm sorry, Rachel. I never wanted to hurt you."

"Then don't. Let me back into your life. Let's make a course correction and continue the journey."

He did an odd double take. "That's . . . weird."

"What?"

"Charley said the exact same thing to me less than an hour ago."

He'd talked to Charley about their situation?

Her posture stiffened. "I thought we always agreed never to discuss our private business with anyone."

"I didn't. He was telling me about Floyd and Gladys."

At the unfamiliar names, she shook her head. "I don't think I've met them."

"Probably not. They're seagulls."

"You mean . . . birds?"

"Yeah." One side of Greg's mouth twitched. "Charley has an eclectic group of friends. In case you haven't noticed, he's a bit on the eccentric side."

"True—but he's also smart and intuitive and empathetic."

"Not to mention a rose expert, from what I gathered."

"Yes. A man of many talents."

The rare touch of levity in Greg's demeanor faded. "Lucky him."

"You're selling yourself short. You have lots of talents too."

"Had—and most of them were physical. Football, wrestling, being a soldier."

"You also have a first-class brain."

"My grades were only marginal in school, Rachel."

"If that's true, it was due to indifference, not lack of brainpower. You have an organized and strategic mind. Look at all the ideas you came up with for the lighthouse campaign."

"Those don't pay the bills."

"We have enough money coming in."

"I don't want to live off the government—or your salary—for the rest of my life. I need to contribute."

"Then let's work together to find a way for you to do that." She held her breath . . . and took a chance. "It might not be a bad idea to pray for guidance. Maybe you could go to church with me again."

He frowned. "Charley suggested that too."

"Like I said—he's a smart man."

"I guess it might be worth a try. Nothing else is working." He straightened up in his chair and motioned toward their food. "We better eat. Our tacos are getting cold."

Yes, they were.

But as the last wisps of mist dissipated and the sun came out on their cooling dinner, her heart was warmer than it had been fifteen minutes ago.

Because she knew two things.

Greg didn't want her to leave—and he was making an effort to communicate.

Those were big steps forward.

Nothing else might have been resolved, but the seeds of hope that had been planted the night he made spaghetti were sending down a few more tentative roots.

And perhaps if they both put a little more effort into prayer . . . if they kept the lines of communication between them open . . . those roots would burrow deep, just as the roots on the rosebush Charley had recommended for her garden were doing in the fertile earth of Hope Harbor.

13

Ben would be here in less than five minutes—assuming he was punctual.

And that was a safe assumption.

From all indications, the ex-army doctor had been born with the responsibility gene.

Marci gave her hair one more disgusted survey in the mirror, huffed out a breath, and tossed the brush onto the vanity. There would be no taming her redhead frizz today. She'd just have to live with flyaway locks.

Besides, what did it matter if her hair refused to cooperate? It wasn't like this was a social visit—even if she *had* spent hours last night making her mom's prize-winning chicken salad, experimented with the corn chowder recipe she'd found in Aunt Edith's collection, and baked a batch of her scarf-worthy espresso brownies.

Offering the man lunch was the least she could do to thank him for his help yesterday and for his willingness to hold off on finalizing the sale of the lighthouse.

It wasn't like she was angling for a date or anything.

Then why did you take extra pains with your makeup? And why are you wearing the new top you got in Coos Bay last week—the one you were saving for a special occasion?

"Oh, shut up."

One of these days, she was going to figure out how to silence that obnoxious inner voice forever and . . .

The front bell pealed, and her heart skipped a beat.

And why did your pulse just go haywire?

Still muttering, she smoothed her palms down her jeans and marched to the front door.

This was ridiculous.

Ben's visit was simply a humanitarian gesture. It was nothing to get excited about. She needed to remain calm, cool, and collected.

With that mantra looping through her mind, she peeked through the peephole—and gripped the doorframe to steady herself.

Wow.

Ben Garrison was one hunk of handsome.

Her heart hopscotched again, and she sucked in a lungful of air.

So much for calm, cool, and collected.

Even the fisheye-lens distortion couldn't detract from the broad shoulders outlined by a tweed jacket, or his overall clean-cut, spit-and-polish appearance.

As he leaned toward the bell again, she jerked away, flipped the lock, shoved back the slider, and pulled open the door.

Double wow.

The man was even more breath-stealing with all the parts in proper perspective.

And when he smiled?

Oh. My. Word.

"Good morning . . . or should I say afternoon?"

Somehow she managed to respond without croaking. "Uh, either will work. Both hands on the clock are straight up."

"Let's go with afternoon then. How's the arm?"

It took her a second to drag her gaze away from his baby blues and process his question.

"It hurts a little, but no other problems."

"You ready for me to change the dressing?"

Right.

He was here as a doctor.

Perspective check, Marci.

"Yes. Sorry to keep you standing on the porch." She stepped back and pulled the door wide. "I assume the kitchen would be the best place."

"Whatever's convenient for you. It won't take long to clean up the wound and put on a new bandage." He held up a small bag. "I brought everything I'll need."

"A doctor who does house calls? I thought you all went the way of the dinosaur." She led him toward the back of the house.

"Some of us make exceptions for special patients."

Special patients?

Did that mean what she thought it might?

Impossible to judge without seeing his face—and turning around to find out would be too obvious.

In the kitchen, she motioned to the table. "I left a clear spot at this end."

He frowned at the two place settings. "Are you expecting someone? We could have done this later in the day."

"No." Her open-weave, bell-sleeved tunic slipped off her shoulder, and she tugged it back into place. Thank heaven for tank tops. "I, uh, thought you might like to stay for lunch. Remember, I told you yesterday I'd like to offer you a proper thank-you for all you've done."

A glint of . . . humor? . . . sparked in his eyes. Curious. "I do remember. But you didn't have to go to this much effort."

"I like to putz around in the kitchen. If you have other plans, though, I under—"

"No." His cutoff was abrupt—and definitive. "After years of army life, homemade food is always a treat. Charley's tacos are terrific, but I'm ready for some variety in my diet."

"Well, don't get your hopes up. This isn't anything fancy."

"I'm not into fancy anyway." He set his bag on the table and pulled out a chair. "Why don't you have a seat and we'll get the unpleasant stuff over fast?"

"How unpleasant?" She sat.

"As long as you don't watch, not very. It might sting a bit while I clean around the stitches, but I'll be quick. Mind if I ditch my jacket first? I came straight from church."

"Help yourself."

He slipped off the sport coat to reveal a dress shirt that hugged his muscled torso as if it had been custom made. Rolling the sleeves to the elbows, he crossed to the sink and leaned forward to wash his hands, the cotton fabric stretching taut over his powerful shoulders.

Ben Garrison might be a doctor who spent his days standing around doing surgery, but based on his athletic physique, he was no stranger to physical activity.

Long before she tired of the view, he returned to the table and set about removing the dressing.

"This might be a good time to look away or shut your eyes."

She did both.

True to his word, in less than three minutes, he was taping a new dressing in place.

"All done."

She peeked at her arm. A much smaller bandage covered the stitches, and there was no blood in sight.

"How did it look?"

"Exactly as it should the day after."

"Was there much blood?"

"Enough to make you squeamish." He rose, disposed of the folded-over dressing in the trash can under the sink, and washed his hands again. "When you change the bandage tomorrow, you shouldn't see more than a few small spots of blood, if that."

"Let's hope so."

"Has blood always had this effect on you?" He replaced the items he'd taken from his bag.

"To some degree, but I only had minor cuts and scrapes as a kid, and my parents didn't let us watch violent TV shows or movies. I didn't realize the full extent of my problem until I was sixteen—on my first date."

He closed the bag. "I sense a story there."

She wrinkled her nose. "Yes—and it's not a pretty one."

"Care to share?"

She shrugged. "Sure. It's ancient history now. But I'll give you the condensed version. I was so excited about the date I didn't bother to ask the guy what movie he was taking me to see. Turned out it was a war flick. I had a feeling I might have some trouble—but since I didn't want him to think I was a wimp, I decided I'd close my eyes during the grisly parts."

"Why do I have a feeling that strategy didn't work?"

"Because you've seen me around blood." She sighed. "The whole movie was one big gore fest. I closed my eyes whenever I sensed blood was coming—but I didn't anticipate the scene where a booby trap ripped off some guy's arm."

He winced. "What happened?"

"I threw up all over my date . . . and the couple in front of us . . . and the person sitting next to me."

"Wow." His lips twitched, as if he was struggling to rein in a chuckle.

"Go ahead and laugh." She waved a hand. "As first dates go, mine was sitcom material. I can laugh about it myself now, but I was mortified for the remainder of my high school career."

"I don't suppose the guy ever asked you out again."

She snorted. "Are you kidding? He went out of his way to avoid me at school. I guess he was afraid I'd pull the same stunt again—and being puked on isn't exactly fun."

"I know. Been there, done that."

"I suppose it's a job hazard for you, but trust me—it's worse if it happens on a date."

"I can imagine."

"So . . ." She rose. "On that appetizing note, are you ready for lunch?"

This time he did let loose with a chuckle—one that was full and deep and rich . . . and set off a bunch of sparklers in the region of her heart.

"In my job, you learn to develop an ironclad stomach. I'm always up for a meal."

"In that case, have a seat." She indicated the chair that offered a view of lawn edged by woods and the gazebo flanked by two lush gardens.

He remained standing. "Let me help in some way."

"The soup is on, and it won't take me but a minute to put the sandwiches together."

"Why don't I get the drinks?"

Ben didn't strike her as a man who took no for an answer—nor did he seem the type to sit while others worked.

"Fine. Glasses are in that cabinet"—she motioned toward it—"and soda and ice are in the fridge."

By the time she'd assembled the sandwiches and ladled the thick soup into crockery bowls, he was waiting for her at the table.

"That looks and smells delicious." He took one of the plates from her and pulled out her chair.

"My compliments to your mother on your manners."

His smile wavered for an instant. "Believe it or not, my dad was the one who taught me my social skills."

"Sorry." She sat. "Sometimes I fall into the trap of assigning gender roles, even though I know better."

"I think in most cases the mother *is* the one who does that sort of training." He joined her at the table . . . but said nothing more.

She peeked at him.

Why hadn't *his* mother handled that chore?

The question hovered on her tongue—but for once, she curbed her inquisitiveness.

"I usually say a short prayer before meals."

He draped his napkin over his lap. "An admirable habit. Please, go ahead."

After a quick blessing, they both dived into their meal.

"This is wonderful soup." Ben ate with gusto. "An old family recipe?"

"I suppose you could say that. I found it among my great-aunt's things after I moved in here."

"Did you know her well?"

"No. My family traveled out here one summer on vacation when I was eleven or twelve, and we stopped in for a visit. That was our only in-person meeting. But she didn't have any other relatives, so we inherited her small estate."

"And you decided to settle here instead of selling the house."

The implied *why* was obvious.

She'd had a feeling that subject might come up again—but she still hadn't decided how much to reveal about her background.

"It's a beautiful area." Best to stay noncommittal for the moment.

"Yes, it is. I always enjoyed my summer visits with Skip. You know . . . I bet I was in town the year you visited. I came every summer from age ten to sixteen, and I'm thirty-five."

"I'm thirty-two—so it's possible."

"Strange to think our paths might have crossed all those years ago."

More than strange.

It was almost like . . . fate.

"We didn't stay long, though." She scooped up a spoon of the hearty soup. "And we spent most of our visit here at the house, with Aunt Edith."

"Was she a native?"

"No. She came here in her thirties. Dad thinks there might have been a tragic romance in her background. He could be right. She never did marry. She spent her whole life working at a nursery and cultivating her love of flowers." Marci nodded toward the window. "After I bought out my sister's share of the property, I had the gazebo repaired and restored her gardens. The house needed major updating too."

"Everything appears to be in tip-top condition now."

"I wish. Most of the cosmetic stuff is done, but the heating system is on fumes. And as soon as the budget allows, I want to tear down the storage shed and build a detached garage. But I needed some assistance with the *Herald* and my PR business more than I needed any of those improvements."

"So you hired Rachel."

"Yes. She's just shy of her journalism degree, so it was a perfect fit." She chased a kernel of corn around the bottom of her bowl. "I didn't realize you knew her and Greg until last week."

"I don't know either of them well. I haven't exchanged more than a greeting or two with Rachel, and I've only talked with Greg twice. I assume you know the story about his leg."

She furrowed her brow. "Yes. From what I can gather based

on the little Rachel's shared with me, I think they've had a rough go of it."

"I agree. How did you connect with her?"

"At church. I sensed she might need a friend . . . and I also got the feeling some additional income would be welcome. She took the job I offered—but she's been less receptive to my overtures of friendship." Marci rested her elbow on the table and propped her chin in her palm. "At least Greg seems to be coming out of his cave. He agreed to serve on the lighthouse committee, and I intend to put him to work."

"That could be beneficial for both of them." Ben finished his sandwich and gathered up the crumbs from the flaky croissant and a small glob of chicken salad with his fork. "That's the best lunch I've had since I arrived—but please don't tell Charley."

"My lips are sealed." She scraped up the last of her soup. "Can I interest you in dessert? Espresso brownies and Oregon-roasted coffee."

"Sold."

Grinning, she stood. "That was easy."

"Chocolate and coffee are a winning combination any day." He stood too, and picked up his plate.

"Why don't we have dessert in the gazebo? Now that the sun's out, I hate to waste those rays."

"I'm game. What can I carry?"

"I'll put the brownies and our mugs on a tray." She rummaged through a drawer, pulled out a dish towel, and handed it to him. "You can wipe down the table and chairs, though. They might be damp from the earlier mist. If Harpo, my resident pelican, is there, just wave the towel at him."

"You have a pet pelican?"

"No. He followed me home from the lighthouse one day and shows up on a regular basis. I think he's taken a fancy to my gazebo. But he doesn't make any noise and keeps to himself, so I'm cool with it."

"Whatever you say." Towel in hand, he walked toward the door while she plugged in the coffeemaker. After twisting the knob, he sent her a quizzical look.

"Sorry. Dead bolt's set. The key's on a hook to your right."

He found it . . . but instead of opening the door, he angled toward her. "You have quite a few locks."

It was a question couched in a statement.

Decision time again.

Should she tell him the reason behind her security fetish . . . which would also explain why she'd freaked out the night she'd seen him climbing a ladder on the tree outside her window?

Or should she brush him off with a simple a-girl-can't-be-too-careful reply?

After several silent seconds ticked by, he hiked up one side of his mouth and turned to fit the key in the lock. "Meet you outside for dessert."

A moment later he slipped through the door.

She was off the hook, thanks to Ben's consideration and diplomacy. Unlike her, he knew when to back off.

Except—why was she disappointed instead of relieved?

Because part of you wants to tell him your story.

Reluctant though she might be to admit it, that was the truth.

But sharing personal information would deepen their relationship—and the closer they became, the harder it would be to say goodbye.

Exhaling, she dumped some beans in the coffee grinder.

What a mess.

Why, oh why, did the first man in two years who'd revved her engines have to be someone who was only passing through?

Working on autopilot, Marci finished preparing the coffee

and cut generous squares of brownie while her mind wrestled with a critical question that had nothing to do with the task at hand.

Should she follow her instincts and share some background with Ben . . . or play it safe and protect her heart?

14

Way to go, Garrison.

As Ben dried off Marci's patio table and chairs and kept an eye on the large white bird with the oversized orange beak that he'd shooed out of the gazebo, he blew out a disgusted breath.

Nothing like introducing an obviously sensitive subject to ruin an enjoyable lunch with a beautiful woman.

Big mistake.

After draping the damp towel over the railing, Ben shoved his hands in his pockets, leaned a shoulder against one of the wooden uprights, and surveyed the gardens.

He'd also made a mistake by assuming Marci wasn't an outdoor kind of person. The well-tended beds spoke of hours of hard labor in the dirt, and the lawn was precision-cut and meticulously trimmed.

He surveyed the ramshackle shed, slated to be replaced by a garage when funds permitted. Given the condition of the structure, that couldn't happen too soon—and a garage would be a welcome convenience.

Yet Marci had taken on the expense of an employee instead, delaying the project.

It was possible she did need help at her office—but it was also possible her motives for hiring Rachel were more benevolent than practical. That she'd recognized a need and stepped in to help, as she had when she'd relaunched the *Herald* and jumped in to spearhead the lighthouse project.

The very sorts of things his grandmother would have done.

A smile played at the corners of his mouth.

Marci was a lot like June Garrison—a spitfire, with spirit to spare.

But Gram had also been all heart—like Marci. No need that crossed her path went unaddressed.

No wonder Marci and Skip had become friends.

Ben wandered over to the other side of the gazebo, following the progress of two gulls as they dipped and soared in perfect sync against the blue sky.

His grandfather might never have mentioned Marci or the column he'd written for the paper, but he'd no doubt found in her a kindred spirit. Someone who'd reminded him of the lively, animated woman he'd loved.

Someone who might fly off the handle on occasion, but who was vivacious and vibrant rather than volatile and vicious.

As Nicole had been.

A shudder rippled through him.

Marci was nothing like the woman who'd made his life a living hell.

Yet she *was* wary. Her over-the-top security precautions proved that.

Was it due to some phobia, like the one she had about blood—or was there a more sinister explanation?

Not a question she was likely to answer today, given her silence in response to his comment about locks.

The door banged shut behind him, and he shifted toward it.

"Dessert's ready."

She descended the single step, balancing the tray, and he strode across the lawn to take it from her.

"Your gazebo awaits. You've done an incredible job with the gardens, by the way."

"Thanks. My aunt kept detailed notes and diagrams about what she planted, what worked, what didn't. It seemed like a nice tribute to her to restore them."

"So you're not an avid gardener?"

"I like flowers—but this"—she swept a hand over the beds—"was an ambitious undertaking. Hi, Harpo." She wiggled her fingers at the pelican.

From his spot on the lawn a dozen feet away, the bird regarded them with a doleful, mute stare and ruffled his feathers.

"Did you know Rachel's a gardener?" He set the tray on the small café table as the bird ambled off, then soared into the air.

"Yes. I tried to entice her to go with me to a new native-plant nursery down near Sixes, with a stop at the lavender farm on the way home for tea, but I couldn't tempt her."

"I wouldn't take the refusal personally. Given the situation at home, I assume she has other priorities." He waited until she took her chair, then sat.

"True." She indicated the sugar and cream. "Help yourself."

"I like it black."

"Not me. As a latecomer to coffee, I like it diluted and sweet. Straight up is too strong and bitter for me." She added a hefty dose of cream and stirred in a generous teaspoonful of sugar.

He broke off a piece of brownie with his fork. "You have a peaceful spot here."

"I agree . . . even if it's a bit on the remote side."

Strange that she'd mention the isolation if she didn't want to talk about her security setup.

Or was she thinking about answering his unspoken question, after all?

Best to play this by ear, let her take the lead.

"I'm surprised this road is so undeveloped."

She blew on her coffee and took a sip. "From what I understand, a speculator bought most of this property decades ago. He sold a few lots here and there, like this one, but the location has its downsides."

"I imagine frequent fog is one of them."

"Yes. Not to mention the wind and the lack of sea views—except out by the light."

"What happened with his grandiose plans?"

"They came to naught. Eventually he went bankrupt, and the property was tied up in litigation for years."

"Is that still the case?"

"I don't think so. Brent told me there's a new house slated to be built down the road—and of course, the person who's interested in the lighthouse is planning to buy a couple of the adjacent lots too. Are you really in the dark about his or her identity?"

"Yes. The offer came through a law firm in Eugene."

Her retro-looking top slid off her shoulder, and he tried not to let the expanse of smooth skin distract him as she tugged it back into place.

Failed.

"Well . . . I wouldn't mind having a few closer neighbors—the lighthouse buyer not included."

Focus, Garrison.

He yanked his gaze back to her face. "Did you, um, ever think about selling the house and moving into town?"

"Yes. I can get easily spooked out here."

"I know."

She wrinkled her nose. "You were right the night you rescued

Annabelle. I should have talked to you through the window instead of calling the police."

"I suppose being in a secluded area like this might be challenging for a big-city girl."

Catching her lower lip between her teeth, she pressed the tines of her fork against some chocolate crumbs on her plate. "It wouldn't have been, two years ago."

He took a measured sip of his coffee.

Careful, Garrison. Don't scare her off.

"Any particular reason for the change?"

"Yes."

She set her fork down, leaving the rest of her brownie uneaten, and wrapped her fingers around the oversized mug. "I had a rather frightening experience in Atlanta."

Based on the tight grip she had on her coffee and the flutter in the hollow of her throat, that was a gross understatement.

Something very bad had happened to Marci.

Tension coiled in his gut, even as he tried to maintain a calm façade.

If someone had hurt this woman, he'd be sorely tempted to forget all about the Hippocratic Oath and beat the stuffing out of them.

Not a very Christian inclination—but that was how he felt.

And it was telling.

He might not have wanted to have feelings for Marci . . . he might have convinced himself she would be all wrong for him . . . he might have career plans that would soon take him far away from Hope Harbor . . . but he couldn't ignore reality.

Like it or not, he was falling for her.

Hard.

When the silence between them lengthened, she peeked at him over the rim of her mug.

Say something, Garrison, or she's going to shut down.

"I suspected there might be an incident in your background that would explain all the locks. Trauma can leave a lasting mark. I saw plenty of evidence overseas. And we have an example much closer to home with Greg."

With an emphatic shake of her head, she set her mug down and folded her hands in front of her on the table. "My situation is far less traumatic—and permanent—than his. In fact, meeting him and Rachel has helped give me some perspective on what happened in Atlanta."

"Is that experience the reason you moved here?"

"No." Her tone was firm. "I wasn't running away. I liked my job, but doing PR wasn't why I'd majored in journalism. After I came here, I fell in love with the town—and once I found out about the *Herald*, I saw an opportunity to create a life closer to the kind I'd always wanted. Run a newspaper, be my own boss . . . it was more providential timing than escapism."

She still hadn't told him what had happened.

How much could he ask before she backed off?

"Have you had any regrets about relocating?" That should be a safe question.

"No. Not one. I knew almost immediately this was where I belonged."

"And you never miss big-city life?"

"Not much. The few conveniences I do miss are more than offset by living in a beautiful setting where your neighbors know and care about you."

A few beats of silence passed.

Looked like he was going to have to take a chance and ask the key question.

"May I ask what happened in Atlanta?"

She studied her knitted fingers.

Somewhere in the distance, a sandpiper trilled while ten otherwise silent seconds ticked by.

She was going to deflect the question.

No surprise, given . . .

"I had a stalker."

It took him a moment to absorb her quiet comment—and as the ugly word hung between them, he gritted his teeth.

"Did he hurt you?" The question was out before he could second-guess whether it was too personal.

"Not physically."

That, at least, was a relief.

"Do you want to tell me about him?"

She massaged the bridge of her nose. "He was the son of one of my firm's biggest clients—and he worked in his dad's company. I met him at a client party. He seemed charming and fun and smart, so when he asked me out, I agreed. Since I didn't deal with that account, there was no conflict of interest. The first date was fun, and I was flattered he wanted to get together again a few days later. That date was fine too. But then he became obsessive—and possessive."

Ben took a sip of his cooling coffee, trying to control the flames of anger licking at his composure. "What happened?"

"He sent a constant stream of letters and cards, along with flowers and gifts. Extravagant stuff, like three dozen roses or a new big-screen TV I'd mentioned was on my wish list. And he'd call a dozen times a day. After work, I'd find him waiting on my doorstep. He started hanging out at the coffee shop I went to every Saturday. He even showed up at my church on Sunday."

She wasn't exaggerating about the guy's obsession.

That was very scary behavior.

"He must have had psychological issues."

"I came to the same conclusion after our second date."

"Did you tell him to back off?"

"Over and over again. On the phone, in person, by email.

Nothing worked. I talked to my boss about it, and he had a conversation with the guy's father. That didn't help, either. In the end, I had to get a protection order against him."

Ben frowned.

He was no lawyer, but as far as he knew, an unrelated victim usually had to have a reasonable concern she was in physical danger—not just trying to stop unwanted attention—to get an order like that.

"Did he threaten you with physical violence, Marci?"

Her throat worked. "Not in words. But whenever he showed up, he'd get close. Too close. Sometimes he'd touch me. And he was tall and strong and . . ." She swallowed again. "I was afraid he *might* get violent."

No wonder her house was under lock and key.

"Did he bother you after the order?"

"Not that I could prove. I did get hang-up calls and a handful of hateful notes, but the police couldn't trace any of them to him."

"What did your family say about all this?"

"I never told them. My sister's lived overseas for years, and we've never been that close. The age difference is too big. My parents are retired in Florida, and they would have been freaked out by the situation. I didn't see any reason to make them worry. There was nothing they could have done to help."

"Except offer moral support."

She shrugged. "At the expense of their peace of mind."

Another example of how this woman put the well-being of others ahead of her own needs.

He stifled the urge to reach over and weave his fingers through hers. "What happened to this jerk?"

"He's still out there, as far as I know."

"Has he bothered you since you came here?"

"No. I suspect he's moved on to his next victim. I found

out later he'd had a similar issue during his college days, in another state."

A serial stalker.

Why, oh why, had this man's life intersected with Marci's?

"How did your firm react?" If the guy was the son of a big client, that could have been dicey.

"They were behind me 100 percent—even though they lost his father as a client. And it was a big account. But my boss had no tolerance for that kind of behavior. When the inheritance came up not long after the incident, he didn't balk at my request for a three-month leave of absence to come out here. He promised my job would be waiting for me."

"But you decided to stay."

"Yes. He was concerned I was making a rash decision based on what had happened, but I wasn't. The truth was, I felt at home here right away."

"Not necessarily safe, though. Officer Gleason told me about the vandalism incident last year."

Her brow puckered. "Yeah. That was a little scary. But it was just a local teen who got his kicks destroying people's property. I was a random victim in that case."

"Unsettling nonetheless."

"Yes—but the fear has receded over the past few months. I might have overreacted the night I called the police on you, but in general I'm not as skittish as I used to be. About my stalker showing up, anyway."

"Why the caveat? What else are you skittish about?"

She moistened her lips . . . and looked straight at him. "Men I find attractive. Like you."

He blinked.

That was direct.

"The trouble is," she continued without giving him a chance to react, "after so badly misjudging that client's son, I'm not confident in my ability to distinguish between normal interest from the opposite sex and some kind of psychotic fixation. I thought this guy was fine the first couple of times I was with him. Either I'm too gullible or he was a master manipulator."

"My money's on the latter. From everything I've seen, your judgment is spot-on."

"I wish I was as certain of that as you."

"Are you concerned about me?"

"Not as much anymore."

"Good. Because you have no reason to be. But I understand your caution. Anyone can be fooled by a person who thinks outside the normal bounds and is an adept actor." As his voice hardened, Marci cocked her head and inspected him—but he rushed on before she could ask the question that had to be forming in her mind. "And for the record, the attraction is mutual."

That was true—but it was also a diversionary tactic . . . and based on the sudden rounding of her eyes, it worked.

Her reply confirmed that.

"Part of me is happy to hear that—but another part is worried. I'm not interested in a short-term or long-distance relationship."

"Me, neither. Nor do I think it's wise to rush relationships."

"So where does that leave us?"

"I wish I knew."

She picked up her fork and played with her brownie. "Too bad your grandfather isn't here. I bet he'd have some words of wisdom to offer."

"No question about it—but since he's not, I think we're on our own with this."

"Not entirely. I, for one, intend to bend the Lord's ear about the situation."

"I'll join you." Maybe reinstituting Sunday church attendance this morning had been smart—for a number of reasons.

"In the meantime, I guess we'll have to take this a day at a time."

"That works for me." He angled his wrist. "Don't you have a lighthouse meeting this afternoon?"

She checked her own watch, and her eyebrows rose. "Yes. In half an hour."

"Let me help you take everything back inside and clean up, then I'll be on my way."

"I can handle the cleanup."

"Nope. I never leave messes behind."

Well, not by choice.

But he wasn't going to think about that now. Not while he was with Marci.

"Has anyone ever told you you're stubborn?" The twinkle in her eyes tempered the criticism.

"That has a familiar ring—but two hands will speed up the work, and you don't want to be late for the first meeting."

He kept the conversation light while they put the kitchen back in order, but his mind was working at warp speed on a more serious issue.

After the personal conversation they'd had over brownies, a simple goodbye or handshake didn't seem sufficient.

Yet neither of them wanted to turn up the wattage yet.

Once they finished, he followed her to the door, where she unlatched all the locks and twisted the knob.

"I'll let you know as soon as we have some ideas about the lighthouse." She pulled the door wide.

"I like how you said when, not if."

She grinned. "I'm kind of like Nellie Forbush from *South Pacific*—a cockeyed optimist."

"The world could use more optimism. *My* world could use more optimism." He reached for her hand and twined his fingers with hers.

Her breath hitched—but she didn't say a word.

"I think we're past a goodbye handshake at the door, don't you?" He stroked the pad of his thumb over the back of her hand.

She nodded.

"So let's move on to this."

Slow and easy, he leaned down, brushed his lips over her forehead—and inhaled.

Up close, the subtle scent of jasmine surrounded him . . . invaded his pores . . . and made him want much, much more than this simple kiss.

Before he succumbed to the temptation to dip lower and claim her mouth, he forced himself to pull back.

Her wide eyes, hazy with yearning, told him she wanted more as much as he did.

Oh, man.

If she kept looking at him like that, his good intentions were going to be swept away as fast as a beach umbrella during one of Oregon's legendary storms.

But one of them needed to be sensible. To keep their emotions under control.

And Marci wasn't the best candidate for that.

He released her hand and backed up. "Thank you . . ." His voice scraped, and he cleared his throat. "Thank you for lunch."

"You're welcome." She was as breathless as if she'd run a hundred-yard sprint. "Drive safe."

Only after he descended the steps from her porch did he turn.

Marci's tunic top had slipped down her shoulder again, and she was holding on to the doorframe as if she needed it for support.

He could relate.

With a wave, he continued toward Skip's truck, her final comment ringing in his ears.

Driving safe wasn't a problem.

But exploring the new territory they'd entered today?

Not so safe.

And until he could figure out how the sparks between them could—and should—play out, he was going to have to be as careful and cautious as those elusive mole crabs he'd never managed to catch during the summers of his youth here in Hope Harbor.

15

"I think that's a wrap." Marci skimmed her sheet of notes again, then surveyed the eight people sitting around her at the table in the Grace Christian conference room. "Let me sum up where we are to verify I got everything. Eric, you're going to handle the legalities of setting up a nonprofit foundation that would own and manage the lighthouse."

The attorney nodded. "Correct. I'll take care of all the paperwork, so we can make it happen fast once we pull the trigger."

"Excellent. Rose, you're going to continue to solicit support from the garden club and also get in touch with the clubs in Bandon and Coos Bay to see if they'll lend a hand until we have the foundation up and running."

"Yes. I know some of the members, and I expect they'll be happy to supplement our ranks on a short-term basis."

"That would be much appreciated." Marci moved to the next item on her list. "Michael, you've agreed to contact everyone on the Helping Hands call list about the project and ask them to contribute their time and expertise to the lighthouse as part of the charitable work they do for your organization."

"The *town's* organization. I'm only the director." He hitched up one side of his mouth. "And yes, I'll email everyone the flyer you designed with the 'See the Light' logo."

"Actually, Greg designed it." She smiled at the younger man. "In fact, we can thank him for all of the support materials—along with the bulk of the ideas we're pursuing."

He doodled on the pad of paper in front of him, a slight flush tinting his cheeks. "Charley did the drawing on the flyer."

"True—but my artwork alone won't save the lighthouse." The taco-making painter folded his arms and leaned back in his chair. "That will take an organized campaign and a coordinated effort. The whole town will have to get behind it . . . and your ideas will help make that happen."

"I agree." Marci continued down her list, shifting the limelight off Greg. "BJ, I'm planning to run a feature article in this week's *Herald*, asking for volunteers to help with the physical work of restoration. May I have them contact you directly?"

"Yes. I'll keep a running list and coordinate with any volunteers Michael rounds up through Helping Hands. I'm also going to call several of my suppliers this week and see if I can convince them to donate materials in exchange for some free, positive PR."

"Which I'll be happy to provide." Marci gave her a thumbs-up.

She concluded with Father Murphy and Brent, who'd agreed to investigate potential private grants and government funding.

After checking off the last item on her list, she set down her pen and paper. "I think we have a strong start here. I hate to pull you all in to too many meetings, but given our short timeframe, I think we should regroup on Wednesday, if that works for everyone."

"I'm in," Charley said. "We need to keep this moving. I'll even provide tacos for dinner that night if it will help convince everyone to give up a weeknight to work on this."

Following a chorus of assents, she linked her fingers on the table. "Everything we've discussed today is important, but two big issues remain. How will we come up with the purchase price—and how will we fund ongoing maintenance?"

"I like the ideas Greg mentioned at the town meeting." Charley smiled at the younger man.

"I do too. I think all of them are worth further discussion. If everyone agrees—including you, Greg"—Marci refocused on the younger man—"I'd like for the two of us to huddle on this and bring some suggestions forward on Wednesday. And of course, additional input from anyone else is welcome . . . especially on how we might raise funds to cover the purchase price."

"Sounds like a plan." Charley closed the small notebook on the table in front of him and pocketed his pen. "Does that about wrap it up for today? My muse is calling."

"The painting muse or the taco muse?" Marci grinned at him.

"Thank you for recognizing that cooking and painting are both creative endeavors." He dipped his chin in acknowledgment. "In this case, it's the painting muse."

"You're going to have some disappointed folks who want a tasty treat on a Sunday afternoon." Father Murphy stood and stretched. "Including me."

"I thought you were having dinner with Reverend Baker?"

"I am—but I could use a snack to tide me over." He tipped his head. "How did you know about my dinner plans?"

"Would you believe me if I said a little bird told me?" Charley stood too.

"I might. You're a regular Francis of Assisi with the animals around here."

Charley chuckled and clapped the priest on the back. "I'll take that as the highest of compliments. See you all on Wednesday."

As he strolled out, the others said their goodbyes and followed suit until only she and Greg remained.

"If you and Rachel have plans for the rest of the afternoon, we could do this tomorrow." Marci joined Greg at the far end of the table, where he'd chosen to sit.

"No. We don't have anything special on the agenda for tonight."

Too bad.

"In that case . . ." She pulled out the chair beside him and sat. "I was intrigued by the concept you mentioned at the town meeting about making the lighthouse pay for itself in the long run. I like the idea of turning it into a special events venue—for weddings in particular. What could be more romantic than getting married at a lighthouse?"

"Rachel liked that idea too."

"There you go. Great minds think alike." She winked at him. "Have you given any additional thought as to how we might implement that?"

"Yes." He opened the folder in front of him, which contained several typed pages clipped together and what appeared to be quite a bit of backup information. "I was going to give you this after the meeting. It's not as urgent as the other items we discussed."

"It's all part of the larger plan, though. I'll be happy to take that and review it later, but why don't you give me a verbal summary?"

"Sure."

For the next ten minutes, she listened without saying a word as Greg walked her through his well-thought-out suggestions about how to generate income on the lighthouse grounds—tours, art fairs, concerts, weddings, rehearsal dinners, family reunion events, corporate functions, bus-tour stop, gift shop . . . the list went on.

And every single item had merit.

Based on a quick flip through the detailed document he

handed her at the end, he'd also put together a polished business plan supported with abundant documentation.

After scanning his proposals and the backup data, she looked over at him. "This is impressive. Do you have a business background?"

"No. I only went to junior college. I don't have a degree."

She set the material in front of her. "Business aptitude can be fostered in many ways. Tell me about your work history."

"I was in the army."

"I know—and that suggests you have discipline and drive. What else have you done?"

"You mean . . . like part-time jobs during school?"

"Yes." The idea beginning to percolate in her mind might not fly—but it was worth exploring. While Greg might not have a degree, practical business experience could be just as valuable.

He ran a finger down the crease of the manila folder. "I didn't have a conventional part-time job."

"I'd like to hear about it anyway."

"Well . . . when I was fifteen, I wanted some spending money. I was too young to get a real job like my brother, so I put together a ninety-minute walking tour of the town for tourists."

Enterprising.

"How did you line up customers?"

"I made signs to put up around town—at Sweet Dreams, the Gull Motel, the Myrtle Café . . . any place tourists hung out. Charley put one on his stand too. I usually had about ten people show up."

"How often did you run the tour?"

"Once a day the first year. At ten bucks a head, I made pretty good money."

A hundred dollars a day for ninety minutes of work?

That was way better than pretty good for a fifteen-year-old.

"I also solicited coupons from businesses around town."

Greg doodled on the folder in front of him, a slight smile curving his lips, as if the memories of his youthful enterprise were sweet. "So tourists got coupons worth more than the price of the tour—which helped promote sales."

Clever.

The idea she was noodling on began to send down some roots.

"You mentioned the first year. I take it you did this for a while?"

"Yeah. The second year I ran two tours a day."

A sixteen-year-old who racked up two hundred dollars a day for three hours of work, doing a summer job he'd created.

Amazing.

And intriguing.

"How did you find enough to talk about for an hour and a half?" Much as she loved Hope Harbor, as far as she knew there weren't enough landmarks to fill out a ninety-minute walking tour.

His eyebrows rose. "This town has some cool history. I found lots of stories after I dug into the research. In my spiel, I highlighted some of the historical characters who lived here—a sea captain, a woman who ran a logging operation, the town doctor who relocated here in 1917 after losing his son in the coyote war."

"Coyote war?" Where had Greg dug up that obscure bit of history?

"Yeah. There was a bizarre rabies epidemic in eastern Oregon for a number of years. I found loads of stuff like that. More than I needed to create a script for every stop on the tour. And I talked about Pelican Point light too."

"How long did you run these tours?"

"Until I went to junior college. The third and fourth year, I hired a buddy who did high school theater to help with extra tours. I wanted to keep the group size small, and the demand kept growing after the paper in Bandon did a story about me. We had people coming from all over the area for tours."

"Why did you stop doing them?"

He shrugged. "I never intended it to be a career. My dad was a firefighter, and my brother is too. That's all I ever wanted to be. It was a family tradition."

"But you enjoyed doing the tours, didn't you?"

"Yeah. It was fun. Not like work at all."

"Those are the best kinds of jobs."

"Depends on your perspective, I guess. For me, the best kinds are the ones that make a difference in the world. Like being a soldier who fights terrorism, or a firefighter who saves lives."

"Creating happy memories for people can make a difference too. You gave visitors a pleasant experience to remember. That matters. Happy times like you provided are what people hold close to their hearts to measure the world against."

He frowned. "I suppose that could be true."

"I know it is. When I'm down, or I hit a bump in the road, thinking about a happy memory can help me get through the day. I bet you've got some special occasions you relive again and again. Like . . . like your first date with Rachel."

"Yeah." The corners of his mouth rose. "That was a memorable night."

"But to an outsider observing your date, it would have seemed ordinary—right?"

"Yes."

"Like your tours looked to passersby. But for all you know, that was the highlight of somebody's visit. It might have whetted a kid's interest in history. Or been part of some couple's honeymoon. Or given someone who was ill a ninety-minute respite from worry. There are probably people who still remember and talk about the fun they had on your tour. Creating special memories is a worthy occupation, Greg."

"I never thought of my little tour in such grandiose terms."

"Maybe you should start." She let that sink in for a moment, then picked up the papers he'd given her and stood. "This is going to be my reading for the rest of the day. May I call you with any questions?"

"Sure." He rose, resting his fingertips on the tabletop to steady himself until his balance stabilized. "It was a productive meeting today."

"I agree. I'm going to put some more thought into finding the initial funding we need, but we're off to a strong start." She angled away, but when he touched her arm, she shifted back.

"I've never thanked you for giving Rachel a job, but I want you to know I appreciate it. The change of scene is good for her, and she enjoys the work."

"I was glad to get her. She's been a huge help—and she's an exceptional writer."

"I know. I've read some of her stuff. I'm hoping that once we . . ." He gripped the back of the chair, and a muscle flexed in his cheek. "That at some point she'll finish her degree. She only needs twenty-eight more hours."

"I don't see why that couldn't happen. More and more universities are offering online programs."

"That's what I was thinking." He picked up the empty manila folder and handed it to her. "Thanks for listening to my ideas."

"Thanks for coming up with them. I'll see you Wednesday . . . and I may be in touch before that."

With a lift of his hand, he walked toward the door.

Though his gait wasn't quite normal, no one would suspect he had a prosthesis. His disability wouldn't stop him from doing much.

Except be a firefighter.

But there were other career options that would dovetail with his innate entrepreneurial skills.

One in particular, based on all he'd told her about his creative town tour and the ideas he'd come up with for the lighthouse campaign.

That was why she'd laid the groundwork for it today.

A lot of pieces would have to fall into place for her notion to work—but that was beginning to happen.

And if it did, Greg might discover that Pelican Point light would end up playing a far more important role in his life than he'd ever suspected when he'd made it part of his town tour spiel as a teenage entrepreneur.

16

A bag of groceries clutched in each hand, Rachel pushed through the door from the garage into the quiet house.

Different.

Usually Greg played music when he was home alone.

Maybe he was on the computer again, doing more research for the lighthouse project. Since the meeting at church two days ago, he'd been burning up the browser.

And that was fine.

He might not have told her in detail about what transpired during the gathering, but Marci had sung his praises at work yesterday, raving about how he'd taken ownership of the project and offered some stellar suggestions.

It was a prayer answered—if his interest lasted . . . and if it lifted him out of the funk that had darkened their lives for the past eight months.

"Greg? Are you here?" She dropped the bags on the kitchen table and began unpacking them.

Her husband appeared in the doorway, and she smiled as

she held up her splurge item. "I got us steaks for dinner. We haven't used the grill on the patio very much, and I thought—"

"Rachel."

At his quiet tone and serious demeanor, her lungs deflated. "What's wrong?"

He moved closer. "Your mom and dad are here."

She froze. "What do you mean . . . here?"

"They're in the living room."

Her stomach bottomed out.

No wonder there was an unfamiliar car parked in front of their house.

But what was going on? Why hadn't they called first? What had prompted this out-of-the-blue trip?

And how much had they picked up about the state of the hasty marriage they'd warned against?

As if he'd read her mind, Greg spoke again, his volume so low she had to lean closer to hear him.

"I figured out pretty quick they aren't clued in to what's been going on in our lives. I just tried to make small talk. We were all very polite, but it's been . . . awkward."

That had to be the understatement of the century.

"When did they get here?"

"Twenty minutes ago based on the clock—but every minute felt like an hour. I tried your cell, but you didn't answer."

"I left it in the car while I was in the grocery store." A bad habit she needed to break.

Would break after this incident.

"You need to tell me how much they know . . . and we need to decide how to play this."

"They don't know anything." She leaned back against the counter and massaged her temple. This was a conversation that required strong cups of coffee and an open-ended timeframe.

Instead, they'd have to cover a large swath of ground fast and plan a strategy on the fly.

"What do you mean by *anything*?" Twin creases appeared on her husband's forehead.

"I haven't talked to them since I called the day after we eloped. All my communication has been through email, and then only to provide mailing addresses. My mom's the one who started phoning, like I told you the night we had dinner on the patio. All she knows is that an injury sidelined you and we relocated here."

"You didn't tell them I lost my leg?"

"No."

"Do they know we've been having . . . issues?"

"No."

"Do you want them to know?" He fisted his hands at his sides.

"No. I . . . I hoped we could fix them before they found out."

He exhaled, and the taut line of his shoulders eased a hair. "Okay." He scrubbed his palm on his jeans and reached for her hand, twining his fingers with hers. "Let's see why they're here."

"This might not be pleasant."

"I didn't pick up any antagonism—but if the discussion goes south, it's two against two . . . and I'm putting the odds on us." He winked and gave her hand an encouraging squeeze. Like he used to do in the early days of their courtship and marriage, when all their tomorrows seemed to be bright and filled with promise.

Back then he'd had an uncanny ability to make her believe that together, they could conquer the world.

He still did.

Her throat clogged, and she sniffed as her vision misted.

"Hey." He again exerted gentle pressure on her fingers. "We'll get through this, and after they're gone, we'll talk. Okay?"

"Yeah." Her response sounded as shaky—and uncertain—as she felt.

What if the arrival of her disapproving parents somehow jinxed the positive turn they'd begun to make in their relationship?

Why couldn't they have worked through their difficulties before her mom and dad decided to show up unannounced and add more stress to their lives?

How should she respond if her parents got all huffy again, Greg retreated—and they ended up back at square one?

Rachel's already crumbling composure eroded another notch.

She didn't want to deal with this.

Not yet.

But with her parents waiting in the next room, what choice did she have?

All she could do was pray she wasn't walking into a minefield that would further fracture her relationship with the people she loved most.

Rachel was trembling.

As they crossed the kitchen, Greg tightened his grip on her hand.

For a woman who'd once been as close to her mom and dad as a daughter could be, the eighteen-month estrangement had to have hurt.

Deeply.

And it was his fault.

He'd been the impatient one, unwilling to wait to tie the knot. Succumbing to his selfish impulses, he'd cajoled Rachel into choosing him over her parents.

But never had he regretted sweet-talking her into marrying him fast—until the IED changed everything.

If they'd waited, as John and Marie Stewart had asked, Rachel wouldn't have been tied to him by her marriage vows. Maybe she'd have stuck with him, maybe not. But at least her choice would have been unencumbered by promises made before God.

Yet despite the guilt that continued to plague him—especially during the sleepless, dark nights when the taste of all they'd both lost was bitter on his tongue—he couldn't be sorry about the marriage. Those first few months with Rachel as his wife had been the happiest of his life.

And the last eight?

Endurable only because she'd stuck by his side—even if he'd never told her that.

He stopped short of the door to the living room, where he'd left her parents stiffly sitting on the couch. "Ready?"

"No . . . but I won't be even if I stand here all night."

"It'll be fine. I promise. Trust me on this?"

She looked up with those wide, emotive hazel eyes that had sucked him in from day one. Searched his face. And despite the slight tremble in her lips, she nodded.

At her vote of confidence, warmth filled his heart.

In spite of the trauma of the past few months, she hadn't lost her faith in him.

That was a gift beyond measure.

Keeping a firm grip on her hand, he straightened his shoulders and led her into the living room.

John and Marie jumped to their feet the instant they entered.

Her mom took a step forward. Caught herself, as if unsure of her welcome. Twisted her hands in front of her. "Hi, honey."

"Hi, Mom. Dad. This is a surprise."

Silence.

Marie nudged her husband.

"Since we, uh, couldn't connect by phone, we thought it might be easier if we all sat down together in person." Rachel's father shifted his weight and shoved his hands in his pockets. "If you can spare us a few minutes, of course."

"You came all the way from Texas to talk for a few minutes?" Rachel stared at her parents.

Another beat of silence ticked by.

"Why don't we all sit?" Greg urged her forward, toward the unoccupied section of the L-shaped couch, and tugged her down, close beside him.

Very close.

And he didn't relinquish her hand.

Once again, quiet filled the small room.

When the stillness grew painful, John cleared his throat, leaned forward, and clasped his hands between his knees. "So . . . we have some catching up to do."

"We've missed you more than words can say." Marie's eyes began to shimmer. "And we'd like to reconnect. Your dad and I have had some long talks over the past few months." She groped for her husband's hand. "Right, John?"

He picked up the cue.

"Yeah. We have. You both know we weren't all that thrilled about how fast you decided to get married."

Greg stifled a snort.

Not that thrilled?

Appalled had been more like it.

But he bit back the retort that sprang to his lips—for Rachel's sake.

There was too much enmity between all of them already.

"It had nothing to do with you personally, Greg. We want to make that clear." Marie leaned into her husband, as if she needed to feel some physical solidarity.

Or she could be sending one of those silent wifely messages.

Like, *Watch what you say, or we could blow this whole visit.*

"That's right." John patted her hand. "We were just concerned that a rash decision might backfire and end up hurting Rachel. But you're an adult now, sweetie. We know that here"—

he tapped his temple—"but it's hard not to think of you as our little girl here." He touched his chest. "We shouldn't have been angry that you chose not to take our advice. And we're sorry we weren't there for your wedding."

A tiny shudder passed through Rachel. "It was hard for me not having you there too. A bride and groom should be s-surrounded and supported by the people who love them."

The tear brimming on Marie's lower lash spilled over. "Oh, honey, I'll always be sorry you didn't have the big wedding you used to dream about, with the beautiful white lace gown and flowers and music, and all our friends and family there to witness the happy event."

Greg's gut clenched.

The simple ceremony he and Rachel had shared had been nothing like the beautiful wedding her mother had described.

There'd been no lace gown.

No music.

No family or friends in attendance.

No flowers to speak of, other than a tiny nosegay he'd picked up en route to the ceremony in a parson's parlor, where the man's wife and son had acted as witnesses.

Apparently he'd robbed Rachel of her dream wedding as well as her relationship with her parents.

The knot in his stomach tightened.

One more regret to add to a growing list.

The squeeze Rachel gave his fingers somehow penetrated his shroud of misery, and he looked over.

She didn't utter a single syllable, but he heard her message loud and clear as they locked gazes.

I love you, Greg. None of those trappings mattered to me because I had you.

The room blurred, and pressure built in his throat.

Sweet heaven, how he loved this woman!

Blinking to clear his vision, he folded his other hand around their entwined fingers and rejoined the conversation.

"I wish we could all go back and change history, but the best we can do is make our peace with the past and move forward. I know both of us want the two of you to be part of our lives again. I'd like to get to know you better, and Rachel would love to have her parents back."

"We were hoping you'd say that." John swiped the sleeve of his sweater across his eyes, his own voice none too steady. "We booked a room for four nights at the Seabird Inn B & B here in town. We don't expect you to change your schedules for us, but we're available whenever you are."

"You're welcome to stay here." Greg didn't know where, exactly . . . but it seemed the hospitable thing to suggest.

"No." Marie shook her head. "We wouldn't think of intruding, especially since we came without any warning. And the Seabird Inn is charming."

"You'll stay for dinner, though . . . won't you?" Rachel's invitation was sincere—but it was underscored by a trace of worry.

Not surprising.

Throwing together a decent meal for four people at the last minute would be a challenge, based on what he could recall of the provisions in the kitchen.

And Rachel would want to do this right.

They also needed to talk before they spent an extended stretch with her parents, make certain they were on the same page about how much they wanted to share.

Thankfully, her mother had the wisdom to decline. "Do you think we could have a rain check and come tomorrow? It was a bumpy flight, with a long drive down from Portland on top of a time change. We're kind of wiped out. We've also disrupted your life enough for one day."

Rachel's relief was almost palpable—to him, anyway.

"That would be fine. I have a job at the local newspaper, but I'm sure my boss will let me off early."

"We don't want to cause problems," John chimed in. "Asking off in a new job might be frowned upon."

"I only work part-time, and my boss is understanding. It won't be an issue." Rachel tightened her grip on Greg's hand and shot him an uncertain look.

He hesitated—but her parents would soon find out he wasn't employed. No reason to hide it. "My schedule is open. I'm still recovering."

"Rachel told us you'd suffered an injury." Marie's tone was cautious. "I hope you're improving."

How to respond?

Her parents must have noticed his limp—but for whatever reason, Rachel hadn't told them about his leg. Would she mind if he did?

He glanced at her, and she gave a small nod of assent.

"I'm making progress—but the injury itself is permanent." He braced himself for their reaction. "I lost my leg below the knee in an IED explosion."

Shock ricocheted across her parents' faces, and her mother's hand flew to her chest.

"We had no idea it was anything that traumatic. I'm so sorry." Marie transferred her attention to her daughter. "Why didn't you tell us? You two didn't have to go through that alone."

Greg would have answered for Rachel if he could, but her reasons for withholding that information eluded him too.

"There wasn't anything you could have done." Rachel picked at a piece of lint on her slacks.

"We could have sat with you. Offered moral support. Done whatever routine chores needed to be done."

"Don't worry about it, Mom. We got through it. But we're glad you came out now." She slid her hand from his and stood.

"I've got cheese and crackers—and some fresh fruit. Let me put together a snack for us."

"Would you like some help?" Greg prepared to lever himself to his feet.

"No. I've got it." Rachel backed away. "You three go ahead and visit for a few minutes." She fled to the kitchen.

Much as he wanted to follow her, Greg resisted the temptation. It was possible she needed a few minutes alone to regroup.

This evening, however, he'd have her all to himself—and he intended to keep his promise to talk through their situation.

No matter the outcome.

What a remarkable day.

Rachel pulled the towel off her hair and blotted her wet locks in the steamy bathroom.

Greg's suggestion that she take a long shower after her parents left had been spot-on. The relaxing, hot spray had been just what she needed to soothe her taut muscles, clear her mind, and lift her spirits.

How incredible was it that her parents had journeyed all the way from Texas to say they were sorry and try to mend the relationship?

And how wonderful to once again be able to call them at will, without the specter of their unhappy parting hanging over everyone's head.

Greg had gone above and beyond during their visit to present a unified front—and as far as she could tell, her parents hadn't picked up on the strain between them.

But if it had been nothing more than an act, it would be difficult to sustain during the four days her mom and dad would be around. They'd soon realize not all was perfect in paradise.

So working through a few issues tonight, as he'd promised they would, was necessary—even if the thought of that discussion ratcheted up her tension again.

Rather than fussing with her hair, she combed it back to air dry. No sense delaying the inevitable. She might as well hear what Greg had to say.

She found him at the kitchen table, brow pinched, two beer cans in front of him.

Her heart sank.

"They're full, Rachel." He picked one up to demonstrate. "These are the last two in the refrigerator. I'm not going to drink them—and I'm not buying any more."

That was the best news she'd had in weeks. "I'm glad to hear that."

"Why don't you sit?" He motioned to the chair beside him and pushed the cans to the side.

"I want to thank you for how you acted while my parents were here." She slipped into her seat. "I don't think they suspected we've been having issues."

"It wasn't an act—and I want to talk about those issues . . . and how to fix them."

She sighed and tucked her damp hair behind her ear. "I have no idea where to start."

"I do. We start with me. That's where the blame for all our problems falls."

"Losing your leg wasn't your fault."

"No, but how I reacted was—and a bunch of things have happened in the past couple of weeks to drive that point home."

"Like what?"

"Like my brother's visit. Dan told me I should appreciate the blessing of a woman whose world has also been rocked but who's stuck around despite my foul moods—and he was right."

So Dan *had* read him the riot act that day.

She definitely owed her brother-in-law a call or thank-you note—at the very least.

"Charley had a few words of wisdom to offer too." Greg pulled a paper napkin out of the holder on the table and blotted up the ring of condensation left by one of the beer cans. "He reminded me that attitude is everything. Made me realize I'd been mired in a glass-half-empty philosophy for too long."

God bless the taco man!

"I also listened to Reverend Baker's sermon last Sunday. His comment about physical blindness not being the only way a person can lose their way—or lose sight of what's important—hit home." Greg took a deep breath. "And then there was your ultimatum."

Her stomach contracted. "That was a desperation measure. I didn't know what else to try."

"I'm glad you did it. It forced me to take stock of my priorities—and to realize that what I wanted most of all in life was you. Losing my leg was bad . . . but losing you would be like cutting out my heart."

As he uttered the words she'd been longing to hear for months, the room grew fuzzy.

"I wasn't even certain you l-loved me anymore." Somehow she choked out the admission.

He took her hand, his firm grip steady and reassuring. "I never stopped loving you. Not for one minute. In fact, I love you more now than I did the day we got married—which is saying a lot. Someday, I hope you'll be able to say the same about me . . . and that I'll deserve it."

"I never stop—"

He held up a hand. "Rachel, I've made your life miserable for months. I don't expect us to get back to normal overnight. To be honest, I can't promise there won't be days I'm frustrated or down and take it out on you again. I'll try hard not to do that, but it could happen."

"I never expected you to be perfect, Greg. All I wanted was for you to love me."

"That I can promise to do. And I'm also going to do my best to turn my life around and be the kind of husband I vowed to be the day we said I do. But I don't expect you to believe that without some proof."

"Your promise is proof enough."

His jaw firmed. "Not after everything that's happened. Let me back it up with some action too."

Action?

She arched an eyebrow. "What kind of action?"

His irises darkened for an instant—and then he flashed her a grin. "Not the kind you're imagining, much as I'd like that." His manner grew more serious. "I think we need to get comfortable together again before we jump back into full-fledged marriage."

He was right.

Lonely as she might be, the sensible course was to take things slow and easy. If this ended up being a false start . . . if for some reason Greg couldn't live up to his promise, or changed his mind . . . it was better to proceed with caution.

She couldn't go through the heartbreak of the past eight months again.

"So what's the plan?"

"I'm going to work on the lighthouse project and think about what I want to do with the rest of my life. I'm also planning to ramp up my physical therapy routine to get rid of this limp. I'll take over more of the household chores. And I'm going to talk to you—really talk to you—every single day. I'm open to other suggestions too."

"I do have one." She lifted their joined hands. "I think we

need to do more of this. Physical affection—even simple gestures like this—help build closeness."

"That will be an easy request to accommodate." He stroked his thumb over her hand. "The hardest challenge will be keeping it simple when I want much more."

"That challenge goes both ways." She tipped her head. "How will we know it's time for more?"

"I'm going to let you make that call."

She rolled her eyes. "No pressure there."

"You'll know, Rachel—and if I think you're rushing it, I'll tell you."

"That would be helpful. Because loneliness can override common sense."

"With your mom and dad back in the loop, maybe you won't be as lonely." He studied her. "Speaking of them—why didn't you reach out to them . . . or tell them about my leg?"

It was a fair question, even if the answer was uncomfortable—and humbling.

"Several reasons." She dipped her chin and traced the fake wood grain on the Formica tabletop. "Pride and stubbornness are two of them. I felt like the wrong was on their side, and I wasn't willing to back down and make the first move toward reconciliation. I thought they should do that. On top of that . . . I was afraid."

"Of what?"

"That if I told them what had happened to you, they might call or come to visit—and I was worried I'd get an earful of I-told-you-so's about rushing the wedding."

"In hindsight, they might have been right about that."

"No, they weren't." She lifted her head, willing him to see what was in her heart. "I love you, Greg. I knew it then, and I know it now. Not being married wouldn't have made me love you any less after the IED took your leg. And without the wonderful memories of our first ten months together to sustain me, it would have been even harder to deal with."

"But you could have walked away, without any strings."

"Wrong." She covered their clasped fingers with her free hand. "Our heartstrings were already entwined."

Moisture spiked on his lashes, and his Adam's apple bobbed. "Man. How do you women deal with all this emotional stuff?"

"Lots of practice." She grinned. "And you get bonus points for hanging in."

"Good—especially if we can talk about food now."

"I have those steaks I mentioned, if you're hungry."

"I'll get the grill going."

He attempted to rise, but she held fast to his hand. "I agree we need to reestablish a trust level and not jump back into the physical side of marriage—but how do you feel about hugs?"

In answer, he pulled her to her feet and wrapped those strong arms she remembered so well around her.

Tucking herself close, she nestled against the familiar broad chest.

And as his heart beat a steady, welcome rhythm beneath her ear, Rachel let out a slow, contented sigh.

They weren't home free yet.

Not by a long shot.

But for the first time, the fleeting moments of hope that had sustained and encouraged her during the past eight months seemed poised to fulfill their promise.

17

Crimping the top of the white bag from Sweet Dreams Bakery, Ben shortened his stride . . . slowed his pace . . . and came to a halt a few doors down from Marci's office.

There was no reason to bother her on this Wednesday morning.

Between her PR work, publishing the *Herald*, and coordinating the lighthouse project, she must be swamped.

But it had been three days since their lunch in her gazebo—and he was missing her.

Bad.

Bad enough to have invested some serious brainpower trying to figure out how their jobs and geographic situations could accommodate a relationship.

So far, he was batting zero.

Marci had been clear that she didn't want a short-term or long-distance relationship—and neither did he.

That meant one of them would have to make some life-altering adjustments if they wanted to test the waters of romance.

And since Marci was only two years into her tenure in Hope

Harbor—a town she loved—it appeared the onus for change was on him.

A huge challenge, given the plum slot waiting for him in Ohio.

"Morning, Ben." Father Murphy called out the greeting from across Dockside Drive, swiveled his head to assess the traffic, and jogged over to join him. As usual, the jovial priest was all smiles.

Maybe he could absorb some of the padre's upbeat mood through osmosis.

"Morning, Father."

The priest sized up the white bag and sniffed. "Ah. A man after my own heart. That's my destination too, on this beautiful morning. There's nothing like a fresh cinnamon roll—or two"—he patted his sturdy midsection—"to launch the day on a happy note."

"They beat Cheerios, that's for sure."

"Or oatmeal—my usual healthy fare." He made a face, then brightened. "But today I'm succumbing to temptation."

Ben hiked up an eyebrow. "Should a priest admit such a thing?"

"Clergymen are human too, you know—and I was born with a ferocious sweet tooth. It's the bane of my existence." He sighed and folded his hands in front of him. "However, in light of our conversation, I'll temper my craving and just buy one today."

"Sorry to ruin your fun."

"I forgive you, my son." Eyes twinkling, he gave him a mock blessing. "And now I'll let you enjoy your own treat." He inspected the bag. "It appears you have enough to share—unless you're indulging your sweet tooth too."

"No. I, uh, thought I'd drop into the *Herald* and exchange a roll for a cup of coffee."

"An excellent plan. I saw Marci conferring with Eric at the crack of dawn in his office while I was taking my morning walk on the wharf. Lighthouse business, I expect. I wouldn't be surprised if she skipped breakfast in order to fit that meeting in." He shook his head. "It was a blessing for this town the day she moved here, but I suspect she works too hard."

"I'll try to convince her to take a short break."

"You do that. She could use a little diversion in her life." The padre tipped his head, his expression speculative. "It's a shame you'll be leaving soon."

Uh-oh.

Was it possible the good father had matchmaker leanings?

"I wish I could stay longer—but I have a job waiting in Ohio."

"Do you have family there? Friends?"

"No. Just a colleague from medical school."

"I see." Father Murphy linked his hands behind his back and rocked forward on his toes. "It's a commentary on our society how people choose where they live these days. Jobs seem to take precedence over every other criterion."

"That's not quite true in my case. My friends are all scattered, and I have no family. One town is as good as another."

"I'll have to disagree with you on that point. A loving community—like Hope Harbor—can help compensate for a lack of family. You should ask Charley about that. Or Luis Dominguez . . . or Adam Stone . . . or Brenda Hutton, the wonderful cook and housekeeper Paul and I share, and her son . . . the list goes on. As for friends—you already have quite a few here. It's a very welcoming place."

"Are you implying I should stay?"

"Not at all. That's your decision. I'm merely suggesting there are many factors to ponder when choosing a place of residence—and *we* have Sweet Dreams." The priest winked and gave him an elbow nudge. "Enjoy your treat and tell Marci I'll see her tonight at the lighthouse meeting."

With a wave, he set off at a fast clip for the bakery.

Eyes narrowed, Ben watched him for a few moments.

Curious how the priest had brought up the very subject that was on his mind.

Turning back toward his destination, Ben spotted Charley strolling by on the wharf side of the street. Heading for the taco stand, perhaps.

The man smiled and gave him a thumbs-up—almost as if he was agreeing with everything Father Murphy had said.

Which was ridiculous.

There was no way Charley could have heard their conversation from that distance.

It was probably just one of the artist's quirky greetings.

Ben waved in response and resumed his trek, for once oblivious to the relaxing harbor scene.

Everything the priest had said made sense—and if he wasn't so far along in the process with the Ohio job, he might toy with the notion of retooling his career plans. But he was in deep already—and passing up an opportunity at such a coveted and well-respected practice would be crazy.

Besides, Hope Harbor had no need of an orthopedic surgeon.

But the practice in Coos Bay does.

Ben frowned.

And the urgent care center here needs a medical director or it's going to fold.

Once again, his pace slowed.

Both of those opportunities were viable—and would be worth weighing, if he was inclined to stay.

In fact, he might be able to arrange to join the Coos Bay practice *and* step in at the urgent care center until a permanent director was found. Many residents used it for their health care needs—including Skip. Hadn't the center recommended the outstanding surgeon in Coos Bay?

Yet much as he liked Hope Harbor . . . much as the notion

of saving the urgent care center for the town was appealing . . . the real incentive to change plans was the woman in the office a few doors ahead.

Except there were two big problems.

It was too soon to know for certain where their friendship might lead—and the job in Ohio wasn't going to wait around for him to find out.

Giving up that opportunity for a relationship this new would be a huge risk. What would he do if he and Marci parted ways?

A billow of gray mist shuttered the sunlight, and out on the jetty, the foghorn issued a long, plaintive warning to harbor traffic.

Beeee. Carefullll.

A caution he should heed as well. There was no need to make a life-changing decision today—or tomorrow.

But now that the seed had been planted, it might not be a bad idea to begin putting out some job feelers.

Just in case.

"Sweet Dreams delivery."

As Ben's baritone voice greeted her from the door, Marci swiveled away from her computer screen to face him.

Whoa.

Did this man ever have a bad hair day?

Not once in all the times she'd seen him had he looked anything but drop-dead handsome.

Suit and tie, jeans and T-shirt, dress slacks and button-down shirt—didn't matter. He was swoon-worthy in any attire, every strand of his thick, dark-brown hair tamed despite the wind that often whipped through Hope Harbor.

If only her hair would behave half as well.

"Any takers?" He held up a white sack but remained by the door.

"Yes. Come in." She stood and motioned to a small conference table off to the side, smoothing down her flyaway locks. "Would you like some coffee?"

"That would hit the spot." He strolled in and glanced around the office.

Thank heaven she'd been born with the tidy gene. An ex-army officer wouldn't appreciate clutter. Her desk might be full of papers, but they were all piled in neat stacks—and Rachel's work space was pristine.

"What brings you here today? Not that I'm complaining, mind you. Anyone who comes bearing Sweet Dreams cinnamon rolls gets the red-carpet treatment."

"I was in the neighborhood and decided to drop in. Is Rachel here?" He surveyed the empty desk.

"No. Her parents showed up so I gave her the rest of the week off."

"Ah. That would explain the unfamiliar car I've seen parked in front of the house."

"Apparently, they arrived on her doorstep without any warning. She sounded happy on the phone, though. They've been estranged, but I'm thinking they've worked out their differences."

"That would be great—for everyone's sake." He set the bag on the small table while she grabbed some napkins and carried over their java.

"Black and strong." She set his in front of him and took a seat.

He joined her, uncrimped the bag, and held it out. "Help yourself."

She took one of the sweet confections, deposited it on a napkin, and licked the icing off her fingers.

At his amused expression, she gave a sheepish shrug. "Sorry. It's too tasty to waste."

"I like a woman who enjoys her food."

"In that case, you've come to the right place." She took a sip of coffee, eyeing him over the rim of her mug. Odd that he'd shown up just when she was thinking about calling him. But what she wanted to talk about was better done in person, anyway. "I'm glad you stopped by. I have an idea I wanted to run by you."

"Shoot." He dived into his roll.

"The lighthouse committee is working hard, and Greg's come up with some inventive ideas about how to make the site pay for itself going forward. Our biggest problem is raising enough money to match the offer you've had from your anonymous buyer."

"It's a chunk of change." He took a paper napkin and wiped some sticky icing off his hands . . . so much more genteel than her finger-lick method.

"I know. And while Hope Harbor is blessed in many ways, most of the residents aren't wealthy in a material sense. Raising funds is a challenge."

Ben took a swig of coffee, faint furrows creasing his brow. "I understand about money being tight. Army doctor isn't the highest-paying job in the world—and buying into a prestigious practice is expensive. Even though I'll work for them for two years before I have to fork over the cash to become an official partner, I won't have saved anywhere near the full price."

"So the anonymous lighthouse offer is a godsend."

"Yes. I'll still have to go into debt, but at least I won't have to start out as much in the hole." He exhaled. "If I could donate the light to the town, I would."

"No one expects you to do that."

"Maybe not—but I wish I could."

"You have to be practical about this. We all get that." She swiped a finger over her roll and sampled a little more icing. Why be couth now? "We're hoping we can come up with a grant or two, but that's not likely to happen in time to give us the funds to purchase the lighthouse. So I'm working on two ideas that would have a quicker impact. I'm planning to discuss them with the committee tonight, but it would be helpful to hear your thoughts first. Do you have a few minutes?"

"Yes. I'm meeting with a realtor at noon to discuss listing Skip's house, but I'm free until then."

"I won't keep you anywhere near that long." Taking a steadying breath, she crossed her fingers under the table and sent a silent prayer heavenward. "You've heard of crowdfunding, I assume."

"I've read about it, but I don't know any details about how it works."

"It's a simple premise—and for certain types of enterprises, it can be very effective. I have a couple of PR clients who've used it successfully. One was a nonprofit organization, the other a start-up business. In the case of the nonprofit, we used a donation approach. With the start-up business, we did rewards—coupons for free and discounted products once the company was up and running."

Ben's eyebrows rose. "It's hard to believe people would contribute based on an online solicitation."

"You'd be surprised. We live in a wired world—and despite what the media might have us believe, generosity and charity are alive and well . . . especially when it comes to good causes. An endangered lighthouse falls into that category."

"So how do you tap into all this goodwill?"

"I design a social media campaign, and once Eric files all the paperwork for the 501(c)(3) foundation, I launch it on a crowdfunding platform. Some of those have tremendous reach. All donations would be sent directly to the foundation, so they'd be tax deductible from the date the organization is created—assuming the IRS application is approved. I don't see any reason why it wouldn't be."

"You've done your homework on this—and the concept is intriguing." He polished off the first half of his cinnamon roll. "What about the second idea you mentioned?"

She shifted in her chair. This was where it could get awkward.

"Actually, Greg gets the credit for this one. But I hate to bring it up, after what you told me about the expense of buying into the practice in Ohio. This could have a direct impact on your wallet."

"You have a receptive audience here. If I can work with you, I will."

"Well . . ." She stirred her coffee again, even though the generous spoonful of sugar she'd added had already dissolved. "It's possible we'll have an overwhelming response to the crowdfunding campaign. It wouldn't be unheard of, and a lighthouse should be an easy sell. A lot of people have a soft spot in their hearts for them. But we may still be short by your deadline."

"Then what?"

"We have two options. If you gave us an extension, we could continue the campaign and hope more funds would come in—or you could take the difference between what we raise and the offer you have on the table as a charitable deduction on your taxes. Any additional donations that came in after you sell the lighthouse to the foundation could be used for restoration or to buy adjacent property to accommodate parking or other needs. The lighthouse footprint isn't that big."

He sipped his coffee as he considered her proposal. "That's an interesting idea."

She squinted at him. "Interesting as in worth some serious deliberation or interesting as in nice try?"

The corners of his lips rose, and a dimple appeared in his

right cheek. "Interesting as in it deserves further investigation. Let me talk to my accountant, get his take. It might be a reasonable compromise—assuming the difference between the two amounts isn't huge."

She yanked her gaze away from that distracting dimple. "Define huge."

"I'll have to discuss that with my accountant before I can give you a definitive answer . . . but I could offer a guess."

"That would be helpful." She held her breath.

When he gave her a number, she exhaled.

The amount he'd suggested would leave them with a challenging fund-raising goal—but it wasn't out of the realm of possibility.

"Considering how hard everyone in town is working to save the light and how much it meant to Skip—not to mention the happy memories I have of it—I'd like to contribute to the effort too. This would be one way to do that." Ben took another bite of his almost-gone roll and motioned toward hers. "You're not making much progress."

She inspected it.

No, she wasn't.

"I tend to get distracted when I'm in the middle of a project. Food falls off my radar screen." She tore off a large piece of the roll.

"No wonder you're slender."

"Oh, trust me. I make up for it between projects." She took a big bite.

"Are you *ever* between projects?"

At the teasing light in his eyes, she grinned. "Once in a while—but not lately."

He popped the last section of his roll into his mouth and picked up his coffee. "What happens with the lighthouse once the foundation owns it?"

"That's where Greg's ideas take center stage."

While she gave him a topline of the thorough business plan Rachel's husband had developed—and told him the story of Greg's teenage tour venture—Ben leaned back, listening in silence until she finished.

"It sounds like he's not only creative but a go-getter."

"That's my take."

Ben pursed his lips. "I wonder if he'd have any interest in managing the site once it's up and running?"

Smiling, she propped her elbows on the table and wrapped her fingers around her mug. "That notion did cross my mind. It's obvious he has an aptitude for this kind of venture, and if he's involved from the ground floor, he'll know all the background, gain useful experience, and grow along with the business."

"Have you broached this with him yet?"

"No. If everyone agrees with the crowdfunding idea tonight, and all the other pieces align, I'll talk to him afterward. I can't imagine anyone on the committee would have any qualms about offering him the slot."

The landline on her desk began to ring, and Ben rose. "I should let you get back to work."

Much as she hated to see him go, she did have a long to-do list—and the top item was gearing up for the crowdfunding campaign.

She stood too, and walked with him to the door, letting the phone roll to voicemail. "I'll let you know the outcome of tonight's meeting."

"Why don't you fill me in over tacos at lunch tomorrow? I could meet you on the wharf at Charley's truck."

A bevy of butterflies took flight in her stomach.

He was asking her for a date!

"What time?"

One side of his mouth hitched up. "That wasn't a hard sell."

"I never pass up a taco from Charley's."

He winced. "Ouch. That puts me in my place."

"Or a date with a handsome man who owns a lighthouse."

"Better." He glanced out the front window . . . checked both directions . . . and bent down to give her another one of those tantalizing forehead lip-brushes that made her yearn for more.

Much more.

"Don't work too hard." He straightened up.

"I'm not sure I . . ." Her voice came out in a squeak, and she tried again. "I'm not sure I can promise that when I'm on a quest to save a lighthouse."

"Understood. But save the noon hour for me tomorrow."

"I'm writing it in ink on my calendar."

"Much better than pencil." He grinned, then gestured out the window. "Looks like I should have brought an umbrella."

She inspected the gray sky and the steady rain that had begun to fall.

Odd.

Usually she noticed if the sun went in and the weather changed.

However . . . it wasn't every day a hot guy like Ben stopped in her office bearing sweets—and bestowing kisses.

"You want to borrow mine? I always keep one here."

"No. I'll run for it. I'm parked just down the block." He pushed open the door. "Enjoy the rest of your cinnamon roll."

"Count on it."

He exited into the rain and began to jog down the sidewalk.

She watched until the wind blew a curtain of moisture her direction and drove her inside.

Closing the door against nature's onslaught, she scanned the gray sky through the window—and a tiny shiver rippled through her.

Odd.

The changeable weather in her adopted town was nothing new. She ought to be used to it after two years. This *was* Oregon. Warm and sunny one minute, with clear skies and views to the horizon. Cool and foggy the next, visibility reduced to a few feet.

Yet the sudden deterioration in the weather today felt like a metaphor for life.

After all, who knew what tomorrow held—let alone the next hour?

Everything in her life *seemed* to be on track at the moment. Her PR business was growing. The *Herald* was beginning to turn a profit. The lighthouse project was going well. Memories of her bad experience in Atlanta were receding.

And the icing on the cake?

She'd met a very eligible, very appealing army doctor who was as interested in her as she was in him.

Life was good.

Not perfect, but good.

Perfect would be if she and Ben could figure out how to deal with the geographic hindrances to their relationship.

But they were both intelligent people. If they were meant to be together, they'd find a way to make this work.

And she, for one, intended to put a lot of thought—and prayer—into that very challenge.

A rumble of thunder rattled the window, and she took a step back, suppressing another inexplicable shiver.

She wasn't afraid of storms—and while her clothes were a tad damp from standing at the door, she wasn't chilled.

The shiver felt more . . . ominous . . . than that. Almost like a premonition—if one believed in such things.

Huffing, she turned her back on the gloomy gray skies and marched over to the conference table.

She'd finish the rest of her cinnamon roll, warm up her coffee, and get to work on the crowdfunding campaign.

And she would *not* let a silly storm spook her.

All the pieces of her life were moving along fine—and there was no reason to worry any of them were about to go south.

18

Apparently he'd been stood up.

Fists on hips, Ben surveyed the wharf, then frowned at Marci's office down the block.

No sign of her.

Yet she hadn't called to cancel.

Strange.

She might be a woman of strong emotions, but she had a first-class mind and appeared to be buttoned up and organized. If he'd ever doubted that, their discussion yesterday about the lighthouse campaign and her crowdfunding idea had been convincing evidence of her business acumen.

So where was she?

He checked his watch again. Five after twelve. Should he walk over to her office, or give her another few . . .

"Can I interest you in an order of tacos? It's a beautiful day to sit and enjoy the view."

As Charley called out to him from behind the counter of the food truck a dozen yards away, Ben strolled over. "That was my plan—but I don't think my date is going to show." He aimed another glance toward Marci's office.

"You wouldn't be talking about our *Herald* editor, would you?"

"Bingo." No reason to hide the fact. For all Charley knew, this could be a business discussion about the lighthouse rather than a social date.

"In that case, I can guarantee she's not going to show. She left early this morning to fly down to Florida. Her mom had a health emergency."

Ben's pulse picked up. "What kind of emergency?"

"Sounded like it could be a stroke."

Ben bit back the word that sprang to his lips.

After everything that had happened to her in the past—and all she had going on in Hope Harbor right now—a family medical crisis was the last thing she needed.

"How did you find out about this?"

"After the lighthouse meeting at Grace Christian last night, I took a walk on the beach, then sat here on the wharf for a while. The light was on at the *Herald*, so I assumed Marci had come back to put in another hour or two."

"That sounds like her."

"I agree. Anyway, she dashed out the door, and I went over to see if everything was okay. She'd just gotten the call from her dad and was running home to pack a bag and catch a red-eye out of Portland. I'm surprised she didn't call or text you to cancel your lunch."

"I'm sure she was distracted." But truth be told, he was surprised too—and disappointed. Friends shared that kind of important news with each other. And he'd have been happy to take her to the airport. It was a long, dark drive north late at night.

"You certain she didn't try to get in touch?" Charley brushed a few crumbs off the pristine serving counter.

"I always have my phone with me, and I check messages regularly."

Or he used to—until the low-key Hope Harbor vibe seeped into his soul and he'd fallen out of the habit.

Maybe she *had* left a message.

He pulled out his cell and pressed the power button.

Nothing.

He tried again.

Still nothing.

"You think the battery might be dead?" Charley leaned across the counter and perused the blank screen.

Ben closed his eyes and exhaled.

Yeah, it was dead, all right.

And no wonder. He hadn't recharged his cell in a few days. Why bother, as little as he used it?

"I need to go home and plug this in."

"Let me get you an order of tacos to take with you."

"I don't want to wait for . . ."

Charley reached off to the side, pulled out a brown bag, and set it on the counter. "A pre-order. But I have time to put together another one before my customer gets here."

As the savory aroma wafted toward him, Ben hesitated. He *was* hungry—and it was slim pickings at the house.

"Are you certain?" Even as he asked, he was digging out his wallet.

"Yep." Charley opened the cooler, retrieved some more fish, and set the fillets on the grill. "Tacos don't take long to make. I'll have another order ready pronto."

Ben counted out the bills and handed them over. "Thanks."

"My pleasure. I know you won't enjoy them as much as if you were sharing them with Marci over there"—he gestured toward a bench beside a planter overflowing with flowers—"but you can always reschedule after she gets back."

"I intend to." He picked up the bag.

"Glad to hear it." His expression didn't change, but the sudden intensity in his dark brown irises was out of sync with his smile. "Sometimes we can let the curves life throws us mess with our internal guidance system. As your grandfather used to say, if you keep your eye on the horizon and focus on your destination, no storm can push you too far off course."

It almost sounded like Charley was issuing a . . . warning?

Then again, the resident sage was known for his enigmatic comments. No reason to read too much into it.

"That sounds like Skip." He lifted the bag of tacos. "Thanks again."

"Not a problem."

Lunch in hand, Ben strode back toward his car. He needed to charge up his phone ASAP. Because unless he'd misjudged Marci—and her feelings for him—he'd find a message or two from her waiting for him.

And while he couldn't offer much more than moral support from thousands of miles away, that might be enough to let her know he was beginning to seriously think they were destined to be more than friends.

What on earth was vibrating against her ear?

Pulling herself back from the oblivion of deep sleep, Marci shifted and . . .

Ouch!

Why did her neck hurt?

Squinting against a beam of light lasering through a gap in the blinds on the window, she gingerly rotated her head.

The vibration continued.

Ah.

It was her phone.

Somehow, while she'd slept, she'd slipped sideways in the utilitarian recliner beside her mother's bed, and her ear had landed on top of her purse.

Shoving her hair out of her face, she straightened up, groped for the cell, and surveyed her mom.

"I'm wide awake, dear. Don't worry about disturbing me if you need to take a call. You should have gone to the house hours ago and gotten some decent sleep."

Other than a few fine lines of strain at the corners of her eyes, her mom looked like her usual self.

Thank you, God!

"I wanted to stay here. And I'm fine." Her fingers closed over the phone, and she pulled it out.

Ben.

Finally.

While she hadn't expected him to check his messages late last night, the silence from his end this morning had been disconcerting. If the situation were reversed, she'd have been on the phone the instant she got the first message.

Her cell buzzed again.

One more ring and it was going to roll to voicemail.

"I'll take this out in the hall, Mom." She pressed the talk button and scrambled to her feet.

"You can chat in here if you like. You won't disturb me."

"Hi." She kept walking as she spoke into the phone. "Can you hold a second?"

"Sure. Take your time."

Just hearing Ben's warm, caring voice chased away some of the doubts that had begun to creep into her mind.

Putting the phone on mute, she turned to her mom. "I want to visit the ladies' room anyway. Where's Dad?"

"He went to get us some real coffee."

"Will you be okay for a few minutes while I'm gone?"

"Of course." She gave an annoyed flip of her hand. "This whole episode was scary, but I'm fine. I feel terrible you made a cross-country trip for nothing."

"I'm glad it *was* nothing. Or not much." She continued toward the hall. "I'll be back in a few minutes."

As soon as she left the room, she put the phone back to her ear and ambled toward the lounge near the bathrooms. "Sorry. I was in with my mom."

"How is she?"

"Doing fine. It wasn't a stroke."

"That's good news. What happened?"

"The doctors called it a complex migraine, even though she's never had a problem with headaches."

"Ah. I saw a couple of those on my ER rotation in med school. A very strange phenomenon. The symptoms can simulate a stroke."

"So the doctors said. Mom told us she hadn't been feeling well all day. Then her cheek and hand went numb, her vision got blurry, and her speech suddenly became incomprehensible. I'm glad I wasn't here for that part." A quiver rippled through her.

"On an optimistic note, in general the prognosis is very positive for those kinds of episodes. In most cases there aren't any residual effects."

"That's what we've been told." She crossed the lounge and tucked herself into a quiet corner. Asking outright why he hadn't called sooner might be pushy . . . but she should be able to get the answer without posing a direct question. "I'm sorry about missing our lunch. I was looking forward to it."

"No worries. We'll reschedule after you get back. Now it's my turn to apologize. I only got your text and voicemail fifteen minutes ago. When you didn't show at Charley's, I pulled out my cell to see if you'd called and discovered the battery was dead."

Propping a shoulder against the wall, she let out a long, slow breath.

Thank you again, God.

"I suppose I could play this coy, but the truth is that makes me feel better."

"As long as we're being candid, I'll reciprocate by telling you that I'm glad it makes you feel better."

Her dad passed by the lounge . . . stopped . . . and lifted a tray with three venti Starbucks cups.

She waved at him and held up a single finger to buy herself another minute.

"That also makes me feel better." She pushed off from the wall. "My dad just passed by with a Starbucks infusion for all of us—and I need some caffeine."

"Have you gotten any sleep?"

"An hour or two. My mom is hoping they'll let her go by the end of the day, so we should all be able to sleep in real beds tonight."

"How long are you staying?"

"To be determined. I can work on most of my projects from here—including the crowdfunding campaign—but I'd rather be in Hope Harbor to keep my finger on the pulse of everything."

"If you need me to step in and help in any way while you're gone, I'd be happy to."

She slouched against the wall again. The lack of sleep was beginning to take a toll. "I'm not certain your bidder would appreciate you undercutting his efforts to buy the lighthouse."

"What he doesn't know can't hurt him."

She gave a soft laugh. "I'll keep your offer in mind, but I've already been in touch with Greg and some of the other committee members. I think we've got it covered for the next two or three days."

"You'll be back that fast?"

"Unless there's a change here—but I don't expect that, based on Mom's prognosis. I don't want to miss an issue of the *Herald*. Rachel's capable and willing, but she's still learning the ropes."

"Let me know your travel plans—and we'll have that lunch as soon as you get back. Now I better let you go join your parents for coffee."

Oh yeah.

They were probably wondering what was keeping her.

"Thanks for calling. Talking to you gave me the lift I needed."

"That goes both ways. Take care, and see you soon." The line went dead.

For a few moments, Marci stayed where she was, replaying the conversation in her mind. Funny how that brief connection with Ben had revived her energy.

Too bad he wasn't here to give her one of those adrenaline-producing forehead kisses of his.

That would be far preferable to a dose of high-octane coffee.

But since java was the only energy booster available, better join her parents and claim her cup.

When she appeared on the threshold of her mom's room, her father smiled.

"We wondered if you'd gotten lost." He plucked the third cup out of the cardboard tray as she entered. "Sweet and diluted—the way you like it."

She reached for it and took a long, slow sip. "Mmm. Perfect."

"Why don't you take the car and go to the house, get some shut-eye?" He pulled out his keys and jingled them in front of her. "It could be hours before your mom gets sprung, and you have to be exhausted."

"To be honest, I think I'm catching my second wind."

"It can't be from the coffee. The caffeine wouldn't kick in that fast."

"Maybe the phone call gets the credit for the boost." Her mom gave her a speculative perusal.

Sheesh.

Her mother's migraine episode might have disturbed the blood flow in her brain, but it hadn't done one bit of damage to her mental processes—or her legendary intuition.

Marci hid behind another sip of coffee, dragging it out as long as she could.

"Did you get some good news?" As usual, her teddy bear of a dad was oblivious to the subtleties his wife homed in on like a divining rod to water.

"No real news. Just a call from a friend."

"Anyone we know?" Her mom's casual tone was at odds with her keen, discerning eyes.

"No. He's only been in town a short while."

"Ah. A man friend."

True to form, her mother had jumped all over the fact she had a new friend of the opposite gender.

"He's passing through, Mom. In three or four weeks, he'll be gone." And she wasn't ready to talk about him to her parents. "You know, Dad . . . I think I'll take you up on the offer of the car. If Mom gets released sooner than anticipated, give me a call and I'll come back to pick you up. Otherwise, I'll try to sleep for a few hours."

"Sure thing, sweetie." He fished the keys out again and passed them over.

She gave him a hug and bent over to kiss her mom. "Take it easy till they let you go."

"I don't have much choice. And you get some rest. Tonight, when we're all home and life is more back to normal, you can tell me about this friend of yours—and give us an update on your save-the-lighthouse campaign."

"Let's play the rest of the day by ear."

But as she left the room, she bumped a discussion about Ben to the bottom of her agenda.

Because her mom would pick up too much—and she'd be astonished to learn that the friend her daughter had referenced was none other than the owner of the threatened lighthouse.

It kind of surprised—and tickled—her too.

And while she was grateful her whirlwind trip to Florida had been for naught, and wonderful as it was to see her parents, she was already counting the hours until she could get back on a plane and return to the town she loved—and the ex-army doctor who was fast making inroads on her heart.

19

So far, this had been a very good day.

Smiling, Ben cranked down the window in Skip's truck, rested his elbow on the edge, and inhaled the tangy salt air as he cruised down Highway 101 from Coos Bay under the cloudless blue Friday sky.

If he wanted to change his resident status in Hope Harbor from temporary to permanent, finding satisfying work appeared to be a cinch.

His early-morning meeting with the owner of the urgent care center had been encouraging. The man had been beyond enthusiastic about the possibility of an army surgeon taking over as director until a long-term replacement could be found. Details would have to be worked out, but the door was open.

And the conversation he'd just had with Jonathan Allen had also been upbeat. The surgeon had been more than receptive to his query about the possibility of joining the growing orthopedic practice in Coos Bay. He'd also introduced him to his partner and promised the two of them would discuss the idea over the weekend.

The sole question mark was Marci.

And she was the lynchpin in his decision.

Tapping a finger against the wheel, Ben passed a slower-moving car. The electricity sparking between the two of them was strong now, but it could fizzle. One, or both, of them might lose interest.

If that happened, would he want to spend the rest of his life in Hope Harbor, knowing their paths were bound to cross?

That could be awkward.

Yet the town did have much to recommend it, as Father Murphy had reminded him the other day. Skip had loved it for all the reasons the priest had mentioned.

Plus, Ben had his own fond memories of the place that had become a refuge during his turbulent younger years after his world flipped upside down.

So what should he do?

Despite his increasingly urgent prayers for guidance, the answer continued to elude him.

All he knew was that he needed to decide soon. If he was going to change direction, it was only fair to let the practice in Ohio know ASAP.

He rounded a bend in the road on the final approach to Hope Harbor, and Pelican Point light peeked at him through the spruce and fir trees, an imposing presence on the craggy headland.

Hard to believe how much his life had changed because of that unexpected legacy. The weather-beaten structure had disrupted his plans, launched him on an unexpected journey, and opened doors to new possibilities.

And who would ever have guessed that a lighthouse would link so many lives?

Strange how Skip hadn't had any takers when he'd put it on the market five months ago, but an offer had landed on the table within days of his demise.

An offer that had rallied the town to save the light, started a romance, and perhaps helped save a marriage.

A grin tugged at his mouth as he passed the Welcome to

Hope Harbor sign. His grandfather would have had a field day with that scenario. Rather than view the events as random, he would have assumed there was a purpose behind them.

Ben wasn't as inclined as Skip to see the hand of the Almighty in everything—but in this case, his grandfather might be right. Everything had fallen into place too neatly to be explained by chance.

Swinging onto Dockside Drive, Ben tooled toward home, one hand on the wheel as he scanned the wharf. Charley's was open for business . . . and for a second he was tempted to indulge in some tacos for lunch.

But the realtor was stopping by again in fifteen minutes. Better keep rolling.

Charley stepped out of the back of his taco truck as he passed, and Ben waved at him through the window.

The man watched him for a moment, then lifted his hand in reply—but there was no trademark flash of gleaming teeth today. Charley seemed almost . . . somber.

A tiny niggle of unease snaked through Ben.

During all their interactions through the years, the local artist had always radiated optimism, his sunny outlook and cheerful nature a balm for troubled souls.

In fact, without him and Skip, Ben wasn't certain he'd have survived his tenth summer. Between the two of them, they'd managed to brighten his world—and fill it with hope.

But he wasn't getting positive vibes from the man now.

Could Charley be having a bad day for once in his life?

He continued down the street, watching the man in his rear-view mirror.

Charley stayed where he was, gaze fixed on the truck, uncharacteristically solemn.

Too bad he couldn't stop and talk to the resident sage. Find out what was going on.

With the realtor on her way, however, he'd be late if he dallied.

Maybe once she left, though, he'd wander back down for a chat with the man. After all the times Charley had cheered *him* up, the least he could do was try to return the favor.

Depressing the gas pedal, Ben picked up speed and completed the short drive to Skip's street in less than five minutes. An unfamiliar car was parked a few doors down from the house, and he gave it a quick once-over as he turned into the driveway. Not the one Rachel's parents had rented. And no one was inside, so it wasn't the realtor waiting for him to get home.

Someone on the block other than his neighbors must have company too.

He pulled to the end of the driveway and swung out of the cab, taking a quick inventory of the house as he approached the back door. The lawn needed mowing . . . but he could do that after the realtor left. A pile of yard waste in the corner was ready to be bagged and hauled away. The fence could use a few repairs too.

Pushing through into the kitchen, he headed for his never-ending to-do list on the counter and . . .

The doorbell rang, and he frowned as he retrieved a pen to jot down the new additions. Much as he admired punctuality, people who came early were as annoying as those who showed up late.

The bell rang again.

Muttering to himself, he tossed the pen on the counter, strode toward the front of the house, and summoned up a smile for the realtor as he pulled the door open and—

The air whooshed out of his lungs, and he reared back as if someone had head-butted him.

"Hi, Ben." Nicole tossed her mane of blonde hair in an all-too-familiar gesture that curdled his stomach. "I bet you're surprised to see me."

Lips frozen—along with his insides—he gaped at the woman who'd sucked him into danger as mercilessly as a riptide.

Surprise didn't come anywhere close to capturing the emotions churning through his gut.

Heart pounding, he gripped the edge of the door and stared at her, the cloying scent of the climbing roses that hid the porch from street view activating his gag reflex.

Her pleasant expression morphed into a pout. "I wasn't expecting you to greet me with open arms, but I didn't think you'd be rude."

Somehow he found his voice. "What are you doing here?"

"We have unfinished business."

"Our business was finished in Germany."

"The army said it was. I don't agree."

"You admitted you lied about me. End of story."

"Not quite." She shrugged. "I might have exaggerated a little about our—"

"You didn't exaggerate. You lied." Fury nipped at his taut words.

"Oh, come on, Ben. You might not have done all the stuff I said, but you were interested in me at first. And I bet you still have feelings for me—like I do for you. Why can't we let bygones be bygones?" She flashed him another smile.

The woman was certifiable.

"The only emotion I feel for you is anger and disgust."

The corner of her eye twitched. "You've found someone new, haven't you? That local newspaper editor, maybe?"

His palms began to sweat, and panic paralyzed his lungs again. "Have you been watching me?"

"I just got here—but my private investigator earned his money."

Sweet heaven.

She'd paid someone to spy on him.

He clenched his free hand into a tight fist and tried to keep breathing as his world began to unravel.

This couldn't be happening.

The nightmare in Germany was supposed to be over.

No, not supposed to be. It *was* over.

He gritted his teeth.

Whatever her sick plan, Nicole was getting nowhere this go-round.

Bracing, he summoned up a fierce glare and ground out his edict syllable by syllable. "I'm going to say this only once. You're trespassing. Get off my property. Don't come back. And don't ever bother me again."

Before she could respond, he slammed the door and locked it.

Without looking to see if she was lingering on the porch, he methodically went through the house and tested the latch on every single window. Closed the blinds. Bolted the back door.

Once Skip's home was as secure as he could make it, he called Lexie Graham Stone.

This was a matter for the chief of police.

"Knock knock." Rachel stopped at the doorway to the spare bedroom, where Greg had been holed up every free minute he'd had since the lighthouse meeting Wednesday night.

He swiveled away from the laptop. "I didn't hear you come in."

"I'm not surprised. You were totally absorbed. Is the grill ready to fire up? Mom and Dad will be here in an hour."

"Yeah. What else can I do to help?" He closed the browser and stood.

"You've already gone above and beyond. Thanks for taking them up to the lighthouse today and giving them a tour of the town while I worked."

He grinned. "I couldn't believe how much I remembered from my old spiel. I'm sorry you couldn't come with us."

"Me too. But Marci's been so kind to me—to both of us—I had to help out during her family emergency. "

"When's she coming back?"

"Sunday."

"Good. We need to keep the project moving."

"Have you given any more thought to the proposal she made to you after the meeting?" Whether Greg realized it yet or not, the job with the lighthouse foundation was a huge blessing that would tap into his natural leadership and entrepreneurial abilities.

"Yes. It's sounding better and better—if I can do it. Dan thinks I should take it."

"Did you talk to him today?"

"Yeah. He called to check up on me. I have one nosey brother."

"Also one who loves you very much."

"I know. I'm going to discuss the job in more detail with Marci after she gets back."

"Sounds like a plan." She started to turn away . . . then swung back. "By the way, that blonde woman who was sitting in her car across the street at lunchtime? She's still there. Did you notice any activity this afternoon?"

"No. I've been glued to my computer." Brow creasing, he crossed to the front window and tipped the blind slightly. "That's weird."

"I agree."

"If she doesn't clear out in a couple of hours, I'll call the police." He let the slat slip back into position. "In the meantime, let's forget about her and enjoy our last evening with your mom and dad."

"I intend to." She leaned against the doorframe. "It's been a lovely few days."

"I'm glad I had the chance to get to know your parents better. They're nice people."

"Yes, they are—but I wasn't just talking about the fact we're all back on speaking terms. It's also been better between us."

He moved toward her, stopped three feet away, and shoved his hands in his pockets. "I told you I was going to work on that."

"And you're proving to be a man of your word—but I already knew that."

He was close enough for her to see the tiny cleft in his chin and the slight stubble from his five-o'clock shadow.

Close enough for her to touch.

Her fingers began to tingle, and before she could stop herself, she took a step toward him and laid her hand on his chest.

His breath hitched, and his irises darkened as he slowly pulled his hands out of his pockets.

"I've missed this." She splayed her fingers against the soft cotton T-shirt stretched over his firm skin.

"That makes two of us." He lifted one hand and placed it over hers, then captured her other hand in his. "I was thinking . . . after your mom and dad leave, why don't we drive up to Shore Acres State Park? Charley said the roses are blooming in the gardens, and we could take a picnic. I'll even provide the food."

Her throat tightened. "That's the kind of outing you used to plan when we were dating."

"Those were happy days—and I want us to get back to that, Rachel. Re-creating some of those dates might help."

"You don't have to twist my arm. I think it's a wonderful idea. Like something from a romance novel."

He cringed—but the corners of his mouth flexed. "Just don't tell Dan about this, okay? He'll approve—but he'll rib me no end about being sappy and sentimental."

"My lips are sealed."

"Not forever, I hope." He gave her a slow, intimate smile that jacked up her pulse.

"Don't flirt with me, Greg Clark—or that moratorium you imposed might not last until tomorrow."

"Is that a threat . . . or a promise?" He waggled his eyebrows.

At his comical antics, a giggle bubbled up inside her. "I'm not sure."

All at once, tenderness softened his eyes. "You know . . . that's the first time I've heard you laugh in months. I'd forgotten how much I love that sound." He held out his hand. "Let's make a vow to put more laughter into our lives."

She grasped his fingers. "Shall we seal that pledge with a hug?"

"I like that idea."

He pulled her close, and she wrapped her arms around him, the worry that had weighed down her shoulders all these months slipping off and evaporating like a Hope Harbor mist.

This was where she belonged.

And absent any new glitches, this was where she would stay.

Forever.

"Ben? It's Lexie Graham Stone. Do you have a few minutes?"

"Yes." Cell against his ear, Ben dumped the remains of his frozen dinner into the garbage.

"Is your visitor still in front?"

"Last I looked—but let me verify that." He strode toward the front of the house and peered through the peephole. "Yeah. Her car's there. I don't have a clear view from this angle, but I assume she's inside. What did you find out?"

"She's staying at the Gull Motel in town. The clerk on duty said she checked in this morning for an indefinite stay."

He closed his eyes.

Not what he'd wanted to hear.

"Anything else?"

"The address on her driver's license is in Omaha—and it's legit. She does have an apartment there. I couldn't find any kind of work history. In terms of criminal activity, her civilian record is clean. I can't speak to her army history."

"I know all about *that* history—at least the part that involved me." So did Lexie. He'd given her a thorough briefing during her earlier visit.

A beat passed.

"This is a tough situation."

He already knew that.

"Is there anything we can do to get her off my back?"

"Civil trespassing charges are difficult to make stick. I can cite her if she breaks any of the laws in town—littering, speeding, parking in a no-parking zone—but otherwise there's not much recourse unless she attempts to inflict harm or begins to manifest severe mental issues. Sitting in front of someone's house or following them with no evidence of physical threat isn't a crime. It's a nuisance—and an annoyance."

As far as he was concerned, it went way beyond that.

But Lexie was in a bind here too. Her hands were tied unless Nicole broke a law.

"Any recommendations?"

"Given your history, I'd say avoid her at all costs. Don't get anywhere close to her unless you're in a public place with witnesses around. Keep your house and car locked. And hope she gets tired of this game and goes home."

"I'm not holding my breath on that. She can be persistent." Not to mention vindictive. "Unless she runs out of money, she could hang around here until she makes my life totally miserable."

"Except you'll be leaving soon yourself, right?"

"That was the original plan—but I've been investigating a few other options. Hope Harbor has a lot of appeal." Including a certain red-haired newspaper editor. "Leaving might not solve the problem anyway. She could follow me to Ohio."

"In view of her obvious mental health issues, I wonder if she's under treatment?"

"Possibly—but if she is, it's not working. And with HIPAA laws, we won't be able to find out anyway."

"True. I'm sorry I can't do more. I'll instruct the officers to do frequent drive-bys on your street, but my presence—and my questions—didn't seem to intimidate her very much earlier."

"That doesn't surprise me." He wiped a hand down his face and broached the concern that had been on his mind all afternoon. "I'm worried about her reference to Marci. Nicole has a very wide jealous streak. In Germany, she shredded the sheets on one of the other nurse's beds and dumped a liter of blood all over it. All because I ate lunch with the woman in the cafeteria."

Lexie murmured a word he couldn't make out. "And *that* wasn't sufficient to convince everyone she had mental issues?"

"It would have been if we could have proved she did it—but she claimed innocence and left no evidence behind that would implicate her."

"Man. This is one scary woman."

"Tell me about it."

"We'll keep an eye on her—and call us day or night if there are any new developments or we can help in any way. You might want to alert Marci to the situation too."

"I intend to. Thanks for giving this so much attention."

"Goes with the job. But I have to say, this is the most unusual situation I've dealt with during my tenure as police chief here. Watch your back—and I'll touch base with you every day."

After one more thank-you, Ben thumbed the off button, slid

the phone back into his pocket, and raked his fingers through his hair.

In thirty-six hours, Marci would be back in town, anticipating a relaxing date with him at Charley's.

Instead, he'd have to walk a wide circle around her. The less contact they had while Nicole was lurking around, the safer she'd be.

But he had to talk to her. Explain what was happening.

And a phone call wouldn't cut it.

This was a discussion that needed to take place in person. He had to tell her the whole story about what had happened in Germany—as she'd told him about her stalker.

Stalker.

As the obnoxious word ricocheted through his mind, the irony smacked him in the face.

All these months, Marci had been worried that the nutcase who'd invaded her world in Atlanta might show up and wreak more havoc in the new, untainted life she'd created here.

Yet it was *his* past that had reared its ugly head and now threatened the future he'd begun to envision.

They could get past this, of course. Nicole couldn't hang around forever. He could wait her out if he had to.

But given Marci's history, would the skeleton in his closet undermine the foundation he'd been laying with her and short-circuit their relationship . . . or did she know—and trust—him enough to believe the story he would tell her when she returned?

20

She was almost home.

Marci turned onto Pelican Point Road and eyed the digital display on the dash. The clock was only closing in on nine, thanks to her three-hour time-zone gain, but it felt like midnight. And after eight hours of flights and layovers, followed by a nearly five-hour drive from Portland, sleep was high on her agenda.

But she'd make time to see Ben, if he wanted to drop by.

Except she wasn't certain he did.

Frowning, she tightened her grip on the wheel as she navigated a curve on the dark, winding road.

Yesterday, and again today during her layover, he'd sounded . . . different . . . on the phone. Distant, worried, preoccupied—it was difficult to pinpoint the emotion in his voice.

Although he'd sidestepped her query when she'd asked if everything was okay, she intended to get a straight answer before she went to bed tonight. If her experience in Atlanta had taught her nothing else, she'd learned that pussyfooting around hard stuff didn't make it go away.

In fact, sometimes it made the situation worse.

If Ben was having second thoughts about them, better to find out now. Without some clarity on that question, sleep would be elusive despite her fatigue—and she needed to be ready to charge full speed ahead tomorrow on the crowdfunding campaign. Given their short fund-raising window, it needed to be poised to launch the minute Eric let her know he'd filed the 501(c)(3) paperwork for the lighthouse foundation.

And given that Ben had asked her to call as soon as she got home, he must want to talk too.

She swung into her driveway, retrieved her overnight bag from the backseat, and let herself into the dark house.

After flipping on a few lights, she pulled out her cell, sat at the kitchen table, scrolled through to his number . . . and hesitated as tension began to prickle in her nerve endings.

Maybe she wasn't ready to hear whatever he had to say, after all.

Finger hovering over the screen, she chewed on her lower lip.

She could always text instead, say she was too tired to talk tonight, and promise to call tomorrow after she got some rest.

Oh, for heaven's sake, call the man, Marci! Don't be a wimp.

Right.

Blood might send her into a tailspin, but she could face whatever he had to say without losing her dinner.

She hoped.

Bracing, she tapped in his number.

He answered on the first ring. "Hi. Are you home?"

"Yes. I walked in the door less than ten minutes ago."

"Long day."

"Too long." Wait. That sounded like she didn't want to talk to him. Better correct that impression fast. "But coming home always gives me an energy boost."

"How is your mom doing?"

"Much better. You'd never know there was an issue. She seems completely back to normal. How's everything been here?"

A couple of beats ticked by, and she tensed.

"Not as normal as it could be. There's been a development I need to discuss with you."

Her spirits plummeted.

Now that she was back in her snug house and all was well in Florida, he wasn't dancing around whatever issue was troubling him—which could mean it was about them. Ben was a considerate man; he wouldn't kiss her off long distance after the scare with her mom.

Sighing, she kneaded her forehead. Allowing herself to hope they could work out some arrangement to explore the chemistry between them despite the geographic challenge had been dumb. She was too old to get all starry-eyed and—

"Marci? Are you there?"

"Yes." She rose. Two aspirin and a glass of water might help her get through this—or at least dull the headache beginning to form in her temples. "What's the development?"

"I want to talk about it face-to-face."

He was trying to be a gentleman and let her down in person.

But it would be easier for her if they did this now. She could hide her reactions—along with any stray tears that might leak out.

"Um . . . like you said, it's been a long day. It might be quicker if we discuss it over the phone."

"I need to see you for this conversation."

Based on his firm tone, he wasn't open to negotiation.

Meaning she'd have to take the initiative and put the difficult subject on the table.

She filled her lungs, steeled herself, and said the hard words. "Look, Ben. It's okay. I understand if this isn't working for you.

The long-distance complication was always an issue, and we both knew it would be a challenge to—"

"Whoa!" His alarm came over the line loud and clear. "I'm not suggesting we end our relationship."

She froze, her hand halfway into the cabinet to retrieve the bottle of aspirin. "You're not?"

"No. This isn't about that. I'm as committed to figuring out the logistics now as I was before."

Before?

Somehow she knew that was key.

"Before what?"

"That's what I need to talk to you about."

She retracted her hand from the cabinet, leaving the bottle of aspirin inside, and returned to the table. "You want to come over?"

"Yes—but not yet."

"What time did you have in mind?" She sank into her chair. It was already after nine—but hey, she could muscle through her fatigue for another hour if it meant seeing Ben.

"This is going to sound weird, but my reasoning will be clear after I explain what's been going on."

"Are you thinking of a midnight rendezvous?" She tried for a teasing tone, but some nuance in his inflection told her this was no joking matter.

"Close—but more like one-thirty."

That *was* weird.

"You mean one-thirty in the morning?" Maybe she'd misunderstood.

"Yes. Please trust me on this. Like I said, once I explain the circumstances, you'll understand. We could both catch a few hours of sleep between now and then. You have to be exhausted."

"I'm more curious than tired now."

"I'll tell you the whole story in four hours."

At the grim tenor of his voice, a shiver spiraled through her. "This is bad news, isn't it?"

"I hope not."

That wasn't too comforting.

"Can't you give me a tiny hint? You're making me nervous."

"I'm sorry." Contrition softened his tone. "I don't want to upset you. I'd wait until tomorrow to do this if I could, but there's a reason we need to talk tonight—and at that late hour. In terms of a hint . . . an incident from my recent past has come back to haunt me. It has nothing to do with my feelings for you, but you need to know about it."

"You aren't an undercover CIA operative or something, are you?"

He exhaled. "I wish it was that simple. Can I come at one-thirty?"

"Yes."

"Thank you. And try to get some sleep in the meantime."

They said their goodbyes, and Marci set the phone down. Rose.

Apparently she *was* going to need those aspirin. Her temples were beginning to throb again.

As for sleep—that was a lost cause.

Yes, she'd go to bed.

Yes, she'd try to convince her body to relax enough to let her doze off.

But with Ben's mysterious visit mere hours away, she had about as much chance of falling asleep as his grandfather had had of winching a full pot of Dungeness crabs from the ocean depths during the spring slow season.

As far as he could tell, no one had followed him.

The Hope Harbor police officer's report that Nicole's car

hadn't budged from the Gull Motel for the past two hours must be sound.

But just to be safe, he killed his lights as he approached Pelican Point Road.

If anyone *was* following him—like that PI Nicole had referenced—they'd never notice him veering off 101 on this black, moonlit night.

It wasn't likely she was still paying her spy now that she was on-site, though. She already had all the information she'd wanted.

Not until he rounded the second curve on the point road did Ben flip his lights back on. No one from the main drag would spot him here, deep in the wooded terrain.

Once Marci's house came into sight, he eased back on the gas pedal, dread pooling in his belly at the thought of the conversation to come.

This could go several directions—some of them not pleasant.

He could only hope she'd listen to everything he had to say with an open mind—and believe he'd been justly exonerated from all of Nicole's claims.

A shadow moved behind a drawn window shade as he pulled into her gravel driveway and set the brake on the truck.

She'd been watching for him.

Not surprising, given his cryptic explanation on the phone earlier. In her place, he'd be curious about such a covert meeting too.

As he approached the door, she pulled it open.

"I want you to know I don't unlatch my locks for just anyone at this hour of the night." Though the backlighting from inside left her face in shadows, her mood wasn't difficult to read.

She was nervous—but trying to lighten the atmosphere.

"I appreciate the vote of confidence." If it lasted.

"Come on in." She swept a hand toward the interior as he ascended the steps to her front porch. "There's a chill in the air, so I turned on the fireplace. I thought we could talk in the living room, over coffee." She motioned to the two mugs on the glass-topped crab pot in front of the sofa. "It's decaf, in case you're worried about sleeping later."

Decaf or regular, he doubted he'd get much shut-eye during the remainder of this night.

He followed her to the overstuffed couch, where she tucked her feet under her, picked up her mug—and gave him an expectant look.

Settling in beside her, he surveyed the room. The glowing flames in the gas fireplace created a cozy, intimate ambiance that would be romantic in other circumstances.

But romance had nothing to do with the sudden uptick in his pulse.

Clasping his hands in front of him, he watched the firelight flicker for a moment. If there was an easy way to lead into his story, it eluded him. Besides, Marci was prepped for bad news. No reason not to plunge straight in.

"We've talked a few times about the night we met—and you've apologized more than once for overreacting."

She wrinkled her nose. "I *did* overreact."

"True—but I did too. And there's a reason for that."

Lifting the mug, she watched him over the rim as she took a sip.

"While I was in Germany, I was involved in a situation with a woman who turned out to be volatile—and dangerous."

"Someone you were dating?"

"No. Or I didn't classify it as that, anyway. We did socialize on occasion at first, mostly because I felt sorry for her. When Nicole crossed my path, she was working at Landstuhl—the army's regional medical center—as a civilian employee for the

Department of Defense. She told me her fiancé had been killed in action the year before."

Marci narrowed her eyes. "That wasn't true?"

"No—but I didn't find out she was lying until much later."

"How did you two connect?"

"I saw her in the cafeteria one night, after I finished a very late shift. She was sitting by herself . . . and she was crying."

Marci's features softened. "I don't suppose a man who rescues hurt kittens would walk away from a woman in distress."

"No—but I wish I had." He picked up his mug, more to infuse some warmth into his fingers than to quench his thirst. "She latched on to me after that. She was new at the base, and I didn't want to hurt her feelings. I could see she was a bit high-strung, but that didn't set off any alarm bells in the beginning. I assumed her emotional state was due to her grief."

"Except she wasn't grieving."

"No. I later discovered she had serious mental issues." He swallowed. "Serious enough to almost ruin my life."

Marci's brows knitted. "What happened?"

This was the hard part.

"She became fixated on me. Kind of like your stalker did with you. I'd done nothing to lead her on, yet she became convinced I'd fallen in love with her. It was fantasy, pure and simple. And I told her that after she began suggesting we do more than meet for an occasional meal in the cafeteria."

"That didn't go over well?"

"A gross understatement." The dark liquid in his mug began to slosh, and he set the cup down on the coffee table. Balled his quivering fingers. "She had a total meltdown the night I finally told her I needed some distance. I hated to hurt her, but her attention was becoming smothering."

The twin grooves on Marci's brow deepened. "I know all about that."

Yes, she did.

But she didn't know anything about the kind of craziness that had happened next.

"There was a difference, though. In the end, your 'admirer' respected the boundaries you'd set and left you alone."

"Only after I got the protection order."

"Still . . . he went away."

"Nicole didn't?"

"No—and she was vindictive." He told Marci the same story he'd shared with the chief of police about the nurse whose sheets she had shredded and bloodied.

"Oh my." As she breathed the words, Marci's cheeks paled. "That's bizarre."

"I agree. The problem was, she covered her tracks well. It was impossible to prove she was the culprit. After that incident, she began to spread rumors about us, suggesting I'd led her on, taken advantage of her, even harassed her."

"How could someone be so spiteful?"

"I don't think a normal person could." He swallowed . . . inhaled . . . and braced. "In the end, she brought formal sexual harassment charges against me."

Marci's complexion lost its last vestige of color. "Did . . . did anyone believe her?"

"It didn't matter what they believed. They had to investigate—because she arranged to have proof."

A hint of wariness crept into Marci's face, and his gut twisted. This was the reaction he'd feared. "What kind of proof?"

"An elaborate, but effective, ruse. Somehow she got into my quarters one night while I was working a late shift and hid. When I returned, I took a shower and headed for bed. No sooner did I hit the sheets than she appeared in the doorway. She was carrying most of her clothes, which she scattered on the floor. Before I could process what was happening, she jumped on top of me and started screaming. The MPs were all over the place in minutes."

"Didn't you explain what happened?"

"Of course. But I couldn't dispute her presence, or the bruises I assume she self-inflicted before she ever got to my room, or her state of undress. Those were facts. The rest was my word against hers."

"All that evidence was circumstantial, though—and surely your co-workers vouched for your character."

"Yes, they did." He scrubbed his gritty eyes. "However, in this day and age, sexual harassment charges are media fodder for any organization. The army is no exception. They had to treat her story seriously while they investigated."

"Were you put in . . . did they arrest you?"

"No—but I *was* suspended from duty and confined to base during the inquiry."

"Is this why you left the military?"

"No. My tour was winding down, and I'd already arranged to go into civilian practice. Except this incident jeopardized the position in Ohio too." He shook his head. "It was a nightmare."

"But you were cleared."

"Yes. The investigation was mercifully fast. My commanding officer put zero credence in her story, and quite a few people came forward to testify about her unstable emotions and give examples of other smaller lies they'd witnessed. There'd been a few blips at her previous job too. In the end, she admitted she might have overstated her case and backed off."

"Could you have pressed charges in return?"

"Yes—but she was fired, and I thought that was the end of it. Until Friday, when she showed up at my door."

"Here?" Marci's question came out in a squeak, her eyes rounding.

"Yes. She had a PI track me down, booked a room at the Gull

Motel, and has been sitting in front of my house ever since. At least during daylight hours."

"But . . . but what's the point? What does she want?"

"Me." He told her about their exchange on his porch.

Marci's mouth dropped open. "You've got to be kidding."

"I wish I was. She has to be delusional to think I'd have anything to do with her after what she put me through."

"Can't the police get rid of her?" Marci set her mug down.

"No." He recounted his discussions with Lexie. "But they're willing to work with me. They're the ones who confirmed her car is at the Gull and the coast was clear for me to come and talk to you tonight."

She squeezed the bridge of her nose. "It's late, and I've had a long day, so cut me a little slack if I'm not following everything. Why do you care if she sees you coming over here?"

"Because of what she did to that nurse's room." He reached for her hand. It was as cold as his. "And because she mentioned you when she came to my door. She thinks you may be a rival. The last thing I want to do is put you in danger."

She stared at him . . . and as her gaze searched his, he prayed she'd believe everything he'd told her—and understand that this late-night visit reflected the depth of his feelings for her. That he was determined to protect her from a woman whose unstable . . . and unpredictable . . . emotions scared the life out of him.

He could handle Nicole now that he'd learned how she operated, but if she set her sights on Marci . . . if she decided the *Herald* editor represented a serious threat . . . who knew what she might do?

"Do you think she's actually capable of physical violence?"

"Yes."

As he gave voice to his deepest fear, sweat broke out on his upper lip and a muscle ticced in his jaw.

He couldn't lose Marci. The very possibility short-circuited his lungs.

And his panicked reaction also brought sudden, crystal-clear clarity to his stay-or-go dilemma.

If he and Marci survived this curve they'd been thrown, he wasn't going to leave Hope Harbor.

He'd stay in the town he'd always loved and trust that everything would work out between him and the woman who had staked a claim on his heart.

However . . . the ball was in her court now.

Even if she believed every word he'd said, she could back off. Given all she'd been through with her own stalker, she might want nothing to do with a man whose life was being disrupted by a woman bent on creating chaos in his world.

He couldn't blame her if she bailed.

Yet as he waited for her response, he sent a silent plea heavenward that she'd stick with him through whatever lay ahead.

21

Marci looked down at their clasped hands as she tried to digest all Ben had told her.

Given his experience with this Nicole woman, no wonder the man had been alarmed—and repelled—by her propensity to fly off the handle. He'd probably been afraid he'd crossed paths with another psycho.

Thank goodness he'd gotten past those initial negative impressions.

And if he'd asked the police to keep tabs on Nicole so he could make a clandestine middle-of-the-night run up here to minimize any risk to her, his feelings must be as strong as hers.

He'd also said he was committed to working out the logistics of their relationship. If he didn't have serious intentions, that issue wouldn't be high on his priority list.

All of which told her he wanted to give this thing between them every possible chance.

But the slight tremble in his fingers told her even more—as did the hint of fear in his eyes.

He was very, very worried the messy situation with Nicole

would raise doubts in her mind about his character. Undermine the foundation of trust they'd been laying.

Those fears, however, were groundless—and her first order of business was to put them to rest.

Shifting toward him on the couch, she squeezed his fingers and locked gazes with him.

"First of all, I appreciate you sharing that whole story. Second, I don't believe anything that woman said about you—nor does the nasty business she instigated change my feelings toward you one iota."

His throat worked, and the taut line of his shoulders relaxed a hair. "Thank you."

"Third, you don't need to worry about me because Looney Tune is in town. Now that I've been warned, I'll be watching my back. And I have a stellar alarm system here. Nicole might have been able to sneak into that nurse's room and your quarters, but she won't get into this fortress. That's one positive outcome from my experience in Atlanta, anyway."

Parallel creases scored his forehead. "I hope you're right—but this is an isolated spot, and you do go outside to work in your garden."

"I always have pepper gel with me, even in the yard. More fallout from Atlanta."

"Which works to our advantage in this situation." He wiped a hand down his face. "I keep hoping she'll get tired of the game and go away once she realizes I have no interest in her."

"You could be leaving for Ohio before that happens."

"Maybe not."

Her heart stumbled. "What do you mean?"

"I've been having some second thoughts about taking that job."

"Seriously?" *Stay calm, Marci. Don't jump to conclusions. Let the man explain before you throw yourself into his arms.*

"Yes." He took her other hand. "I think we have a whole lot

of potential, and you've been clear you're not interested in a long-distance romance."

Yeah, she *had* said that.

But in light of her growing feelings for Ben, she'd bend that rule if it would smooth the path ahead of them.

"I, uh, might be willing to renegotiate that."

"You don't have to. While you were gone, I put out a few job feelers—and I think I could have a satisfying career here."

As he told her about the conversations he'd had with the urgent care center and the orthopedic practice in Coos Bay, her spirits soared.

If Ben had gone to all that effort to try and line up an alternate career path in Hope Harbor . . . if he was willing to give up a plum practice in Ohio . . . his feelings *did* run as deep as hers.

Cue the "Hallelujah Chorus"!

Except . . .

She frowned.

Much as she'd rather ignore the concern strobing across her brain, it wouldn't be fair to Ben. He was the one with the most to lose.

"What's wrong? Don't you want me to stay?" He released her hand and traced a finger down her cheek.

"Of course! It's just that I . . . what if we don't . . . I mean, we're only at the beginning of this relationship, and . . ." Her voice trailed off.

"You're worried the fireworks might fizzle."

She nodded.

"I've already considered that—and I don't think it's going to happen. I'm convinced the odds are in our favor."

"But what if you're wrong?"

He shrugged. "There are no guarantees in life, and I accept that. If by some chance the two of us go our separate ways,

Hope Harbor has other compensations—like Charley's tacos and Sweet Dreams cinnamon rolls." He winked and gave her a slow smile that set off another round of those fireworks he'd mentioned.

Given all the rockets and sparklers going off inside her, it was *not* easy to engage the left side of her brain—but she tried her best to analyze his response. Was he making a compromise he wasn't entirely certain about and might later regret?

Hard to tell, with her mind in a muddle—but he seemed sincere. Looked sincere. Sounded sincere. And the warmth in his eyes *felt* sincere.

Still grinning, he tapped the tip of her nose with his finger. "Stop thinking so hard. This is what I want to do—and I'm not changing my mind. Subject closed."

In that case . . .

"When you put it like that, how can I argue?" She scooted closer. "So what's the plan with Nicole?"

His lips flattened. "Wait her out, I guess. We can't force her to leave. But until she does, I think the two of us need to be discreet and keep our distance. Since she already suspects I'm interested in you, I'd rather not fuel the fire by her seeing us together."

"So we're going to let her run our lives?" Marci backed off a few inches and crossed her arms. Allowing other people to dictate their behavior stunk—and she'd vowed never to do that again after her experience with Jack.

"No." In contrast to her huffiness, his tone was calm and reasoned. "We're going to be smart and let this go away all by itself. I'd rather she leave on her own than force her hand. It will be far tidier—and less dangerous."

"Maybe if she sees us together she'll realize her pursuit is a lost cause and leave sooner."

"Or she'll get mad and do who knows what."

"It's hard to be invisible or get away with much in a small town. And the police could watch her."

"Not every minute of the day and night. Hope Harbor doesn't have those kinds of resources. Very few police departments do."

She scowled. "I hate letting her have this much control over our lives."

"It doesn't sit well with me either. I'm not one to run from a fight. But I've tangled with her once and she doesn't play by any rules I learned. Will you do it my way for now?" He stroked a finger over her lips, leaving a trail of warmth in its wake.

Mmm.

Nice.

"I think this borders on coercion." She tried not to purr as her eyelids drifted closed.

"Is it working?" His husky question sent a tingle down her spine.

Oh yeah.

"Uh-huh."

"Maybe this will work even better."

Before she could open her eyes to gauge his intent, he lowered his mouth to hers.

Oh.

Man.

The scent of earthy, intoxicating sandalwood surrounded her as he tucked her firmly against his chest while his lips worked magic.

As soon as she could gather her wits, she wrapped her arms around his neck and matched him stroke for stroke, touch for touch, nip for nip.

Bliss.

When they surfaced a few minutes later, she was breathing hard.

"That was . . ." Her voice wobbled, and she swallowed. "That was some first kiss."

"I agree." He nuzzled her neck, his touch electrifying every pore in its wake.

"I, uh, don't think we have to worry about fireworks petering out." She fanned herself with her hand. "At least not on my end."

He lifted his head, his irises the same intense cobalt hue as the fathomless waters of the deep. "Mine either."

"I'm glad we're on the same page." Forking her fingers through the thick hair at the back of his neck, she grazed the stubble on his chin with her lips.

A low growl rumbled in his throat. "Quit tempting me." He eased back, and she let her hand slide to lie flat against his chest, where the hard, rapid pounding of his heart throbbed against her fingertips. "It's the middle of the night, we're here alone . . . and I'm not a saint. We need to stop."

"You started it."

"Guilty as charged." Although he didn't appear to be in the least repentant. "Are you sorry?"

"Nope."

"I probably shouldn't have." He played with a tendril of her hair. "But I didn't want to leave any doubts about my feelings, and it could be a while until we can do this again."

Because of Nicole.

Some of her euphoria faded.

She was liking the woman less and less with every passing minute.

"Are you certain you can't convince her to leave?"

"I tried the day she arrived. She was *not* receptive to my message. And both Lexie and Eric have advised I not speak with her again."

She hiked up her eyebrows. "You talked to an attorney?"

"I'm trying to cover all the bases."

"Has she bothered you since that first day?"

"Other than sitting outside the house and following me wherever I go, no."

Marci suppressed a shiver. "This is very creepy."

"Yeah." He twisted his wrist and squinted at his watch. "I should leave. It's getting really late, and you have to be exhausted."

"Not as much anymore. My adrenaline is pinging like crazy—in a very pleasant way, thanks to you."

He grinned. "Should I apologize?"

"Not a bad idea. But why not let actions speak louder than words?"

She tugged his head back down.

He didn't resist.

When they at last separated, she rested her forehead against his chin. "Okay. You're forgiven."

A soft, deep chuckle tickled her ear. "If this is all it takes to make up with you after a fight, we're never going to be mad at each other for very long."

"I'll hold you to that."

With superhuman effort, she finally extricated herself from his arms. "Much as I hate to break this up, I do have a full agenda tomorrow—today—and top on my list is the crowdfunding campaign. I'm hoping we see some initial results before our committee meeting on Wednesday . . . but if I log less than six hours of sleep, I'm not going to be very productive."

"Duly noted." He stood and held out a hand. "There may not be much we can do about Nicole, but I can relieve your mind on one score with the lighthouse. I talked to my accountant, and if you can raise the amount we discussed last week, I'll donate the difference between that and my other offer as a charitable contribution to the foundation."

"Yes!" She pumped her fist in the air and did a little happy dance.

Ben chuckled. "Gee . . . I was hoping you'd show a *tiny* bit of enthusiasm."

"Sorry. I do have a tendency to get carried away when I hear good news." She gave him another hug. "Thank you."

"You're welcome." He hugged her back, then took her hand and walked her toward the door. "I'll stay on the porch until I hear the beeps from your alarm system."

"I thought you said Nicole was at the motel."

"Last report, she was—but humor me. This woman is a master manipulator. I wouldn't put anything past her." He tipped the shade on the window adjacent to the door and scanned her front yard.

"I know you want us to keep our distance, but will you stay in touch by phone?"

"Count on it." After stealing one more quick kiss, he slipped through the door and shut it behind him with a soft click.

Some of the supercharged air in the room exited with him . . . and all at once the house felt very, very empty.

And very lonely.

Odd.

For two years she'd been perfectly fine living here alone—and she'd resolved to never again give any man a smidgeon of control over her state of mind.

Yet as she ran up the stairs, set the alarm, and watched from the upper window while Ben strode toward his truck under the security lighting, she faced the truth.

If you cared for someone, they *did* affect your moods . . . and your feelings . . . and how you viewed the world.

And she cared for Ben.

A lot.

In fact, if she hadn't already fallen head over heels for him, she was on the verge of tumbling.

So as soon as Nicole was out of the picture and it was safe for them to get together again, she intended to take some hands-on action to accelerate that process.

If she could wait that long.

22

Nicole was gone.

At least her car was.

Glass of OJ in hand, Ben tipped the slat in the front window blinds a tad more and gave the street a sweep in both directions.

There were no vehicles parked on either side this Wednesday morning.

Was it possible she'd tired of her game after only five days? Gotten his message, given up, and left town?

It was almost too much to hope for.

But it was worth checking.

He set his glass on the table by the front window and tapped in Lexie's number.

After four rings, he prepared to leave a voicemail—but she answered at last, sounding sleepy.

"Ben. Hi." She cleared her throat. "What's up?"

"Did I wake you?" He peered at his watch. Cringed. Maybe eight in the morning *was* a bit early to call her personal cell.

"I was pulled into a county-wide situation late last night that cut into my sleep, but I was about to get up. Trouble with your visitor?" The last vestiges of slumber vanished from her voice as she asked the question.

"No. That's why I called. Her car's not in front this morning. I was wondering if you or one of your officers could drive by and see if it's at the motel."

"Sure. But checkout isn't until eleven. She might be sleeping in. Stand by."

"Thanks."

Ben slid the phone back in his pocket. If wishing could bring it about, this episode would end quietly—but he had a feeling Nicole's absence today didn't mean she'd called it quits.

Lexie confirmed his suspicion when she buzzed him back ten minutes later, while he was shaking some Cheerios into a bowl.

"She hasn't checked out of the motel, nor given any indication she's planning to. However, her car's not there. Has she shown up at your place?"

He retraced his steps to the living room and surveyed the street again. "No."

"She might have gone out to eat or do some shopping."

A logical assumption—but nothing about Nicole was logical.

"That's possible."

Based on Lexie's next comment, she shared his skepticism. "Given what you've told me about her, I'm not convinced, either. I'll have the patrol officers keep an eye out for her."

"I appreciate that. Sorry again to bother you so early."

"No worries. Call anytime. Being police chief in a town this size is a 24/7 job."

Ben wandered back to the kitchen and ate his cereal standing by the rear door. All quiet in the backyard too.

Considering his schedule for the next few hours, Nicole had picked an optimal window to disappear. Having her shadow him to his meeting at the orthopedic practice in Coos Bay would be more than a little disconcerting. Likewise if she followed him to his official interview this afternoon for the urgent care center position.

But unsettling as it would be to have her on his tail while he made his rounds, the question strobing across his brain like a red alert was just as unnerving.

If she hadn't checked out of the motel . . . and she wasn't watching him . . . where was she—and what was she doing?

Unbelievable.

Marci stared at the crowdfunding website tally for the lighthouse fund. Yes, she'd done a social media and PR blitz to announce the campaign—but could it actually have generated 20 percent of the funds needed to purchase the landmark in less than a day?

"I'm going to clock out, Marci, if that's okay."

She continued to ogle the screen as Rachel spoke. "Sure. Fine. Listen—take a look at this number and tell me I'm not seeing things."

Her assistant circled the desk and leaned down to skim the screen.

Rachel's jaw dropped.

"Wow! You only launched this eight hours ago."

"I know. I can't believe it. I mean, I was ready to move the minute Eric called to let me know all the foundation paperwork had been filed, but still . . ."

"You said all along people have a soft spot in their hearts for lighthouses. This proves it. Not to diminish the campaign you put together, of course. Your press materials and social media stuff were fantastic. They obviously piqued the public's interest and drew attention to the crowdfunding effort."

"I never expected such fast results, though. I'm stunned." A wave of exhilaration swept over her—almost as heady as the one she'd experienced in the early hours of Monday morning, after Ben's kiss.

Almost.

"Everyone will be thrilled when you tell them the news at the meeting tonight." Rachel perused the screen again, as if she, too, needed to convince herself the number was real.

"I know. At this rate, we might get everything we need—and more—in the first few days. Wouldn't that be something?"

"Fantastic. Greg will be pumped."

"Especially since he agreed to manage the site for the foundation." It was mind-blowing how the campaign to save a lighthouse had saved so much more. "I can't tell you how happy I am he took the job."

"Not as happy as I am." Rachel played with the hem of her knit top. "I want to thank you for offering him the opportunity—and for going out of your way to be kind to both of us. Also . . . once the lighthouse situation is settled, I'd like to cash in that rain check for a visit to the nursery down in Sixes and tea at the lavender farm. If you still want to go."

"Absolutely. We'll pick a date soon."

"Well . . ." She took a step back. "I need to get going. Greg's cooking dinner again tonight, and I don't want to discourage his culinary efforts by being late."

"He's becoming quite the chef. What's he making?"

"Stew."

"Should be a tasty meal. I need to squeeze in dinner before tonight's meeting too . . . if I can tear myself away from watching the crowdfunding results come in."

Rachel caught her lower lip between her teeth. "You know . . . Greg mentioned earlier that the recipe would leave us with leftovers for a week. Why don't you join us?"

Well . . . how about that?

An invitation from the woman who'd seemed in such need of a friend.

Another prayer answered.

When she didn't respond at once, Rachel spoke again. "Sorry. I didn't mean to put you on the spot—and to be honest, I can't guarantee the results. But everything he's concocted up to this point has been palatable." A twinkle sparked in her irises. "I think he's as surprised about that as I am."

Much as she was tempted to accept, a fledgling cook might be upset about having an impromptu guest—and no way did she want to cause a setback in what appeared to be a robust reconciliation.

"I appreciate the offer—but Greg might not like having his talents on display at this early stage."

"I'll call him if you'd feel more comfortable, but I guarantee he won't have a problem with it. And it would give you two a chance to talk about the lighthouse project before the meeting."

"Why don't you run it by him—but tell him it's fine if this isn't the best night."

Rachel pulled out her phone and perched on the edge of the desk.

While her assistant relayed their discussion to her husband, Marci refocused on her computer screen. She didn't try to listen as she jotted some notes for tonight's meeting, but it was hard to tune out Rachel's side of the conversation.

"Yes . . . That's what I said . . . Oh . . . No, I doubt it—but I'll ask. Hang on a sec. Marci?"

She turned. "Not the best night?"

"No. He said that based on a preliminary taste test, the stew is edible. But he wanted me to let you know he also invited Ben. Do you mind?"

Mind having dinner with Ben?

Was she kidding?

Of course, Ben might not be too thrilled about her visiting his neighborhood with Nicole lurking around—but when he'd called earlier, he'd said she hadn't shown today. Meaning their dinner together shouldn't be an issue.

"I don't mind in the least." Despite her attempt to contain it, a trace of excitement crept into her voice. Hopefully Rachel would attribute her enthusiasm to the lighthouse fund total.

"She's in, Greg."

"Tell him I'll swing by Sweet Dreams and find something sinful for dessert. We deserve to splurge, with money already rolling in for the lighthouse foundation."

"She's bringing dessert to celebrate some exciting news." Rachel smiled. "I'll let her share it after she gets there. You'll have to be patient." As soft color rose on her cheeks, she angled slightly away and lowered her volume. "I know. Me too . . . Yes. I'm leaving now." She ended the call and stood. "Greg told Ben six o'clock, but I think everyone's flexible if that doesn't work for you."

"Six is fine."

Rachel slid the strap of her purse over her shoulder. "If anything changes, let me know. Otherwise, we'll see you soon."

As the door shut behind her assistant, Marci swung back to the computer to marvel over the donations again.

Another hundred dollars had come in over the past fifteen minutes.

Incredible.

Even more incredible?

She was having dinner with Ben.

Her mouth curved up.

This meal definitely deserved to be topped off with one of Sweet Dreams's decadent double-chocolate flourless tortes.

There was a car parked on his street again—but it wasn't Nicole's.

It was Marci's.

What was she doing here?

Frowning, Ben swung into the driveway, glanced at his watch, and blew out a breath.

If he'd known his meeting with the management of the urgent care center was going to last most of the afternoon, he'd never have accepted Greg's invitation for dinner. After a full day of intense discussions, first in Coos Bay, then here, he was beat.

And now he had to worry about Marci.

He parked at the back of the house, let himself in, and strode to the window that offered a view of the front porch.

No sign of his favorite newswoman.

Might she be at Greg and Rachel's house? A business visit, perhaps?

Didn't matter.

If Nicole cruised by and happened to spot her—or her car—she'd assume Marci was here to see him.

And that would not be good.

After giving his hands a quick rinse and running a comb through his hair, he let himself out of the house and secured the front door. From behind the rose trellis, he checked both directions for any sign of Nicole's car.

Clear.

He broke into a jog and covered the distance to his neighbors' house in a few dozen steps.

Greg answered on the first ring and ushered him in. Women's voices chatted and laughed somewhere in the background.

One of them was Marci's.

"Sorry I'm a few minutes late. I got caught up in some meetings." More laughter from the direction of the kitchen.

"No worries. The longer stew simmers, the better it tastes—according to the recipe. And Rachel and Marci need a few more minutes to finish the biscuits they're making."

"I saw Marci's car out front. I didn't know she was coming tonight."

"Neither did we." Greg grinned. "Rachel issued an impromptu invitation about two hours ago. But there's plenty of food. Enough for a party."

The man was in high spirits. And based on Rachel's laughter, she was too.

Perhaps her parents' visit had helped clear the air between the almost-newlyweds.

"Hi, Ben. Glad you could join us." Rachel appeared in the doorway, Marci on her heels. Both women's hands were dusted with flour.

"I'm always happy to have a home-cooked meal." He shifted his gaze to Marci. "I didn't expect to see you here."

"I appreciate a home-cooked meal too—and I have some exciting news to share. I'm glad you'll be among the first to hear it."

"Rachel told me that on the phone, but I haven't been able to get her to spill anything." Greg arched an eyebrow at his wife.

"The news is Marci's to tell."

"I won't keep you waiting too long. Once we sit down for dinner, I'll give you all the details."

"In that case . . . let's get this meal started."

"The biscuits aren't finished baking yet." Rachel motioned toward the oven behind her.

"They will be by the time we fix drinks and say a blessing. Come on back, Ben, and claim a seat. Sorry it's a little crowded. There's supposed to be a leaf for the table somewhere in the house, but we haven't found it yet."

Ben followed him back to the kitchen. The round table *was*

on the small side—but as long as Marci was beside him, that wasn't a problem.

While Greg and Rachel finished the final meal preparations at the counter, he held out a chair for Marci. She sat, and he took the seat next to her.

As the younger couple conversed in subdued tones across the room, he leaned close to his dinner partner. "Coming here might not have been the best idea."

"I drove up and down before I parked." Her breath was warm against his cheek, like a Hope Harbor breeze on a bright summer day. "If I'd seen a car parked on the street, I would have called Rachel and bailed. But no one was here. Do you think she's gone?"

"She hasn't checked out of the motel."

"Drat." Her face fell. "Why do you think she backed off on watching you?"

"I have no idea. She must be changing her strategy."

"Well, let's not worry about it tonight. I, for one, am thrilled to have a chance to see you." Her leg brushed his, and he hiked up his eyebrows. "Hey . . . it's the best I can do in public."

He smothered a chuckle with his napkin as Greg and Rachel joined them.

After a brief blessing, Greg dished up the savory-looking stew. The first bite verified that it tasted as good as it smelled.

Greg fielded the compliments, then turned the spotlight on Marci. "I've been waiting two hours to hear the news Rachel hinted at over the phone. Don't keep us in suspense."

"I won't." Marci buttered a flaky biscuit and set it on the edge of her plate. "I posted our campaign on the crowdfunding site this morning. You won't believe how much money had come in by five forty-five, when I left the office."

Greg tossed out a guess. Ben shrugged. He hadn't a clue what to expect.

When Marci gave them the figure, he suspected his eyes were popping as much as Greg's.

"You're kidding." Greg gaped at her.

"No. At this rate, we might not even need you to donate the difference between what we raise and your original offer, Ben." Marci beamed at him.

"The donation stands. If extra funds come in, use them for restoration . . . or marketing . . . or to buy an adjacent lot or two for parking or any buildings that might be in the master plan. I want to contribute to Skip's legacy too."

"Thank you." She gave his leg another nudge.

In response, he reached over and squeezed her fingers under the table.

A lively discussion about the lighthouse project dominated the conversation during the remainder of the meal, and once they'd all had a generous slice of the cake Marci had supplied, she and Greg had to make a mad dash to Grace Christian for the meeting.

Rachel walked her and Ben out while Greg went to the office to gather up his notes.

"Hold on a second." Ben pressed a hand against the door to stop her from opening it and scanned the street through the sidelight.

No unfamiliar cars.

"We're clear."

Rachel's eyes thinned. "Does this have anything to do with that blonde woman who's been sitting in a car on our street?"

So far, he'd told only the police and Marci about his unwanted visitor—but it wasn't surprising his neighbors had noticed her presence.

"Yes."

"We spotted her on Friday. Greg reported her to the police later that night." Rachel waited, giving him a chance to explain—or not.

Dredging up the overseas episode wasn't on his agenda for the evening—but it wouldn't hurt to give his neighbors a topline in case Nicole showed up at their door for some reason.

"I knew her during my army days in Germany. She has some serious emotional issues. I'm hoping she gets tired of whatever game she's playing and goes away."

Greg rejoined them in time to hear the abbreviated explanation. "If it's any consolation, I haven't seen her all day."

"She's still in town, though." And probably up to no good. "If she comes around again and I'm gone, I'd appreciate it if you'd let me know."

"Sure. Sorry you have to deal with such a hassle." Greg pulled out his keys. "If there's anything else we can do to help, let us know."

"I appreciate that. Marci, why don't I walk you to your car?"

After another round of thanks, they exited.

All was quiet in the neighborhood as they followed the flagstone path to the street. Two seagulls soared overhead. A child's laugh floated through the salty air. From the jetty, the muffled, measured blare of the foghorn echoed.

It appeared to be a normal evening in Hope Harbor.

He hoped appearances weren't deceiving.

Marci hit the autolock button and paused next to the driver's door, swiveling away from Rachel and Greg's house to hide her face from their view.

"I've missed seeing you." He rested his elbow on the roof of her car and angled toward her.

"How long are we going to keep this up?"

"I wish I knew."

She sighed. "Maybe we'll have to arrange another midnight rendezvous."

"I don't know. I'd hate to interfere with your beauty sleep—and I'm not certain I trust myself alone with you in the middle of the night again."

"*I* trust you."

"That makes one of us." He hitched up one side of his mouth to let her know he was kidding.

Sort of.

She slanted a look toward the house. "Do you think they're watching us?"

"Hard to say."

A raindrop landed on her cheek, and she lifted her chin, smiling. "Thank you, God." She bent down, retrieved an umbrella from the passenger seat, opened it—and tilted it toward the house. "A rudimentary cloaking device."

He grinned. "A fellow *Star Trek* fan. I knew there was a reason I liked you."

"Yeah?" She gave him a saucy shoulder prod. "Prove it."

Adjusting the umbrella, he dipped his head and stole a quick kiss that only left him wanting more.

But it would have to do for tonight.

For a long moment after he straightened up, her eyelids remained closed.

"Mmm. Too short." Her lashes finally fluttered open.

"Sorry. Best I can do under the circumstances."

"I know. I'll take what I can get for now—as long as I can look forward to more later."

"Count on it." He closed the umbrella and handed it back to her. "Call me after you get home from the meeting?"

"Yes." She slid behind the wheel. "Expect to hear from me by ten, unless we run long."

"Be careful."

"Always. Talk to you soon."

With a nod, he closed the door and moved back.

She started the engine and drove away, flashing her lights in farewell.

He lifted his hand in response, watching until she turned the corner.

Seconds later, Greg pulled out of his driveway and followed her down the street.

Once both cars disappeared, Ben strolled back to Skip's house, giving the neighborhood one more inspection.

No sign of Nicole.

Where was she?

He wished to heaven he knew.

Because nervous as her presence had made him for the past five days, her absence was more disconcerting. At least while she was parked in front of his house or following him, he knew what she was up to.

Now?

It was anyone's guess.

Unless Lexie or her crew had spotted her somewhere and were willing to give him an update.

It was worth a call, anyway.

23

"That should wrap up tonight's meeting, unless anyone else has another item to discuss." Marci surveyed the eight members of the lighthouse committee seated around the conference room table.

"I have nothing to add except to say I think this is moving along splendidly." Father Murphy smiled at her. "On behalf of all of us, I want to thank you for taking on this project—and commend you for the tremendous results we're already seeing from your crowdfunding appeal. This wired world we live in is astonishing."

"I agree that the ability to reach huge numbers of people in our short window was a godsend."

"A perfect word." The priest's smile broadened.

"But without everyone's efforts, we'd never have gotten this far. I wouldn't have tackled the project alone. BJ and Michael lined up the volunteer crew for the restoration work. Eric handled all the legal stuff at warp speed. Rose has gardeners far and wide chomping at the bit to dig into the dirt up there. The rest of you have been phenomenal too. If ever there was a group effort, this is it."

"It's gratifying to see so many people rally to save a town landmark. It would have been terrible to lose a structure that was a beacon of hope for decades." Charley linked his fingers on the table.

"I think everyone realized that once it became a real possibility." Marci tapped her papers into alignment. "I'll keep you all informed of the donation tally by email. Other than that, why don't we all continue with our various jobs and meet again next Wednesday?"

After a murmur of assent, everyone stood and began filing out.

"Marci, do you need me to stay for any further discussion tonight?" Greg joined her at the head of the table.

"No—but I'll be in touch later in the week to talk more about the job, now that everyone has put their stamp of approval on you. And if donations keep coming in at this rate, we might be able to put you on the payroll sooner rather than later."

"Don't stretch the budget until there's some cushion. Uncle Sam is taking care of me for now, thanks to this." He indicated his leg. "Not that I want to rely on government assistance forever, but it's okay for a while."

"You earned whatever compensation you're getting."

He shrugged. "That's what Rachel says—but I wasn't raised to let someone else take care of me." He tucked his file folder under his arm. "If we're done, I'm going to head home. Rachel's spent too much time alone these past few months, and I'm trying to make up for that."

"By all means, go. I'm leaving myself."

She didn't have to urge him twice.

Only Charley, who was doing a final circuit of the room and collecting a few stray candy wrappers, remained.

"Another productive meeting, Marci."

"Thanks. I can't believe how fast all of this is coming together."

"You can claim the lion's share of the credit for that."

"I think it had more to do with the fact that the threat to Pelican Point was imminent."

"Could be. It seems sometimes we have to almost lose a blessing before we realize its value." He deposited the discarded items in the trash can. "Why don't I walk you to your car? Safety in numbers and all that."

She slung her purse over her shoulder and squinted at him. Had Ben told Charley about the situation with Nicole?

"I never worry much about being safe in downtown Hope Harbor." She watched the man for a clue.

"I don't either. It's a special place. Other than that vandalism spree a year ago, trouble's bypassed us for the most part." His amiable tone and placid expression didn't suggest he knew anything about the unwelcome woman who'd invaded their town. "But I'm leaving too. Why not walk out together?"

"Works for me." She picked up her files, and he fell in behind her as she exited the room and walked toward the front door of Grace Christian's fellowship hall.

Once she secured the lock, she turned to find Charley doing a sweep of the parking lot and the adjacent road. When his eyes narrowed, she gave the area a quick scan too.

As far as she could tell, no one else was around. Nor did she see anything to cause concern.

When she looked back at him, his usual pleasant countenance was back.

"After you." He motioned toward their cars, which were parked side by side.

"Your mother—or father—taught you excellent manners."

"Grandmother, actually. And yes, my abuela did instruct me

in the finer points of etiquette. We were dirt poor, but wealth doesn't make a lady. Character does. And she had it to spare."

Marci studied him.

In all their conversations during the two years she'd been in town, he'd never mentioned his childhood in Mexico.

Strange that he would offer a peek into his past now.

He waited while she got into her car, then touched the brim of his Ducks cap and took a step back. "Drive safe. Stop by for some tacos soon."

"That's my lunch plan for tomorrow, if you're cooking."

"If you're coming, I'm cooking." He winked and circled around her trunk to his own vehicle.

Her thoughts already on the phone call she was going to make to Ben once she arrived home, she put the key in the ignition and turned it.

Dead silence.

She frowned and tried again.

Zilch.

Was it possible she had a dead battery?

But how could that be? She'd replaced it days before she'd set off on the cross-county drive west to become a permanent Hope Harbor resident.

She twisted the key with more force.

Nothing.

Apparently her five-year battery had decided to give up the ghost three years early.

Of all the inconvenient times for this to happen.

With a huff, she peered at Charley through the darkness. He glanced toward her . . . got back out of his car . . . and circled around her Civic again as she opened her door.

"Car problems?" He leaned down.

"It won't start. I think the battery's dead. You don't happen to have any jumper cables, do you?"

"No. Sorry. And Marv's is closed for the night."

"I thought he ran a body shop."

"Also a garage. He has a magic touch with engines. Why don't I give you a lift home, and he can come by the lot tomorrow morning and jump it for you."

"I don't want to take you out of your way."

"You won't. I have to pass by Pelican Point Road to get home."

That's right. His house and studio were north of town, on the coast.

"Well . . . if you're sure you don't mind."

"Not in the least. I'll treat you to a ride in a genuine classic."

She eyed Charley's 1957 silver Thunderbird, its white top gleaming in the moonlight. His vehicle was almost a town landmark itself. Unlike the lighthouse, however, it was in pristine condition.

"I don't think I've ever ridden in a car this old." She followed him around the trunk and waited while he opened the passenger door for her with a flourish.

"Not old. Timeless. Wouldn't want Bessie here to take offense." He patted the fender.

"Sorry. No insult intended." She slid onto the roomy seat.

He closed the door and joined her a few moments later. The engine purred to life as he turned the key.

"Sounds like she's in tip-top condition."

"She is. But when I bought her, she was a mess. I spent two years restoring her. As with most things—and most people—though, a generous application of TLC worked wonders."

The conversation shifted to gardening as they made the short drive to her house, and Charley surprised her yet again with his breadth of knowledge on the subject.

"Is there anything you don't know about?" She shot him a teasing look as he pulled into her driveway.

"Algebra, for one. It baffles me. I'll get your door."

She let him. It seemed appropriate after sharing a ride in a stylish car like this with such a chivalrous driver.

Not only did he open her door, he walked her to the porch.

"Thanks again, Charley."

"Would you like me to give you a lift back to your car in the morning? I could open the taco stand a little early."

"No. I've already put you to enough trouble. I'll ask Marv to come get me when I call him about the battery—or phone someone else."

"I doubt Ben would mind swinging by."

He might—given the woman who was lurking in the shadows.

"I'll keep that as an option. I'm going to call him tonight anyway to give him an update on our meeting."

"Sounds like a plan. Enjoy the rest of your evening." With another touch to his Ducks cap, he strolled back to his car.

Marci waited for him to leave, but once he got in the car, he focused on the dash, as if he was adjusting his radio. Finally she went in, deactivated the alarm, and relocked the door.

By the time she looked out again, he was gone.

After dumping her tote bag and notes in the kitchen, she called Ben.

"I've been waiting to hear from you. Any problems tonight?"

"Other than a dead battery, no."

"Bummer. How did you get home?"

"Charley dropped me off. I'll call Marv at the body shop in the morning and have him give me a jump."

"I could pick you up and do that if Nicole continues to lay low."

"Still no sign of her?"

"No. I talked to Lexie, and she said the patrol officers haven't spotted her car."

"I'll take that as a positive sign. If the coast is clear and you want to swing by tomorrow, that would be appreciated."

"I'll give you a call about eight—unless that's too early."

"Nope. I'm always up long before that."

"Is your alarm system armed for the night?"

"Not yet. I'm downstairs."

"Why don't I wait while you go upstairs and set it?"

"She really has you freaked out, doesn't she?"

"You'd feel the same if you were in my shoes."

"Okay." She gave him a recap of the meeting as she shut off the downstairs lights. "I'm climbing the stairs now. The alarm"—she punched in the numbers—"is also armed."

"I hear the beeping. I'll sleep better knowing you're safe."

"I will too—based on everything you've told me about her."

After a lingering goodbye, Ben ended the call.

Marci put her phone in the charger beside her bed and ambled over to the window. As she'd done the night Ben had attempted to rescue Annabelle, she peeked through the shades.

Same as on that occasion, she saw nothing. The pools of illumination from her security lights were empty. The only sounds filtering through the screen in her open window were the wind in the trees and the plaintive hoot of an owl.

It was a night like any other here in Aunt Edith's cottage.

But unlike her distant relative, who'd never married, she might not live out her days here alone—thanks to the arrival of an ex-army doctor who'd traveled thousands of miles to claim a surprising inheritance.

And if all went as she hoped, maybe she'd alter the plans for that detached garage she was planning to build from single car to double.

What was that sweet scent?

Rachel gave a contented sigh and snuggled deeper into her pillow.

Mmm.

It smelled like roses.

What a lovely dream.

Her nose began to tickle, and she wrinkled it. Something soft was grazing the edge of her nostril, and she lifted her hand to brush away the . . .

"Happy birthday, sleepyhead."

Her eyes popped open.

A mass of velvety, crimson petals filled her vision.

She might be in bed—but that heavenly scent hadn't been a dream.

It was as real as the man whose handsome face appeared above her once he moved the vase of roses aside.

She scrambled into a sitting position and touched one of the perfect petals.

"Wh-where did you get these?"

"Budding Blooms on Main Street. They opened early for me. And there's more." He set the vase on the nightstand and disappeared out the door.

She was still gawking at the gorgeous bouquet when he returned with a tray bearing two mugs of coffee, another small vase bearing a single rose, a plate of melon and strawberries, and two Sweet Dreams cinnamon rolls dripping with icing.

"I thought you deserved breakfast in bed on your birthday." He set the decadent treat on the bed beside her and pulled up the straightback chair that sat against the wall. "With company."

The room blurred, and she groped for a tissue from the box on the nightstand. Never in a million years had she expected him to indulge her like this on her birthday.

Truth be told, she hadn't been certain he'd even remember the occasion, after all they'd been through.

"Hey." He touched her cheek. "No tears today. We have a packed agenda."

"Like what?" She dabbed at her eyes.

"Like that picnic in Shore Acres State Park I mentioned last week. The gardens there are blooming, our lunch is packed, and Charley told me about a perfect, secluded stretch of beach we'll probably have all to ourselves for our picnic."

"Sounds like a perfect birthday."

"That's what I'm aiming for. Now let's eat or these rolls will get cold. I picked them up while they were fresh from the oven."

Within fifteen minutes, every scrap of food on the tray had disappeared.

"I guess breakfast was a success." Greg removed the tray from the bed and stood. "Let me get rid of this before the next surprise."

"What surprise?" She called out the question as he disappeared down the hall again.

"Stay put. I'll be back in a minute."

Hmm.

A dozen long-stemmed roses with baby's breath. Breakfast in bed. A romantic picnic.

What more could he have up his sleeve?

He didn't keep her in suspense long.

In less than a minute, he returned with a flat box wrapped in silver paper.

"I'd sing 'Happy Birthday,' but as my high school music teacher told me, my superb breath control would be better applied to a wind instrument than to voice." He grinned at her and handed over the box.

"You didn't have to get me a present too."

"Yes, I did. Especially this one."

She weighed the box in her hand. Too large for jewelry, too small for clothing.

What could it be?

"Go ahead. Open it." Greg sat back in the straightback chair beside the bed and folded his arms.

She ripped off the paper and lifted the lid.

Nestled in tissue paper, she found a file folder.

She peeked over at him.

He crossed an ankle over his knee. "Remember—good things come in small packages."

In silence, she pulled the folder free of the tissue and flipped it open.

Inside was a stack of clipped pages. Printouts from various websites, based on a preliminary skim.

University websites.

All of the material in the file related to journalism degrees.

She looked up at him.

He leaned forward to clasp his hands between his knees, all traces of levity gone. "Marci said if the money keeps rolling in, they might be able to get the paid position at the lighthouse up and running sooner than expected. Even if it doesn't happen that fast, though, we're not hurting for money. I want you to finish your degree."

Funny.

She'd been thinking about that lately too. Her work on the *Herald* had reminded her how much she enjoyed journalism.

"I want to do that too, but I'm in no hurry. I can wait until our life is a bit more normal."

"No." He gave an emphatic shake of his head. "We're not going to push this off. I did some research, and the University of Oregon has a journalism program at the Eugene campus. There are also a bunch of colleges that offer online programs. I want you to enroll somewhere this fall. You gave up enough when you married me. I don't want your degree to be one more item on that list."

Her throat tightened, and once again her vision blurred.

"You're wrong." She took his hand and twined her fingers through his. "I didn't give up anything. I re-prioritized and traded up."

His eyes began to glisten. "Thank you for that. But I got the best end of the deal." He squeezed her fingers and swept a hand over the file. "There are some outstanding programs in there. Please promise me you'll pick one and do this. I know you already have a job at the *Herald*, but the credential of a degree will open doors in the future if you want to explore other options in journalism."

There had been times she'd wondered if he realized how hard it had been for her to walk away from college at the end of her junior year, leaving that dream in limbo to marry him.

Now she knew.

He'd understood far better than she'd given him credit for.

"I promise. And thank you. This is the most thoughtful gift I've ever received."

"I'm glad to hear that—but there's more to come. Can you be ready to go in half an hour?"

"I can do better than that. How does twenty minutes sound?"

"Perfect."

He started to lean forward . . . like he was going to kiss her. Jerked upright. Stood and backed toward the door. "I'll, uh, load all the goodies into the car."

With that, he spun around and disappeared.

Fast.

Like he didn't trust himself to keep his hands to himself if he stayed around.

Rachel swung her legs off the bed. Fingered the rose petals and inhaled the sweet perfume. Smoothed a hand over the file folder in her lap amidst the silver paper.

He'd suggested they rebuild their relationship slowly—but he'd left the timing on their full reconciliation to her.

Yet after the birthday he'd given her so far—and a romantic picnic yet to come—she had a feeling taking this slow and easy wasn't going to be easy at all.

And maybe she didn't have to try too hard to do that.

Maybe it was time to listen to her heart.

24

Chirp. Chirp. Chirp. Chirp.

As the familiar ringtone penetrated his sleep-fogged brain, Ben jerked awake. Groped for the cell on his nightstand. Pressed it against his ear after peering at the screen.

"Lexie. Hi."

A beat passed.

"I think I'm the one who should apologize this go-round. I just checked my watch. Sorry for the early call."

He tried to focus on the digital display of the clock next to the bed. Two minutes after seven.

Yeah, that was kind of early for his post-military life.

"No problem. I needed to get up." Not a lie. He owed Marci a call. "What's going on?"

"One of my patrol officers spotted your friend in the parking lot at the Gull last night about eleven. She changed rental cars."

No wonder Nicole had been under the radar.

"What's she driving now?"

"A silver Chevy Impala with dark-tinted windows."

"Where is she?"

"Car's still at the motel."

"Okay. I'll keep an eye out for her. Thanks for the update."

"Not a problem—but sorry to wake you."

"My alarm was about to go off anyway. Will you let me know if there are any new developments?"

"Of course."

"Thanks."

Ben set the cell back on the nightstand and stood. No sense trying to eke out another few minutes of shut-eye. He was wide awake.

Twenty minutes later, after downing a large glass of OJ and finishing off a bowl of cereal, he punched in Marci's number.

"Good morning." She sounded wide awake and cheery.

"Morning." He leaned back against the kitchen counter and gave her the bad news about Nicole.

"Oh, shoot." She blew out a lungful of air. "I was looking forward to seeing you this morning."

"Likewise. I wish I could swing by and give you a lift, but I'd like to find out what she intends to do next before I risk letting her see us together."

"She already suspects we're involved."

"Based on whatever her PI passed on. She hasn't spotted any evidence herself as far as I know—and I'd like to keep it that way."

Silence.

"Marci?"

"Yeah. I'm here." Another sigh. "Letting her run the show isn't sitting well, Ben."

"With me, either. If there was any legal recourse, I'd take it. But she can't keep this up forever—and we have a lifetime ahead of us. We can afford to wait her out."

More silence.

A niggle of unease snaked through him.

The woman he was falling for had many fine qualities—but her emotions did have a tendency to get the better of her.

"Marci?"

"I'm here."

"Let's be patient, okay?"

"I'm trying. So what are you going to do today?"

He frowned.

Her abrupt change of subject didn't leave him feeling warm and fuzzy.

"I have a stack of paperwork to fill out for the two jobs here, and I want to get the Oregon licensing process started. I also need to contact a few references—and call the practice in Ohio to let the partners know I've changed my mind about joining them."

"You'll be busy." Her voice warmed. "But it's a good busy—from my perspective."

"From mine too. Hope Harbor always felt like home. Now it really will be." He strolled over to the kitchen window as Greg and Rachel came out their back door, a picnic basket in hand. "Hey . . . I think my neighbors have a date." He relayed the scene.

"Nice. It's Rachel's birthday. Sounds like Greg stepped up to the plate to make it special."

"When's your birthday?"

"Not for months. I was almost a Valentine baby." She gave him the date.

"Ink me in for that day."

"I like a man who knows what he wants and plans ahead." She exhaled into the phone. "I guess I'll ring Marv for a lift. Call me later today?"

"Guaranteed. In the meantime, be careful if you spot a silver Chevy Impala."

"I haven't seen any sign of Nicole since she arrived. I think I fell off her radar."

"I hope so." His lips quirked as Greg gave Rachel a hug. The two of them definitely seemed to have mended their fences. "Talk to you soon."

As he ended the call, he watched the younger couple next door pull out of the driveway for whatever adventure they had planned for the day.

Lucky them.

He'd be planning similar outings with Marci if Nicole wasn't in the picture.

Gritting his teeth, he expelled a breath and began to pace.

Was it possible he was playing this wrong?

Should he confront the woman, goad her into taking some kind of unlawful action?

That sounded appealing—in theory.

But he'd been burned by her on the legal side once.

Badly.

Thank heaven he'd escaped with no more than a few scars.

If it happened again, however, he might not be as fortunate.

That was why Lexie and Eric had both advised him to avoid her at all costs.

So what *could* he do?

Hard as he tried to come up with an idea or two that might solve his dilemma, inspiration eluded him.

He did know one thing, though.

Marci wasn't the only one who was frustrated.

Biding his time and letting Nicole dictate how they lived their lives was getting very, very old.

This was getting old.

Fuming, Marci began to pace in the parking lot of Grace Christian while Marv jumped her dead battery.

This Nicole chick who'd tried to ruin Ben's life was beginning to grate on her nerves.

Big-time.

What on earth was she up to?

And why would she switch cars?

If she was hoping to observe Ben secretly, she was delusional. Staying under the radar in a town this size was next to impossible.

Or maybe the explanation was simpler. Perhaps her other car had developed mechanical issues.

Except nothing was simple with this woman, based on what Ben had told her.

Marci let loose with a loud huff.

Instantly, Marv stuck his head out from under the hood and sent her an apologetic look. "Sorry to hold you up. I'll have you back in business in less than five minutes."

"No worries. I've got messages to check." She waved her cell at him and tried to conjure up a reassuring smile despite her bad mood. It wasn't Marv's fault her battery was dead—or that some unstable woman was wreaking havoc on her budding romance.

He disappeared back under the hood—and true to his word, he had her engine humming before she finished responding to emails and texts.

"That should take care of the problem." He detached the cables. "A battery this new shouldn't be giving you grief. I think she'll work again without any hassles. But to be safe, you might want to drive around for fifteen minutes to recharge it. If the car won't start next time you use it, the battery isn't holding a charge and will have to be replaced. That shouldn't happen, though, unless you've got a dud."

"Thanks." She unzipped her purse. "Let me write you a check."

He waved her offer aside. "I'll send a bill to the *Herald* office. I don't expect you're going to disappear and leave me with a bad debt."

"No worries on that score. This is home."

"That's what I figured. See you around." With a jaunty salute, her morning chauffeur ambled back to his tow truck.

Marci slid behind the wheel of her purring car, put it in gear, and backed out of the spot in Grace Christian's parking lot. With fifteen minutes to tool around, why not drive up 101 to the scenic lookout that offered a glimpse of Pelican Point light? It was a beautiful view, and she might even be able to snap a few photos she could post on the *Herald*'s Facebook page to remind residents that the See the Light campaign was in full swing and dollars were pouring in from the crowdfunding campaign.

Decision made, she pulled out of the lot, aimed her car north, and tuned the radio to an upbeat station.

The cheery music lifted her spirits—until she happened to glance in her rearview mirror halfway to her destination and spotted a silver car in the distance behind her.

Her pulse picked up.

Was it a Chevy Impala?

Given her limited interest in and knowledge of cars, only an up-close-and-personal inspection of the grille or the hood or the trunk—or wherever the brand name was displayed these days—would provide the answer to that question.

Keeping one eye on the silver car, she finished the drive and turned into the overlook.

Doors locked and engine idling, she waited.

Sixty seconds later, the silver car with dark-tinted windows rolled by . . . and kept going.

She let out a slow breath.

It had taken her two years to tame her paranoia after the Atlanta debacle, and letting it resurface was *not* an option.

The silver car was nothing more than a coincidence.

Leaving her Civic running, she dug around in her purse for the camera she kept on hand for potential *Herald* stories, walked to the edge of the stone wall, and managed to shoot a dozen usable shots of the lighthouse in the distance.

And she only looked over her shoulder three or four times.

Task accomplished, she got behind the wheel and retraced her route back to Hope Harbor.

No silver car followed her.

See?

Overactive imagination.

But an hour later, when she strolled past the window in her office after refilling her coffee mug, the silver car parked two doors down *wasn't* a figment of her imagination.

It was all too real.

As was the blonde woman wearing sunglasses, seated across the street on a bench by the wharf—but staring her direction rather than toward the view.

Marci's stomach flipped.

Apparently Ben's nemesis had decided to watch her instead of him.

Why?

They'd been careful not to be seen together. Other than that middle-of-the-night rendezvous at her house, they'd kept their distance from . . .

Wait.

After dinner last night with Rachel and Greg, they'd walked out together, assuming the coast was clear.

But that was before they'd realized Nicole had switched cars.

Was it possible she'd been lurking nearby? Could she have witnessed the cozy parting they'd taken pains to hide from Rachel and Greg with a discreet tilt of her umbrella?

If so, it would have confirmed her PI's report that the man

she'd targeted was getting friendly with the local newspaper editor.

Fingers clenched around the mug, Marci backed away from the window and sank onto the edge of her desk, the story Ben had told her about Nicole's revenge on that nurse playing through her mind.

Was she now planning some similar vengeance on the woman her twisted mind considered a new rival?

Or was she waiting to make her move until she had further proof her suspicions were sound?

Anger bubbling up inside her, Marci mashed her lips together. Stood.

She was *not* going to be a sitting duck.

She was *not* going to let this woman intimidate her.

She was *not* going to pussyfoot around and wait for the other shoe to drop.

She was done letting Nicole call the shots.

But . . . what sort of proactive measures could she take?

Chugging a fortifying gulp of coffee, she returned to the window, brain firing on all cylinders. There had to be a way to force the woman's hand.

She discarded the first preposterous ideas that sprang to mind . . . but then a solution that seemed to have serious potential took root.

Yeah.

That could work.

And as far as she could see after weighing all the ramifications, other than some capital outlay, there were no downsides. It would be simple to implement, and it might put an end to this fast—assuming Nicole was as volatile as Ben said.

Even if it didn't work, at least she'd be *doing* something.

To get this rolling, though, she did need some assistance—but hopefully her query would be kept confidential.

Besides, she wasn't going to say *why* she needed the information.

Shoring up her resolve, she crossed to the *Herald* phone, picked it up, and dialed Lexie Graham Stone.

Rachel's birthday had been a success.

As Greg lowered himself to the side of the bed in the guestroom he'd occupied since they'd moved to Hope Harbor, a smile played at his lips.

His wife had loved the roses, the breakfast in bed, the college catalogs, the picnic. She'd been glowing by the time they'd wended their way home and parted for the night with a simple hug in the hall.

Only one thing could have made the day more perfect.

But after promising to let her set the pace on their full reconciliation, pushing would be wrong.

He leaned over and began to remove his prosthesis.

She needed to be the one to make the first . . .

A soft knock sounded on the door, and he looked up. "It's open."

Rachel cracked it a few inches and peeked around the edge. "I thought you might be asleep."

He would be under normal circumstances. It was closing in on eleven. But holding Rachel's hand for most of their day together—and sharing a final hug—had juiced his adrenaline. Even *thinking* about sleep had been impossible until fifteen minutes ago.

"Not yet." His prosthesis was half off, so he bent back down to finish the task, trying for a light note. "If you're after more birthday presents, I'm all out."

"I hope that's not true."

He lifted his head—and the breath jammed in his lungs as she slowly pushed the door open.

His wife had exchanged the yoga pants and oversized T-shirt she'd worn to bed since they came to Hope Harbor for the filmy negligee that had knocked his socks off on their wedding night.

She remained in the doorway as he tried to rein in his galloping pulse.

Her invitation couldn't be any more explicit.

And if he had two sound legs, he'd jump to his feet, sweep her into his arms, and give her the present she clearly wanted.

Not an option now that he'd removed his prosthesis.

And maybe that was better.

With him stuck on the edge of the bed, she'd have a few moments to rethink the step she was taking much sooner than might be in her best interest.

She twisted her fingers together in front of her, and a soft pink hue flooded her cheeks. "Sorry. I didn't mean to put you on the spot. We need to be on the same page for this." She backed up and started to turn away.

"Wait!" He pushed himself to his feet, balancing on one leg as he grabbed for the crutch propped against the wall beside the bed.

After a brief hesitation, she angled back.

"We're on the same page." He locked gazes with her. "I can't think of a better end to this day. But it might be too soon."

"For me . . . or for you?"

"You. I don't want you to rush into anything you might regret. You haven't given me long enough to prove myself."

"Didn't we agree I'd decide the timing?"

"Yes . . . but I want to make sure you're thinking clearly about this." Even if every instinct in his body was urging him to be less than noble and take what he desperately wanted.

"I *am* thinking clearly."

That made one of them.

"Are you certain?"

"Yes." She walked toward him, her pace slow. Deliberate. "I know we've had a rough stretch—but I've never stopped loving you. And my heart tells me we're out of the woods." She stopped two feet away, reached for his hand, and twined her fingers with his. "What does yours say?"

For several seconds, he studied her.

There wasn't one ounce of doubt on her face—or in her radiant eyes.

Thank you, God!

Instead of responding with words, he tugged her close, wrapped her in his arms, and gave her a birthday kiss to remember.

Greg had no idea how long it went on.

But somewhere along the way, they ended up on the pillows, Rachel's soft curves molded against his harder planes.

Like in the early days of their marriage, before an IED changed everything.

And as her birthday waned . . . as he demonstrated just how much he loved this woman who'd stood by him with love and fidelity through all the difficult months they'd endured . . . gratitude overflowed in his heart.

It might be his wife's special day, but the gift she'd given *him* was one he would treasure every single moment for the rest of his life.

25

Ben drew in a lungful of the bracing salt air and forged up the path to the lighthouse, waiting for the invigorating hike to work its usual magic and take the edge off his nerves.

But on this bright Saturday morning, the strenuous climb wasn't reducing his stress level one iota.

Not yet, anyway.

Halting at the halfway mark up the path to Pelican Point, he surveyed the placid sea and fisted his hands at his sides.

It had been bad enough to find Nicole on his doorstep eight days ago.

But he could deal with that far better than he was handling her sudden interest in Marci.

The very notion that the woman who'd captured his heart was in the sights of the blonde troublemaker chilled him to the core.

Yet the *Herald* editor hadn't been at all perturbed when he'd called yesterday to pass on Lexie's news that Nicole had staked out a bench on the wharf across from her office. Apparently she'd spotted Nicole herself on Thursday afternoon and hadn't considered it worth mentioning to him.

Nor had she seemed too concerned that one of the Hope Harbor police officers had seen the Impala parked on Pelican Point Road, near her house.

Another shiver rippled through him—and it had nothing to do with the cloud that scuttled across the sun, blocking the warming rays.

Ben shoved his fingers through his hair. This hike was a lost cause. He wasn't going to relax until Nicole was gone.

But who knew how long she planned to hang around?

Farther up the path, another hiker lifted a pair of binoculars and focused on a fishing boat churning the waters offshore.

Binoculars . . .

He propped a foot on a nearby rock as an idea began to percolate.

Maybe it was time for some intimidation tactics of his own.

Instead of standing by passively while Nicole watched them, why not start watching *her*—and be very visible doing it.

After all, two could play the stalking game . . . and as long as he stayed in public view, where there were witnesses, she couldn't launch another smear campaign like the one she'd manufactured in Germany.

The strategy might accomplish nothing—but it was better than letting her call all the shots, as Marci had said a couple of days ago.

Resolve firming, he retraced his steps down the path and followed the coast trail until it merged with Sea Rose Lane, at the edge of town. From there, he headed toward the wharf. Marci had said she was going to work most of the day on lighthouse business, so if Nicole was still on her trail, that's where the woman would be.

As he reached the tiny park on the north edge of town, the smell of tacos wafted his way.

Charley was cooking.

Food wasn't high on his agenda, but that aroma was hard

to resist . . . especially in light of the meager bowl of Cheerios he'd wolfed down hours ago.

The taco chef raised a hand in greeting as he caved to temptation and veered toward the food truck. "Morning, Ben. I was beginning to think I'd lost a customer."

"No way. I've just been . . . occupied. With matters far less pleasant than one of your tacos." He surveyed the wharf as he spoke. A blonde woman was sitting on a bench near the *Herald* office. Her back was to him, but he had no doubt about her identity—or what she was doing.

"I've noticed some unsettling vibes in town myself the past week or so."

Ben pivoted around to find Charley scrutinizing Nicole too.

"Have you met her?" No sense pretending he didn't know the woman.

"She stopped in for an order of tacos once." Charley looked back at him. "And she asked a lot of questions."

"About what?"

"You. And our *Herald* editor." Charley inclined his head toward the grill behind him. "Would you like some lunch?"

Yeah, he would—but he was far more interested in what Charley had told Nicole.

"Sure." He checked on her again before picking up the conversation. "She and I have an unpleasant history."

"So I gathered." Charley pulled some fish fillets out of the cooler.

"She told you about us?" Why would she do that, when all of her claims had been invalidated?

"No—but people communicate in many ways that don't involve words." He sprinkled the fish with some of his special seasoning and studied Nicole again, faint creases denting his forehead. "She's a troubled soul."

At the very least.

"Also dangerous."

"Those kinds of people often are. You should be careful."

"Trust me, I am. I'm more concerned about Marci." No reason to pretend he wasn't interested in the local newspaper editor. As soon as Nicole was history, the whole town would know. "She tends to be a bit on the impulsive side."

The corners of Charley's eyes crinkled. "Ah, but impulsiveness has its charms—and its merits. She dived headfirst into the lighthouse project, and look where that led."

"I'm not saying it's a negative trait. I love her spontaneity and enthusiasm. But with someone like that woman"—he nodded toward Nicole—"it can get you in hot water."

"I'm sure Marci realizes that."

As if on cue, the *Herald* editor appeared in the doorway of the office down the block and strode their direction.

Ben straightened up.

If she was in the mood for tacos for lunch too, he needed to get out of here.

Fast.

Either that, or hope she noticed him and altered her route.

A few seconds later, Marci did glance his direction.

But instead of beating a hasty retreat, she lifted a hand in greeting and crossed the street—on a collision course with him.

His heart lost its rhythm.

Hadn't she seen Nicole?

"Um, Charley, I think I'll pass on those tacos." He backed away from the truck as he spoke. "Give my order to Marci."

Without waiting for a reply, he strode away from her.

"Ben!"

At her summons, he picked up his pace.

"Ben! Wait up!"

He peeked over his shoulder.

She'd broken into a jog.

Short of sprinting away, there was no way to avoid her.

He stopped and swiveled around. In the distance, Nicole rose, her attention riveted on the two of them.

Great.

"Hi." Marci stopped three feet away and gave him a sunny smile. "I was hoping to run into you today."

"Marci . . . Nicole is watching us." He kept an eye on the blonde. "She's on the wharf."

"I know. She's been on that bench all morning."

"I thought we agreed to wait her out."

"I agreed to consider it—but my patience has worn thin. So I decided to be proactive."

He furrowed his brow. "Define proactive."

"My pleasure."

In one giant step, she erased the distance between them, threw her arms around his neck, and kissed him.

Right on the mouth.

Where anyone in the vicinity could watch.

Including Nicole.

A wave of panic crashed over him.

What in creation was she thinking?

"Marci." He wrenched his lips free and tried to pry her hands off his neck.

She tightened her grip and locked gazes with him. "I'm tired of playing by her rules, Ben . . . and following her timeline. If she wants proof we're a couple, this should do it. Now the ball's in her court."

"This isn't badminton. She plays hardball." His alarm ratcheted up another notch, squeezing his windpipe. "You could get hurt."

"No, I won't. Trust me on this. I've got it covered."

He squinted at her. "What does that mean?"

"It means you don't have to worry about me."

"I can't *not* worry about you. That's what happens when you lo . . ." Whoops. Too soon for that word. "If you care about someone."

"Then why don't you play bodyguard?" Her eyes began to twinkle. "We can be together *and* you can keep me safe. That's a win/win in my book."

"I'm not trained to be a bodyguard. I'm a doctor, not a special ops soldier."

"I don't need a special ops soldier. All you have to do is follow me home from work today—and pick me up for church tomorrow. My house is a fortress, so I'm safe once I'm locked inside for the night. Besides, after this"—she snuggled close again—"I don't think she's going to wait long to make her move—if she even follows through. For all we know, she'll accept the fact you're taken and disappear."

If only.

"I wouldn't hold my breath on that score."

"I believe in being optimistic."

Of course she did.

That was Marci.

And now that she'd deep-sixed his hands-off strategy, he'd *have* to follow through on his idea and keep Nicole in his sights—at least until Marci was safely locked inside for the night.

If he was lucky, that tactic would freak the other woman out and make her rethink her own plans.

"Hey." Marci nudged him. "You still with me?"

"Always." He bent and claimed another kiss.

She smiled up at him. "I'm glad you got with the program."

"You didn't leave me much choice." He draped an arm around her shoulders. "Why don't I buy you some tacos and walk you back to the office? When you're ready to leave tonight, call me and I'll follow you home."

"Will you stay for dinner?"

Not while Nicole was sticking close.

"Can I get a rain check? I have a few chores I need to take care of this evening."

"Anytime." She slipped her arm around his waist and tugged him toward Charley's stand. "Let's eat."

Ben let her tow him along, sending Nicole a defiant stare over her head. He might not have chosen to tackle their dilemma as directly as Marci had, in her sometimes headstrong way, but the damage was done.

All he could do was keep Nicole in sight—and hope Marci's optimism for a positive outcome wasn't misplaced.

What the . . . !?

Marci bolted upright in bed and clapped her palms against her ears as a piercing alarm ricocheted off the walls in her bedroom.

She might be groggy from the deep sleep she'd finally tumbled into hours after Ben had followed her home last night, but one thing was clear.

Someone was breaking into her house.

And only one suspect came to mind.

Not what she'd expected—but Ben had warned her Nicole was unpredictable.

Vaulting out of bed, she snatched her phone off the nightstand. The security company would already be alerting the local police, but she wasn't about to part with her lifeline.

She dashed to the bedroom door and double-checked the slider lock.

Set, as usual.

A big, burly guy might be able to kick down the heavy

wooden door, but she doubted Nicole would be capable of that feat.

All she had to do was stay cool and wait for . . .

She frowned.

Sniffed.

Was that . . . smoke?

She sniffed again.

Yes.

Definitely smoke, drifting in through her open window.

As the reality slammed home, her heart stumbled.

The alarm ringing in her ears was for fire, not burglary.

It seemed Ben's worry that Nicole might be capable of causing physical harm had been merited.

But setting a house on fire?

Definitely not what she'd expected.

Minor vandalism, yes—but the woman must be unhinged to take this kind of drastic action.

Marci gripped her phone tighter.

What to do now?

The volunteer fire department in Hope Harbor would need a few minutes to assemble once it got the alarm. . . and Nicole could be lurking nearby.

Pulse hammering, Marci crossed to the window. Peeked out.

All was dark.

No sign of flames.

She returned to the door and felt the wood panels.

Cool.

The fire wasn't close to her room yet.

But the smoke might be.

And that killed more people than flames.

Shifting into fast-forward, she yanked on her jeans and stowed the phone in the pocket. Then she jammed her feet into her slippers, eased the door open, and sniffed again.

A very slight haze hung suspended below the ceiling—but the air was breathable.

Get to an exit.

Now!

Excellent advice.

As long as her shaky legs didn't give out on her.

She hurried down the hall, the shadowy light spilling from the bedroom behind her providing only marginal illumination.

Stumbled when the peppy melody of "Zip-a-Dee-Doo-Dah" erupted from her phone.

Forcing herself to pick up the pace again, she pulled out her cell and scanned the name on the screen.

Let out a relieved breath.

Help was close at hand.

She put the phone to her ear. "It's Marci."

"Where are you?"

"Approaching the stairs. Is it safe to come out?"

"Yes. I'll watch for you. I alerted the fire department."

"So did my alarm company. Where's the fire?"

"In the back."

She started down the stairs. "Did you get everything?"

"More than you'll need."

"I'll be out in a minute."

She slid the phone back in her jeans. Exhaled.

There would be damage to contend with once the smoke cleared, but her gamble had paid off.

Nicole was history.

Middle-of-the-night phone calls were never a good omen.

Ben felt around for his cell and tried to clear the fog from his brain—but as Lexie's name registered on the screen, his mental murkiness evaporated as fast as a Hope Harbor mist chased away by the sun.

"What's wrong?" He swung his legs to the floor and snagged the jeans he'd tossed on a chair after returning home from the Gull at ten o'clock. Nicole had taken a swing by Marci's house during the evening, but as far as Ben could tell, once she'd pulled into the Gull, she'd called it a night.

Maybe that assumption had been wrong.

"There's a fire at Marci's house. The call came in ten minutes ago. I thought you'd want to know."

His heart missed a few beats.

Yeah, his assumption had been wrong.

"Is Marci safe?"

"Yes."

"What happened?"

"I'm on my way to find out."

In the background, the siren of the town fire truck began to wail.

"I'll be there in fifteen minutes."

"I figured you'd want to join us. See you soon."

The line went dead—and he went into action.

Years of trauma work overseas had taught him to move at warp speed, but he broke his own record getting to Pelican Point.

In ten minutes flat, he was on-site.

After pulling in behind a police car on the side of the road, he sprinted toward a cluster of people standing out of the way of the firefighters. Lexie, Officer Gleason, Marci—and some tall, lanky guy dressed in black that he didn't recognize.

Marci saw him first, and she broke away from the group, jogging toward him as fast as she could in . . . he peered at her feet . . . bunny-shaped slippers?

She launched herself at him from three feet away, and he absorbed her weight, wrapping her tight in his arms.

"Are you okay?" His question came out in a croak.

"Uh-huh." The words were muffled against his chest. "And best of all—Nicole won't ever bother us again."

"If we can prove she did it."

"That won't be a problem."

As Lexie spoke, Ben reluctantly loosened his grip on Marci. She turned but stayed within the circle of his arms.

Where she belonged.

"What do you mean?"

"We have pictures—thanks to Marci and Mr. Young here." Lexie indicated the lanky guy, then addressed Marci. "When you asked me for the name of a reputable PI, I had no idea what you had in mind. I thought you were researching some story for the *Herald*. If I'd known your plan, I would have discouraged you."

"It worked, though."

"I can't argue with that. It appears we have irrefutable evidence of her illegal activity."

"What plan?" Ben puckered his brow.

Marci shrugged. "I got tired of waiting for Nicole. So I had my alarm company add a few cameras to my setup, hired Steve"—she motioned to the PI—"and gave her a reason to go after me sooner rather than later."

Ah-ha.

Her seemingly impulsive move at the taco stand hadn't been impulsive at all, but part of a well-orchestrated strategy to exert some control over the situation.

"So that's what the kiss yesterday was all about."

"Guilty as charged . . . and not in the least repentant."

"What if I hadn't shown up at the wharf?"

"I had plans to get you there."

Yeah. She would have.

"You put yourself at risk."

"I'm fine." She waved a hand in dismissal. "And it brought this whole nasty business to a head. Although I have to admit I didn't expect her to resort to fire."

Lexie pulled out her phone and skimmed the screen. "Excuse me a minute." She walked a few yards away, cell to her ear.

"I think my work here is done." The PI extended his hand to Marci. "I'll make sure the police have everything they need."

"Thank you." She clasped his fingers and did a belated introduction.

Ben shook hands with him too—but as the man walked over to talk with Jim Gleason, he gave her a stern look. "You could have told me about this, you know."

"You wouldn't have liked it."

"True."

She caught her lower lip between her teeth. "Are you mad at me?"

"Good news, folks." Lexie reappeared, giving him a reprieve on that answer. "We already picked up your friend. She went back to the motel, with no apparent suspicion her activity here was monitored and documented. You won't need to worry about her anymore. The evidence we have will put her away for a very long time."

"That's a relief." Marci inspected the house. "How bad is the damage?"

"Minor, according to the fire chief. With all the rain we've had, the wood is damp, and that inhibited the effectiveness of the accelerant she threw on the siding. You've got some serious scorching, but your smoke alarms picked up the fire fast. Other than minimal repairs in the kitchen, the house shouldn't need much work on the inside."

"That's a relief. Can I stay here tonight?"

"It will take a while for the fire crew to finish. They'll want to make certain nothing is smoldering. You might have a long wait." At a summons from Officer Gleason, Lexie excused herself to join him.

"There's a guest room at Skip's house with your name on it." Ben twined his fingers with hers.

"Sold. Let me collect a few essentials."

"I'll wait for you in the living room. And bring those." He motioned to her feet.

She dipped her chin . . . and flushed. "Whoops. I usually keep these hidden—but they were the handiest footwear."

"They're cute."

"Silly."

"I stand by cute—and whimsical and charming and fun and playful. In other words . . . they're you."

"When you put it like that . . ." She grinned and started toward the house, holding tight to his hand. "Give me five minutes."

"No problem."

Because truth be told, he planned to give her far more than that.

A fact he intended to make very clear before this night was over.

"Mmm. That was perfect, Ben. I wouldn't have expected you to have herbal tea on hand." Marci took another sip of the soothing blend and appraised the man beside her on the couch. Now that she'd showered the smoke smell off her skin and out of her hair and was dressed in her most comfortable fleece sweats, she felt human again—even if it was close to two in the morning.

But Ben had been awfully quiet during the drive to the house . . . and since their arrival.

"Skip always kept some on hand."

Her companion was still too subdued.

Maybe she could lighten the atmosphere.

"I was going to call you first thing in the morning, but there's no reason to wait to share the news. As of last night before I went to bed, we've officially exceeded our crowdfunding goal. Better yet, the money is continuing to come in. Pelican Point light will live on."

That earned her a small flex of the lips. "Skip would be pleased."

Drat.

There could be only one explanation for his restraint—and she might as well address it head-on.

"You're mad about the trap I set for Nicole, aren't you?"

He toyed with a strand of her hair. "I'm not certain how I feel about it, to be honest. I admire your initiative—and your willingness to put yourself at risk to resolve the issue. I'm disappointed in myself that I didn't come up with a solution first. I'm also worried you might go off on your own and pull another stunt like this in the future if a dicey situation arises—and that the outcome might not be as positive."

"I don't expect us to face anything this dramatic again, do you?"

"No. But life has a way of throwing curves and handing out surprises."

"Will it make you feel better if I promise never to implement a plan like this in the future without first talking it over with you?"

His fingers stilled. "Never is a long time—if you're assuming we'll be together years down the road."

Her stomach knotted.

Was he having second thoughts about them already, thanks to this escapade?

Curses on the red hair that had gotten her into more scrapes than she cared to admit.

"I am." She swallowed, gripped her mug—and forced herself to ask the question preying on her mind. "I thought you were too. Have you changed your mind?"

"No. After tonight, I'm more certain than ever we belong together. When Lexie called and told me about the fire, I couldn't . . ." His voice broke, and he sucked in some air. "I couldn't breathe. Losing you would be like losing a part of myself."

The tension in Marci's stomach uncoiled.

Ben wasn't quiet because he was mad or had lost interest in her.

He was quiet because his fears for her safety, however misplaced, had taken the wind out of his sails—to use one of Skip's colloquial phrases.

She set the mug on the coffee table and scooted closer to him. "For the record, I plan to stick around for a very long time. I have a lighthouse campaign to finish, a paper to publish, a PR business to run . . . and a handsome man who wants to woo me." She looped her arms around his neck. "I'm not going anywhere, buddy."

"Is that a promise?"

"Yep. This girl is ready to be romanced. Think you're up to the job?"

A chuckle rumbled deep in his chest. "I don't know—but I'd like to give it a shot."

"What did you have in mind?"

"Roses, candlelight, picnics on the beach, impromptu lunches at Charley's. How's that for starters?"

"Not bad. But you better add lighthouse rehab to that agenda. I told BJ to put both our names on her volunteer list."

"Without asking me?"

"What? You don't want to put some sweat equity into restoring your grandfather's lighthouse?"

"I'd rather romance you."

"What could be more romantic than scraping paint off a lighthouse?"

He grimaced. "I can think of a few things."

"There'll be time for those too." She leaned in and waggled her eyebrows. "You want to practice one of them now?"

His answering chuckle erupted into a full-fledged laugh. "Why do I think life with you will be a grand adventure?"

"Is that good or bad?"

"It's very, very good. Skip told me once that marriage can be a beautiful adventure if you find the right woman—and that some feistiness can add tang to a marriage."

The air whooshed out of her lungs. "Is that . . . a proposal?"

"Nope. Skip also told me to take my time, ask the Lord for guidance—and cross my fingers. That's what I plan to do over the next few months. You okay with that plan?"

"Sounds perfect to me."

"Glad to hear it. But I'll let you in on a little secret. If I was a betting man, I'd lay money on the outcome. Now . . . about that romance."

He pulled her close—and Marci didn't resist.

Because Ben was irresistible.

And as he offered some persuasive evidence to support the outcome of that bet he'd mentioned, she gave thanks for the winding path that had led her to Hope Harbor . . . for an abandoned lighthouse in desperate need of TLC that had brightened multiple lives . . . and for the special man in her arms who was destined to play a starring role in her future.

Epilogue

"Can I steal you away for a few minutes, Mrs. Garrison?"

Mrs. Garrison.

A delicious trill rippled through Marci as she turned toward her brand-new husband, movie-star handsome in his elegant black-tie wedding finery.

She held out her hand. "You may—but they'll need us for the first dance soon."

"I'll have you back in time for that."

He twined his fingers with hers, and she followed as he led her out of the large white tent that had been erected on Pelican Point and down the gravel path toward the lighthouse, edging around a couple of seagulls huddled together.

One of them cackled as they passed.

Marci stared at the bird.

Was it possible these could be the same two gulls that had hung around months ago when she and Ben had had a less-than-cordial exchange in this very spot?

Ben slowed, and she glanced over at him. He, too, was eying the birds.

"That sounded like . . ." His voice trailed off.

"I know. Kind of weird, isn't it?"

"Yeah. But what are the odds?"

"Slim to none—and I'm not going to waste another thought on laughing seagulls." Marci lifted her face to the late-afternoon sun. "I'd rather give thanks for such a gorgeous day. November can be iffy, but this feels like summer."

"The sun wouldn't dare play hooky on such a beautiful bride." Ben smiled at her as he resumed walking, the love in his eyes as bright as the illumination from the Fresnel lens in the Pelican Point lighthouse that had once offered a ray of hope to storm-tossed ships.

They continued past the neatly tended flower beds, kept weed-free by several area garden clubs, until he stopped at the base of the refurbished lighthouse.

"I never get tired of this view." She slipped her arm around his waist and scanned the vast blue sea.

"And now it will be available for future generations to enjoy, thanks to a certain redhead I know."

"Thanks to a *lot* of people—including you."

"I was going to sell it."

She lifted one shoulder. "A lighthouse didn't fit into your plans seven months ago."

"True. I thought it was a white elephant."

"Understandable. But you did have a change of heart. Not only did you sell it for a bargain price, you're serving on the board. And look what's been accomplished." She swept a hand behind the lighthouse as she gave the scene a slow sweep.

The white tent hosting their reception occupied the spot where construction would soon begin on a permanent banquet and hospitality facility featuring huge, vaulted windows that framed the lighthouse.

In the background, half hidden behind shrubbery, a parking lot was situated on adjacent lots purchased with excess crowdfunding money . . . far more than they'd expected, thanks in part to the lower price Ben had accepted for the lighthouse.

And closer at hand, a small structure designed in the style of traditional keeper's quarters housed Greg's office.

"It's hard to believe how much we've done in a handful of months." Ben completed his own perusal and refocused on her.

"I know. Greg told me a few days ago that he's booking two years out."

"He was an inspired choice for the job."

"I agree. However . . . much as I've loved this project, I'm not in the mood to discuss business today." She sidled closer. "I'm hoping you brought me out here to steal a kiss by the lighthouse that started it all."

"That's on my agenda. But there's another item I want to take care of first. Give me one minute." He bent down, swept his lips across her forehead, and pulled a key out of his pocket. "I need to retrieve a package that has your name on it."

With a wink, he circled around to the front of the structure and disappeared from view—just as the band behind her launched into the classic strains of "Unforgettable."

The corners of her mouth tipped up.

How appropriate.

Because the man who'd stolen her heart fit that description.

And no matter what surprise he was about to present to her, she already had the best gift of all.

Ben himself—for always.

Maybe every groom felt the same on his wedding day, but he really *was* the luckiest guy in the world.

Throat tightening, Ben picked up the box Greg had stashed

in the lighthouse for him earlier today, slipped back outside, and circled around in the opposite direction.

His stunning bride was standing where he'd left her, gazing out to sea, her filmy veil floating on the breeze as it trailed from her upswept hair, the elegant, form-fitting lace gown that dipped into a deep V in the back showcasing her slender figure.

She looked perfect.

In fact, *perfect* was the ideal word to describe the woman he'd promised to love and cherish all the days of his life.

Not perfect as in flawless, of course. Like him, she had her faults and peccadillos.

But she was perfect for him.

And that was all that mattered.

As if sensing his scrutiny, she shifted toward him, the dipping sun casting a golden glow on her already radiant face. "Sneaking up on me, I see."

"No. Admiring the view."

"The view's that way." She motioned toward the sea.

"One view is—but I'm enjoying the *best* view."

Laughter danced in her green irises. "Flattery will get you everywhere."

"I'll remember that." He strolled toward her and held out the shoebox-sized package wrapped in shiny white paper and tied with a white satin bow.

"You already gave me a wedding present." She touched the string of luminous pearls clasped around her neck.

"This is a bonus gift. One that has more sentimental than monetary value."

"Now I'm intrigued."

"Then I won't keep you in suspense. I'll hold it while you open."

She dispensed with the wrappings in quick order.

"Oh . . ." She breathed the word as she gently touched the

elaborate mother-of-pearl inlay on the lid of the mahogany box. "This is gorgeous."

"There's a story that goes with it."

"I love stories."

"I know. That's why I thought you'd appreciate this." He stroked a thumb over the edge of the box. "This started life in the mid-1800s as a case for a sextant. It was owned by a Captain Jeremiah Masterson and went with him on numerous voyages all over the world. He passed it on to his sole heir, a daughter who used it to store jewelry and keepsakes."

"How did it end up in *your* hands?"

"Patience, dear wife. I'm getting to that."

She wrinkled her nose. "I'm still working on that virtue."

"No kidding."

"Ha-ha." She elbowed him and grinned. "Go on."

"Masterson's daughter married a fellow by the name of George Newton."

Her eyes widened. "The Pelican Point lighthouse keeper in the early 1900s?"

"One and the same. After Skip bought the lighthouse and began renovating, he found this in a concealed storage area under a loose floorboard. I came across it in the closet in his spare bedroom, along with notes he'd made after researching its history."

"Was there anything inside when he found it?"

"A few crumbling letters and some rusted, corroded costume jewelry. Nothing he could salvage—until he discovered the box had a false bottom."

"Ooh. A secret compartment. I love this!" Her face lit up and she clapped her hands. "Was there anything inside?"

"A love letter Captain Masterson was in the process of penning to his wife, dated 1892—during his last voyage."

"Why didn't he finish it?"

"I haven't a clue. Maybe a storm sidetracked him. Or he arrived home faster than expected. But the half-finished letter remained in the box. The daughter may not even have known about the secret compartment." He opened the lid to reveal a folded piece of parchment paper. "Go ahead and read it."

Marci carefully lifted out the antique sheet of vellum and opened it.

Over her shoulder, he skimmed the document again.

My dearest Priscilla,

I don't know when I shall have a chance to send this letter on its way to you. Soon, I hope. I want to know that your fingers have held these same pages, and that we are connected if only through mutual touch. For as my years have lengthened, my days at sea have begun to grow long and wearisome. I wish now only to be with you, my love.

You wondered when last we were together if I would miss the sea. I told you no, but I am not certain you believed me. My darling, it is true. I have loved the sea . . . but I have always loved you more, and my heart longs for you each day we are apart. Here on the ship, the sextant guides my course. But you have always guided my life with your sweetness and grace and kindness—and I miss you more than words can say. I long to feel your soft cheek against mine, and to walk with you on the sand and watch the sun set. You are my everything, and one day soon we . . .

The letter ended there.

Marci looked up at him, eyes glistening. "This is beautiful."

"He did have a touch of the poet in him."

"Why would his daughter leave this in the lighthouse?"

"According to Skip's notes, in their later years she and her husband took a trip east to visit family, and while they were there, he died. She never returned here. Their belongings were boxed up and sent to her . . . but since this was hidden, it must have been overlooked."

"Well, now that it's come to light again, it will have a place of honor in our home."

"You should put this inside too." Balancing the box in one hand, Ben extracted a folded piece of paper from his tux jacket and handed it to her. "I can't hope to compete with Jeremiah's poetic language, but I thought it fitting to add a note of my own to the box."

She opened the sheet, but he didn't have to read along on this one.

The words he'd penned were etched in his mind.

My dearest Marci,

The sentiments Jeremiah wrote to Priscilla almost 125 years ago are timeless—and it would be hard to improve on them. Which goes to show that love isn't bound by eras or social norms or chronological age. It's universal and unchanging.

I feel about you exactly as Jeremiah felt about Priscilla.

Although this box once housed navigational tools, I don't need a compass to find my destination—for I arrived at it a few hours ago when we exchanged vows and I became your husband. And every single morning from this day forward I will thank God for the gift of your kind, caring heart and contagious enthusiasm. You have brought me a joy I never knew existed, and my life is brighter because you fill it with laughter and love.

When I came to Hope Harbor and discovered Skip had bequeathed me a lighthouse, I considered it a yoke around my neck. But today, as we stand man and wife in the shadow of this structure that for more than a century guided lost souls home, I recognize it for what it really was.

A beacon of hope that led me home to you.

I love you, Marci—and I always will.

Sniffing, she refolded the letter and nestled it in the box beside its antique counterpart. "You're ruining my mascara, you know. And I paid big bucks for this professional makeup job."

He closed the lid, set the box on one of the new benches that lined the walkway, and took her hand. "I'll love you even if you have raccoon eyes." He handed her his handkerchief.

"That'll look great in the photos." She dabbed around her lashes as Rachel stepped out of the tent and waved to them.

"That must be the cue for our first dance." Ben acknowledged the other woman with a lift of his hand. "It will be fun to see which comes first with her—the baby or her degree. I predict a photo finish."

"That's what Greg says—with a big grin every time he mentions the subject. I'm happy for both of them."

"So am I. But today is about us." Ben took both her hands. "And I have one other item on my agenda before we rejoin the festivities."

He started to bend down, but she leaned back.

"Wait. I need to say . . . Your letter is . . . The box was so . . ." She blew out a breath. "You know, despite the fact that I work with words every day . . . and as fast as my emotions can bubble to the surface . . . and as easy as it is to trigger my temper . . . I'm not very good at sappy stuff."

"That's okay. You don't have to say anything. I know what's in your heart."

He leaned down again to claim his kiss.

Once more, she held him off, her expression as earnest—and

determined—as he'd ever seen it. "No. I want to say this." She gripped his hands tightly. "You, Ben Garrison, are my light in the storm. You brighten my days, and even when it's cloudy, my life glows because of you. You're as stalwart and dependable and solid as this lighthouse, and if I live to be a hundred I'll never stop thanking God for sending you my way. Priscilla may have married a fine man—but I married the *best* man."

As the horizon behind Marci blurred, Ben somehow managed to choke out a response. "Thank you."

"My pleasure." Her reply was soft, her face luminous.

"Do you think we could have that kiss now?"

"Yes." She wrapped her arms around his neck and rose up on tiptoe. "You're on, Dr. Garrison."

He dipped his head, and the two seagulls behind his bride fluttered into the air and glided away, leaving them alone in each other's arms.

And as their lips melded . . . as he held her close beneath Pelican Point light . . . as the setting sun unfurled a gilded ribbon across the sea and turned the sky into an impressionistic canvas of gold and pink and purple . . . Ben telegraphed a silent message of thanks to the grandfather he'd loved.

For always knowing what he needed most.

For standing with him through life's storms.

And for an unexpected legacy that had brought him home to Hope Harbor . . . and led him to a woman whose sweet love would enrich all his tomorrows.

Read an excerpt from
HIDDEN PERIL

All is well in Kristin Dane's life until, one by one, people connected to her local fair trade shop begin to die. It's up to Detective Luke Carter to find and stop the ruthless mastermind behind the killings before it's too late.

AVAILABLE EVERYWHERE FALL 2018

A Monastery Near Al Hafar, Syria

Why was a light burning in the workshop at midnight?

Suppressing a shiver, Brother Michael Bennett peered at the sliver of illumination seeping under the bottom of the heavy wooden door at the end of the long, vaulted passageway.

There could be only one explanation.

The monk who'd closed up the shop for the day had forgotten to turn it off.

He wiped a hand down his face and leaned a shoulder against the rough stone wall. That wouldn't have happened on his watch. Last chore before he left each night, he flipped the switch.

Eyeing the door, he gauged the distance. Could his legs handle the detour? Questionable. The bug that had felled him at noon had left his muscles wobbly as Jell-O. If his parched throat wasn't screaming for some chipped ice, he wouldn't be making this taxing trek to the kitchen.

Fuel for the workshop generator, however, was expensive.

And they had better uses for the funds entrusted to their care.

Shoring up his waning strength, he pushed off from the wall and trudged down the drafty passage, the February chill creeping into his Florida-born-and-bred bones . . . as it always did in winter.

Yet not once in the past ten years had he regretted his decision to join this simple religious community in the shadow of the Qalamoun Mountains. Christianity had flourished amid the harsh beauty of this high desert for centuries, and it was an honor and privilege to make a contribution to that tradition . . . no matter how small or insignificant.

Life might not be easy here—but it was good.

Tonight, however, he could have done with a few luxuries.

Like room service.

And heated hallways.

Another shiver rolled through him. It wasn't as cold in here as it was outside, where the temperature was probably hovering near freezing—but it couldn't be much above fifty.

Then again, no one was supposed to be wandering the halls at this hour.

He picked up his pace.

At the door to the workshop, he paused to catch his breath. All he had to do was flick off the lights, continue to the kitchen for his ice, and return to his warm bed.

The sooner the better.

He twisted the knob . . . pushed the door open . . . and froze.

A dark-haired man was hunched over a workbench against the far wall, a high-pitched whine abrading the midnight stillness. It was impossible to identify him from behind.

But whoever he was, he shouldn't be here.

A prickle of unease skittered through him, and he gripped the edge of the door to steady himself. "Hello?"

His raspy greeting was no more than a hoarse whisper.

He raised his voice and tried again, wincing as the words scraped past his raw throat.

The whirring noise stopped abruptly, and the man spun around.

"Khalil?" Brother Michael stared at the refugee who'd arrived on their doorstep two years ago, one of the many desperate souls who'd lost everything in this war-ravaged land. He switched to Arabic. "What are you doing here?"

Beads of sweat broke out on the twenty-six-year-old's forehead. "I'm working."

"At midnight?"

"I wanted to finish a . . . task."

God knew the small contingent of brothers needed all the help they could get to keep the place running, and Khalil was a hard worker. That was one of the reasons he'd been allowed to stay on as a volunteer in exchange for room and board.

But no one expected him to toil at the expense of sleep.

"You don't have to put in nighttime hours. You more than earn your keep as it is." Brother Michael leaned against the doorframe. Ever since he'd pled Khalil's case with the abbot and other monks, he'd taken the refugee under his wing. "This can wait until tomorrow."

"As you wish. I'll just clean up before I leave." The man gave a slight bow, his back brushing against the workbench.

A flutter of shavings drifted to the floor.

Too many, given the nature of the work they did here.

Odd.

And what had produced that whine he'd heard when he'd opened the door?

Certainly none of their usual equipment.

Brother Michael's pulse quickened.

Something wasn't right.

He needed to check that workbench.

"I'll help you with the cleanup." He forced himself to walk toward the bench, each step a supreme effort.

"No." The sweat on the man's forehead glistened in the overhead light. "You're sick. I'll take care of it."

"I insist." The workshop was his responsibility. *Khalil* was his responsibility. If the man was using the space for questionable purposes after hours, the issue needed to be addressed.

He continued toward the bench, stopping a few feet away, waiting for his protégé to give him access.

For several seconds they locked gazes. A parade of emotions

darted through the younger man's eyes. Panic . . . fear . . . resignation. And then resolve.

Without a word, Khalil moved toward him, stepping aside as they exchanged places.

Now that he had a clear view of the bench, Brother Michael scanned the items on the wooden surface. Added them up. Gripped the edge of the worktable.

Dear God!

How could he have made such a terrible mistake?

Khalil wasn't here to support their mission.

He was here to—

A shattering pain exploded in the back of his head.

Brother Michael staggered.

Groped for the edge of the bench.

Missed.

Legs crumpling, he slumped to the stone floor.

And in the scant few moments before the darkness swirling around him snuffed out the light, he sent a silent, desperate plea to the Almighty.

Please, God, let someone—somewhere—discover the truth and put a stop to the evil deception that is defiling this holy place.

——Six Weeks Later——

Brother Michael was dead.

Kristin Dane gripped the edge of the corrugated, travel-worn shipping carton that had logged more than six thousand miles on its journey from Syria to St. Louis, blinked to clear her vision, and forced herself to reread the letter.

Dear Ms. Dane:

I am pleased to send you the 50 pillar candles you ordered from our humble workshop here in the cradle of Christianity. We are grateful for your willingness to support our humanitarian work by selling the labor of our hands in your shop. As you know, every dollar we receive is used to help victims of the terrible violence here, Christians and Muslims alike. We continue to be amazed at the resilience and strength of the remarkable Syrian people, who have suffered so much.

And now I must pass on some sad news. Brother Michael has, quite suddenly, gone home to God. On February 16, he grew ill and took to his bed. The next morning, we found him on the floor in the workshop. We believe he rose during the night and went to the shop for some reason. It appears he tripped, or perhaps grew dizzy, and fell backward, hitting his head on the corner of a workbench.

I know this will be a shock to you, as it was to all of us. Our American brother spoke often of your kindness to him when you met two years ago while he was visiting your city.

Here at the monastery, we are already missing his selfless work and the deep spirituality and trust with which he lived his life. And we grieve the shortness of his days. Forty-four seems far too young to die.

Please pray for the repose of his soul, as we will continue to do here in the land he adopted—and loved.

With gratitude in Christ,
Abbot Jacques Gagnon

"Kristin?"

From a distance, a voice penetrated her shock.

Refolding the single sheet of paper, she lifted her chin. Susan Collier was standing in the doorway between WorldCraft's stockroom and the retail section of the shop.

"Are you okay?" The woman took a step toward her.

"No. I'm trying to . . . to absorb some bad news." She relayed the contents of the letter to her part-time clerk.

"I'm so sorry." Sympathy deepened the lines at the corners of the other woman's eyes. "From everything you've told me, he was a fine man."

"The best. A saint among us." Kristin traced a finger over the hand-lettered label on the box. "Meeting him was an amazing experience. He had an incredible ability to draw people in."

"Some men are very charismatic."

At the hint of bitterness in her words, Kristin looked at her. "I meant that in a positive, spiritual sense. Brother Michael exuded holiness. Not all men are like your ex."

"I know." Susan's features relaxed a hair. "I keep reminding myself of that. Brother Michael sounded like one of the good guys." She motioned toward the box. "Do you want me to put those on the display for you? I know you usually like to do it yourself, but you're already cutting it close for the wedding."

Shifting gears, Kristin checked her watch.

Her clerk was right.

In less than three hours, the bride would be walking down the aisle. And since she was one of the two people standing up for the groom, she couldn't be late.

Letting Colin down wasn't an option.

"Yes, thanks." Kristin set the letter from the abbot on the desk wedged into one corner of the stockroom. "If you need me for anything later today or Monday while I'm at the small business seminar, call or text."

"I'll be fine."

"I know." She summoned up a smile. "In the year you've been

with me, I've come to rely on you for much more than clerking duties. You've been a huge asset to WorldCraft."

Cheeks pinkening, the mid-fortyish brunette smoothed a renegade strand of hair back into the sleek chignon at her nape. "Thanks. I appreciate you giving me the job. If it hadn't been for you and Kate Marshall, I don't know where I'd be."

Kate Marshall . . . Kate Marshall. Oh, right. The director of New Start, the agency where Susan had gone for career counseling after she had finally walked away from her abusive marriage.

"You would have been fine. With your background in retail, someone would have snapped you up."

"I don't think so. My skills were rusty after being on hold for two decades."

"Not true. Your volunteer work with the handicraft co-op kept them fresh—and dealing with that kind of merchandise was perfect background for the fair trade goods I sell here." She retrieved her purse from the desk drawer. "Now I'm off to be best woman."

"You earned that title in my book the day you hired me."

"Don't give me so much credit." She squeezed the woman's arm. "I just recognized talent when I saw it. Thanks again for working extra hours on Monday to cover for me."

"No problem. Have fun at the wedding."

"I'll give it my best shot."

But as she left by the rear door and crossed to her Sentra, even the sunny skies on this second day of April couldn't chase away the pall hanging over her.

Brother Michael was dead.

Not from militant bullets or bombs or blades as she'd always feared, but from a tragic accident.

Why would God take a man who'd left behind everything he knew to do desperately needed work in a dangerous land?

It didn't make sense.

And it felt all wrong.

But as Colin always reminded her when she raised such questions, trying to understand the mind of God was an exercise in futility. You had to trust in his goodness and accept that he saw the bigger picture, even if your own lens was murky.

Bottom line, at some point you had to let questions like this go.

Depressing the autolock on her keychain, she closed the distance to her car in a few long strides, slid behind the wheel, and started the engine.

This was one of those times—at least for the next few hours. She couldn't allow her gloom and grief to ruin the biggest day of Colin's life. She and Rick owed their best bud 100 percent of their support and focus.

So she'd fix her hair, do her makeup, slip into the knockout black dress she'd splurged on for this event, and smile for the world.

Even if her heart was aching.

Author's Note

Welcome back to Hope Harbor—where hearts heal . . . and love blooms.

When I wrote the first book in this series, I wasn't certain it *would* be a series. I hoped readers would fall in love with my special little town on the Oregon coast, but until the numbers came in, I had no idea if there were more Hope Harbor stories in my future.

As it turned out, readers embraced this charming town and its wonderful residents. So much so that every book to date has been a bestseller. Translation? There are more Hope Harbor books in the works!

I'd like to thank all the people who have played such an integral role in my writing journey. I couldn't have hit—and passed—the fifty-book milestone without their support and assistance.

My husband, Tom, who believes in me even on days when I'm certain I'll never think of another compelling plot, and who does so much to smooth out the bumps in our life so I can concentrate on the stories in my head.

My parents, James and Dorothy Hannon, who have been in

my corner from day one—my ever-faithful cheering section. Dad's still out there rooting, and even though Mom's gone now, her unwavering support and the joy she always took in my achievements are sweet memories that will sustain me all the days of my life.

My publishing partners at Revell, especially Dwight Baker, Kristin Kornoelje, Jennifer Leep, Michele Misiak, Karen Steele, and Cheryl Van Andel. I am honored to call you colleagues and friends.

And finally, all the readers who choose my books. Your support has allowed me to build a career telling the stories of my heart.

I hope you'll return with me to Hope Harbor in April 2019, when a woman who runs a lavender farm/tearoom crosses paths with a man who's in over his head juggling a new life, a grieving little girl, and a rambunctious dog who happens to like digging up lavender plants.

In the meantime, if you like romantic suspense, please watch for book 2 in my Code of Honor series, *Hidden Peril*, coming in October 2018. I guarantee it will keep you turning the pages late into the night!

Irene Hannon is the bestselling, award-winning author of more than fifty contemporary romance and romantic suspense novels. She is also a three-time winner of the RITA award—the "Oscar" of romance fiction—from Romance Writers of America, and is a member of that organization's elite Hall of Fame.

Her many other awards include National Readers' Choice, Daphne du Maurier, Retailers' Choice, Booksellers' Best, Carol, and Reviewers' Choice from *RT Book Reviews* magazine, which also honored her with a Career Achievement award for her entire body of work. In addition, she is a two-time Christy award finalist.

Irene, who holds a BA in psychology and an MA in journalism, juggled two careers for many years until she gave up her executive corporate communications position with a Fortune 500 company to write full-time. She is happy to say she has no regrets.

A trained vocalist, Irene has sung the leading role in numerous community theater productions and is also a soloist at her church. She and her husband enjoy traveling, long hikes, Saturday mornings at their favorite coffee shop, and spending time with family. They make their home in Missouri.

To learn more about Irene and her books, visit www.irenehannon.com. She is also active on Facebook and Twitter.

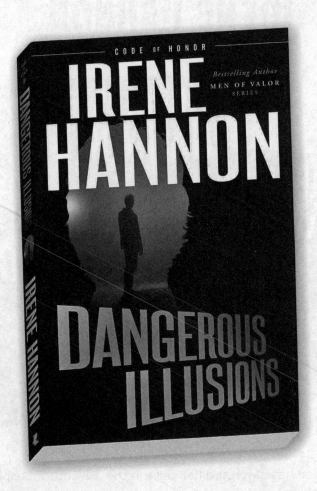

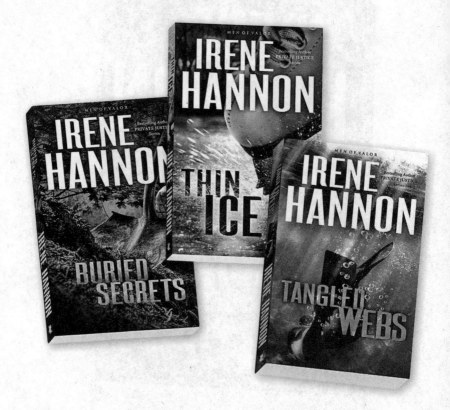